Hunger

A TOM DOHERTY ASSOCIATES BOOK
NEW YORK

Hunger

Jane Ward

HUNGER

Copyright © 2001 by Jane Ward

This book is printed on acid-free paper.

Design by Heidi J. M. Eriksen

A Forge Book
Published by Tom Doherty Associates, LLC
175 Fifth Avenue
New York, NY 10010

www.tor.com

Forge® is a registered trademark of Tom Doherty Associates, LLC.

Library of Congress Cataloging-in-Publication Data

Ward, Jane (Jane A.)
    Hunger / Jane Ward—1st ed.
        p.   cm.
    "A Tom Doherty Associates book."
    ISBN 0-312-87754-4 (alk. paper)
    1. Mothers and daughters—Fiction.   2. New Hampshire—Fiction.
3. Women cooks—Fiction.   4. Restaurants—Fiction.   5. Cookery—
Fiction.   I. Title.

PS3573.A73354 H8 2001
813'.6—dc21
                                                        00-048456
                                                             CIP

First Edition: April 2001

Printed in the United States of America

0 9 8 7 6 5 4 3 2 1

For John

A person cooking is a person giving:
Even the simplest food is a gift.

—LAURIE COLWIN

Contents

PART ONE

Proofs

Over a congratulatory dinner one evening in early January, surrounded by friends around a comfortable dining table, I look up and find my husband taking a small snooze. His plate rests in front of him; the salmon with avocado salsa—his favorite, since the dinner is in his honor—is untouched. He drifted off during a discussion of foreign films playing at the Biograph Theater, and slept through a good deal of the conversation. Our guests, with their eyes, direct my attention to Michael, seated to my left. I turn in my chair, my head bends toward him now, and I stare. How often had I kidded him about being dead on his feet after putting in long hours for years to achieve partnership in his law firm? And here it is: proof.

His lashes are long and thick like a darling young boy's. They cast a shadow over his cheekbones, and I watch his shoulders move up and down in the regular slow breath of sleep. My guests, taking their cue from me, relax as I smile at my husband. They must believe I feel tenderly. I don't; I feel smug. I think, *I told you so*.

We have Julie and Jim down from Michigan; Barnaby and his second wife, Maddie; my friend from work, Colette, who is a food stylist; and her photographer boyfriend, Tom. Colette and I work together at a food magazine, where I was hired nearly seven years ago as a food analyst for the test kitchen. Most of my day is spent breaking foods down to their basic parts; I analyze everything.

I invited Colette, although she is more my friend than Michael's, simply because I need someone here who shares my interests. Michael's lawyer friends, some like Jim and Julie, whom he's known since day one of law school, talk shop when they congregate—theoretical discussions, comparisons of current cases and clients—thus ignoring the nonlawyers in the bunch, which is usually just me. Then Maddie, too, when she came along. Michael seemed to think we would hit it off, but she is new to the group and difficult to draw out, which makes me diffident around her. Colette, Tom, and I—food stylist, photographer, food scientist—can talk about food and about our work when the conversation around us becomes too exclusive.

Barnaby may be Michael's closest friend. He's been our lawyer for years, and Michael trusts him like a brother. They met at the firm, and their friendship solidified during weekends spent on various Chicago area golf courses. Since his remarriage, Barnaby walks taller and his brow has cleared. He is a happier man to be near. We took a trip or two with Barnaby and his first wife until they began bickering, and the anxiety hung in the air around us like a noxious cloud. At the time I decided I knew how to spot a marriage in distress: by the bickering, the loud and robust arguments each partner would instigate. Now I see how little I truly understood.

Jim and Julie were, with Michael, founding members of their law school study group. The three provided support and coaching during three otherwise cutthroat and competitive years, and they remain a tight, an impenetrable, circle. This is what I think: that they formed a unit while I became the diversion. I feel that Julie hasn't much patience for me or my role in Michael's life. She continues to make much of my past foray into temp work and test labs full of refrigerator dough, my penchant for dark clothes, and the fact that I now only work three days a week.

When we met I was newly married, and she summed me right up. "Let me get this straight," she said when we were introduced. "You have a degree in food science? What is that exactly? Are you going to be a home ec teacher? I remember in high school, back when the girls took home ec and the boys were shuttled off to shop. Not that I wanted shop, either," she continued, with a glance down at her perfectly French-manicured nails, "but I certainly knew even years ago how sexist it was to stick us automatically in home ec."

"No," I explained, "I'm more of a lab person, a chemist," thinking that "chemist" sounded both understandable and impressive. "A chemist who studies and works with food."

"Well, then, is that what the dough is all about?" she concluded, referring to the night job I held, testing the pH levels of refrigerator dough for a huge food manufacturer. It wasn't much, but I worked diligently, albeit unhappily, during the law school years to keep us paying our rent and eating. She then eyed me for about a minute and turned to someone else presumably more interesting; I was dismissed.

I remember looking at Michael across whatever table we were sitting at—bar, pizza parlor, coffeehouse—while my husband shrugged and rolled his eyes in something like sympathy.

But he craved their company, and their shared experience forged a very strong bond. I thought I'd seen the back of them at graduation, but Jim accepted a job in Grand Rapids, Michael in Chicago, and we got into a twice-yearly routine. So of course when Michael's partnership became official, no question, they were present to share in the celebration.

For our dinner I had diced seedless cucumber, red peppers, plum tomatoes, red onion, and an avocado uniformly; tossed them all together with lime juice, cilantro, salt, and pepper; and then placed a few spoonfuls on each plate. After removing stray bones with my needle-nose pliers, I had brushed a huge, bright orange Pacific salmon fillet with grainy mustard and grilled it quickly, divided it into eight pieces, and set each on top of the salsa. Earlier in the day I had made a potato salad, laced it with a roasted-garlic mayonnaise and some dark green scallions and capers, and turned it out into my best majolica bowl. The table was perfectly set. When our guests arrived, Michael took them to the living room, where they nibbled almonds I had sautéed in butter and sprinkled with sea salt. Michael, the perfect host, poured drinks: white wine, kirs, gin with bitters.

While the others talked, Colette visited me in the kitchen, arm in arm with Tom, who put his fingers into the potato salad for a taste before dinner. He looked at me instantly, like a guilty child, but I smiled and told him, "Go ahead." He groaned with pleasure at the taste, which made me beam. He was about to lick the last bits of dressing from his fingers when Colette said, "Wait." She took his hand, saying, "Let me." And she licked the last morsels from his fingers. "Anna, that's gorgeous," she crowed. But I turned away, blushing, mumbling my thanks, feeling as if I had intruded on something more intimate than the sharing of food. I was excluded, an outsider, a stranger to whatever it was that had just passed between them. In that moment, my appetite, so fickle lately, fled.

Now, as I watch Michael sleep, conversation temporarily suspended, my smug amusement soon gives way to a familiar, random anger—anger as slippery and as hard to pin down as mercury. Anger slides around within me in oily beads, shooting out in many directions without any single target, and the best I can do is keep chase in an attempt to harness it. I rein in the anger with the voice of reason, the voice I carry with me always, which tells me to keep calm, be quiet, be good, bear up, maintain the appearance of smooth, seamless perfection. I pretend to be content to let him rest on with his eyes closed.

I rise slowly and begin clearing plates, trying to keep the clatter of dishes and silver to a minimum, but I leave Michael's meal at his place in case he is hungry when he wakes. Julie rises after me, stops next to my husband, and seems to consider removing his unfinished meal.

"Wait," I instruct her. "He may want to finish when he wakes up. Why don't you all go into the living room while I get the coffee," I suggest, and I carry dirty dishes to the kitchen with Julie in tow.

"Let me help," she says, lifting a dessert plate and turning it over to see its mark. "Quimper? This must have cost Michael a fortune."

"Actually, it cost me somewhat less than a fortune," I reply.

"Did you get these in France?" she persists.

"Yup. In the Paris flea market. They're used," I feel obliged to qualify.

"Paris." Julie lets the word linger in the air. "You've been quite a few places."

"I guess. Not recently, though, not since Sara was born." I pause to scrape food scraps into the sink.

Julie asks, "Shouldn't we wake him, Anna? I mean, won't he be mortified that we went on without him?"

Let him, I think, for I am not feeling very tenderhearted. Instead I shrug and say, "Michael's been tired lately, but I've never seen him fall asleep at dinner before. I've told him he's overworked."

"The old 'I told you so,' marriage's finest bit of communication?" Julie asks. "What's your opinion? What do you think this spontaneous sleep is all about?"

I recognize from my experience with Michael the buildup of questioning, each question carefully worded to elicit evidence, proof. "I think he's well, if that's what you're asking." I pause, leaning my side against the sink as I set the dishes down and wait for her to get to the point. "Where are you going with this?"

"Do you think Michael's depressed? Has he said anything?"

"Depressed?" I shake my head. "If anyone's going to get to be depressed around here, can I be first in line?" I attempt a smile, but Julie wants no part of my humor.

"Why would *you* be depressed? I'm serious, Anna, Jim's tired. I am very familiar with tired. Michael looks beyond tired, he looks unhappy."

"Okay, seriously then, he's just finished jumping through hoops for seven grueling years. I'm sure it's catching up with him," I answer.

She lays her hand on my arm, circles my wrist, as I try to finish the task of scraping the dishes under the running water. She turns the water off and makes me stop working. Looking me squarely in the eye, Julie asks, "He's in the middle of celebrating his promotion and he falls asleep, and you won't look any deeper than simple fatigue?" When she puts it this way, I sound both self-centered and blind. Before I can answer, Julie continues, "Can I give you some advice, Anna? I mean, I understand the stresses Michael's under. Jim and I are both in busy firms; we've had to get the kids involved in the routine of day care. But now everyone understands their role, their part in running the family's days successfully." She picks up a coffee cup, rubbing her thumb over the painted folk figures on its outside. "Take the pressure off; let Michael set the pace. Maybe structure your days a little more, then he'll feel you're working with him. Sara won't take up so much of your time, his time. I think," and with this she sets the cup down and clasps her hands behind her back. I see her persuasive, courtroom pose. "I think," she repeats, "Michael could relax if he didn't feel torn between his work and your need to be . . . entertained."

I've never considered Julie my friend, but I admire her loyalty to my husband; still, this concern, however touching, burns me, like the incompatible chemicals of an exploding science experiment at my core, burning cold and smoking. Her words, assuming such a personal knowledge of my marriage, a knowledge I apparently don't have, eat away at my flesh until nothing is left but the resentment, frigid and static.

" *'Entertained'?*" I echo, incredulous. "And *'pressure'?* What pressure do I put on him? I never *see* him. Have you been talking about me?" I ask suspiciously. "Has Michael told you he feels pressured, or is this just your observation? Are you here as his emissary or his legal counsel?"

Julie holds up her hands, as if calling for a truce. "His friend. I'm here as his friend. He didn't ask me to say anything to you; Jim and I have been there, and we can see all the signs."

Folding my arms across my chest, I drum my fingertips against my upper arms. I look away—at the floor, the sink, the messy countertops, anywhere so she won't see me roll my eyes as I itch for her to finish.

"Oh, for God's sake, Anna," she sighs, "don't get upset. This isn't personal, and you know what I mean. The man is obviously torn between needing to spend time at work and the pressure he feels to be at home. If you let him know you're not quite so needy, he could relax. I just thought I could help my friend."

" *'Needy'?* So you think I should stop pressuring Michael to spend so much time with his wife and daughter?" I ask angrily. "Do you have any *idea* how much he's home now? Or how *little* I actually say about it? He comes home most nights at nine and continues to work after dinner, and I've said nothing. I'm not a nag."

"I'm trying to be helpful." Julie lowers her voice, reminding me as she does of my guests down the hall and my husband asleep in the next room. "If you'd stop being childish and think about it," she continues, "you'd see I was right. You don't have to say a word, it's evident in all your superhuman efforts. Take this dinner for instance." With a broad sweep of her arm, she gestures back to the dining room and then around the kitchen, pointing out the traces of our meal scattered across the counter.

"What about dinner?"

"You never relax, you're out in the kitchen all night making one thing after the next. It all has to be just right, look just perfect. It's as if you're trying to anticipate Michael's every last whim. It's overwhelming, Anna, it's claustrophobic. 'Look at me, notice me,' you seem to say," and she waves her hand in front of my face like an eager student at the front of the class. "No one can live with this kind of pressure."

Breathing deeply, I answer, "I won't apologize for Sara needing her father around, and when I see my husband I'd kind of like him to stay awake."

"Exactly," Julie answers, sounding relieved, as if I've finally gotten her point. "We just see different ways to achieve that goal. If you push him, if you keep waving your hands in his face, so to speak, he'll just retreat even further. My advice? Relax, back off, make your own days, and Sara's, as full as you can. Okay?" she asks, patting me on the shoulder. She reaches for the stack of dessert plates and coffee cups. "Jim and I will put out the dessert dishes in the living room, so why don't you go wake Michael?" she suggests as she walks from the kitchen.

Before she gets too far away I am tempted to wrest the dishes from her, drop them, and watch the slivered shards scatter across my kitchen floor. The satisfying crash would mimic the chaos in my head, yield a sound as fragmented as my anger. But I know I won't; she's touched a nerve, finally, come a bit too close to a very basic truth. *Look at me, notice me*, the attitudes of an attention-starved child, my dinners the equivalent of standing on my head. Humbled like the child I once was, I accept the reproach because doing so is in my nature. I can continue to bend and bend until I've prostrated myself; I'm revisiting old territory.

I lie on my back on the grass beneath the cherry tree in my backyard. My knees are bent and I have a book lying facedown on them. August is not cooling off, but the grass under the tree is damp and shaded. Behind me my mother's forsythia stands thick and green in front of the fence. It has long since shed its flowers, yellow and starlike; in the spring I cut some branches without Mother's permission along with some shimmering pussy willow, wrapped the ends in wet newspaper, and gave them to my next-door neighbor, Mrs. Klein.

I like spring best because the most interesting things happen: Leaf and flower buds appear; my friend's chickens hatch chicks that feel like ticking yellow clocks in my small hands; my father lets me dig in the wet soil by flashlight for nightcrawlers, which he takes with him in a bucket when he fishes. Summer is too hot, and I often find myself on my back seeking shade, like today, when I am also escaping the airless quiet of the house. I have little to do; most of my friends are away with their families. My mother has closeted herself upstairs, leaving me to amuse myself.

I began visiting my next-door neighbor in the spring, and I think I will see her today. My neighbor, Mrs. Klein, is dying. She has cancer, something that makes her thin and weak. Her hair falls out, and she wears a wig. She doesn't mind that her hair has fallen out, she tells me; many Jewish women shave their heads on purpose and then wear wigs. She says she likes to pretend it is Orthodoxy and not chemotherapy that is responsible for the lack of hair. I have seen her without her wig. Almost completely bald, she has some wisps of light brown hair remaining on a silvery scalp. Her head is not round like the circles I draw on figures in my art class drawings, but oval and elongated.

When I visit, usually her husband is at work. Her two children, older than I, are away at camp—"music camp," she's told me proudly. While we are in the house together she lets me try food that eager relatives and friends from her temple bring to tempt her appetite. "It's no use, Anna," she sighs, "I don't keep anything down." My mother often wonders why I am not very hungry at lunchtime. I never tell her I have filled up on noodle puddings, some savory, others sweet with raisins; kasha with bow-tie pasta; grainy chopped liver and cold slices of brisket. I develop quite a taste for the cold root vegetables served with the meat. To me it is all very exotic. When Mrs. Klein tells me she is tired I go home, but she always thanks me for the pleasure of my company.

I can see into her screened porch on this day in August, can see her sitting with her potted plants, the awnings full out over the screens to keep the sun off her. She looks as lonely as I feel.

My parents argue heatedly before my father leaves for work. I pretend to be asleep, but I hear. It is an argument about time, and not enough of it. Their arguments lately seem to center on demands on Father's time, and therefore on my mother's time. Today my mother cannot work out how she will manage it all and me, too.

"I am always saddled with this child. There's not time to get anyone to watch her. No one's even around to call."

I hear Father say calmly but decisively, "You'll think of something."

As I feign sleep, I hear his coffee cup settle on its saucer, his chair push out from the kitchen table, its legs rough on the tile. I hear the creak of hardwood floors as he makes his way to the front door. I recognize her lighter step on the stairs; she's rushing up and away as behind her, my father leaves and gently closes the front door.

As it latches, my mother calls, "I always have to think of something. And I didn't even want her in the first place. You *made* me. *You* think of something!"

I roughly shove the kettle under the faucet and start the water for coffee. Leaving the water to heat, I set up the Melitta and walk through to the dining room, where Michael's chin now rests on his chest. His breathing is heavier, rhythmic. Soon he will be snoring, and I will pack him off to bed. Leaning over him, I listen for a moment to his breath. I put my hands on his shoulders and massage his neck. He wakes at that moment, but easily, not startled, and reaches up to me, lets his fingers brush my face. He is vulnerable, open to me, and a tenderness creeps in to replace the heat in my chest. Looking around, Michael sees that the table has been cleared.

"Aw, hell. How long have I been out?" he asks.

"A few minutes, maybe more. We just looked over, and you were asleep."

"Why didn't you wake me?" He is clearly perturbed, but with himself or me I can't tell.

"I just did," I answer and I finish the back rub with a couple of firm slaps on his back. "Finish up your salmon," I instruct, moving back toward the kitchen. "We're having dessert in the living room. I'm just getting the coffee now."

"That's okay, you can take my plate." He pushes his dinner away.

"But your dinner," I point out. "Aren't you hungry?"

"It's cold, Anna. It probably tastes like shit by now." He pushes back his chair. "I'll go splash some water on my face. Meet you in the other room in a bit." Michael stands to go; I stand in the kitchen doorway, frowning.

"What's the wrinkled forehead for?" he asks.

Our words, our movements and expressions, exist on a surface, a flat plane, a place where polite words can gloss over a churning undercurrent of fear and resentment. Right now, though, it is easier to exist here, easier to pretend all is well. So I say, "Nothing, I guess," softening the scrutiny and letting the familiar paralysis settle in. It is so much easier than confrontation, so much neater than letting the angry words fly.

Michael turns his back to me, stretches, yawns, and heads for the bathroom. I prop up the doorway for a few more seconds, then turn into my kitchen to wait for the kettle to whistle.

I hate like hell to throw this fish away. I think of the strength of this fish, once swimming like silver lightning, darting and licking underwater, carrying around its curious overbite, which keeps the salmon on the wrong side of beauty. The delicate lateral line running its length is the only darkness marring the skin's iridescence. The fish has never had a chance to fertilize or spawn. Instead I've grilled its skin to a leathery toughness; when I removed the fish from it, the edges curled. I've seen wallets made from the skin, not quite a hide but as durable as leather. I've seen slippers, too, no longer silver but bearing the spots and striations in dry liver-colored splotches.

I take a bite of Michael's meal, and the act of chewing calms me a little. So I eat his dinner, or part of it, at first forcing myself because I'm slightly bilious from cooking and looking at all this food during the afternoon and evening. The chilled salsa has gone tepid and the sizzling fish is now cold, meeting somewhere in the middle, but sometimes the flavor of things is dulled or immured by too much chill, too intense heat. When I lift a forkful of vegetables they glisten like faceted jewels, uniformly cut. Their liquid has leached into the lime juice; it drips between the tines of the fork, down my chin, and onto the plate I rush under my chin. I taste, trying to tempt the appetite that so often fails me these days. I have the desire to prepare the food, to make it look and taste good, until a meal is in front of me, and then my esophagus chokes closed in a perverse response to the tempting smells. The fish is moist on my tongue, breaking down and smoothing out between my tongue and palate, sliding easily down my throat. After my own sketchy dinner, my stomach growls a bit with the first taste. I eat as I couldn't at the table in front of guests, and with an appetite I haven't felt in a long while, stopping only for a moment to wipe my chin, tasting as I do the peculiar soapiness of cilantro so piquant as it has reached room temperature. I am proud of myself for feeding eight people so well; this pride edges a smile to the corners of my still-moist lips. With these raw ingredients, I know what I am doing. At least that's something.

Michael startles me as he passes through the kitchen to join his friends. I set his plate down hurriedly, the fork clatters, and I stop to wipe my mouth.

"Hungry?" he asks, pausing a moment.

A mother can ask her child this, determining the child's appetite for mealtime. You can ask this of a spouse as the sun goes down and a gnawing teasing emptiness begins to tickle your stomachs. Or as you pass an ice cream parlor on a warm day, meaning, *Wouldn't ice cream taste good right about now?* Or after a picnic, meaning, *Are you finished?* You're lazing on the grass, sated, you want to bring an end to the meal, an excuse to pack up the basket, drop the lid, and lie on your back gazing into a perfect sky.

Strange how his one word makes me feel like a glutton.

The kettle whistles, and I pour water through the cone filter. I hear the voices in the front room, increasing in volume, in liveliness, as Michael steps through the door. From my place at the stove I see Colette and Tom alone in a corner of the room; away from the rest they look insular, complete, whole. Maddie sits silently with her hands folded on her lap. Barnaby sits on the arm of her chair, his hand rests on her left shoulder. Michael sits on the couch, his back leans into the cushions, his legs stretch long and lean in front of him. Between Michael and Jim, Julie talks animatedly with her hands. She prods Jim's knee, and I see her give Michael's upper arm a playful slap with the back of her hand. I think of hovering birds, like hummingbirds, wings in constant flickering motion. It isn't me, I think as I watch them, who hasn't changed. I am tired suddenly, watching all the activity, vicariously tired because I do nothing here but stand and watch and wait.

I am uneasy, off balance, unsure of myself once I leave my comfortable kitchen to join the social scene. But I want everything to look nice and therefore be nice, so I continue to concentrate on my guests and cook nice meals. Any less would be admitting defeat, which I am not yet prepared to do. There is a burst of laughter as I walk into the room, and my arrival causes it to subside. *Interloper*, they say, by the way their mirth sputters and trails off at different rates: Michael stops short, Julie gives a last trill of giggles. Until, finally, there is empty air, into which I announce, unnecessarily, "Dessert."

I slice a chocolate cake. For a moment I think I could eat this cake, I could take a spoon, break into its soft sunken middle, and greedily scoop up the silkiest molten bits for myself. Instead I pass a sauceboat full of crème anglaise, and its eggy yellow wiggle looks slightly obscene, and the desire dissipates.

Colette leaves her pleasant nest with Tom and comes to stand behind me. She offers me strength by placing her hands on my shoulders. Despite her gender, she is my stalwart knight this evening, and I am instantly grateful for her protection. Tom comes and sits at my feet and talks to me of work—how he would photograph my cake if I would let him. I laugh, exclaiming how many cakes I'd need to bake, how many pounds of butter, chocolate, how many dozens of eggs, to get one cake just right for the camera.

Michael demonstrates pouring the sauce, floating a slice of cake on top, and our guests follow his lead. Except Maddie. She, like me, passes on cake. I offer her coffee before the others, since they are still maneuvering plates and silver. She declines, and I note a smug smile flicker over her lips a moment before her mouth resumes its usual sweet placid pursing. I see now what keeps Barnaby interested. He must love to kiss that sweet mouth, I decide, hoping to find the surprise under its calm expression.

And then something about the secretive look of her smile strikes a familiar chord with me: I've had that secret, too, when I alone held the knowledge of Sara growing inside me. I, too, refused coffee and chocolate and tea, wine, and any other threats or poisons. Maddie sees the recognition on my face; it would be hard to miss. She looks straight at me, benign smile in place as perfect as her hair, her makeup, the colorful scarf around her neck artfully tucked into the neckline of her dress.

My husband, my guests, are digging into their cake. They are talking, laughing; Michael has revived. Julie asks if anyone minds if she smokes. She's lit the match and the end of the cigarette already, ex-

pecting no resistance. I say, "Better not. I think Maddie might mind."
Turning to Maddie, I ask, "Isn't that right?"

"Maddie, what were you and Barnaby thinking? A baby? Why didn't you
tell us?" Julie chides. "And how did Anna guess when the rest of us
had no idea?" She looks at me, puzzled.

"But Julie, we're so excited about the baby! We wanted to surprise
all of you."

"That you did," Michael assents. "Congratulations," he says, offering his hand to Barnaby. "It's the beginning of so many new experiences."

Barnaby leans forward in his seat and asks, "So, Costello, is it all
true: no more sleep, huge adjustments?" His words carry an elbow's
nudge to the ribs.

"You don't want to know," Michael kids.

I correct Michael, adding, "Besides, we adore Sara, can't remember
life without her now that she's here."

"I remember life before kids," Julie says wistfully. "Sundays in bed,
reading the newspaper, drinking coffee without fear of being pounced
on."

Jim picks up her thread, "Dining out, spending eighty dollars on
bottles of French chablis instead of disposable diapers. . . ."

Colette says, "The more I hear, the more I'm glad my husband
and I didn't have kids. I'm just too selfish, I guess. All the sacrifice
would have pissed me off."

"Probably for the best," Michael adds. "Custody is the messiest
part of divorce."

Colette agrees, "That too."

As I look across at pregnant Maddie, I question all the talk about
childbirth and parenthood, subjects best steered away from expectant
parents. I tell her, "Don't pay any attention to these voices of doom.
Yes, your life changes, but in wonderful ways. I can't think of anything
better than seeing the world through your child's eyes. It's like a second
chance—"

Michael cuts in, "You're romanticizing. Maddie, Sara barely slept for something like six months. And the crying? I remember the evenings I used to come home late to find Anna swaddling the baby in a receiving blanket in the rocking chair. Seems to me, Anna, all you did back then was watch a lot of late-night television and cry yourself."

I frown at Michael. "But Sara's crying couldn't have bothered you, you were hardly home. Anyway, she grew out of that eventually."

"Things got better, right?" asks Maddie.

I nod, but Michael continues, "Even after she grew out of the colic she still hated certain things. Like car rides. Anna, do you remember when she was ten months old? The baby pictures?"

Michael expects an answer, so I turn to Maddie and Barnaby and explain, "I wanted a formal baby picture for Michael's birthday that year. Thirty car-ride minutes later, I was drenched in sweat when we pulled up to the studio."

"You should have known better than to choose a photographer in Oak Park." Michael relaxes in his chair, stifles a yawn, and smiles.

Maddie asks, "What about the photographer? Finish about the pictures."

I look at Michael, he looks back, yields me the floor with a gesture of his hands. I don't trust the bland expression on his face; something lurks behind his composed features. Suddenly I feel we are skating, and I can't judge the thickness of the ice. One wrong step and one of us will be mired in icy water, but I continue, speaking rapidly, intensely, to bring this story to a close. "The camera flashed. Sara turned, startled, eyes wide. Then again, flash! She began to cry. The light from the bulb frightened her. We took our time between snapping pictures, but we never caught a smile. In my mind's eye I could see the proof sheets already: in every frame either surprise or fear or tears. At some point I wondered why I didn't just gather her up and head for home. But I didn't.

"I think I probably lost five pounds that day and forced years off my baby's life.

"Weeks later the photographer mailed our proofs. As I expected, they showed a very unhappy baby. But there was no question of going through the shoot a second time. Michael and I chose two pictures, out of maybe twenty-four, in which she wasn't crying."

"That's probably enough," Michael warns. "I think you've made my point."

"It wasn't all like that, though—it wasn't all tears," I insist.

"And then what?" Maddie leans across the table. I think she may grab my hand, but instead she pours Barnaby more coffee, twisting the coffee cup on its saucer until it grates. I pick up on her nerves and fold the edges of my napkin, once, twice, over and over, until I have a circle. I begin to open my mouth to answer her question.

"Anna, darlin'," Michael laughs, using his endearment, dropping the *g*, which I used to think made it so much more intimate, "please. Shut up."

Only Julie laughs with him, although Jim smiles. Barnaby is embarrassed. Only Maddie is pale, truly distressed by our stories. Colette, still standing behind me, begins to massage the muscles at the base of my neck. She moves her hands outward slightly, manipulating the tendons and tense sinews along my shoulders. I am so thankful for this touch, gentle yet insistent, that I could cry. She keeps me in my seat when I could easily have fled.

We finish the evening and a warm fallen chocolate cake in forced high spirits. Our guests, remembering Michael's fatigue, send one another signals that it is time to go home. Colette offers to stay and clean up with me, but I send her on her way. We linger at the door saying our good-byes. Michael is offered another round of congratulations and warm hugs. I put my arm around Michael's waist as we stand at the door waving good-bye to our guests, until they drive off into the night and he steps away and closes the front door.

"I'm going to bed," Michael says through a yawn, and he turns his back to me on his way to the bedroom. At the sight of Michael's back as he walks down the hallway, I feel like a mother with a child who won't finish his meal. I feel the mounting frustration of participating in a struggle I know I won't win. But I do know I need to speak.

"Why did you ask me to tell that story? Are you so angry with me that you didn't care what we were saying to Maddie?" I ask him.

Michael stops, I see his shoulders heave in a sigh. He turns, rolls his head around, and loosens his shoulders in a show of tension. "I'm not angry, I'm tired. Anyway, you could have stopped anytime."

"But I felt egged on, Michael, like you wanted me to tell the story for some reason. Look," I suggest, "come do dishes with me. Or sit while I do them. We can talk; I want to talk."

While we were students, when we'd throw parties, large herds of people tramping through a cramped apartment, we'd walk together, Michael holding a large green trash bag following me as I picked up paper plates and cups, the detritus of a successful evening. We would talk, Michael and I, about who drank too much, who said something funny, who would not be invited back.

In the paper plate days, I felt I could grab Michael and kiss him in any room of the apartment as he tidied up. He'd be dumping ashtrays, and I'd take his arm and make him plant the ashtray firmly on a table. With amusement tickling his face, he'd grin, put down the trash, and lift his arms over his head. I'd help him off with his jersey, and somehow we'd end up in a tangled wrestle on the floor, neither one of us calling for relief.

We've graduated to breakables and stainless steel and can no longer clean up by tossing out; I can no longer entice Michael even to stay in the same room with me. Our time in the kitchen filling the dishwasher, scrubbing pans, and storing leftovers might give us room to talk, to meet again after our party faces have been put away, but he begs off from the cleanup, and I remember his sleepy boy's face above his dinner plate.

"Michael," I say. I stop him in the doorway as he turns again to leave for bed, before I have a chance to reconsider my question. "Do you want a divorce? Are you thinking of leaving me?"

For a moment, his back to me, he doesn't move. Then I see his hand reach up to the hair over his ear as he runs his fingers through it: thick, dark hair that I've had my own hands wound in; hair that I can feel, even in memory, to my nerve endings. Its coarseness, its wave.

He turns slowly, he exhales, his shoulders slump. "For God's sake, Anna. No. No, I don't want a divorce, I'm not thinking of anything like that. I hardly have time these days to scratch, let alone think about starting over again."

"Because sometimes . . . ," I begin haltingly, "sometimes I feel like you've already left. You can tell me," I prod. "At least that's something I can understand."

"Believe me, there's nothing to tell. And understand? There's nothing to understand, either."

"But there is, there must be, otherwise why are you never home? And why would you fall asleep at dinner tonight, on the rare occasion that you are home? Why am I always simmering inside? *Please.* Talk to me."

Addressing me, Michael speaks slowly, "You know what?" he asks. "I think talking is vastly overrated in marriage. The way I see it, you work hard, you settle down, put down roots, raise a family, create a history together. Simple. I don't see much point in dissecting every last thing. I do enough of that at work. Something in my life needs to be easy."

"I don't think it's that easy," I reply. "What happens when simply going along is not enough? I need this; I need to talk. What about what I need?"

He deflects my question with one of his own. "Just what do you need, Anna? When you look around you, what is it that you think is missing?" Like Julie with the sweep of her arm, Michael makes me look around my home. Looking at my possessions, I feel greedy. I own so much; why isn't it enough?

"While you were sleeping, Julie told me I was too needy. Is that what you think?"

"What I think is I need to concentrate on work. I need my family to support me; I need you to keep things going at home."

"After Julie lectured me, after she left the room, I remembered my mother. And my father," I tell him with my voice steadily rising. "I hated it when she called after him, tried to make him listen to her. She knew he wouldn't respond, he never did. He remained calm and walked away. Is that what we've turned into?" I ask him.

"I'm not your father."

"And I don't want to be like my mother, but I feel like I'm either screaming for your attention or locking myself in my own quiet place."

"Will you calm down?" Michael pleads. "Jesus! This will change, Anna. We have the rest of our lives together."

"What if I don't want to wait for our lives to change? What if I think we need to do something about it instead?" I demand.

"There's nothing we can do about it tonight, so can we not talk about this now? I'm exhausted, and I want to get to bed."

"When, then, when can we talk?"

"I don't know," he says. "Soon. Once I settle into the new routines at work."

And there is nothing more I can say in the face of his fatigue, so I send him off to bed with a wave of my hand and without a kiss.

I stand at the sink scrubbing the wine glasses by hand. Soon, I think, with the partnership under his belt, he will have a routine to hold on to, and a rhythm will be restored. Is this what he is telling me? Is this what I must believe?

Speaking of Paris with Julie made me remember that Michael and I used to like to travel. Maybe we should go away, be together, talk. Maybe he needs a vacation; maybe we both do. Now I think of a vacation reverently, as if it's a cure for a terrible illness: We could talk and maybe reconnect, get rid of whatever is surging within us. Maybe. At least we could talk without the distractions of work and a child and the endless socializing, and talk is what I sense we must do.

I decide right then I will suggest a trip to Michael, but my mind comes back to him snoozing over his half-finished dinner, his one vague word, "Soon." I reach for a wine glass under the suds and my hand lights on a slicing knife instead. I bring my bleeding thumb up to the faucet and run it under cold water until my flesh is numb. I wrap my finger in some paper towel, then leave the dishes in a kind of blind funk to wash up, bandage myself, and down a couple of pain-killers to numb the ache I know is coming.

On the way to join Michael in bed, I stop in the living room to turn off the lights. With my tightly bandaged finger I find and stroke the frames surrounding the portraits of Sara we talked about earlier. When the enlargements were ready I drove back to Oak Park to fetch them, but this time I went to a different address. I found Suite 107, as directed, and it was a plastic surgeon's office, our photographer's husband. My daughter's pictures had been wrapped in heavy paper and awaited us on the reception desk. I remember making small talk with the secretary as I wrote out my check. I looked around the office as I waited for a receipt, noticing the walls were covered with photos of children, beautiful children in black and white, perfect children. Flawless, really. At the time I felt uneasy with all these faces looking back at me, and, holding my baby closer, I couldn't wait to leave. Once outside, I breathed in some cold, brisk air until I felt better.

Sara's portraits hang in my home now, and many people remark on their beauty—the round, soft, baby beauty of my daughter. But Sara was more beautiful to me in her person, with her wrinkled forehead and the rash on her cheeks. She is not perfect but she is mine. Her lovely face and others—Michael and I sharing hopeful smiles on our wedding day—remain static behind glass, frozen in those moments.

Around the room are more of the beautiful things I've collected over the years just to please my eye. From our trips I've brought home pieces of other, foreign, richer cultures: the Quimper from Paris; from Italy, majolica covered in its circus colors; jars of jam made in England from fruits nearly unknown to American palates; cut glass from Ireland that seemed to catch and then refract light, generously throwing rainbows onto my table. Maybe Julie has a point; maybe I have learned well how to spend Michael's money. But maybe that's because it is what he gives freely.

Sometimes my things make me feel connected to other countries, places that care so much about beauty that their artisans continue to produce exquisite things; sometimes, surrounded by richly colored Belgian tapestries on my walls, I feel happy because my eye is satisfied.

But at other times I know that if I touch my things they will crumble to dust; if so, they will no longer nourish me.

Now as beautiful food passes my lips and colors light my plate to coax my stomach, as my fingers caress, like Julie's, the raised paint on my plates and intricate cuts in glass or the Braille of woven threads, nothing here breathes or moves or responds. Like those captured children in that suffocating office back in Oak Park, like the photos on my own walls. But as I look around I think: All of it is mine. I know what I possess.

 In the morning Sara will eat her toast if I cut it into nine small squares; she just wants it buttered today. I am so tired, and she is so agreeable that I give her an extra-long hug and a chapter of the book we are reading, a rare treat on a workday. She will be tired, too, maybe cranky after eight hours at the preschool, so I soak up her tenderness now, bask in it, so I can keep going in the face of tantrums later.

Michael is long gone, and Sara and I sit on the couch, side by side. She won't sit on my lap any longer, but she will throw her leg over mine, rest her shoulder into my arm. I can smell her hair, the Tide scent of her clean clothes. The sleepy-skin smell of a warm body held under rumpled sheets. She tosses her arms up over her head when she sleeps, like she's surrendering.

I hold her close as I read, fearing as I do that I love her too much, hold on too tight, smother with my love because I don't want her to see any storms raging below my surface. Her smooth, untroubled brow, her peaceful concentration as I read, these touch me.

" 'Sometimes the sea's rough, sometimes it's calm,' " I read, " 'but down underneath it's always the same. And life's like that, there.' "

We are very close to the end of this book about a mermaid, a hunter, and the family they create out of a bear, a lynx, and an orphaned boy.

"What does the mermaid mean, Mama?" Sara asks.

"I guess that ocean life is familiar to her; it's easy under the ocean. I think she means she likes it on land because it's harder for her there. And if her life is harder, then it's also different. And she likes her life when it's different."

"Why?"

"Imagine trying to move around on land with a tail. Or touching fire for the first time. Those things could really hurt, couldn't they?" I ask. "But then maybe she feels more alive." I close the book now, marking the page with my finger, and pause to check my watch. "Hey, Sara, we should get going. Can we finish the last few pages before bed?" I ask.

"But what will happen next?" she asks. "I want to know." Her voice sings with anticipation.

"I want to know, too," I admit, "but it's getting late and I need to be at work. Can we find out tonight?"

I see in her eyes how she considers my suggestion before nodding her agreement, and then she smiles, igniting my heart with her easy emotion.

On the bus after I drop Sara at her preschool, I think briefly of our storybook, of life under the ocean as the mermaid describes it, easy and familiar. Looking at the people climbing on board the bus, I wonder about these fellow passengers, some buried in their books, men hanging on to overhead straps, women in their Reeboks and business suits, the same faces crowding on after jerking stops and starts, all following the same routines. Were any of them passive participants, content to swim their marriages like the mermaid's ocean, or was someone, somewhere, getting it right?

When I reach the magazine offices, I stop in first to see Colette. She is recently divorced, and spends most of the day hiding from management and sneaking off with Tom under the pretense of photo shoots.

"I deserve this," she tells me as I poke my head into her office.

"Deserve what, exactly?" I ask.

"Come all the way in," she tells me, waving me into her spare chair. "These kisses, to answer you, with Tom. I haven't kissed like this, just for the sake of kissing, since about junior high school. I used to sit in the back of the movie theater and kiss Billy Wallace until our tongues hurt."

"Oh," I say. "You were one of those girls."

"What?" Colette asks. "Doesn't everyone have this memory?"

"I don't."

Colette looks at me. "Aw, get *out!*"

"I don't," I repeat. "I didn't know Michael until college. When we met everything just went *boom!*—beyond kissing." I pause, searching for the right words. "I was always just too disdainful of most boys, young boys. I mean, they did the dance, hung around, got their friends to talk to me, but I never encouraged them. So I guess when I met Michael, all that was stored up or something. We just went past the silly stuff."

" 'The *silly* stuff'? You mean to tell me," Colette asks, incredulous, "you've never just made out, never necked in the backseat of a car?" She is amazed, her eyes wide.

"Never. I led a sheltered life." I reply piously, hand over my heart.

"That's not sheltered, that's just beyond weird. And to think I actually like you."

She is right; sheltered doesn't even begin to describe my youth. I had kissed prom dates chastely, had hung my arms around the necks of my share of boys during slow dances. I'd felt a choking in my throat well up and travel down my sternum. I knew no way to direct that ache, no idea what to do, no person to do it with. Until Michael. Colette's phone rings, and as she picks up, she motions to me to wait for her to finish. I settle back into the comfortable seat. Until Michael, I think.

We met during the first week of college. The biology lecture hall was full of students from all majors, but Michael was probably the sole history major immediately fulfilling his science requirement. He took the seat next to me. He said later that out of all those students he'd felt drawn to me. I told him magnetism had nothing to do with biology; he ought to have signed up for physics. I was a tough nut to crack back then, inexperienced and defensive and therefore sarcastic.

But when this good-looking boy with the dark hair and eyes leaned over to whisper to me, I felt electrified. We were the male and female of the species at ripe reproductive age.

The random wonder of it all overwhelmed me. Michael could have enrolled in botany or astronomy, two popular sciences for the nonscience major; if he'd been a procrastinator, he might have put off enrolling in any course. His eyes could have lit on Elizabeth Lister, front row center, who, after all, called more attention to herself with her hand swinging in the air than did quiet Anna Rossi. But, as Michael explained, he watched my pen fly over my notebook, touched by the reams of notes I took as hair fell in my eyes, by how carefully I transferred them to my binder. He liked that I looked solemn and sober and in a hurry to learn.

We met later in the month, departing the library at closing time. Michael followed me to my dormitory, explaining his history studies all the way. It felt good to listen to him. At the front door to the dorm, Michael kissed my quiet mouth. I weighed the key in my hand. I measured the kiss and my physical response. In that moment, Michael looked beyond me into the black night. His faraway eyes hooked me, and I wanted them back on me—close, not distant.

Very calculatedly I asked him to my room. I surprised this dark-haired boy. In disbelief, I think, he followed me upstairs to my fourth-floor room. If we had been alone in the building I would have removed clothes as we traveled up the stairs. Instead, I leaned over the railing and stopped him with a kiss. I let my tongue find his mouth and tasted tobacco and peppermints and the underlying sweetness of tender human flesh. His teeth felt smooth and even. If I could have consumed him I would have, I was that hungry. I pulled back and found that Michael's eyes were still closed, his lips parted. When he realized I had moved away, his eyes opened and again I saw surprise.

He took two stairs at a time to reach me and passed me by a step to stand over me, looking down. I shot past and raced him to my door.

By the time I met Michael, my body felt like a cage holding pacing tigers on the lookout for the merest break in the gates.

He was an intelligent and passionate student, he knew so much, and he was willing to share knowledge with me. He would leave class to come and tell me what he'd learned, like the history of the Vietnam War, which had not existed in my home, from France's early involvement in Southeast Asia to the war's bitter, divided, unresolved end. He spoke to me over cups of coffee of politics and economics and law; he interrupted my thoughts with passages from books: Foucault, Heidegger, Tocqueville. He understood semiotics and deconstructionism, and I was a receptacle, a willing listener.

His passions spilled over to include me, and I wanted to be what he was: strong, smart, committed, and responsible instead of naive. I felt younger, certainly, than Michael in experience, despite being the same age. I watched him over sticky marble tabletops, selecting a cigarette from a collapsed packet, lighting it with a confidence I did not possess, too frightened still of parental disapproval to take even a drag, utter a swear word, or drink anything stronger than a glass of wine. Michael himself was an intoxicant: nicotine, alcohol, forbidden language, and the allure of illicit sex in one provocative package. And once I had him in my bed, if he ever seemed far away, I learned I only needed to ask him a question to start him talking about his studies, or kiss him in a certain way, or place his hands under my shirt, and he was with me again.

I liked sex instantly, from the first time; in bed, desire that had been long bottled up flowed out freely. On a cold night between frigid sheets, our skins could go from gooseflesh to warm to the overheated chill of sweat in a matter of minutes. I discovered how much the tactile sense pleased me; finally understood why, as a child, I always needed to feel or taste something to know it. And how often that touch or taste was discouraged. But with Michael I could touch and taste at will with no limits or rebukes. I suddenly knew how deprived I had been. Fine hairs, coarse ones, the satiny undersides of arms, the sinewy muscles across an upper back, facial skin toughened by wind and shaving, salted sweat, tobacco, a skin oozing garlic after a rich meal.

By the time we married my father had died; I had no one to give me away. But I wouldn't have wanted that anyway, and eventually my mother gave in, worn down in the absence of my father. Although it was unconventional, it was what I wanted, and Michael's presence gave me the strength to persist. My grandmother did not come because the ceremony was not in a church and there was not even a priest in sight, because I wore ivory not white, because I had no veil on my head. A litany of excuses. But my smile on that day said, *Screw you. Who cares?* It really did.

Michael wore a suit. He smiled, too, although his smile said to me, *I'm glad you're here*, and it was accompanied by reassuring hugs. No sweating brow, no furrows, no questions, no distance.

Family, friends, flowers, food, music. Photographer. Candid shots, no portraits, so all I saw when I looked back over the wedding proof sheets was Michael and me, our guests, talking, laughing, dancing. No posing. The many shades of red: dendrobium orchids, rubrum lilies, raspberry mousse, wine. And the aunts, uncles, parents, Michael's brother, our friends, umbrellas, tables, sunshine, an oasis in the city. The string trio played Cole Porter, Benny Goodman, Glenn Miller, and Gershwin, and the bassist winked at me as I floated by. I could have winked back; instead I laughed. There were presents: boxes; envelopes; unbelievably, a chair with a huge white bow; white elephants, unexpected treasures, all for our home, all much loved. There was advice to be listened to, from sages, the experienced. Or laughed off. We didn't need to pay attention. We were sure, confident, certain.

We knew it all.

Our honeymoon was a long weekend at a chalet borrowed from friends on the edge of the White Mountains of New Hampshire. We arrived the morning after our wedding and hiked the entire day. Climbing Black Cap, I felt as light and graceful as the sun streaking through the pine needles and branches. From the mountain trails, the streams looked thin, simply hairline fissures in the earth. We heard animals all around as we sunned ourselves on the bald peak; there was no such thing as silence up there despite the expanse of peaceful sky, always a twitch or a rustle or a chirp from the treeline just below us.

Back at the chalet we climbed the stairs to the loft and quietly pushed two twin beds together to make one. The August night held the bite of fall, and we lay close together and shared body warmth. Lying very still, I curled into Michael's arms in the cold loft on top of the two beds pushed together.

In these early days of our marriage, we met in a heat, and febrile skin was the common denominator. We were hungry, and we fed each other through tactile contact, skin against skin. Never enough. We knocked our front teeth together in our haste to meld our mouths. Once we pulled back from a painful kiss, the root nerves of our front teeth zinging. Simultaneously we each brought a hand up to our mouth, looked at each other, and laughed. But we went back to each other quickly; I slid my hands up Michael's back and tried to pull myself as close as I could. I wanted to wear him, and he wanted to be under my skin.

"Anna? Anna?" I hear Colette's voice breaking into my memories. "You were far away. Is it anything you want to talk about?" she asks when I turn to the sound of her voice.

"Yes," I agree. "I've got to clear my head. Maybe over lunch?" I suggest.

"Okay, then, we'll have a good talk at lunch. I'll tell you all about my day with Tom yesterday. You won't believe what we did after the spread on desserts. That should cheer you." She looks closely at my face. It is grim, I bet, because she adds, "Or maybe we'll just talk about what's bothering you. I saw that look on Chicken Little's face in a book from my childhood. 'The sky is falling! The sky is falling!' Hello? Anna?" She reaches over and knocks gently on my forehead. "That was supposed to be funny," Colette teases.

"I'm sorry. I'm not much company today, I'm afraid," I say, giving her a half-smile. "It was a late night with the party, and cleaning up after. Sure I'd like to hear about Tom."

"Let's take a two-hour lunch then, and get you over this brooding," Colette suggests.

I leave her office to work alone in the kitchen, and I am happy for the solitude. I am working on a project developing low-fat substitutes for cooking and baking; it has been taking me a long time to get products ready to use in recipes, but I have a deadline. The special low-fat issue will be ready for print soon, and the precision of my work gives me something to focus on. Concentrating on the ingredients, the weights and balances, the liquid measures laid out before me, I lose myself in my routine, a blank scrim.

What I first notice about Michael is his breadth: He is broader across the shoulders and taller than any boy I have ever known. He has a heavy beard, which begins to grow back within six hours of his morning's shave. I know this because I watch for him outside class, around campus at all hours of the day. I feel an electrical current, a buzz traveling through me when I catch him looking back at me. I feel the power I have stored all those years, the secret I have held on to, and I know it has been for him, or someone very like him.

When he talks to me after class, at the library, when I pay attention to the topics he discusses, I carry around a wetness between my legs until I know I can't stand it any longer. By then I am taking birth control pills because I want to sleep with Michael; I have long since abandoned any Catholic beliefs and any residual guilt. Yet I know if I sleep with him, I will get pregnant because of the way my body feels: so welcoming and warm, blood lined.

I knew about sex by the time I got my first period, but not from my parents. The longer they remained silent about my puberty, the more curious I became. At the library I read and read about intercourse until I was more knowledgeable than my friends. I lay in the dark of my bedroom, passed my finger around the hole of my vagina, until the strong muscles yielded to my pressure; its walls were both rock hard and velvety. My finger held my blood, and I knew what the blood was there for. Sitting at a study carrel in an isolated corner of the library, I read books about a woman's body, about sex and lovemaking, and I began, at twelve, to sense the difference: one clinical, one mysterious. I heard boys say "fuck" at the bus stops, on the pathways behind the school. "Fuck you," they would say to one another as I watched them play ball and fight in empty lots. I knew what that word meant, too— the crudity, the violence, the physical longing, the recreation all implied, inherent in the word, the act.

With my new breasts and my leaking body, I watched boys and they watched me right back. At twelve I moved my finger further forward from my vagina to part lips, finding my clitoris. When I touched it, it became swollen under my finger. I read the word "clit," and I liked that better because it was a short, quick word, which described how I first made myself come. It took so little time, so little pressure until my muscles spasmed that I was surprised, panting, unaccustomed, and quite unprepared. So I did it again. I couldn't imagine boys doing this for me, like the books described, couldn't imagine any boys I knew having penises harden and swell and then push into me. When they tried to kiss me I kissed back, and then I laughed, knowing what I knew about me, about them, about fucking. I also knew then I would not kiss them any longer. They were bewildered, pressed on briefly, but I was moving past them; behind me their eyes were large and full of questions. Instead I went home, lay on my bed or the floor of my bathroom, felt for my clit, and thought of the day I would meet someone who was not a boy, fumbling and bewildered.

So I leave the library with Michael knowing that I will sleep with him, I stand with him by the front door of the dormitory as his kiss confirms what I know. After we reach my room, while we kiss, while his mouth is on my neck traveling from front to back, I ask him questions. I long to hear about his experience, I whisper the question I want an answer to, I ask him how many girls he has fucked. He pauses at the word, searches my face. He takes my hand and brings it down to the front of his pants. I say the word, use it carefully. "Are you going to fuck me?" I ask.

He answers, "Tell me what you want."
And I say, "I want you to fuck me."
At that moment I remember everything I have read, I feel for

myself every place I want his hands, and I show him. I take his pants by the fly, unbutton, unzip, slide them down until he stands and they drop to his ankles.

"I want you to fuck me," I say, as I remove all my clothes, as he kneels on my bed in front of me, as he pulls my hips to meet his, as he lowers himself, takes my hands in his and brings my arms up over my head, as he pushes in and I read joy on his face, as his pushing quickens and my hips move to keep up. I feel his muscles tense; mine wrapped around him begin to contract, and I whisper, "Please." The feeling within is familiar, and I know I need only a bit more of this to make me come. And he pushes again, his eyes close, his face contorts, and I feel his hand travel between my legs, it reaches down, grabs his penis, steals it from me, holds it over my belly until he yells and comes and I feel something warm and wet on my skin. My fingers touch the puddle trapped in the concave hollow between my hipbones. Reading hasn't prepared me for this, and I wonder what it might have felt like inside, I wonder if we would have come together. My own muscles are suspended somewhere between coming and relaxing, and I tell Michael, "Please," I guide his hand, his finger.

As we lie wrapped together, his penis warm between our two bellies, I tell him it would have been okay to stay in. I tell him I am taking birth control pills, and he says he didn't even think, no one ever had before.

"Catholic high school girls." He laughs as if this explains everything.

"Next time," I say, "please stay in, please come inside me."

"Will there be a next time?" he asks, one eyebrow raised.

And I say, "Oh yes, yes, there will," and I stroke him, touch the small of his back, feel the veined, tightened skin of his balls; I run my hand across his chest and watch, wide-eyed, as his nipples harden like my own; I push him onto his back, look him straight in the eye. "Oh, yes," I say again.

Later Michael tells me, "I am in a state of thrall. I've never seen a girl completely naked before you. Before you it was always just fumbling through layers of clothes in the dark," he says. When I look the word "thrall" up in the dictionary, I am not sure I like its definition. But in so many ways I feel in control. Michael assumes I have so much more sexual experience than I actually do.

"I've never known anyone like you."

"What do you mean, like me?" I wonder aloud.

"Experienced, sure of herself."

"Why do you think I'm experienced?" I ask.

"You know what you're doing. Aren't you? Experienced?" He looks slightly embarrassed as he asks.

"No," I answer, "I've never done this before." I put my arms around him in my bed. "It feels good, that's really all I know. I've been thinking about sex, imagining, reading, and I do what I think will feel good."

"Reading? That's a little weird," he says. "You never ever slept with another guy?" he asks.

And I answer with a shake of my head, never certain that he believes me. Sometimes when I look back, even I don't believe my lack of experience.

As I grow up my family works together like the parts of a clock: My father is the winding stem, starting the motion; my mother the cogs; and I am propelled by their actions. I quickly learn to be self-contained, well behaved, observant, and economical with my words.

Before our first communion my best friend twirls to show me her store-bought dress and veil. It nips in at the waist, the wide skirt appears as if from nowhere, absurdly fluffed out by a stiff netting she calls tulle. Her veil rises from a comb, puffs above her head, and falls to her shoulders. My mother has sewn my dress, white wool gabardine. A straight shift, it pulls over my head and buttons with three flat white buttons at my left shoulder. On my head I wear a square lace scarf— a mantilla, my mother says, giving it an exotic air it does not possess. I think it looks like a lace version of one of my father's pocket handkerchiefs. I am a nun among brides: simple, pious, disdaining all earthly vanities.

We line up, boys and girls, on separate sides of the church. We have been rehearsed, instructed to follow directions while at our pew for standing, sitting, kneeling, praying, approaching Father at the altar. I sit between my mother and father, and my father rests his heavy hand on my shoulder as I kneel in my rehearsed prayer. When the priest commands, "All rise," the congregation stands. My father comes to his feet next to me but his hand remains on my shoulder, applying pressure, keeping me kneeling while everyone else follows the service. I do not sit or stand at all; I do not obey Father but Father.

The only time I am able to rise is to receive communion, my first. We have been taught we are ready to receive the Body of Christ. My father looks unconvinced but allows me to go with a wave of his fingers. My friend whispers to me in line, asking why I keep kneeling. I do not know. My father tells me to ask forgiveness, but I do not know for what. I have no answer for her.

Years later, after I make my confirmation, I vow never to return to church. I pretend to go with my friends to the early folk mass for teens, but I sit at the back of the parking lot on a curbstone in all kinds of weather.

This is my secret disobedience.

I have been invited to a birthday party, a pool party, my first with boys and girls. My friend, Cathy, is turning twelve; I was twelve in March. Last year's swimsuit doesn't fit because I am growing breasts sooner than many of my friends. I think my waist has slimmed and my hips are developing, but no one talks to me about this and I am too self-conscious to ask. I spend a good deal of time assessing my new body in my bedroom mirror. Although I like my new curves, and all my friends are envious, I wish my mother would say something so I would know I am normal.

I see a two-piece swimsuit I like. Many girls wear two pieces, have done since I was in single digits. But my mother says no. "Your father wouldn't like that; he is old-fashioned," she explains, and she directs me to yet another one-piece tank suit with the substantial back straps of my swimming-lesson years. In the store I do not question what she's said; nevertheless I do not understand what old-fashioned has to do with a swimsuit. Why I can't wear what everyone else wears. I try it on quickly in the dressing room, and it is just like all the others, cinching, modest. I feel trapped.

When I try my new suit on again at home, the firm stretch material binds my breasts down, flattens them until they—I—feel imprisoned. As I look in the mirror, I begin to understand what my mother meant.

Six of us walk in the dark in the wooded area behind our school. There is a dance tonight, and my friends carry a bottle of premixed vodka-and-orange drink—screwdrivers, they're inexplicably called. Everyone quietly passes this bottle around, but I take only a token sip, then decline any more. It smells to me like a bottled orange punch or baby aspirins, its strong chemical taste and smell remind me of cough medicine and sickly sweet bug spray.

I know it is wrong to drink: First, it is illegal because we are only fifteen; but also, I could lose control.

Once, at a family reunion, my grandfather drank too much. "It was only a drop," he explained to my father.

But my father turned his back when his father asked for a ride home. "Get control of yourself," he hissed. "You won't get in my car with my child in your condition."

I could see my grandfather as we drove away from the party. At first he walked alongside our car, and then as we gathered speed he couldn't keep up; he was small and insignificant in the distance. I thought I could see his lips pursed in a dejected whistle, but that might have been my eyes playing tricks.

As my friends drink, the once-silent circle rapidly becoming giddy with alcohol and wrongdoing; I don't care about the excitement or the opinion of my peers. I can, however, picture my father coldly locking the doors against me, I can imagine having nowhere to go, and I am certain I never want to see his unreachable, unbending stony profile.

We study reproduction and genetics in high school, hatching fruit flies at the school lab, and now I need to write up a report of our findings. The telephone is on the kitchen wall, so after I help clear our dinner dishes I bring out my notebook and call my partner, Robert DeCola. We have worked well together; he is fairly serious for a sixteen-year-old. Some of my friends have been paired with boys who take great pleasure in releasing fruit flies all over the school.

"Hello? May I speak to Bob, please?" I ask. At that moment I see my father pause at the doorway between the dining room and the kitchen.

"Who is that?" he asks.

"My lab partner," I tell him as I wait on the line for Bob to pick up.

"Give me the phone." His lips are white; I remember that.

"What?" I ask. "But I need to talk to him. Our project—"

I relinquish, my father takes the receiver from my weak hand, holds until Bob is on the line.

"Hello," he begins calmly. "This is Mr. Rossi. I'm afraid Anna can't speak to you right now. She'll see you in school tomorrow." And he gently replaces the phone on the wall, breaking the connection.

"Anna," he says, facing me, "you don't telephone boys."

"But I need to write a report with him. It's for science lab." I think this might be funny if I didn't recognize the force behind his words. He means what he says.

"Beverly," he calls, and my mother appears from the other room. She looks from me to my father. "Tell Anna that she is not to call boys. *Ever*. It's cheap, and I'm not raising her to be cheap." That is Father's last word on the subject, and he leaves the room. Beyond the kitchen I hear the television switch on, the volume rising as the set warms up.

"Anna, your father doesn't want you calling boys," my mother parrots.

"No kidding, Mother. I have ears. I heard what he said."

"Don't talk back to me," she says, and I feel the sting of her hand on my face. I bring my own hand up to my cheek in surprise.

"This is so unfair," I cry, fleeing to my room. "It's a stupid science project, not some giggly phone call." I want to slam my door, yell some more, hear my voice bouncing off my walls.

I don't even like boys, I want to call out. *They're stupid and juvenile, and anyway I'm waiting for someone older.* Instead I close my door quietly, not inviting any more slaps or threats. In the end I give nothing away, and my parents like this about me: my silence. I take my hand from my face, look in the mirror at the red streak left there, and it occurs to me that despite my silence maybe my father knows what I'm waiting for.

For the next three years of college Michael and I are inseparable, into the routine of eating, studying, and sleeping together. As we become so close I know the determination within Michael, his drive, the single-minded concentration he gives to reaching his goal, which, I learn, is to practice law. Occasionally I feel him pull away from me mentally, although physically we remain inseparable; sometimes while we are together his mind is just very far away.

One evening I perch on my bed as Michael slouches on the floor hunched over his notes. A few times I reach out to stroke his neck, his shoulder blades, but he removes my hand, telling me, "Later."

But I want him right then, want to feel him in my arms, to slip into bed with him at that very moment. "You have such self-control," I tease.

He turns around and glowers, "Please. I need to get this finished."

"I'm bothering you."

"Yes, you are. Don't you have work of your own to do?"

"Of course I have something to do; the problem is the something I want to do instead." When he doesn't respond, I say, "I'm only telling you how I feel." But I feel silly, sex-obsessed, and as stubborn as a thwarted child. So I return to my studies, dissatisfied; I hate the silence in the room, the attempt at companionable quiet. "Why are you here, then," I press, "if you'd rather be studying alone?"

"It was something I thought we could do together: just sit together and work," Michael explains.

"But we're not doing anything together," I answer. "You're buried in your work, and I'm just waiting, making things up to keep busy. That's about as separate as we can be."

"Do you want me to go? And come back later?"

"Can't we just talk for a while and then get back to work?"

"What do you want to talk about?" he asks, shutting his notebook with an exaggerated sigh.

"I really don't know," I answer, laughing because I am at a loss.

"You're crazy," Michael informs me. "You're like a five-year-old." He opens his course work, which pisses me off. I look over at him, the familiar broad shoulders, the slope of his neck bent over a book, his lean legs stretched out in front of him. Maybe, I think, even as I desire his body, maybe I should have other relationships, against which to measure this one with him.

"Michael, do you really like being here with me? I mean, that wasn't a very nice thing to say."

"What wasn't?" he asks, without lifting his eyes.

"That about me being childish."

"Okay, you're not childish."

"But why would you say it if you didn't mean it? Unless you're just trying to get me to shut up?"

"That's exactly what I'm trying to do." The truth is unmistakable, and it stings.

"Maybe we should stop seeing each other for a bit. Since I'm such a pain."

"Anna, cut it out."

"I mean it. Maybe we should see other people for a while. Maybe this just isn't working out."

"It's worked for the past three years. C'mon, I'm sorry. I'm under a lot of pressure, and I didn't mean what I said. I love you. I don't want to go out with anyone else."

"Why, Michael? Why do you love me?"

"I don't know. You're fun, different from me, lighter. You make my life less serious." He looks at my closed face. "This is why I didn't want to talk. Talking always becomes fighting, and I don't want to fight. I have too much on my mind right now, finals . . . ," his voice drifts off, stating the obvious school pressures. Michael stands, puts his books and notebooks into his backpack. He takes a seat next to me on the bed, puts his hand on my back, and massages my spine up and down until I shiver. "I don't get it," he says. "We're together every day; then I turn around, and you're leaving me."

"I just want to be sure we're right for each other."

"Sounds to me like you want to sleep around. Sanctioned by me." He takes his hand from my back. I slap his face.

"You need to leave," I speak through clenched teeth. "Now."

During the next day I fume as I replay every syllable of our conversation in my head. My outrage builds recalling the insults, and I plan pithy retorts for when the apologetic phone call comes. I am prepared. But he doesn't phone. Not a word. When I pass him on the quad nearly twenty-four hours after our fight, he is with some friends and his eyes rise briefly, locate me, then look away; he makes a show of the conversation he is involved in, pointedly ignoring me. I stand watching, waiting, but his group moves on.

Back in my room I go over our fight again to assure myself that I am in the right. I feel justified.

Twenty-four hours become forty-eight, which then drag into a week of silence. By then I don't care about apologies; I just want to hear his voice. I miss him. Nothing could have prepared me for the emptiness of my bed. I begin to think, with so much solitude, that perhaps I misspoke, perhaps I could have handled the situation better, that I could have made myself understood without threats. I hurt him, I think. His silence proves that.

In my loneliness I forget, or choose to ignore, his final words; but words spoken in anger, are they to be trusted? So as the implied words *slut* and *whore* form in my mind, I quickly squash them down. I pick up the phone and dial Michael's room.

"Can you come over? I miss you," I blurt out when he answers. "I'm sorry."

Ten minutes later he is at my door, and all it took was my phone call. He loves me, I think. I let him in, and we grasp at each other as soon as the door closes. We tear at clothes until, standing, we are both naked. He'll touch me, I think, hold me, love me, and as I back into the wall, Michael lifts me onto his erection and slides in; we cling together, kissing, not moving, just standing connected. I whisper in his ear, I tell him, "slower faster stop more" until he withdraws, lifts his mouth from mine and pulls me into his arms with my back against his chest. Michael pushes into me from behind so I can't see him, holding my hips steady. I am shaking as he grinds into me, and he comes quickly, his legs stiffen until he is way in deep, reaching for something I imagine far within me. I think, He is here with me. I reach my hand down and touch the stickiness between my legs, bring a finger to my mouth, paint it with the stuff, and turn my head to kiss his swollen lips. "Here," I offer, "taste yourself."

In this way, we take possession of each other; there is no turning back.

We decide to marry the week my father dies. He dies over Christmas break during our senior year, shortly after Michael learns he has been accepted to law school and as we both prepare to graduate.

I have been in the house for only two weeks of the midyear break when my mother wakes me after she hears my father fall in the bathroom. I try to reach him as he lies across the cold tile floor, but he blocks the door with his body, and it will take the paramedics removing the door from its hinges to reach him.

I want to step in and reach my father. I hope he isn't sad or scared as he lies alone; I hope he has no awareness at all. I feel he needs someone with him, so I stand at the bathroom door after dialing 911. His rasping intake of breath assaults my nerves. It comes farther and farther apart, dissipating into gurgles, faint rattles, and then nothing. I know, before anyone reaches the house, that he is dead.

A paramedic sits with my mother in the kitchen asking questions, diverting her eyes, blocking the view of invasive equipment meant for reviving my father entering the house. My mother is only temporarily diverted.

"Does your husband have a history of heart disease, Mrs. Rossi?"

"Beverly." She pauses. "Is he dead? Are you telling me he's dead?"

"How long have you been married?"

We won't hear definitely until seated in the emergency room waiting area, after answering medical histories and insurance questions, after glasses of water and aspirins, that he died at home, had not been revived. At home later I sit with my mother, thinking of Michael, needing someone close to be with me, just for me. I call and wake him and ask him to drive to me.

"Don't feel guilty, Anna," Michael says to me as I sob the details into the phone. "There's nothing you could have done, other than just being with your mother." And he leaves his home to come to me.

There is no desire in those days between death and the funeral, after my frantic pleading phone call brought Michael to me. The casket is open for the wake; the dead body is a certain deterrent to desire. At the funeral home many people weep for my father; many chat, forgetting that his dead body is in the same room. I think everything feels strange, from socializing to standing in this home that isn't our home.

Michael stands across the room talking with a group of my aunts and uncles. I speak to no one but ruminate, alone, over funeral directors and floral arrangements. There are so many clashing colors, and an overabundance of perfumes from the bouquets. Some are just too fussy for the sleek gunmetal gray coffin my mother has chosen. I wonder why we bothered to select coordinating sprays since, after all, friends and relations sent whatever their florists had assembled.

Instead of crying I think of all these things. I was up all night with my mother on the night of Father's death, and didn't sleep much in the days that followed. After he was pronounced dead of a heart attack, Mother and I sat together and waited for the sun to come up. On the day of the funeral, therefore, I am too tired to cry.

As I stand between Michael and my mother in the church's service, Michael's hand rests on my back, and after the funeral he asks me to marry him. Later that night, after he feeds me and I say, yes, I'll marry him, we drive to the beach. He has a blanket in the back of his car and spreads it on the uneven sand up in the bluffs, over a spate of coarse beach grass. It is rough beneath my back, poking up through the loose weave of the blanket as I lie under Michael. I lie there feeling every roll of the waves as if the icy Atlantic lived in my innards, black, choppy, and chill.

I am rubbing my eyes with the heels of my hands when Colette knocks at the door. Hours have passed, and it is lunchtime already. She sends me to tidy up and makes me pass a tough once-over before she allows me to accompany her to lunch. In the ladies' room I can see why: There is a huge oil stain on the breast pocket of my white coat and I've just rubbed eyeliner around my lids. Fortunately the stain hasn't bled through to my clothes, and my black shirt and khakis look presentable enough for a casual lunch. I quickly deal with the makeup, pass the once-over, and leave the building with Colette.

We find our favorite lunch spot emptying out after an earlier rush. Colette makes me sit while she goes to the counter to order. When she returns, she's holding a deep dish of bread pudding. When I realize this is what she has selected for my lunch, I break out laughing.

"Comfort food," she pronounces, and I dig my spoon in. "I'll get you another when you've finished this. You look like you can use it. What's going on?"

"Dinner was hell last night," I blurt out. "You know, Julie cornered me in the kitchen to tell me that I'm too needy. That my life has moved into a new phase, and I'd better deal with it. As if I couldn't tell." I rest the spoon alongside the dessert dish and fiddle with my napkin, unable to look my friend in the eye.

"She is a real piece of work." Colette shakes her head. She pushes aside her own lunch and reaches across the table. She gently turns my face in her hands until she has my attention; she touches the sides of my face and I feel the warmth of her fingertips. "News flash: Your husband's friends are assholes."

"Thanks for that." I reach up to take her hands in mine and hold on for dear life. "It's why I love you. I mean it; I begin to wonder if it's just me."

"You are not an asshole. I speak the truth: They're jerks." Colette pauses and looks directly into my eyes. "Let's cut the crap here, Anna. What's really going on? My ex-husband may have had his low moments in my history with him, but he never told me to shut up. At least not in front of company."

Tears fill my eyes. With our fingers entwined, we sit for minutes as I try to think of what to say. But I have no answer for her. "I don't know what's going on except that I am angry all the time," I admit. "Michael works constantly, and I am lonely. When he comes home he has more work to do, and I'm still lonely. When he comes to bed, sex—if we even have it—is . . . awful! . . . and then I'm lonelier than ever." The words, the tears flow out over lunch, over my clothes. But it feels better. Colette passes me her napkin to wipe my face.

"The worst of it," I continue, "is that our days have been like this for so long, I can barely remember anything different. I've let it get this far."

"So talk to him, talk it over," she urges.

"I've started to. I decided 'that's it, I've had enough.' I told him I thought we needed to talk. Last night after dinner I asked him if he wanted a divorce."

"And?" Colette prompts.

"And he brushed me off, said things will change. But do I think he wants to leave? What I think is he finds everything more seductive

than me: work, money, other people, and the web of connections between them. He said right now he needs me to keep things smooth at
home, no making waves," I tell her, mimicking Michael's terse voice.
"Just a fancier way of saying what Julie did: I'm too needy."

"We're all needy, Anna. There's really nothing wrong with needing
to feel loved, especially when you're married. There's absolutely nothing wrong with giving or needing affection."

"I know that, I really do, but when I say, 'Michael, I'm unhappy,'
the minute the words leave my mouth I feel so lame, so emotional. I
feel Michael's disapproval, like he expects me to be only rational and
logical and strong."

"You're not going to like what I have to say," Colette warns.

"Say it."

"You and Michael can dance around this issue indefinitely, take
the roles you each expect of each other, and play out the rest of your
lives. But do you want to live like that? I'm guessing no, otherwise you
wouldn't be here talking to me."

"Listen," I begin. "I'm thinking about asking Michael to take a
vacation with me. We haven't been anywhere in years, and maybe the
time away—just the two of us—would be good."

"A vacation?"

"I thought we could go back to New Hampshire, where we honey-
mooned. It's a comfortable place for us, maybe we could talk there.
Figure out what's going on. Look," I say, seeing the questions in Colette's eyes. "Something's telling me to work at this, that I'll go crazy
if I keep quiet. And there's Sara, she deserves a mother who isn't crazy,
she deserves a better family."

"You can suggest therapy—I'll give you the name of my guy. He
was great." She reaches across the table to squeeze my hand.

"Yeah, and you got divorced."

"So what? He didn't tell me to get divorced. But I was able to see
it as an option, and it happened to be the right one. Is that what
you're afraid of? Divorcing?"

"Of course I'm afraid. I've never been on my own. Michael was
my one walk on the wild side, and I married him. How wild is that, I

ask you? I was trying to get away from my parents, do the bad things, the forbidden: drinking, smoking, cussing, sex," I count off on my fingers. "Back then what I really wanted was someone who wanted to touch me. But I think we had good sex once," I add wistfully.

"Well, good for you. Good sex is great. In fact," she continues with a wicked grin spreading across her face, "I think sex should be like a good meal, and you should never leave the table hungry."

"And these days, when I leave the table? I'm starving!" I proclaim.

The people at the next table turn shocked faces to us, and we put our heads together and giggle like schoolgirls. It is a relief to be able to laugh.

"My one big rebellion. So what?" I ask when the laughter subsides. "How am I any different now? How is the grown-up Anna any different from the well-behaved child?"

"You're not stupid. You have all the answers, you just don't know what to do with them. Talk to Michael, talk to someone. Don't be afraid; you've got people around you to help you."

"Like my mother? You know, there's been exactly one divorce in my family. A Catholic shame. When the family gets together, no one talks about my cousin and her ex-husband. It's like they no longer exist."

"Sounds lucky for them. Seriously, I mean me, you ninny, your friends. You have lots, you know, all over the place. You don't give yourself enough credit. You mentioned getting away, so do it. Let your mother take care of Sara for a few days. Like you said, get off to some comfortable, neutral place, get all the bullshit out of the picture— work, socializing—and talk to him."

When I decide to suggest this trip to Michael, I pick a clear Sunday later in January and plan a family breakfast at one of our neighborhood's restaurants. The restaurant sings with people out for Sunday breakfast. Cinnamon rolls in the front case entice; the smell even reaches the street. Seated, Michael faces street side; the sun streams in the window and hits him squarely in the eyes. Sweat beads break out on his forehead as the warmth of the sun and the excessive glare distress him. Sara and I flank him around the table, and I offer to switch places. I enjoy the warmth, I tell him. Michael declines; instead, he shades his eyes with his hand. His mouth tenses, and all color and animation leave his face. I recognize this face of tension. I stare, trying to catch his eye, but Michael glances furtively around the room, searching for another empty table out of the glare of the sun.

"Where is the waiter, anyway?" he demands.

I feel the vibration through the floor from Michael's bouncing knee before I actually notice his body shaking slightly. He is making me edgy, but I believe if I keep my eyes trained on him until he speaks, until we make eye contact, then we can smile together, relax.

"What?" he asks, finally meeting my gaze. "Could you please stop staring?" he insists.

A waiter arrives with menus, and Michael asks for a glass of water and juice for Sara. Sara bounces in her seat when the juice is set down before her. There is no break in the sun or in Sara's happy chatter.

"Daddy, want some of my juice?" she asks, holding out her glass and straw.

Michael, startled by the sound of her voice, turns sharply and knocks into the glass with his shoulder. Juice sprays his forehead and his shirt sleeve, and Sara laughs. Even I have to hold my fingers over my own mouth before I begin wiping the spilled juice with my napkin.

"Jesus," Michael quietly curses. "Sara, quit waving around your cup. Anna, can you make her stop? And pass me some more napkins; I'm soaked."

"Michael, it was an accident," I try both to appease him and release Sara from some responsibility. Her eyes are wide, her lip is quivering at his sharp voice. "You're not that wet."

"I've got to get out of here," he tells me, standing, giving a final brush to his sleeve. "Why don't you have your breakfast, and I'll see you at home later."

"Where are you going? I don't want to stay if—" I begin, but he cuts me off.

"Stay." He holds up his hand. "I'm going in to work for a few hours. I'm crazy sitting here because I've got a ton of work on my desk. I can change into a clean shirt once I get to the office. I'll see you at home," he repeats.

"I wanted to talk to you, though, about an idea I've had."

"We'll talk later." He looks into my eyes. I am pleading; my eyes flicker all over his face. "I promise, we can talk tonight," he assures me as he grabs his jacket.

Michael walks out into the street, he hunches into his overcoat, then stops to light a cigarette before turning westward to the El tracks.

"Why'd Daddy go?" asks Sara, her eyes wide and questioning.

"He had to go to work, sweetie," I tell her, turning from the window to focus on my daughter. "Work to do. Well, what do you say to pancakes?"

"I'm not hungry."

"Right, neither am I, I guess." The bloated feeling returns. "Let's go home." With my hand on the back of her head, I shepherd Sara away from the table after leaving a huge, guilty tip. At the counter I pay for the juice, pick up some cinnamon rolls for later, and we take hands for the short but cold walk home.

I am not surprised when Michael returns much later in the day, in time for a late dinner. I've fed Sara earlier; she and Michael play briefly; he reads to her and gets her ready for bed as I finish putting our dinner on the table. We eat dinner late, my husband and I, at least four nights a week. Michael sometimes suggests that I don't wait to eat with him. He thinks maybe he should have a sandwich at his desk as he works into the evening. He begs me not to go to too much trouble, for a late dinner means a late night cleanup.

While I set the table, light candles, test the chicken's internal temperature at its fleshy thigh, I think about these sandwiches he speaks of so casually, and imagine piles of pink, fatty meat, heart-attack-prompting cold cuts. Or maybe he means a hamburger from a fast-food place, uniformly gray and tasting of steam and warming lamps and paper wrappers and, if he's lucky, sharp yellow mustard. Onions that smell like the insides of athletic shoes. Surely he doesn't mean a thinly sliced, marinated chicken breast with a small bit of Tabasco-laced mayonnaise, with a crisp but buttery leaf of lettuce and a slice of garden tomato that has never seen the inside of a refrigerator? Or something Mediterranean, like oil-packed tuna mixed with capers and sliced red onion, held together with a bit of lemon juice. Nothing tremendously fussy, but satisfying. Tasty.

It's not a burden, I tell him time after time; I don't mind cooking or cleaning up. In fact, after a day of coming up with vegetarian protein exchanges, for example, I enjoy being a little more creative. I've always enjoyed cooking and working with food. I tried to persuade my parents to let me attend a culinary school when I was eighteen, but they insisted on college; my science grades were too good to ignore. For my father, a chef just didn't have the same cachet as a doctor.

And he had no interest in food, none beyond my mother's over-cooked dinners. At the table when I mentioned cooking as a profession, he told me about his mother, the grandmother I had never known, who could ruin Jell-O because she wouldn't follow the package directions; as I chewed and swallowed down something dry and taste-less, he spoke at length and in gory detail of the many undercooked chickens, birds still oozing blood at the joints, that he ate as a child.

"Do you see," he asked, turning to my mother but addressing both of us, "why I need everything well done?"

The talk of bloody meat made me feel queasy myself so I agreed; I acquiesced to stop the haranguing. My mother, too, nodded.

But for me, working with my hands didn't mean poking at someone's innards. I was a child who had sneaked into a neighbor's yard to steal garden tomatoes, eating them like apples as I stood hidden behind a flowering cherry tree. Where had I sprung from? Mine was a home of foods spiced with onion soup mix. With my innate love of flavors and the look of foods, there was no place for me in a home where we ate only to stay alive. I compromised with the chemistry-based degree in food science, but what I love to do is cook.

So I tell Michael I don't mind dining late because I'd rather have him home; I need to feed my own family something good. Often the meals my father demanded were depressing: tough, dry, stringy meats, the well-fed muscle contracted completely as all its moisture was cooked out. After years of sampling overcooked gray meat and bland foods as a child, I would always feed my family well.

Tonight, with Sara already in bed, it is another quiet meal, the end to a stressful day for both of us. There is no attempt to discuss our work; every day has been pretty much the same for a long time. We limit our talk to Sara. Our love for our child is safe ground. As we sit together I wonder, Has he noticed the seasonings of sea salt or the smoky sweetness of Hungarian paprika? As I watch Michael eat, mechanically filling his mouth until he's no longer hungry, I ask myself if he's recognized the fresh thyme I tucked under the chicken as it roasted. With each question our meal becomes bigger and weightier than simply delicious food on a prettily set table.

As Michael sets down his silver, resting knife and fork on the rim of our delicate china, my dinner remains largely untouched. I am unable to swallow, but I already know what everything must taste like. I've spent hours ingesting the aromas. Instead I drain my wine glass and rise to clear the table. Michael touches my arm as I pass by with stacked dishes. He tells me he has some work to do and excuses himself. From the kitchen I imagine I hear the click of the briefcase locks, and then as an afterthought, the door to the study closing with a heavy push. It is swollen, sits poorly in its frame, and needs some weight to close it. It is about ten o'clock as Michael settles in to work, and I have a kitchen to clean up.

Why, I ask myself as I recork the wine bottle and wrap the leftovers, do we sit at the table with nothing to say?

I knock softly on the study door and enter when I hear Michael's voice. He's pouring himself a gin and tonic, no ice, no lime, and it's late for a drink, nearly midnight. Tomorrow's Monday; I have to work in the morning and so does he. My mind reels at the thought of six hours of sleep and hustling Sara out the door. I make a silent wish that she's cooperative in the morning, for I know my patience will be slim on little sleep.

This is when I propose to Michael, finally, the idea for a trip over his birthday, just the two of us.

"We can go away to be alone," I suggest, "to get away from all the crazy routines we've created for ourselves. In February, for your birthday.

"Neither one of us has had a break since Sara was born," I urge, "and she just turned five. My mother is dying to take her for the week, we can stay at the Chapmans' inn, see some friends. I talked to Nora and Hugh, they have a room for us."

"This'll cost a fortune."

"Not a fortune. Anyway it'll be worth it. It's your birthday, and a vacation from work besides. It'll be good for us."

"Have you got this arranged already?"

"Well, I had to speak to everyone, to make sure we could swing it. Remember the chalet? How beautiful everything is in the snow? And Stanley's? I'll even throw in blueberry pancakes at Stanley's."

Michael rubs his eyes after I finish talking, takes the last few sips of his drink, and shrugs his assent, slowly, reluctantly agreeing to my plan after we go back and forth over the details. I move to his desk, riffle the papers a bit, then close his folders. He doesn't object; he's tired, and I decide to bring him to bed. I want to reach him, hoping I will find some bit of what used to be between us.

But I don't. When we're in our room, I close the door firmly behind me, turn down the lights. Michael is in washing up. When he comes out of the bathroom, he's still in his clothes, so I begin to undress him, starting with the buttons of his shirt. This is our usual routine of making love, so he stays still, doesn't do the work himself. Now we forgo the touch, the taste, the appearance—even the scents of each other exist only in memory—and we move directly to the rhythm of fucking. Now we move right to the gentle rocking hypnotizing motion, dulling the world around us.

When we're in bed and I move on top of Michael, I try to clear my mind. His eyes are closed with fatigue, but he's moving against me and I try to concentrate on the back-and-forth, up-and-down motions. Before long, though, my mind is reviewing a million details for work tomorrow. Grilling eggplant instead of frying. How much lemon to replace salt, how much applesauce will replace shortening, how much egg substitute will I use instead of whole egg? Cookies for Sara's class. Peanut butter. Carrot muffins for the party or chocolate cupcakes? Ideal temperatures for baking muffins, proportions of whole grain flour and unbleached flour. New grains to work with: buckwheat groats, quinoa, flaxseed, bulgur. Barley pilaf instead of rice, brown rice instead of white. How to season tofu to replace chicken in a stir-fry. Quick soak of dried beans, black bean burritos instead of meat. How little oil can I get away with? How much vinegar in a dressing? Calculating calorie counts, portion sizes, balances, protein exchanges. Good spices, less salt, vegetable broths for cooking, olive oil, canola. Use less.

Michael comes beneath me, and he can sleep. Before I rise to wash up, my earlier question knocks around my head as loudly as if I'd shouted it in a bare room. But the room is quiet, and Michael sleeps on.

Fresh yeast looks like chalk against my wooden tabletop; a gray brick, it breaks up like the strata of sedimentary rock. Yet it gives, squishes under my thumb and forefinger as I crumble it into a bowl. Unlike dried yeast, it won't take very hot water, so I'm careful to test for warmth with my fingers: If they begin to tingle, then throb, within ten seconds of immersion, the water is too hot. It should feel like a baby's tepid bathwater, and it does, so I pour water over the yeast and wait for a slow foam. Some people think that you need sugar to proof yeast, that only by seeing the yeast bubble as it devours the sugar can you really tell if the bread will rise. But it's not necessary if you know what you're doing, and I usually skip that step.

Since I can't sleep any later than four-thirty on Monday morning, I decide to bake bread to start the day. The sour smell reaches my nose within seconds of adding water to the yeast. When I was pregnant, the smell made me feel ill, reminded me of the yeast of puked-up beer or unwashed bodies on an overcrowded subway. So I bought bread. Now I make my own. I think that Michael and Sara will be nourished by the good flour, water, and sea salt; take strength from the energy I massage in with my hands now strong themselves from so much kneading. Bread dough can feel like flesh, the malleable and soft outside holding something even softer, more fragile within. Straight from the oven, the inner crumb can be torn apart, steamy, slathered with sweet butter or jam, or both if I am feeling indulgent.

The kitchen is warm from the oven. The aroma of fresh bread travels through the house and seeps through imperfect seals at my windows and doors and hovers outside, suspended in the air. The smell draws Sara to the kitchen, to my side. I want to feed them, Michael and Sara, with good things that I make, and my heart expands when I watch Sara reach for a slice of bread. She asks for honey. We get this English honey that is thick and cloudy, and Sara calls it fuzzy honey. It spreads like jam, so I let her knife it on generously. Michael rolls his eyes as he walks through the kitchen.

"Her teeth," he reminds me.

"We'll brush," I reassure him. "Have some breakfast."

"Can't," he replies, ignoring the toast already on a plate at the table. "I'm late. Can you pour me some coffee?" he asks, holding out his thermal mug, its lid in his other hand.

I take the cup from him, place it on the counter, and pour coffee from the pot. Steam rises, soon captured by the lid. Michael grabs his cup, kisses my head, blows Sara a kiss from the doorway. It makes me feel better to imagine him standing just outside the door, stopping briefly, breathing in the scent of warm bread before rushing to the El. Thinking about what he's passed up, perhaps, his stomach rumbles in hunger, responding at once to the scent reaching his nose. I watch him for a moment as he turns the key in the lock, his posture perfect as he walks down the few steps and onto the sidewalk. It is an assured walk, upright, erect, open to the world around him but oddly invulnerable, unapproachable.

"Sara," I say, "how about those teeth?" As I've been watching out the window she's been sneaking extra honey on her finger straight from the jar. And hands, too," I remind her as she runs from the kitchen. Once I hear water running, I take the bread I've sliced for Michael, toasted for him, to the back door. Yes, it does smell wonderful out here. Breaking the bread into bits, I throw it to the winter birds that flock the frozen, unyielding ground, grateful for easy food.

PART TWO

The Man Who Ate with His Hands

 We flew into Boston today from Chicago, rented a car, and now begin our journey north with a stop in the suburbs to settle Sara comfortably in my mother's home. Sara spends the thirty minutes before Michael and I leave opening cupboards and drawers: fondling, snooping, asking questions. A writing mass of impulse, she is a breath of fresh air in my childhood home. My mother's patience, surprisingly, is boundless; her gentle way with my daughter catches me off guard. Sara is not scolded for looking, touching, asking, and when she comes across some old photo albums, my mother sits with her on the couch telling her something about each picture.

When I come out of the kitchen with cups of tea, Sara is studying a picture of me at six, not much older than my daughter is now. "Mommy," she exclaims, "you look like me." And it's true, she has my face, the face I had as a young girl. My mother agrees. "She has Michael's mannerisms—she stands like he does—but she is the picture of you." To Sara she says, "And your mother was a very pretty little girl."

I look closely at the picture. In it I am smiling, showing big new teeth that look like I've borrowed them from someone else, ill-fitting hand-me-down teeth. My hair is cut way up on my forehead, short around my ears and neck. A pixie, the cut lives up to its name: I look more like a waif than a pretty girl. But I am secretly pleased my mother thought I was pretty. Looking closely I see the hint of cheekbones, the tease of my older face. Already in my early thirties I've lost the roundness, and can sometimes see the contours of my skull when I look in the mirror.

I feel relaxed as I sip my tea. My mother is so monopolized by Sara that her cup is untouched, and the tea is chilling. Michael excuses himself to get Sara's small suitcase from the car. He'll use this time to have a cigarette, I'm sure, for he knows my mother hates them in the house. When we visit they play this game: My mother knows he smokes, but as long as she doesn't see him, she can pretend he has no bad habits. Michael obliges; he doesn't mind smoking on the sly. It's a comfortable game for us all, and I'm amazed at how polite we can be.

Watching my mother with Sara, I long to have a mother I could confide in, I long for us to sit with our cups of tea and talk about my marriage, the reason for this trip, my fears, while Michael smokes out back, shadowy and distant. I'd like to be comforted, enfolded in a pair of arms, stroked, supported. Still, I should be happy: Our relationship has settled into a calm one, easier, less rigid since my father's death.

At Sara's age I, too, had sat on the same couch with my mother, open books on our laps. I had just started school, and my father had begun a new job. A promotion, my mother explained as she took breaks between books to dress for dinner in a restaurant with a new boss and new clients.

As I sat with my mother, she absentmindedly stroked the inside of my arm. Every time she turned a page she stopped, until I demanded, "Again, again." I told her, "That tickles, Mother. I like that," and pleasure radiated from my young face. I squirmed with being petted; I loved it, loved the tickling that ran up my arm and made me shiver. At that moment I loved my mother so purely and simply for making me feel this good, and I snuggled my face into her breast. She was soft there, and warm, so soft that I brought my hand up to touch. My mother stopped running her fingernails along the inside of my arm like butterflies and removed my hand. "Stop that," she said.

We heard the car pull into the driveway, heard the car door open and close as my father got out to open the garage. Mother sat up straighter, she straightened me next to her as we listened for his footsteps in the kitchen. From the couch I heard ice filling a glass, cupboards opening, liquid pouring, the fizz that comes with loosening a soda bottle cap.

"Beverly?" Father called.

"I don't want you to go," I whined, and as my mother listened distractedly, I returned to baby speech, to lisps and truncated words.

"Stop that whining," she said firmly. "It cuts through me like a knife. He needs me, Anna, and you need to sit here quietly like a good girl while we change for dinner. Not another sound, do you understand? Or your father will put you in your room."

I nodded and lay back on the couch with my eyes closed and rolling back in my head like death. I heard my father's wingtip shoes on the uncarpeted oak floors. Without a word to me as he walked by, I heard the ice clattering in his glass as he ascended the stairs.

He liked it when I kept myself quiet for longer and longer stretches; I liked the challenge of keeping still better than being removed to my room, alone with my disgrace until the babysitter arrived. When I really tried for my father I could stay very, very still.

The silence is a screen between us in the front seat of our rental car, an uncrossable barrier. Our thoughts just hang around us, unspoken. I want to lay my hand on my husband's shoulder, but I refrain. In the car's interior—no music, no talk, just the dull sound of wind shear and tires on the road—I become lulled by the passing scenery. We quickly leave the busy highways of Massachusetts, pass the state border liquor stores, the industrial cities of southern New Hampshire, and enter long stretches of expansive wooded areas, mountains in the foreground beckoning us to come closer, teasing in the distance. The mountains take me by surprise after our last seven years in the Midwest. I am sorry for anyone who's never been here, sorry for myself for staying away for so long.

Out the car window is nature, a foreign land. My landscape for a number of years has been buildings, some of the tallest in the country, congested highways, row houses. Even the parks along Lake Michigan, though tree-filled and grassy, are surrounded by high-rises, people living in stacks looking out over a lake that resembles an ocean until you notice it barely moves unless there's a storm. Here the trees are tall, and the woods are dense. There are marked trails in the woods—for hiking or cross-country skiing—but it's so dark in there I could get lost. In the past I had entered these woods, blindly trusting the trails; I had walked alongside mountain streams and come out to clearings on the other side. You can't get lost in a city constructed on a grid if you have your map, and there are always taxis to find you and take you where you want to be.

I want to get out of the car and look out over the valley because it is dark and clear and I can see the first stars, my first in a long time. But since we are only fifteen minutes away from the inn and it is getting late, Michael wants to press on. There is a scenic pull-off, and for once I implore Michael to stop. His lips stretch out in a thin line, but he does this for me. I open Michael's door, pull him out into the night. I hold his hand as we stand at the railing, flimsy protection against a rough drop. The dark, my fear, are exhilarating, and I thread my fingers into Michael's, and I think I feel him squeeze back, applying a bit of reassuring pressure. We stand together, facing the mountains' outlines, which lead our eyes down to the black void of the valley.

We pull into the White Horse Inn late Friday evening, just before eleven.

The tavern is open and lively with rounds of Bass ale and a serious game of darts. I can see Michael is fatigued from the flight and the long drive; it shows in the grim set of his mouth. But we are quickly sucked into the crowd, and gregarious Hugh Chapman presses pints of beer on us. We recognize very few people other than our old friends, the Chapmans. But of course it's been a long time.

Hugh and Nora Chapman have owned the inn and tavern for years. They were, in fact, our biggest source of conversation and speculation during our newlywed days. Hugh is British-born, a former New York stockbroker. From listening to his pub stories, Michael and I assumed Hugh gave up the fast life for his own business in New Hampshire. We played at inventing their stories, getting carried away with outlandish details until we finally believed everything we made up, even long after they became close friends. In the past Hugh always had a pint in hand, egging on the darts competition or playing dominoes with us. He always drank a bit too much, leaving Nora to run the kitchen and make the guests comfortable and welcome. And this hasn't changed. I'm surprised, somehow, to find them still here, still together, just two hardworking innkeepers.

Tonight, not long after we've settled at a table, Hugh leaves Nora at the bar and sits down with us. "Well, Judge," Hugh says to Michael, "last time you were up here you were living the life of a student. How does it feel to be playing with the big boys? Are you here to relax?" Hugh christened Michael "Judge" when he started studying for his law degree.

" 'Relax,' " echoes Michael. "Man, this is the first vacation Anna and I have had in about five years, which she bluntly reminded me of not too long ago. And you know what? I'm too tired right now to tell you how 'relaxing' feels."

"Hold on," says Hugh, and he hustles to the bar to bring back more beer, which Nora has ready for us on a tray.

"How about a smoke, Judge?" asks Hugh when he finishes handing out the second round of Bass. I'd forgotten these two smoked heavily as the beer went down. As an afterthought Hugh offers the Dunhills to me. I've never smoked beyond a drag on Michael's cigarette years ago on a dare, but I take him up on his offer. Hugh leans across the table, extending his lighter, and I catch its flame, inhale shallowly and recognize the taste of my husband's mouth. Michael lifts an eyebrow but doesn't betray me. I think I am doing fine, haven't choked, and it feels comfortable in my hand. "So you're tired? More reason to be on vacation. Nora," he calls, motioning for her to come to the table, "these people are tired. Haven't had a break in years, they tell me. So, should we all raise our glasses, or have a good cry in our beer?" Hugh's eyes sparkle as he teases us.

"You shouldn't joke about it, Hugh. Michael has a habit of falling asleep wherever he happens to be sitting. Despite the scintillating company." Hugh turns a questioning eye to Michael, but Michael is looking at me with something simmering on his face.

"Once," he says, locking eyes with me. But I don't back down. Maybe I should have taken up smoking long ago; I feel like a different person. Or maybe the beer has gone to my head. We stare into each other's eyes until laughter erupts from my mouth. My eyes crinkle, and it feels so good to be this happy teasing my husband, even better when seconds later he is able to laugh, too.

"Once," he explains to Hugh between sips of beer, "once, man, I fell asleep at dinner. It was a long week."

"I never look back and regret leaving all that madness behind me," responds Hugh. "But I can see you've still got that manic look in your eye. What? Are you still charged up with work?"

"I love work," Michael replies. "It's so much more satisfying than school. The mind games, the intellectual tug of war, constructing the better argument. It's something, Hugh, working on this adrenaline."

"A male thing," I observe wryly. "A real testosterone rush."

"Everyone feels it, Anna, the men and the women," Michael retorts.

"So it's like sex?" I ask. "Only without the actual sex? Much neater, I suppose, between men and women."

Nora steps over to join us and piles empty glasses on the tray in her hands. Hugh grabs her by the waist until she sets down the tray to sit for a moment on his knee. "I think I arrived in the middle of a very weird conversation," she observes.

"Sex." I nod. "Men and women. Very weird." I blow smoke into the air and stub this cigarette out.

Michael drains his glass. "If the brain is the primary sensory organ, why can't intellectual intercourse," he continues even as we collectively groan at his pun, "be as powerful as sex?" Despite his joke's reception, Michael smiles. He loves the wordplay.

"Maybe at times it can be as powerful as sex," I agree. "But great sex? Great sex should start in the brain and then travel to other parts of the body."

Hugh laughs out loud. "Sounds like you have a working thesis. Only think of the experiments, the research!" he exclaims.

"I'd love to try, Hugh," I say, "if only someone would give me the chance."

"I'm sure you could find volunteers." He turns to Michael. "In the interests of science, of course."

"That's my cue to leave," Nora tells us. "You three are crazy. Anyway, I've got to close up, shoo off these stragglers," she refers to the last few drinkers at the bar. "But you all stay right where you are. We'll talk a little longer, and I'll get you settled upstairs."

As she leaves, Hugh jokes, "If you let her, she'll turn down the bedcovers and tuck you in, too." He drains his glass. "Although I tried telling her you'd probably figure out how the bed works all by yourselves. The second honeymoon thing isn't lost on me. Which reminds me, now that we've gotten rid of the masses, let me break out something special."

Hugh goes to the bar and dips into the refrigerator under the counter. Holding up a bottle, he says, "A nightcap." He grabs four small glasses in the other hand and rushes them back to the table. Nora locks the door and shuts off the bright overhead lights. We're sitting in semidarkness, our table lit by the lamps over the bar and the fire in the fireplace.

"Aquavit." He shows us the bottle. "Danish schnapps. You drink it down cold, from the freezer, and ten seconds later heat explodes in your chest. Amazing." He pours, lifts his glass in a toast, "To marriage."

Except for Nora, we've all had two beers apiece. It's nearly one in the morning, and I'd like to go to bed, but I accept the shot glass, bring it to my nose, and sniff. I smell, faintly, caraway and thick, black Magic Markers, so I sip with caution. Michael and Hugh have swallowed quickly, and Hugh pours another round. I decline; Nora holds her hand over her glass.

"So what will you do while you're here?" she asks me.

I set my glass down. Talking is an excuse to stop drinking. "We haven't made too many plans. That was kind of the point," I explain, "to get away from planning every last minute. I'd like to spend some time out of doors. It's not so cold that we couldn't go cross-country skiing on one of the trails."

"The last time we went skiing, Anna, you couldn't keep up," Michael reminds me.

"That's because the group we were with decided it was a race instead of a leisurely trek through the woods. Just the two of us, we could take our time. You wouldn't have to leave me behind."

"I didn't leave you behind," Michael protests. "You couldn't keep up."

"Same thing," I tell him.

"Not quite," he replies, smiling.

"Hair-splitting," Hugh breaks in. "Why don't you just hang around here? Sit by the fire, read some books. Do a whole lot of nothing for the next couple of days." Hugh pours two more shots of Aquavit. "You don't even have to leave your room if you don't want to." We sit in silence for a few minutes as the men finish their drinks.

It was in an open field, six or seven years ago, that I watched my husband and his friends, men more than six feet tall and experienced women skiers, take off down a trail marked Expert. This was my first ski, there was no one with us who was as inexperienced. No one to keep me company, although Michael offered. I saw him look down the trail after making the offer so I told him, "I'll be okay alone."

He gave me the keys to the truck. "In case you get cold, waiting."

They enjoyed the sport, narrow trails, uphill jogs. I simply liked the trees, the snow, the sunshine warming my face, my neat tracks in the pristine snow, the heat under my sweater as I kept moving. I skied for about an hour, staying close to the clearing, and that's when I started to wonder how long they would be on their trail. Maybe hours. Maybe they'd get lost or someone would get hurt, and I would be here waiting and waiting.

My feet began to sting with the cold, even when I kept moving. I made my way back to the truck, but I was afraid to turn on the engine, fearing asphyxiation or draining all the gas, so it was just as cold inside. I piled discarded jackets over my legs and felt a bit warmer. Worrying, though, drained the blood from the outer edges of my body. Nerves rested up under my ribs, in a flutter. I strained my ears for human noise, but it was quiet in here, like a locked room.

When they returned, they found me asleep under jackets. The sun was starting to go down. "I was worried," I told Michael, and tears fell down my face in a frustrated rage.

He laughed at me while wiping my face with his scarf. "You were sleeping pretty soundly for someone so worried. C'mon, we were fine. It was great, a great trail."

They began telling me, over the noise of the ignition, the heater turned up high and blasting heat, all about the adventure. Everyone told a bit, the next person finishing the sentence, telling a bit more. I thought of the game I played as a child, a party game called Gossip. You would whisper something to the person next to you, and the story passed along and along until the last person spoke it aloud. In the end, the story would be embellished, outrageous, like the ones Michael and his friends were telling me: each exploit, each trick in the trail better than the last.

Finally the conversation died down as they reflected on the day. As we pulled out to the main road, Michael asked, "What about you, darlin'? Did you have a good time?"

I nodded, I told him about the tracks I made in the snow before I began to get cold and worried.

"Maybe you can try the trail next time. Won't be so dull for you." He patted my knee; he was humoring me. He knew I wouldn't be able to keep up.

Under the table Michael, relaxing with the last sips of his Aquavit, presses his leg against mine. The feeling is so unfamiliar that I flinch and move my leg away involuntarily, a reflex. He notices the jump, and catches my ankle with his foot.

"We haven't done nothing in awhile, have we?" he asks me, moving his arm over my shoulders in a kind of lazy, slow stretch. His eyes, as he turns them to me, are glassy. It was a mistake, I think, staying up so late, drinking, talking after our flight and long drive. Nora notices, too, and adds, "Or you could just catch up on your sleep. We've kept you up too late; it was selfish. There'll be plenty of time to visit later."

She rises, discreetly whispers in Hugh's ear. He averts his eyes, nods, and leaves. Michael and I watch as he heads up the stairs to bed while Nora begins cleaning up the glasses, capping the bottle.

"Here's your key," she shows me. "Top of the stairs, turn right, and all the way to the end of the hall." Nora, tired, leans over and kisses me on the cheek. I must look pained, for she says, reassuringly, "Get some rest, sleep as late as you like. Anyway, it's good to see you two back here again. It's been too long."

Michael is waiting for me at the top of the stairs. He takes the key from me but can't manage to get it in the lock. Before he gets frustrated I hold out my palm for the key; my suppliant hand asks "Please" nicely. So he places it without argument in my hand, and I get the door opened swiftly.

Our bags are just inside the room, I feel them with my foot, see their outlines in the moonlight coming in at the window. I feel along the wall for a light switch, feel Michael's hands behind me holding me by the waist, moving me into the room before I find the light. He closes the door with his foot, his hands still hold me, and he pulls my back against him, kisses the back of my neck, the side, my shoulder. He whispers to me in the dark, "Is this the kind of experiment you had in mind?"

Michael relaxes his hold, lets out a heavy sigh, and I smell his breath like a pendent herbal cloud in the air around my mouth and nose. I turn, hold his hands low on my hips, try to kiss him back. I find his lips in the darkness, go exploring around his mouth. His hands leave me to unbutton his shirt, his jeans; he's moving fast, his clothes drop off but our mouths are still together. I touch his face, hold it closer to me still kissing his mouth. Michael moves his hands back to my sides, moves them slowly up along my ribs. I feel his fingers edging into the spaces between the bones, a place I loved having tickled as a child. He takes a breath from our kiss, rests his forehead, his nose, against mine. His fingers move along my rib cage and he whispers into my mouth. "Your bones," he says. "You are too thin." The touch is assessing me, judging. He takes my shoulders instead, gives me a tight kiss with his mouth closed, pulls back, moves the hair from my forehead, where it is always falling into my eyes. He kisses my forehead, like he does with Sara, then leaves me so he can lie down.

"Christ, the room is spinning," he tells me in the dark. It is the last thing he says before he passes out.

Plenty of cars down here," says Michael as he cruises around, looking for a place to park.

"Yes," I answer. The downtown is hopping, a tourist mecca in contrast to the serenity we've left seven miles up the road. We squeeze into a space in front of the restaurant.

"Wait, wait," calls Michael as I reach for the door handle, and he leaps from the driver's seat. He's going to open my door, I realize with surprise, something I don't recall he's ever done. We walk into the teeming restaurant, noisy with vacationers, the kind of sparkling, crackling chatter that simulates electrical current with zaps and zips that make their way to my ear in snatches. The place is alive, the sum total of every individual in the room, and as we enter, our evening promises to be moved along by its gathering force. Through the noise I hear my name. Turning, I see our friend, short, sturdy, dark-haired Ben, the chef-owner of this lively place, opening his arms to embrace me. Years ago Ben, sensing in me a shared appreciation for food, took me by the hand, led me behind the scenes, and showed me all the preparations within his kitchen.

At first I cling to him awkwardly, but soon we're laughing and hugging some more. He smells of thyme and roasting meat, even hand soap that I smell when he takes my face in his hands and kisses both cheeks. He shakes Michael's hand and keeps hold while leading us over to a table. Wine is chilling in a bucket next to the table, but Michael asks for some gin, and Ben calls a waiter over to take his order.

"It's good to see you both. It's been way too long," Ben tells us as he pulls out my chair for me to sit.

"It smells wonderful in here, Ben, all winy and spicy. And garlic!" I exclaim. "It's making me hungry. Even you smell good enough to eat."

"Business looks good," Michael adds.

Ben answers, "This time of year, yeah. These skiers are kind of a captive audience. And of course, it's the only place in town to get real food."

I smile at his easy assessment. He looks so proud, standing over us, and rightfully so, for he works hard and feeds his customers well.

"The only problem with the tourists is," Michael begins, leaning in conspiratorially, "they are too fucking loud."

Ben laughs heartily at this, and Michael raises his drink before taking a sip. "Still a great martini. I suppose I can't smoke in here?" he asks.

"Up at the bar, if you really have to. But those things will kill your taste buds," Ben warns.

"Can you stay and talk a bit?" I ask Ben.

He puts his hand on my shoulder and shakes his head. "Someone's got to get working in the kitchen if you want to eat. If I leave those lazy bastards alone too long, they tend to forget we have hungry people out here. Seriously, I've got a couple of things I want to make specially for you. I'll come back later, though. Promise." I reach up and squeeze his hand, which is clean and warm.

Alone now with Michael as he finishes his martini, I wonder why he's drinking this much, why all weekend he's been filling up with alcohol, and I make small talk to keep him from upending his glass so quickly. But in the middle of my chatter, our waiter returns, opens our

wine, and pours some into glasses that soon begin to drip with condensation. I smell cut grass and hay and take a sip with my eyes closed.
We don't have to look over menus, make decisions, talk about choices:
Ben has planned the entire meal for us. But perhaps it doesn't matter,
perhaps after years of cigarettes Michael can't taste a thing.

I lean across the table and tell Michael in a low voice, "I hope
you like your dinner. I hope it tastes—" I repeat but without finishing
my thought because our first course arrives. Wild mushrooms, earthy
and musky, crisp phyllo pastry, chive sauce. As I taste the butter in
my first mouthful, I can't recall what or when I last ate. Something for
breakfast in the late morning as I visited with Nora in the kitchen;
coffee, my stomach reminds me, and I eat slowly, relishing every bite.
Across the table, Michael has set down his silver. It takes me a minute
to realize he's asked me a question.

"Excuse me?" I ask since I haven't heard him.

"I said, could you pour me another glass of wine?" I look down
and his glass is, indeed, nearly empty.

"Sure, but why don't you take it easy? The wine's not going anywhere, and we have—"

Michael cuts me off. "I'm fine."

"Okay," I answer, holding up my hand. I remind myself that we
are here to relax and talk, not to start fights, especially not here, not
tonight, not this weekend. Instead, his accomplice, I fill his glass and
push the bottle back into the ice, ice moves up the bottle and slides
up the side of the wine bucket, displaced by the force contained in my
hand.

As we finish our first course I talk to Michael about the food,
talking sauces, techniques, varieties of mushrooms. Babbling, I begin
to feel flushed with trying too hard, with too much rich food too
quickly. Michael looks at me as he chews, only nodding as I talk on,
and I detect a slight moisture building along my upper lip.

"Can you excuse me?" I ask.

I need to splash water on my face, my wrists, maybe the back of
my neck. In the ladies' room at the sink I take a minute to blot my
face with a damp paper towel until I feel cooler.

On the way back to Michael I slink around tightly spaced tables to stop at the bar for a cold drink, something to bring my body temperature down. I smile at the bartender, "Hi, I'd like—" I begin, but he interrupts, saying, "If you want another bottle of wine, I'll send your waiter over."

"No, I don't want any more wine," I tell him. "What I really want is some soda water."

"Perrier?" he asks.

"No, just soda is fine. Lots of ice."

As he siphons my water, I check my watch: We arrived at nine, and it is now after ten. When I look up the glass is in front of me. Taking a cool sip, I notice a man seated next to me, maybe my age, alone. His shirt is worn threadbare at the collar and elbows, the fabric is limp from too much wear. He sits with a poorly kept, cracked leather jacket on his lap. His jeans are torn, his hair mussed, but he has a smile for me as he acknowledges my stare, a brilliant smile that makes the tatters seem insignificant. He reaches over the bar and plucks a slice of lime from a bowl. Holding it above my glass, with his eyes, the lift of an eyebrow, he asks if I want some in my water.

"Go ahead," I tell him, and he squeezes the juice into my glass, floats the peel on top of the ice. It is a strange, intrusive offer, but, I realize, it is just what I wanted; the lime is refreshing. He motions at the bartender with his head, "He never puts lime in unless you ask."

From the kitchen come two large white bowls; they are set down, along with a plate of sliced bread, in front of my neighbor. Mussels steamed in white wine with garlic butter, and an empty bowl for shells. "Dinner," he explains as he eats, tearing the shells open and discarding them, dipping the bread in the broth, and eating hungrily. The ritual, his fingers, fascinate me. I forget my drink and my own dinner and watch him instead.

"Would you like some?" he asks, laughing at me and my unwavering gaze.

"No, thanks. I'm sorry I'm staring."

"No need to be sorry. You looked hungry, that's all." He finishes off the mussels and then the broth with the last piece of bread.

"No." I shake my head emphatically. "I'm not. I should go . . . my husband, my dinner's probably waiting."

"You're Ben's friend, aren't you?" he asks, placing me as he stands down from the bar stool. He puts some money on the bar and picks up his water glass.

"How did you—" I start to ask.

"Saw Ben at your table. I work here. Your mushrooms?"

"My mushrooms?" I repeat, thickly uncomprehending.

"Your first course, the wild mushrooms," he reminds me. "I made them."

"Oh. They were good," I tell him.

"Good?"

"Very good."

"Very good," he mimics, amused by my limp praise. He laughs at me again and it is a laugh full of delight, deep and resonating below the hollow at the base of his throat.

Oddly, I am not embarrassed this time. I tell him, "They tasted of the earth. Of the roots of trees breaking through the ground and of the damp undersides of rocks."

He turns to me, again offering that smile. "Like you said, very good."

He holds his water glass and his hands over the empty bowl that once contained the long black ovals of mussel shells, steamed open and edged with deep purple lips, and he pours water first over one hand and then the other, washing the butter, the wine, and flecks of herbs off with ice water without spilling a drop on the bar. He wipes his hands, grabs his dishes, and leaves through the kitchen.

With the swipe of a damp cloth the bartender further removes any traces there might have been.

"You were gone awhile," Michael states, pointing at the dinner set out on the table: veal chops. Michael's is already half eaten; mine rests on what was, when hot, a creamy puddle of polenta and meat *jus*. "The waiter didn't want to leave your dinner to get cold, but I told him to go ahead. I didn't think you'd be this long."

"I needed some water. I was getting warm," I answer sullenly. Also in my absence, the wine bottle has been emptied, Michael's glass topped off, and the dead bottle inverted, neck down. A bottle of wine contains at best five glasses. I begin a scoreboard in my head: Anna two, Michael three, plus one gin equals four drinks. Instantly I am angry that I've begun to count my husband's drinks, to hold each one of them against him. Angry at him for drinking, angry at my anger. "And then I got to talking with one of the cooks at the bar. We talked awhile about mushrooms."

"Mushrooms?"

"Mushrooms, and what they taste like," I explain. "What about you?" I ask him. "Are you enjoying your dinner, Michael?"

"It's fine, it's good."

"Good, I'm glad," I say.

Good, I think, good dinner. Very good mushrooms. He can't taste, and I can't eat, I think. What a pair. I've come back to the table with a bad mood developing, looking at cooling food, half-eaten meals, dead bottles of wine, smeared wine glasses, water glasses, scattered used silver, a drooping yellow freesia, candlelight flickering through the openwork of a hammered aluminum holder and shining on a spotted tablecloth, even my discarded linen napkin, crumpled upon my departure and left next to my plate. So many things on such a small table for two. So many things between us and not one of them simply very good. Especially not this conversation, which is hardly what I planned when I suggested that we needed to talk. But I am incapable of stopping the momentum of my anger.

"And the wine? Did you enjoy that too?" I ask.

"What's the matter, Anna? Are you angry because I finished the wine?" Michael asks, scrutinizing my face, looking for confirmation of the sarcasm he hears in my voice.

"Never mind," I tell him, "it's not important. As long as one of us is sober for the ride home."

For a moment neither of us speaks. All around us, plates clatter, silver rattles; I even hear the sound of a match striking as a waiter relights the candle at the next table. I watch as Michael absorbs the impact of my words. His face is absolutely blank, no expression, no anger. He gives me nothing. Very carefully he places his knife and fork on the side of his plate. He wipes his mouth, lays down his napkin. His face is remarkably composed. "I'm just me, Anna. Christ, you've known me for nearly fourteen years, you know who I am. What is it you want from me?" he asks.

I answer, "I don't know."

Michael rises and collects his coat from the rack near the door. It occurs to me I could call after him, take my words back, apologize: "I'm sorry. I'm sorry. I'm sorry." These words sound familiar to me, part of my lexicon, part also of my past. Instead, finishing my soda water, I watch Michael leave, watch him shoulder his way through the crowd at the entrance. I see a shadow on the table, sense a body behind me. When I look up expecting to see the waiter, I see instead Ben. He, too, watches Michael leave, disbelief coloring his strong face.

"Can I?" he asks, pulling out the empty chair.

I nod in answer.

"What happened?" Ben questions. He puts his hand across the table, takes the empty glass from my hand, sets it down, and takes my hand in his. This quiet gesture of friendship makes my eyes fill with tears.

"I think for the first time in my life I was a bitch," I tell Ben, which makes him smile.

"First time, huh?"

"Probably not the first, no. But maybe the last." I continue, "We haven't exactly been getting along. I got angry because we aren't able to talk so instead, I told him he was drinking too much."

"Ouch," Ben winces.

"And he left. Actually," I speak on, "I thought all this might help," and I gesture at the table. "But nothing's turning out the way I expected."

"Nothing ever does. Hardly ever." With me tonight, Ben is a man of few words. He continues to pat my hand until the stinging behind my eyeballs and the pressure in my throat disappear.

"I hate the way my marriage is falling apart, so I got angry at his drinking tonight. That makes a great deal of sense."

"About as much sense as walking away when you get pissed off. So is it?" he asks.

"Is it what?"

"Falling apart," Ben reminds me.

"Did I say that?"

"You did indeed."

"I think my memory's been playing tricks on me. I think something has to exist before it can fall apart. Forget it," I say when I see Ben's puzzled look, and we sit without speaking for another few seconds.

Ben asks, "You okay? How will you get back?"

When I remember the rental car, I wonder if Michael dared drive it back to the inn, and my mind fills with horrifying images of twisted metal and broken bodies. But even if he walked or got a ride somehow, I still don't have any keys.

"I could call . . . Nora, maybe . . . ," my thoughts trail off, "but I think they were going to a movie or something tonight. I wasn't really paying attention earlier."

"If you hang out here, I can give you a ride in about an hour, maybe sooner. Kitchen closes at eleven, I can leave around then and come right back to close up."

"Maybe I'll take you up on that," I say, rising. "I'm going to go for a walk, clear my head. If I need a ride I'll be back here by eleven."

The air is bracing as I step out into the night. Diners leaving the restaurant have spilled out onto the sidewalk and stopped, congregating in a large group I must maneuver around. I slow down and look for another place, quiet and alone. I remember the roadside turnout is just ahead a half mile or so. I walk to the clearing off the road, bound by a viewing rail and overlooking the large expanse of the valley. In the still, cold night, I can see my breath; in my mind I can see my life with Michael, as ghostly and vaporous as the warm breath mingling with the cold air around me.

When Michael takes me to the beach after my father's funeral, a mediocre deli sandwich is roiling in my stomach. I did not want to eat so I picked apart the bread, the meat, licked mustard from my fingers, and forced down a few bites. All I can taste is fat, the waxy heavy mouth feel of animal fat coating my tongue and upper palate. Michael insists I finish, and I oblige with one slice of bread. A caraway seed lodges between my molars, and I attempt to wash it out with beer.

Bill paid, we leave through the front doors to find Michael's car on the street. "What do you feel like doing?" he asks. "We should go back to your mother's house, be with your mother."

"Drive," I tell him. "Just drive."

It is January, damp and raw rather than snowy. We drive to Manchester-by-the-Sea, to Singing Beach. Off-season, there are few parking regulations, so we pull right up to the sand's edge. The air feels good, smells fresh and salty. Maybe I'm a bit carsick after the long ride, a bit overwhelmed with the emotion of the day, maybe I've had too much beer, but there is a sick heft in my esophagus threatening to buck the peristaltic wave. I tell Michael I want to sit on the sand, breathe in the fresh air for a bit.

"Are you sure?" he asks. "It's pretty cold and windy."

"That's okay; it won't bother me, and it won't be for long," I promise.

He pulls a blanket from the trunk of the car as I walk on ahead to a bluff I know in the direction of the Magnolia cliffs. Michael follows, lays the blanket at my feet, sits with me, and we stare out at the sea. The waves mimic the sound of my stomach.

Michael pulls his knees up, says, "We haven't had a chance to talk, it's been so hectic. All the plans keep everyone from thinking about what's happened."

"Yes," I agree.

"Anna, I can't imagine what you're going through," he begins. After all, I have found my father stretched out on the floor, past help.

"No, you're right," I say. "You can't."

"I'm sorry, I know you loved your father," he says. It's what everyone says.

"That's the thing," I tell him. "I don't know how I feel. No, that's not right, I don't feel anything, really."

"That's called shock," Michael says.

"No, Michael, it's called absence of feeling.

"He was a difficult man," I explain, "and I was probably a difficult daughter. I always wanted so much more than I was ever given. He was cold, logical."

"Yes," agrees Michael. "I always liked talking with him because of his logic. He was a good persuader, he made a good case."

"Yes," I nod, "imagine growing up with that, though." I pause. "Do you love your parents, Michael?" I ask.

"Well, yeah, tempered with the usual amounts of guilt and frustration, I guess I do."

Again I nod. "Me? I just don't know what I feel." The ocean rears up, slams the shore, pulls back. On my face I feel mist carried by the wind.

For the funeral my mother chose a full mass to accompany the service, complete with readings, one of which she asked me to make. I declined, which elicited an angry exhale from my mother.

"But I can't," I pleaded. "I can't possibly stand in front of all those people and say anything." My Michael, good Irish Catholic boy, stepped in and offered to take my place. His voice traveled down to my pew, clear and deep and full of expression. How my mother loved him at that moment; her eyes glowed for him as he stepped down from the altar. Walking into our pew, he stepped past me to sit at her side; he squeezed her hand. He had the poise of someone twice his age, and he was not uncomfortable in this role.

We stood, sat, listened, prayed. I recognized the rites involved in communion—the chalices, the plates, the altar boys, the blessings—but not much else, since I hadn't been to church in a while. Turning to us, the priest began, "Lord I am not worthy to receive you . . ." My mother stood to form the line for communion. Michael rose behind her, but I sat it out. The line snaked up the center aisle; people approached the priest with their hands outstretched to receive the sacrament. I had never seen this practice and it stunned me. I recalled as a young girl standing, tongue out, after the amen. As a ritual, it was a powerful feeding for a supplicant, mouth open, humbled, and willing. Now even the priests didn't want to be this close to my body, to anyone's orifices. Instead it was the recipient's own hands taking the body of Christ, just one remove from intimacy.

At the beach I tell Michael, "Make me feel something. Right now." I think he understands what I am asking.

"But it's freezing. We'll freeze."

"I don't care; even cold is something."

Somehow we get the blanket both below and around us. Michael moves on top of me, and with practiced hands hikes up my skirt, slides my black tights down. He opens his zipper, his underwear fly. We've never done this with so many clothes on, and my fingers fight in vain against fabric for the familiar feel of his skin. It's over fast; when Michael finishes he kisses me, tells me he loves me, struggles to zip up his pants under our blanket.

"Can you get me some tissue from the car?" I ask. "I can't get dressed until I clean up a bit." He doesn't complain and when he leaves, I sit up, dig a small hole in the sand by my side, and retch into it: my sketchy meal, the beer, my bile, even mustard, mingle in a puddle beside me, which I then bury. I do feel relief after vomiting although I'm cold, my stomach's still slightly upset after the motion of sex, and I'm a little sore with the pain of friction since I was dry inside—so many feelings, just as I'd hoped, and I give them all the same name: desolation.

When he's back, we sit side by side again and he proposes marriage. Is it so surprising that I say yes? So surprising that when I do say yes, it is to a man like Michael who so effectively takes charge, who knows just what to do with me? I am adrift. Cut loose. How good of Michael to do what I ask, even better that he's thought of this marriage thing on his own. By now, my stomach is rocking so, I might as well be riding the waves I see in front of me. I never want to admit this, that my father's death has disturbed me so deeply. I have told Michael I feel nothing but, again, I am inaccurate. I feel dissatisfied. I try for so many years to be independent, I achieve a sort of freedom, but my father dies before I can show him anything I have become.

Together Michael and I can move ahead. Maybe now my life can stretch out, begin. I think to myself, it's something I can do. So I say yes.

My father dies in January, and by July I am married. When we announce our engagement to my mother in February, she asks, "Why?" She is unsure if six months is a proper amount of time; she would like us to observe a period of mourning; she thinks Michael should finish law school first.

"But that's three years!" I wail. Once he's asked me, I want to marry as quickly as possible, I want to hold on to him, I want to wake up every morning with someone I know so well.

Michael remains calm, he puts his hand on my knee under the table to signal to me to lower my hysterically rising voice. "Ordinarily I'd agree with you, Mrs. Rossi. I used to think you should get school out of the way first, then settle down. But the thing is," and he looks directly at my mother, "Anna and I have been together about four years. This way, she can work, and we can put some money aside while I am in school."

My mother nods; this makes sense to her, I can see. It is so logical that I, too, nod in agreement, my words no longer at the back of my throat waiting to be barked out.

"I had a feeling Anna was being impulsive," my mother says, "so I was worried."

"I've given it a lot of thought, Mrs. Rossi," says Michael. "I wouldn't do anything that didn't make sense."

"Good, good," answers my mother, and her voice is now contorted with tears. It rises an octave as she manages to squeeze out, "That's the way I'm used to doing things." And I know she is thinking of Father, missing him, the plans he made so thoroughly and so well. As Michael is now, for me.

I sit there watching them, Michael comforts my mother with his calm presence and her quiet tears abate.

"Thank you for reassuring my mother," I tell Michael later, when we are alone. I am sitting next to him in his car, in the crook of his arm. "Thanks for smoothing that out."

"I meant it, it's the right time," he answers.

"It feels impulsive, too," I reply, "but in a good way, like I'm following an instinct. You feel right, it doesn't matter when." And I move in closer, smelling the aftershave he's wearing, the damp wool smell of his sweater. My hand slides around his waist into his lap and lingers on the fabric of his jeans.

"I think I know what she means," he explains. "I've never been irrational or impulsive, either. I've known for a long time what I wanted to do with my life, always pictured myself working, then finding someone who could be part of my life. But then I met you." He smirks.

His statement, his grin, irk me, like I am a roadblock, or a detour on his arrow's path. I feel he means there are about a million women he could have plugged into the equation that explains the life he imagines for himself. Briefly he reminds me of my own dubious equation—*It's something I can do*—but I push that thought away and concentrate instead on my anger. "But," I begin, sitting up from the comfort of his body, "falling in love isn't rational; you can't plan everything."

He feels my temperature rising and asks, "What difference does it make, the reasons why, whether we even have different reasons? I found you, that's what matters. That's all I mean. We can have a great life together. Don't get upset."

"Don't get upset." These words bring my father back to life for me. Messy feelings distressed him; he wouldn't allow chaos. From an early age I am allowed into the family's circle only if I remain quiet, controlled. Childhood tantrums are not tolerated; I learn this the hard way, through separation, banishment. I am, therefore, an easy child, offering so much less resistance than I could have if given the chance.

When I am seventeen, when we discuss what my father expects, we have our first true disagreement. I am less willing to sit and listen, especially as I begin to see my future as an independent one. Sending me to my room will not be an option, he knows that, too, maybe sees it in my eyes during our discussion.

So, when my blood is boiling, when I try to explain my interests calmly, when I hear his refusals and begin a slow burn, he speaks those words, too: "Don't get upset." His words are accompanied by a small, amused mouth, as if my temper is his amusement. He is canny, though, he can compromise, make me feel powerful and still get his own way. He suggests the science which is, after all, what I do love, chemistry because it makes sense, explains so much of life. I get to believe I am just biding my time, that soon I will have my freedom.

Now I think I see my freedom in Michael, dark and smart. Sitting in Michael's car I rationalize: He is not laughing at me, he cares about me, he doesn't want to upset me. I push all comparisons deep down, bury them like old bones, because I do not want to see my chosen, my intended, cast in my father's shade.

Michael spends more time at the library or with his study group. He quite often comes home after eleven and flops on the couch to watch the late news or a talk show. Sometimes I am already in bed, asleep, or perhaps I've just put out the light. I am plenty tired, too, after late, solitary nights with my ridiculous pH samples. But if I hear him come home, I get out of bed and join him for a bit. We sit, side by side in the darkened room, without talking. I like to watch the flickering re-flection of the television in our living room windows more than I like the programs. I like sitting quietly with Michael.

If I ask no questions about his day, his classes, he lets me sit endlessly, holding his hand or resting my head on his arm. Of course he is busy and stressed with studying hard, but I miss the sound of his voice talking or reading to me, I miss his presence. Yet I never tell him so. Talking seems a doorway into some frightening land, a door best left closed. Quiet is a new phase, a temporary one, I bargain, and I learn to live within its structure.

On the nights I hold Michael's hand to the glow of the television set, I try to persuade him to come to bed. I feel like a cheerleader at times, trying to muster enthusiasm from my crowd of one. But sometimes I leave Michael sleeping on the couch while I return to bed alone.

If, instead, he stays awake long enough to turn the set off, I have him by the hand, trailing me. I help him out of his clothes, lay him down, and run my fingertips along his spine. I climb on top of my husband and make love to him. I can feel him relax into me; my singular achievement these days is that I can fuck a tired man and help him sleep.

Years before, while dating, we went two-stepping at the only country-and-western bar around Boston. Michael dragged me to the dance floor and made me laugh my way through our own clumsy dance interpretations. I hadn't much rhythm, but I never minded looking silly. Sitting next to him by the glow of the television set I recall the look in his eyes at the Blue Star. He never looked away then, never would have watched a television show instead of me. Christ, he never wanted to take his hands off my waist! He'd pull me back by the belt loops of my jeans if I got too far from him.

On the Tuesday and Thursday nights Michael has his study group, I stay a little later at work. The group likes to meet at our house because of the married couple's well-stocked refrigerator. At first, Michael asked if I would make them snacks, sandwiches or something. I told him that although I will cook for parties at our apartment, I will not play the hired help for a group of his friends. Instead I usually arrange to be out or at work when they arrive, and now there is never any question about my role.

The group is four, sometimes, five, law school classmates: Michael, Julie Holcomb, Jim Bova, Peter Markson, and occasionally a quiet woman named Roberta Johnston who, Michael tells me, prefers to study alone except before exams. I hate these years of law school, I hate the small hick town we live in, hate my pointless dead-end job. I have no friends of my own, and I begin to regret marrying Michael. I begin to wonder if I married out of fear, fear of losing him, of being alone if he left me behind to go off to school. But now I ask myself, Which is worse? Being alone by yourself, or being alone with somebody else? Perhaps this is what I hate most about these years: all the quiet time I have to chew on my doubts.

One night I come home to find the study group of five sitting around my kitchen table, drinking the beer I worked to buy, laughing over some inside joke. For me the evening has dragged, monotonous, no different from any of the rest in the lab. I arrive home with an attitude; nothing going on in my kitchen will dispel it. I head upstairs to wash. When I enter the kitchen to pour myself a glass of wine, Michael asks, "How was your day?"

"Oh, you know," I answer, "nothing exciting."

"Nothing exciting in the world of dough?" Julie asks. "What a surprise. I don't know how you do it, Anna."

I shrug. "As far as I can see," I answer her, "it beats law school. At least there the doughboy can't talk back." And I leave the kitchen with my drink.

Without considering any dinner, I take my drink and head for the bedroom where I pick up the books I am reading, a collection of essays by Richard Feynman and the latest novel by Margaret Atwood. Shortly after I settle down with my books, I hear a car engine start up outside, I hear Michael's voice calling presumably from the front door out into the night. Then there is a faint rap at my door, it opens and it is Michael. "Julie's staying a little longer, and then I'll drive her home," he explains. "Everyone else had to leave but we still wanted to go over something."

"Fine," I reply, holding his gaze for a moment before I turn back to Feynman's essays, hoping some of his humor will rub off on me.

Michael lingers at the door. "She didn't mean anything," he says.

"You mean what she said?" I ask.

"Yes, she feels terrible," he explains, "like she offended you."

"Michael, you have to care to feel offended. What Julie thinks doesn't affect me at all. I'm tired, so why don't you get back to work," I suggest. And he closes the door softly as he leaves.

I begin to make a dent in the glass of wine. Maybe I've overpoured, maybe my head is dizzy from fatigue or lack of food or all the hate I'm carrying around today, but the alcohol goes right to my head. Soon, words are swimming on the page and I feel lightheaded, I hear our front door open again, soft voices on the pathway. My bedroom over-looks the front where our car is parked, so I go to the window to see Michael helping Julie into the car. Once he gets in they sit for a while, talking, it looks like, and I wonder why they don't drive or why they didn't just continue their conversation in the kitchen. Too dulled from my drink, I just don't catch on until I see Michael lean over Julie's lips, her face obscured to me by his head, but I know they're kissing. I blink, as if that will erase or correct my vision but no, they're still kissing, and I look on until something makes them part. Michael starts the engine and they leave.

He isn't gone long enough for much of anything to happen. I imagine maybe another kiss outside her door. Michael enters our bed-room as I think, the kiss could be the beginning of something or the end. There could be a raging affair going on that I don't know about. I haven't a clue. I had put my book down and turned the light out soon after our car pulled away, so Michael enters our bed in the dark, whispers my name to see if I am awake. "Anna." He strokes my arm, pushes his erection against my back, which is turned to him. Briefly I wonder if the erection is for me or Julie, and then I decide I don't care. It's been so long since I've been touched, so long since he's made the first move, that any sex—even a guilt fuck—will feel fine. I turn to him, let him do what he wants.

I consider divorce near the end of our three years of law school; I am strung out, tense, and hating life, which is unlike me. I actually contact a lawyer from my hometown for information. He tells me I must file where I live, must speak to a lawyer here.

"Wait," he says. "Someone I went to law school with practices out your way. Hold on, I'll get his name and number for you." So I hold until he gets back on the line. "Brian McNamara," he says, reading off the phone number. "He's a good guy, and if he can't help you, he'll find someone who will."

Thanking him, I hang up. I stare at this name on a scrap of paper for a long time, imagining the web of people between Mr. Pistorelli in my hometown and Brian McNamara or whomever he thinks suitable, all lawyers who probably once hated one another in school, all helping people between here and there to dissolve their marriages. Suddenly it seems like so much work to pick up the phone, put the paperwork into motion. I see myself moving to another apartment, staying in this awful town maybe testing more dough, mountains of dough, until all the legal stuff is finalized. I see myself stuck here until I want to scream.

By now Michael is interviewing for jobs. I consider what this news would do to him, how it might affect his concentration. He's excited about a firm in Chicago, seems to believe the city would be a cool place to practice. Imagining Chicago, I begin to realize there will be a new job for me, too, places to go to like museums, libraries, symphonies. And I slip the paper into the back of my desk calendar, not ready to act but not yet ready to give up this name.

After law school graduation, after Michael takes and passes the bar exam, we drive one thousand miles across the country from Boston to Chicago. We've been married just over three years, and for the past six months, Michael has been finishing school, flirting with potential employers, and prepping for the exam. When all of the hoops have been jumped, with so much air travel between the two cities under his belt along with his permit to practice law in Illinois, we pack our meager belongings between a Ryder truck and the back of Michael's old mustard-colored Corolla. We plan our route on two maps: one for me in the car, one for him in the truck. I will lead the way. We work out signals for each other, in case we need to make rest or fuel stops, and then we set out for the apartment Michael has rented.

"This place will be good while we get settled," he tells me after he returns. "It's not too expensive, the neighborhood's safe enough and convenient. Maybe in a year or two we can buy something. God, I feel like I'm really moving forward, getting started." His enthusiasm is intoxicating.

On our way we pass through New York, Pennsylvania, Ohio. I've passed trucks all day, long-distance haulers. I am tired and bored behind them; there is no working radio, no tape player in the car, so for fun I wait for the right moment, pull out, and pass the eighteen-wheelers. Behind me Michael is stuck; the Ryder truck reaches a maximum speed of fifty miles per hour so heavy is it with our things. I move ahead until I am in danger of losing track of Michael, draw back, begin the game all over again.

I like the road until we reach Cleveland. On our route this is my first taste of passing directly through a big city's traffic; driving along the curve of the lake, I reach a point where, irrationally, I feel that if I continue in a straight line I will drive right into this gray pool. I feel nervous, my hands clench the wheel, and I sit up straighter, not seeing until I get there that the road curves inland. Finally I can relax. When we stop for gas just beyond the city, Michael tells me Chicago is like this: Lake Shore Drive twists around the eastern border of the city from north to south. I haven't been there yet, so as I fill up the car I think of Cleveland, and I try to imagine living in Chicago without being afraid of the roads, a place that looks like Cleveland, and I think I will hate it.

So I am unprepared, once Gary is behind us, for pulling into the southernmost borders of Chicago. It sprawls, bursting with people even this far south. The buildings shoot up in front of me, almost like the mountains of New Hampshire: the Sears Tower, the Standard Oil Building, other landmarks I've only seen in pictures.

I get onto Lake Shore Drive near the Museum of Science and Industry, near the university, and I let it lead me in a serpentine meander up the coast. And I am instantly in love. There is a vitality, and not just from the cars pushing north. I see lights pulsing from the skyscrapers, and sailboats dotting the lake tied up in marinas from Grant Park north. Here, I drive along twisting S curves but feel nothing but awe and intense excitement, building in my head and traveling down my spine until I could bounce in my seat as I drive; the city welcomes me; such a large vibrant place speaks promise to me, hope.

Moving to Chicago I see now was like filing for an extension on a tax return. At first you think, How clever, I'm out from under, but you've really just bought yourself a new deadline, a new set of stress.

When winter moves into Chicago it is swift and relentless. I am not yet working, and for weeks around Thanksgiving it is all I can do to get out of bed at a reasonable hour just to stare at the stainless-steel-gray skies that hang low and ponderous over me, my home, the city. I begin to creep downtown on the number 22 bus when Michael is at work. I walk along Michigan Avenue, Oak Street, Chestnut Street; I look in the windows of the designer shops, watch people flood in and out of office buildings, sometimes find a gourmet shop for a peek in at glistening salads, at rows of wine bottles, at heavy cheeses. When I step back outside the sky overhead is not only dull gray, it is darkening early. The wind whips up the cross streets from the lake, bites my ears. After these solitary expeditions I end up in the lobby of the Drake Hotel, find the magnificent rest rooms that are now so familiar to me, take refuge in a stall, and cry quietly. The heavy skies depress me, as if they are physically pushing me lower and lower as they descend over the city.

After I've dabbed my eyes and come out of the stall to splash water on my face, I walk back to my bus stop and go the length of Clark Street to my home. I hate the city in the late fall and winter, so soon after I've arrived. It lied to me, Chicago did, with its lingering summer in September, the sun flashing off the lake in Morse code, the white sails before the boat owners brought them in for the season. Now I am reduced to shedding a few lonely tears in a hotel rest room.

When Michael comes home at eight, I am curled in a corner of my new sofa, reading a book. He drops his briefcase and slips to the couch next to me.

"You won't believe this day," he says.

I close my book, turning over a page corner, and I rest it on my lap. "What happened?"

He mentions a name—asks, "You remember him?"

And I do: a thin, high-strung man from a cocktail party we attended back in Michael's first month of work; he's been there three months now.

"He's lead counsel on my case? Okay, he's on the train from Evanston this morning, almost in the city, when he feels chest pains. So, when the train stops, he hails a cab and—in the throes of a heart attack—takes the taxi to Rush Presbyterian. He's had a mild heart attack, Anna; the guy's thirty-six years old." Michael gives a short bark of laughter. At twenty-six we think we are untouchable.

"Is he all right? What about a wife? Isn't he married?" I think I recall a wife.

"She left him about six weeks ago. He's got no one, nothing but work. He wants to come back right away. I mean, he's calling us from the freakin' hospital bed. What an idiot."

"I suppose he just feels terribly responsible."

"Bill's reassigning—I think that's what he feels. It sucks to be removed from a case. It's like a swirling vortex from there; he'll most likely never get another chance like this again. It's the beginning of the end."

"Just because he got sick?" I am incredulous.

I think of racehorses, shot when their legs are broken, no longer useful. Surely we don't do this to people, too. I am overwhelmed with dislike for Bill Kunkel, so cavalierly cutting a man out of the picture. I recall Bill's hearty laugh when I met him, his welcoming outstretched hand, the look of a computer behind his eyes: I watched as he seemed to photocopy my face, repeating my name, so that if he saw me again he could pull up the picture from his database, place me, ask me some relevant questions as if we were old pals. I see it all as false, a front.

I look over at Michael's profile; he's moved on. His head is on the back of the couch, his eyes are closed.

"I'll get your dinner," I tell him, excusing myself.

"Okay," he answers, dozing on. When I am in the kitchen, he calls, "What about you? What'd you do today?"

Before answering, I compare my self-indulgent tears to the outlines of a man in a hospital bed, threaded to monitors, his ear attached to a telephone. I find it impossible to complain, so I lie.

"I went to check out some cooking classes," a white lie, since I've been considering them for a while.

"Good, that's great. Hey, maybe you should think about working now that we've more or less settled. Actually, Bill's wife told me you should call her. Seems she's got some contacts at a food magazine."

"When were you talking about me?" I ask him as I come into the room with his warm dinner on a tray.

"Earlier this week she stopped in, asked how you were doing. I told her you'd gotten us squared away and that you might be feeling sort of bored."

"Sort of," I agree, but I'm not so much bored as I am distraught.

"Anyway, she asked what you do, and I told her as best I could, and that's when she mentioned the magazine. You ought to call her, I think she was sincere."

Two days later I am back at the Drake, this time having afternoon tea with Michael's boss's second wife, Liliane, and her magazine publisher friend. For the first time I test out the powers of networking, relying on a connection to find work rather than on my skills. For the moment, no one cares about my credentials, education, or experience. I am being viewed, like new clothes, for fit, as all around me china clatters and tea sandwiches and cakes are trotted out on multitiered dishes. It is sybaritic and appealing, being coddled and pampered, being drawn out by these two charming women in their immaculate designer suits. When we leave the hotel, Liliane's arm linked in mine like an old friend, I notice that for the first time in weeks the sky is clear. Night is descending on the city but the sky is clear; it will be blue-black and, somewhere away from the city lights, full of stars. Up along Michigan Avenue white Christmas lights glitter in the rows of trees stretching for what seems forever.

We leave each other, laughing over our success; I shake the hand of my new boss, sealing our agreement, and wave as she steps into a waiting taxi. I stand a moment looking down Michigan Avenue, my eyes follow the strings of lights, taking in the beauty of a gleaming city night. I am, once again, seduced.

And for a time I am taken in by the city, my new job at the magazine, my new friends. If Michael works a lot, I take on new trappings, too. I find myself invited to wine tastings, wine dinners like the Beaujolais Nouveau celebration in November at the Ritz; I am invited to dinner parties for the magazine, various restaurant and trade-related shows at McCormick Place. So if I see my husband alone maybe once a week, if we have sex maybe once every week or two, I don't have time to notice. Days pass quickly. There are my cooking classes, Friday-night daiquiris with Colette. We entertain, we drink a lot, we try out new restaurants alone and in groups. It seems we have a lot to talk about, Michael and I; we are always talking, catching each other up at the end of a week over drinks, over the newest Thai food in town.

The city provides an infusion of energy and affluence, as if we were poor and now we're instantly rich, and I don't mean just the new salaries. Experience—there is a wealth of it—so much to be pored over, and we compare, smile at each other, so busy, so happy. For two years we are so diverted. One day I dig through old boxes, cleaning house for the move to our new coach house. I find my old datebooks, now replaced by my computer day planner, and I riffle through them for anything I may wish to save. Out falls my scrap of paper, my lifeline for a while. Brian McNamara. I throw the whole box away.

I am in the kitchen of our new coach house, cooking dinner for a group of the associates in Michael's firm. I have taken cooking lessons, have been working at the magazine for about two years; I am confident in the kitchen, gifted, and I work swiftly. Everyone now remarks on my talents. No one knows—how could we?—but I will become pregnant with Sara tonight. We've always been very careful, haven't even entertained the thought of children beyond my nebulous, "Wouldn't it be nice . . . ," but we won't be so careful tonight. As my husband and guests all drink beer and wine with abandon, I am sipping, too, in the kitchen as I cook. The men let loose after a long workweek. Michael is standing in the living room with a bottle in hand, telling a story, keeping them entertained as I finish making our meal.

I turn back to the counter, chopping herbs and garlic. There is a burst of laughter from the other room, and shortly after I feel a warm pair of hands on my hips. I smile, flushing with pleasure. I welcome Michael's touch, I have missed it. Except it isn't Michael; it's one of his coworkers, a fellow attorney, and I am surprised, frozen still under his hands.

"Came for more beer," he tells me. He doesn't try anything but he doesn't take his hands off me either.

"Let me," I say, and I move out of his grip to the refrigerator. I take out a six-pack, hand him the whole thing. Maybe, I've convinced myself, his hands mean nothing more than a friendly embrace. I have missed touch, always liked it, so I relax. He takes the beer from my outstretched hand, he takes my hand, too, smells the fingertips.

"Garlic," he says, smiling at the strong scent of my fingers.

Although he's kept this within the boundaries of proper, it feels as intimate to me as if he's touched an unclothed breast.

Hot, yeasty breath inflamed like the inside of an oven baking bread. Sour. It's my own breath I smell, my teeth fuzzy from food and alcohol. I was too heavy headed to make it to the bathroom to brush my teeth before bed, and now my nose wants to shut down at the smell of my own mouth. Instead I turn my head, bury it in a pillow, a place that smells of laundry soap, not stale wine. First I hear a voice, suspended in the dark, disembodied. And then a mouth finds mine, breathing words, insistent words that tell me what to do, words that urge me to wake up. My mind drifts in and out of consciousness, aware of making love with my husband but in a dream or through a screen or on another universe; it's hardly real.

But it is real. Michael's in me, and I close my eyes tighter and picture the green river splitting down the middle of the city, full of algae and scum and flowing unnaturally west, away from the lake.

My back hurts, my legs ache from holding on so long; he won't come. It's artificially hot in our house, close in our bedroom with the door and windows shut, close with sex and beery breath and an impending sulfite headache. Sweat pours from Michael's forehead, rolls down the side of his face, hits my lips, until it's over, he's tired, and he rolls away from my tired body, both of us asleep and snoring within minutes.

This was so long ago I'd almost forgotten.

Four weeks later I learn I am pregnant. I remember all the wine I've been drinking—during those four weeks we socialized and drank a lot—and I am frightened. I haven't told Michael, about either the baby or my fear, and I carry both around with me like heavy weights. Along with the suspicion that this unplanned pregnancy will be, for Michael, also undesired.

Colette notices circles under my eyes. I've been tearing my nails and I look gaunt. Except for my breasts which miraculously swell and feel tender. I must wear a bra now for the first time in my life or they ache. This, I think, the addition of an undergarment I usually shun, this Michael will notice and question, but he doesn't notice my clothing or underclothing; in fact, I see him less and less. I begin to daydream. Between thinking about the baby, a lonely tadpole-like swimmer, developing leg buds, arm buds, losing a yolk sac, becoming a person, I think about sex. Standing at the kitchen sink I think of Michael's coworker who, just a few weeks ago, had touched me. I fantasize that he will call me on the phone one day, will ask to meet me. I cannot, however, see beyond the clandestine meetings or the hands on my hips. Cannot picture, for example, being in bed with him. I don't even find him all that attractive, although the lower part of my body aches with longing when I think of sex, and my legs feel weak and wobbly.

Finally I tell Colette I am pregnant, feeling a small amount of guilt that it is not Michael who hears first. I do not tell her, though, that I got pregnant while drunk, yet I blush when I tell her about my sexual feelings, about the pull between my legs.

"Relax," she reassures me, "it's just hormones. It's natural, enjoy it. The first sex you and Michael will have without worrying about getting pregnant," she reminds me.

Later that week I decide to tell Michael. When he gets home at nine, I fix him a small meal, some homemade chicken soup, toasted bread, and a crisp apple. He smiles wanly after dinner, runs his hand though his hair until it stands up in the front. Smiling at him, I reach my hand up to smooth his hair down. I touch his hair, his brow, trace my fingers over his ear until he contracts his neck.

"That tickles," he says, removing my hand from his neck and kissing my fingertips before releasing my hand.

"I've got some work to finish up. Long day," he adds. "Leave the dishes and I'll clear them on my way to bed." He pushes his chair back.

"Michael, before you go, I need to tell you something.

"I'm pregnant," I say before he can rise, "about four weeks. The baby's due in November."

His body, tensed to stand, remains still for a few seconds, caught in a crouch like a sprinter. "A baby." Michael restates the fact, maybe as a stall for time while he takes in my news. Although he tries to relax back into his seat, he seems uncomfortable, confused.

I nod. "I guess you could say it's an accident."

"You're pregnant?" he asks, as if what I've said is still unclear. "You're sure?"

I nod again.

"Wow," is all he finds to say, and I try to pick up his hand and lace his fingers through mine. "Four weeks?" he asks. And he sets my hand down and rubs his fingers over his brow, his eyelids. I detect a small groan, as if in doing the calculations, he's figured out the conception day.

"But it's an accident, I've been worried because we hadn't planned . . ."

"Wow," he repeats. He stops to consider. "I suppose I can rack up some more hours, which in the long run will be good for the partnership race."

There's so much to acknowledge, and this is what he chooses to say. I say nothing.

And then there is Sara.

I stop drinking, give up coffee and tea, even chocolate. When Michael's home, he smokes out on the deck. In this way I manage my heart-stopping fear that I've somehow damaged my child. I'll be perfect from now on, and all will be well, she will be well.

So on the nights I am alone, I make myself small, comfortable nourishing meals. Whole rolled oats with brown sugar and light cream, chicken soup with pastina. I try mashed potatoes with roasted garlic whipped in, which tastes lovely but seems to give me heartburn, so I resort to mealy baked Idaho potatoes. I try macaroni and cheese in small oval baking dishes, soft-boiled eggs and white toast triangles, Welsh rabbit, pots of whole-milk yoghurt, plates of angel hair spaghetti with just butter and grated Romano cheese. One night I eat rice pudding with stewed rhubarb.

I never feel sick but I have cravings: dry, floury pretzels, the large hard ones; ice cream; sliced tomatoes with salt and olive oil; avocado scooped out of the shell; asparagus quickly sauteed until slightly browned; ripe Bartlett pears; even applesauce. Michael phones from his office, his voice low and solicitous although it's always just a quick check. "Everything okay? Have you eaten? Don't wait up. Get your rest. I'll be late, so we'll have breakfast together."

I take care of myself, hugging my stomach as it grows rounder, holding in my baby, rocking her, keeping her safe.

After Sara comes we are so tired, yet Michael stays even later at work.

"I am on the promotion track," he says, so he spends hours at work, comes home late, works some more, and flops into bed. And as tired as I am with a new child, I feel I have to entice Michael. I believe he works late because he does not find me as attractive; I think it is about the pregnancy, the changes in our lives brought by a new baby, maybe the changes in my body. So I stop eating, sleep poorly, run on reserves, and lose the baby weight plus a little bit more.

It is easier than I thought, losing weight. Food tastes like nothing, as insubstantial as air. I am able to make it look pretty but can do nothing about the taste buds in my own mouth. I wonder if they no longer work, in some freak hormonal response to childbirth, like hair loss or postnatal depression.

I no longer have the ripe breasts of pregnancy because I can no longer tolerate the taste of milk, even skim milk; thinking of emulsified fat globules swirling around in my mouth, I am repulsed. I fear Sara isn't getting enough nutrition when she nurses, so I begin giving her bottles. I miss her mouth on me, sucking, and occasionally I will offer her my nipple, anticipating that first tug, which always causes me to catch my breath before I settle into the rhythm of her eager mouth.

When Michael comes home one night, he finds us rocking; I hold Sara to my breast, my shirt is unbuttoned to my waist with both breasts exposed. "I thought you'd stopped that," he says, coming to sit next to us. He touches Sara's head.

"Every once in a while," I answer.

He draws my blouse up over my shoulder, up over my unused breast and covers it. Looking at Sara's head, her lips now motionless as she's fallen asleep, Michael says, "But it looks like you've got nothing left." He reaches down to stroke Sara, runs his finger along her cheek, which is curved and clefted like a peach as she rests against me. I hear the faint suctioning pop of her gums, her lips, as her red mouth turns instinctively to follow the feel of Michael's finger. "You're pretty thin," he tells me.

Soon she does not want my flesh nipple, preferring the accessible, flowing milk through the rubber one; soon my breasts dry up, and I am back into my old clothes, my lush breasts a thing of the past for all of us.

Memory is, indeed, a tricky thing, and mine's been a regular practical joker. Looking back and back along its flat, uncontoured surface I think I see some perfect happinesses: falling in love, first sex, a wedding day, a honeymoon, our child. But as I stand here, as I shift my view, see all the same memories from different angles, the perception alters and the pictures change. My life with Michael is so much more complex: All my memories, even the happier ones, are tainted with something— a feeling, a gesture, a word—both uncomfortable and wrong. We've held this knowledge all along, we knew our own history yet ignored it, we married, we became cohorts, and now we are so culpable. And I am becoming responsible enough to feel stupid with the mistake: the waste of ten years' time on my conscience.

I turn from the railing and head the hundred or so feet to the road, considering a walk to the inn in spite of Ben's offer. I feel like the miles will be my penance, as if a long hard walk, like a few Hail Marys, will save my wretched soul. It is dark, but I can make out the headlights of an approaching vehicle slowing down at the curve. Hugh and Nora Chapman call out to me from the pickup's cab. Nora says, "We thought it was you. We were coming back from the movies, and I said to Hugh, 'Slow down, that looks like Anna.' "

"Lord, girl," speaks Hugh, "what in hell are you doing out here walking at this time of night? It's bloody cold. And you're lucky it was us. What were you thinking?"

I cannot answer. How can I possibly explain all that's gone on this evening and over the past few years? What can I say that they would even want to hear? I simply answer that I needed to spend some time alone looking up at the mountains. "I've missed them," I explain.

"Where's Michael?" asks Hugh, bewildered.

"He went on ahead."

At this Hugh and Nora exchange a look but don't ask questions. We've been away too long; maybe they don't feel comfortable asking. Maybe, though, they hear the evasion in my answer and decide to respect my privacy.

"Hop in," Hugh instructs. As I climb into the pickup, he asks, "Chicago's rather flat, then, isn't it? Maybe we'll visit someday. We don't get into cities much these days, Nora and I. We don't want too much more than what we've got out here."

Nora nods, adding, "We're lucky, really." As they smile at each other, they remind me how much of an outsider I am to this kind of communion.

"Is it luck?" I ask. "Or have you two cracked the code?"

We pull on to the main road heading for the inn. "What code?" Nora wonders.

"For happiness. Together."

" 'Happiness' is a tough word, Anna. If you mean a successful marriage, it's part luck, finding the right person is sometimes a matter of luck. But making sure the two right people want to stay together? That's hard work."

"I suppose you can't simply rely on forward momentum? The passing of time?"

"You're not talking about us, are you? Let me tell you a story," Nora begins. "When we decided to move out here, I knew it was the right thing to do, for Hugh—he was going crazy in the city; work was driving him crazy. But even though I knew this, even though I wanted to move for his sake, I went through a period of depression. I missed our friends, missed walking out the front door to find shops, bakeries, culture.

"When I walked out the front door here, I'd find . . . snow to shovel or leaves to rake. I had to start all over, make new friends. It was even an affront to get into the truck and drive seven miles for groceries! I remember reaching the breaking point, yelling at Hugh because it was so difficult just to get food." She laughs. "I was so angry with Hugh, for leaving a life that I thought was easy because it was familiar.

"And I still find it difficult, and Hugh does too; we really have to work to find things to do. But you learn there's really nothing wrong with working to find your happiness. Working with the big picture in mind."

"The big picture?" I ask.

"The reasons you stay together, the reasons to go on. You know, the big picture, the future. There's something to be said for these pleasures that are a little hard to obtain."

"And they are sweet," agrees Hugh.

"That is, I suppose, one of the truest, wisest things I've ever heard," I say to them.

We drive the last few minutes in a companionable silence until we pull into the gravel drive. "Such a short ride, but you'd've been walking all night." Hugh laughs.

"Yes, I know," I agree. "I guess I'm lucky, too. Thank you for stopping."

"And it looks as though your husband decided to wait back here for you," Hugh points to the parking lot. Indeed, there is the car. Michael made it here safely, and I wonder how long he has been back. The three of us are out of the pickup in a hurry, sprinting in from the cold.

 Michael is in a booth at the back of the bar, smoking; a pile of dominoes in front of him, he makes patterns on the table in a solitary game of matching dots. I remember this quirky game, which, oddly, the four of us were passionate about playing on slow nights. I ask Nora if I may use the phone to call Ben, tell him I got a ride.

When I finish on the phone, I look over to find Nora, Hugh, and Michael sitting together, shuffling dominoes. Michael spots me, calls me over to the table. He acts as if he has forgotten the past couple of hours, or at least is not acknowledging any of it. I am curious; his composure draws me.

The bone tiles click on the wooden table as Hugh flips them over for the draw. The four of us draw our seven tiles each and take turns building a twisted chain on the table in front of us. We concentrate on our game for a time, and I finish placing all my tiles first, which gives me time to watch the others. Nora and Hugh are curious about our separate rides back to the inn—I watch their eyes dart back and forth between us—but good friends, they will not ask directly. Michael stretches and yawns, the only one of us not visibly tense and upright in his seat. It is now after midnight, and the bar begins to clear. Nora leaves for a minute to speak to the bartender about clearing the tables and closing up.

"We hire people to help out, so we can maybe go out once in a while, but there's still work to do," Hugh explains. More customers leave, and the tiles get turned over for our second game. Waiting for Nora, we make idle conversation, the banal question-and-answer of filling time.

"But it was a break, right?" I remind him. "Did you enjoy your night out?"

"Movie was okay, not great but okay. But you're right, it's good just to have a break, do something different, have something different to talk to each other about besides when to place the beer order, what piece of equipment is breaking down, and whom to call to fix a leaking roof."

Nora returns to the table, selects her dominoes, and asks, "So how was dinner?" Without waiting for an answer, without looking up at us, she adds, "Ben's got a good business going. He's always busy, even in the off-season."

"It was packed. He did everything just right for us. The meal was beautiful," I assure her.

"Beautiful," Michael echoes. "Although I didn't stick around for dessert. Did you?" he asks me.

My eyes are cast down, looking at the table, concentrating on the game in front of me, but at his question I lift them fractionally, enough to see Nora and Hugh again exchange inquisitive glances. Yes, they know, they understand, I can tell, their eyes reflect both the question and the answer: *What happened at the restaurant tonight? Maybe they fought, someone walked out, obviously they each finished the evening alone.*

I do not envy them their seats here, between us, caught in the middle of our loaded conversation, our weighty marriage.

"Does anyone want a drink?" Hugh asks, making to rise and walk, perhaps sprint, to the bar.

"No," Michael and I answer in unison.

I pause a moment to turn over my dominoes; quitting the game, I thrust my tiles into the center of the table. "After you left, I went for a walk," I tell Michael. "To the scenic vista, the turnout on the main road. Where Nora and Hugh eventually stopped for me."

Hugh asks, "Are you sure you want out of the game, Anna? Why don't we have one more friendly game, then get to bed?" he suggests.

Michael across from me corrals the remaining tiles into a pile in front of him. He stands them up in a row on their narrow end, punctuating his speech. "And what did you see in the dark?" he asks, speaking down to the tiles while continuing to build a chain.

"It was dark, like the night we arrived, and the valley appeared bottomless. But what did I see?" I repeat, postponing my answer. "Pictures. From the last ten years. I saw my life."

"*Your* life?"

"Ours, together."

Michael has stopped snaking dominoes across the polished surface, over and around the indelible rings made from sweaty glass bottoms. His pattern, like a figure eight, bisects itself but veers off from its curve to infinity to teeter instead at the edge of the pub table.

"Instead of another game," Nora suggests, "why don't you get some sleep now, and talk this out in the morning." But seeing our resolute faces, our figures firmly planted and squared off in our opposite chairs, Hugh and Nora finally give up and beg off from the table. They take cover in the busywork at the bar.

"Tell me what you saw, Anna," Michael presses.

"I saw everything, everything I've avoided or ignored over the past ten—no, fourteen years, really. Standing at the railing I thought if I looked back far enough I could find . . . the seed . . . I thought I could remember something right between us.

"I saw me, hungry, terrifically hungry for physical contact, so hungry I could have picked anyone. And I picked you. You were available, taken in, seduced. Then you shut yourself off to me when I got too close or needed you too much. And I put up with it. I saw it all, Michael, things we should have seen as warnings before we got married."

"What else? Did you see me working hard all those years to build something secure for my family? Did you remember all the times we had to pull together, like when Sara was sick, like the time her body was covered with a scarlet fever rash, and we beat ourselves up because we didn't catch the strep in time?

"The point is," he explains, "we married—for whatever reasons—and we stayed married. We have a life together, and now we have a child."

"We have something that resembles a life. I stood by the side of the road, and it was like I had stepped outside myself. I watched us wake up, head to work, I saw you bill clients and come home to pay our bills and then continue working. I could see the money fly out the door on a house, a car, credit cards, clothes, day care, cleaning woman, the things we—I—collect, entertaining. Friends or bosses sitting with us, demanding your attention and my cooking, second wives or latest girlfriends and their talk of hairdressers and play groups and bikini waxes and health clubs. Our heavy, pointless meals and enough alcohol to deaden our senses.

"I mean, look at all this stuff we've put between us. We have ten years and a child and a bunch of shit between us, cleverly constructed to look like a life. But all it does is keep us from actually dealing with each other. Is this enough for you, Michael? Do you think, do you ever think it was a mistake, us marrying?"

Michael points his finger at the top of the domino chain but doesn't push. "Your questions are like my finger," he explains, "and I think they're better left unasked. Why bother shaking things up when you know what'll happen. It's a waste of time and energy, especially since in the end, all we really want is someone to stay with us as our minds and bodies start to fall apart."

Rising from my seat, I look around the bar, over at our friends who are trying their best to ignore our disagreement. I feel enormously sorry for Hugh and Nora. The room is quiet except for glasses being stacked and a labored breathing I suddenly recognize as my own. With his elbow on the table, Michael rests his chin on his hand; he's finished; he's made his point. But in his eyes, buried under the triumph of a well-constructed logic, I see for the first time fear.

I feel my fingers contract, curl, nails digging into my palm, skin stretched tightly, tensely, across my knuckles. Without thinking, I react, bringing my fist down sharply on the table, toppling and scattering dominoes. Yes, he's made his point. But now I've made mine.

I am sitting by the window of our room when I hear a light knock on the door and, a second later, the rattling turn of the doorknob. Michael stands in the doorway. The bed looms large between us, reminding us of our problems, mocking us. We cannot bring ourselves to look directly at each other; I look away, my mind on the bland decor of the room instead. The color and clean lines please me. The floral drapes could use an airing, however, and dust blurs some of the color in the folds.

"You know, Anna, I was thinking downstairs. About what to say after I finally propelled myself up the stairs after you." Michael speaks, breaking the quiet. He steps into the room and takes a seat on the end of the bed. I watch as he lights a cigarette, hearing every last scrape as he strikes his match. He takes a few drags before continuing, catching the ashes in his cupped hand. I look around at the open closet and see my clothes hanging, just as I put them in when we arrived yesterday.

He picks up the conversation in a tired voice, turning a pale face toward me. It's so late, and we're so exhausted.

"Anna, do you remember that one time I helped a client with his divorce? Gave him advice? We were handling his patent work and he came in, started talking to me about his marriage. Now, he knows I'm not a divorce lawyer, but he told me anyway how his wife left. He wanted to hold his marriage together, but his wife was already gone.

He broke down and cried, he was a big guy, too, burly and masculine and sitting in my office crying like a baby.

"I remember looking at him thinking, You stupid fuck, you sorry bastard. Pull yourself together. I told him, 'Go home, look at yourself in the mirror, and repeat, "My marriage is over, my marriage is over, my marriage is over" until you believe it. Because it is.' That was my advice. I knew if she'd already left then it was over."

Michael stands and puts his cigarette out in the ashtray, and he comes to stand next to me at the window. His voice is low and familiar in my ear. "You know, I look around me, and I see some people living the life I want, the life I always saw myself having: work I love, a wife, kids. Like my parents did, raising us until they were finally able to sit outside their house at the beach. That's what I see, what I want: to one day sit like they do—Dad dozing in the sun, Mom reading the newspaper next to him. Then I see all the others, screwing up. How did we get to be the screwups? I'm just so tired. Tired of you watching me all the time, watching, waiting for me to make a wrong step. You think I drink too much, I work too much; hell, I couldn't even enjoy dinner enough for you. Why can't it just be easy?"

Just a short while ago I would have chosen to sit now, in a dull harmony with my husband. Even now I see how I could reach a sort of truce: an agreement to go on with a new awareness of and polite respect for our differences. Maybe this subtle shift in knowing each other would cause the drinking to stop; even the sex could get better. Maybe. I imagine myself lying with Michael again; I could sleep with him now; part of me still feels attracted to him, and I know his body almost as well as I know my own. And Sara. Obviously Sara needs her father around. I can see, as Michael says, how attractive easy might be.

"Because it isn't easy," I answer. "I don't think your parents are able to sit together now because their lives progressed effortlessly and seamlessly."

"No, I know you're right. There were years when Dad worked all hours and never saw any of us. Mom was practically raising us alone, me and my brother. They actually worked very hard to get where they are, dozing side by side. The thing is, you have to want to work, you have to have something worth working for." Michael turns to me, takes my face in his hands to look at me briefly, then he pulls me to him and holds me close. Over his shoulder I look into the indigo sky. "So, Anna, do I need to look in the mirror?" he asks in my ear. "What do I need to tell myself?"

I move my hands up along his sides, I clutch him beneath his shoulder blades where he feels muscular and strong. "Michael, I thought we would be comfortable here, comfortable enough to talk."

"We are finally talking," he agrees. "You were right, though, I haven't wanted to talk. It's easier not to."

"We're not very happy together, and avoiding that, not talking about it, doesn't make the unhappiness go away.

"I've needed to tell you I'm tired, too, of feeling like an annoyance, of feeling like I'm misbehaving every time I want your attention. I'm not a wife with you, Michael, I'm a child again." I kiss the side of his neck, breathing in the smell of his skin one more time. "I thought we could use our past, remembering good times in the past, to help us out of this miserable place we're locked in. But there's nothing here in New Hampshire; there's probably been nothing really good between us, ever."

"I know," he says, burying his face in my shoulder until through my shirt I feel wet tears.

"You have to believe I didn't take this trip knowing, intending, that our marriage would end. But it is, I think. Finished." And at this moment, I realize how utterly unprepared I am; I have not anticipated this feeling of bewilderment and the physical pain, the emotional rending even as we stand still clinging to each other. The shock hits me like a flu: my shoulders ache, my eyes and head throb. I am laid low, needing my bed to crawl into, someone to pull down the shades. The meaning of my own words hits me like a chink of light creeping in through those shades simply to annoy my fluish eyes. I think of Sara, but I cannot see what I will do alone with her, where we will go.

Then I remember Nora in the truck telling me how the best things are not always the easiest, and I imagine myself walking on land with a tail or touching painful fire for the first time. And finally I remember my hand hitting the table—the catalyst, the vibration, the stored energy—all such good, basic science, knowledge so comfortably at home in me, things I've known all along.

Over my husband's shoulder I look out through the window at a sky full of stars. Closing my eyes, I imagine Michael in the rental car pulling out over the gravel and snow to the road. If I concentrate I imagine I can hear the gravel crunching beneath the tires as he pulls away. Beyond him are the mountains and the valley, all in blackness but magnificently and majestically there. The sky is clear and full of stars. Beneath my closed eyelids I watch him until, with the curve of the road, I can follow him no longer. I imagine Michael, with the mountains and stars surrounding him, driving south to the airport, flying out to Chicago. I remember Sara at my mother's outside of Boston, and I wonder where we'll be come Monday.

Opening my eyes I step back from my husband's embrace; my face is composed.

On Sunday, nearly noontime, I stand in the empty reception area, so considerately emptied for my private use, I reach for the phone, and I make my calls. My mother, soon to be surprised by a visit from Michael, is first.

"I will not tell your daughter this news," my mother insists when I tell her about our decision to separate. "What are you *thinking?*" she demands.

"*Please* don't criticize," I beg. "Please? It's hard enough. And right now Michael is on his way down there to see Sara before he goes home. Will you please let him see her?"

"You know he's welcome here. Do you really need to ask?"

I tell her that I will be there tomorrow, that I need some time to figure out what to do. "Fine," she answers, then she hangs up. One word spoken miles away and I can see her tight lips, feel her strong disapproval.

I make one more call—to the answering machine in my house,

Michael's house, talking back to Michael's prerecorded voice, advising him to contact me through my mother until I am settled somewhere.

Mercifully I am alone, so when I place my forehead on the cherry-wood desk, no one sees me. My brain feels swollen in my head, and I require a good night's sleep to rid myself of this dull, hungover feeling. Neither of us slept after Michael packed his bags last night. We had had our brief embrace, holding each other tight as we admitted our marriage was over; now sleep was painful, impossible. We lay side by side for what we knew was the last time, holding our bodies' muscles still and tense as we waited for morning and the release from our joint incarceration. What touched as we lay supine? Sometimes elbows, or a toe met a toe as a foot twitched, the leg muscles in revolt against staying so contracted. Once we both shifted simultaneously and a left shoulder brushed a right shoulder after which we muttered low, embarrassed apologies, like strangers next to each other on a crowded bus.

Once the sun rose, Michael prepared to go on ahead without me, to visit with Sara at my mother's before returning to Chicago to somehow begin carving out a new existence. "Sara!" he repeated, with tears once again springing to his eyes and mine, his voice pushing out from his throat, a cross between a moan and a wail.

But now Michael is gone, my eyes are puffy, my head is thick, and I have no concrete plans for myself beyond putting one foot in front of the other. I rest my forehead on the highly polished, cool wood of the reception desk, rocking gently back and forth. I smell Pledge, which only makes me pause for an instant before resuming the rocking.

When I lift my head off its resting place I see stars, feel light-headed, I've stood up too soon. Blood rushes in my ears, but when it clears, the peace around and within is crystalline and pure, tangible and solid. The gears of thought grind, bump, start slowly, but start nonetheless. Behind me are pegs holding room keys; some pegs are empty, a reminder we weren't the only guests this weekend. Lives go on all around me.

I think of one more phone call to make. Local: Ben. It's lunchtime, he should be there although I'll be interrupting his work. Someone answers in the kitchen. "Hang on," I hear, then the rocking of the receiver left dangling against a wall. For a couple of minutes all I hear is movement—of people, pots, swinging doors, shouted voices. Maybe, I think as I hang on the line, Hugh can drive me down to Boston for Sara. Or I could borrow the truck and do it myself. And then there's Ben finally on the phone, deep-voiced, inquiring, terse, rushed. I suck it up and say what I am thinking.

"Ben, it's me, Anna. I wonder . . . I think I need a job." And then the tears. They come.

PART THREE

Learning to Eat

I am a mess.

I've been a mess since Michael and I separated, since I brought Sara up here and started working. For the first two weeks I sit in our small, nearly bare apartment after long hours adjusting to both a new job and a new life and dream longingly of my home, my collected cookware: stockpots, *sauteuses*, Dutch ovens, *sauciers*. I wonder about my mandoline, my *chinois*, and the million other gadgets I own but rarely use; I think of my faience, majolica, crystal from Ireland, tea sets, breakfast dishes, and original Fiestaware, all collecting dust, their colors and sparkle dulled.

I am at times sorely tempted to go back and surround myself with the familiar. My belongings have always made me feel contented and complete. But despite the dreams of wrapping myself in our silk rugs and tapestries, I refrain. I walk straight on, a plumb line, into something new: the unknown.

It is March; I've been working three weeks. One of the first things I buy is a bathroom scale, along with a clear plastic shower curtain dotted with tropical fish because it delights Sara, and a looped cotton bath rug in turquoise because its color delights me. The scale, however, is stark white, and I keep it in the cupboard under the sink.

I buy the scale because my clothes now hang off my body in ways I've never imagined even after years of a spotty appetite. The waistband of my jeans stands out in the back, inviting glances at my underwear; the seat of my pants sags; when I peel off my shirt and can count bones under my breasts, I decide to check my weight, which is something I've avoided in the past. I know my body well, have never shied from looking at it or touching it, and this doesn't seem like mine anymore. It horrifies me.

As I step on the scale, watch the needle hovering at 105, I feel certain that this shell is no longer mine; it is foreign, another's, one I am merely renting, a discarded carapace to fit my shriveled soul. Oddly, my body matches this alien apartment with its Spartan appeal. I've never been overweight, certainly I've been quite thin for some time, but I've also never had a glorified image of the wraith, no desire to force myself into anorexic frailty. But even innocuous toast tastes like sharp razor blades as it teases my esophagus. I think of ice cream, recall its taste, its cold richness, the cold too often numbing the flavor, so that I wait until it's melted to the right consistency in the bowl. But even then it tastes too sweet; the spoonfuls of frozen cream and egg yolk make me gag.

For the first month or so our days go something like this: We wake at eight or nine; when the sitter comes at three, I leave for work. In the mornings Sara and I play, perhaps out in the snow or with other children at a play group I've discovered. Or we make a daylong project: cook something, make homemade play dough, or take a snowy hike and build snowmen along the trails. When I roll in from work around midnight, I pay the sitter, a robust nineteen-year-old with freckles and endless patience. The sister of one of our waiters, Trish is taking some time off from college and is happy to have the job. Sara is in bed, has been since eight, so when I go in to kiss her, when I kneel down at the side of her bed to listen for her breath, she rarely stirs. Sometimes she is remarkably peaceful, although she may wake later in the night with bad dreams. Sometimes, though, I think I detect a small catch, an irregularity, a hiccup almost—the sign she's cried herself to sleep. Laying my hand on her forehead, I feel her cool skin beneath my fingers, which surprises me; I guess I imagine she'll be burning with fevers because I have not been here to watch over her. Her chest rises and falls with each exchange of air, and I watch her small body as it participates in the comfort of sleep, the temporary suspension of thought, speech, and emotion for the day. Thank God for sleep, I think, kneeling beside her bed with my elbows resting on the covers and my palms on Sara's fragile arm. During the day she is sometimes stricken with bad moods and temper tantrums, but she teaches me patience I never knew I possessed. When she is sullen or passionately in a temper, I sit with her silently, hold her, reassure her. Sometimes, in my own despair, I forget how Sara's world has been torn apart, then stitched together so inexpertly. I do the best I can.

When I rise a few minutes later and leave the room, some of the rhythm of Sara's sleep has found me, smoothed out the wrinkles of worry beating from my heart. My pulse rate has slowed, my blood pressure, too.

I can't mislead; I am unspeakably lonely on these long cold nights. I take a book to bed and wait until maybe one or two, when I feel tired enough to sleep. I am physically exhausted, unused to being on my feet, working five or six days, but my brain needs time to wind down. At night my brain is a child listening to a bedtime story, as I concentrate on every word trying to coax my thoughts into a straight line toward sleep.

In these hours, if I can't focus on my book, I find myself thinking of Michael, of how any body right now would be warmer than this empty bed. I can make myself quite angry at night because of my longing; I find myself questioning what made me decide my marriage was over. If I were alone in an empty, flat land instead of this small apartment I would scream long and loud to let this rage escape my body. But with my daughter sleeping in the next room and neighbors above me, I must keep it in, sleep with it. The irony is, I thought the anger would leave me as soon as I split with Michael, that it might pass through my body's pores into the atmosphere and I would be rid of it. Sometimes my anger at myself overwhelms me, I feel like hurting myself or, alternately, dropping into a corner to weep. People who burn themselves with hot irons or mutilate themselves with sharp objects, those who drink themselves out of consciousness—they are my friends. I understand the impulse. Maybe not being able to eat has something to do with this, too, as if I can just make myself disappear.

When I do eventually sleep, my dreams are scattered with men: sometimes Michael, but mostly faceless men, teasing me, keeping me at arm's length. I wake, feeling as if a hard penis has been inside me, I can feel where my lips have grasped it, but now it's gone, leaving me empty and unsatisfied. Sometimes when I'm waking from these dreams Sara cries out in her sleep, herself haunted by nightmares, and her cries shame me as if I have woken her with screams of my own. When I go to her, kiss her, stroke her hair, I whisper, "It's okay, Mommy's here," over and over. As I do this for her, I do it for me, too. I do it to drain all the residual longing from my body, rid myself of the aches. I become Mommy, free from desire, once again just a loving, warm, sexless presence. I decide that my answer lies in celibacy, in throwing myself into work, into healing Sara, into creating new routines she can count on to get her through with minimal pain.

Only then am I able to creep back to my bed and sleep.

In the morning after a night like this, my head hurts from lack of sleep. Erratically and with little warning, Sara may cry over her breakfast cereal. On these difficult days Sara asks, "When are we going home? Daddy thinks we should all go home. He said in his letter that he misses me." In her mind this makes a neat resolution, the missing puzzle piece: We miss each other enough, so it's time to end the grown-up nonsense.

"Sara," I remind her, "you and I have talked about this before. We are here because Daddy and I aren't happy when we live together."

"I'm happy with you and Daddy," she says simply. "Why did Daddy say he misses me if I can't go home?" she demands.

"I know you would like to be back with him, in your own room, in your own house. And he is lonely; of course he misses you. But that doesn't mean Daddy and I would stop arguing if we went back to Chicago now."

"Well, I like Daddy. And I think you're mean."

Black and white, the lines are drawn. *Nothing, Sara,* I long to say, *nothing is that simple.* Instead I agree. "I know you're upset with me. It's okay that you're angry." And I try to touch her hand, but she pulls it away. Withholding love is an effective punishment; we've all done it, and I am chastened. But I will not force her to deny her true feelings just to make me feel better.

On a day like this, when Trish arrives so I can go to work, our stony, intractable faces greet her, tell her everything so she doesn't need to ask. I bend to kiss Sara good-bye but her lips are turned from me, her cheek cold and the muscles hardened as she grits her teeth.

Through all these days of adjustment Michael writes to Sara—to me, too, since I must read most of the words aloud to her. Between the lines I hear a fervor, a kind of single-minded frenzy for a connection with his daughter, and I wonder what is happening to him during the days of separation agreements leading up to divorce and custody arrangements. But I don't need these letters to remind me of what Sara is going through. She reminds me with her questions about her daddy. She still calls for him after bad dreams; it's always, "Mommy! Mommy! Daddy!"

Through his letters, though, I sometimes feel I understand him in a small way, as if the distance is freeing him from restrained speech. I, too, am free, able to stand and observe, released from participating or merely reacting to him. I listen to him speak to Sara about the things that matter to him, both now and when he was a boy, things he wants to share with her: his love for the natural world, the ocean in particular. He finds her weak places—her nightmares—and he makes them his; they are his; he admits his fears. He gives her the empathic part of himself that I remember until I am awash with a nostalgia, and also an anguish for the miles between father and daughter.

There have been only two things keeping me going, Sara and work. In Ben's restaurant, even with its unhappy memories of the last night with Michael, I feel useful. I work with busy, productive people.

But within a week my experience as a food scientist in a test kitchen fails me when faced with the hustle of a working restaurant kitchen. Work, which should be safe, reliable, and comprehensible, is

JANE WARD

foreign. The first weeks are hot and tiring. I am unused to working late into the evening, taking orders as part of a team, unused to creating a meal on demand rather than breaking it down into its parts. All the anxiety, the foreignness, catches up with me, and I find myself crying on Ben's shoulder.

"Look, Anna," Ben says firmly, "you don't see me pampering anyone else on staff. You can't do this. I sure don't have time to do this."

This knocks some sense into me. "I didn't mean . . . ," I stumble, "I'm just overwhelmed right now. I'll pull myself together, I swear."

"Hey, you're my friend," Ben goes on, holding me by the shoulders. "I'm happy to help you out right now with a job, and I'm not angry with you. But it's not enough just to love food; that won't get meals on the table. You have to know what you're doing. Anyway, it's my responsibility to give you some training instead of throwing you into the thick of things. You can train with James, help him out, and he'll show you the ropes. Okay?"

"Ben, it's not as if I don't know what I'm doing . . . ," I protest but my words trail off into nothing. I haven't spoken more than ten words to James since the night of Michael's birthday dinner, the night we separated, and my face burns at the thought of working with him: He was so relaxed that evening, tearing open mussel shells, and I was stunned and awkward, my world coming apart.

Ben calls James over. He immediately takes responsibility for me and solemnly leads me from Ben's side to his work area. I notice that his hands, rough and chapped from frequent washing, are nonetheless gentle on my elbow as he leads me away. We stand side by side at a stainless-steel counter, and with very few words passing between us, James starts me working.

He works quickly and efficiently while I watch; then sometimes he gives me brief instructions, which I follow. James assumes I know what he is talking about, and I very easily fall into his routine. He is a good, quiet teacher. I quickly perform better in the kitchen, and soon Ben gives me increased responsibilities. My workdays become purposefully busy; I am tired but happy; I have no time to feel inadequate. I think I am catching on, being accepted.

A few days later I overhear someone from the staff talking at the door of Ben's office while I am washing my hands at the sink. When I turn the water off, I hear the voice I recognize as James's. He's telling a story so I pause to listen, entranced by his voice because he usually speaks so little to me.

"I see her," he is saying, "across the kitchen. She is like a bird, nervous and full of quick, sharp movements. I'd like to see her slow down, quit jerking and flitting from one place to another, but I don't know if she can. Right now it ruins the flow of the place, gets the guys upset and working out of sync."

I should stop eavesdropping but I am rooted, curious.

"Man, if I had say over the staff, I'd fire her sorry ass. I know, I know, you've got some kind of connection, and you're trying to get her out of a bad place. And she's good-looking, so I can't blame you. But I think you're probably being way too kind."

This is how our kitchen works. Ben is executive chief and owner; he makes the creative decisions and hires people. He has a sous-chef, a kind of second in charge, James, who sees that everything gets done the way Ben wants it and makes sure the staff is working together. Then there is the garde-manger, who watches over the pantry and cold food preparation, and a few line cooks, who each have a responsibility for getting meals on the plate. So far I'm a floater.

James is telling Ben someone is not measuring up. From my spot I picture Ben taking it all in, turning the decisions over in his mind. What is best for the restaurant. He doesn't like me, I think, meaning James, because it is obvious he is talking about me. His patience, his instruction, all of it, means nothing; he doesn't like me, wants to fire me. I am frightened of losing this job, my attempt at independence a failure, but mostly I am enraged. I hate James for lying to me, offering me help when all along he expects me to fail.

I wait at the sink until the conversation breaks up. When James walks by I grab his sleeve, clutch the white twill full in my clenched fist. I expect to startle him but he stops easily, waiting for me to say something.

"Don't ever, *ever*, talk about me behind my back. Again. If you're having a problem with me, tell me about it." My voice is steady, even, threatening. Then I toss off his arm and walk away.

I face a pile of artichokes this afternoon, all of which need to have the leaves stripped off, the choke removed, leaving only the tender bottom and heart. Angrily I move around the globe, bending leaves back until they snap, working farther and farther in until the furry center is exposed. One after the other, I work steadily. I know James is watching me, but for once I don't care, I finally lose myself in the rhythm of my task.

We work during the rest of the evening, since I overheard him urge Ben to can me, in a professional tenor. James instructs, orders, demands, and I do. I watch as all around me everyone works, peppering their arduous work with off-color jokes and screaming, cursing tantrums when the tension gets high. I do not participate; I have no role yet in this dialogue, no part in the camaraderie. I work, and I work, and I avoid speaking to James about anything but work-related questions. Somehow I know I can get better at the job; I can feel it; I'm not imagining this. I have a near-defiant confidence, focus, and direction, as if I've accepted a dare.

Later I find myself alone with him at the back door of the kitchen, taking a break from this hectic evening. With a mug of coffee warming my hands I'm still shivering with the cold of a March evening.

"You have a temper," James says.

"No, I do not," I answer back.

He finds this extremely funny.

"There's nothing wrong with getting angry. Actually, it seems to be helping you. You're doing okay, much better."

"Uh-huh," is all I can manage to reply, then, "Think I'll go back in; I'm too cold."

From inside Ben calls, "O'Brien!"

"Looks like I better get in, too," he tells me. "Sounds like trouble."

But it isn't. As we walk in together, James holding the door for me, Ben hollers over, "How 'bout a beer tonight? We all thought we'd go out after work. This has been one hell of a shift."

James shrugs his assent. I realize I haven't been invited, and because of my exclusion I desperately want to be included. I ask Ben if I can tag along.

"There's no good reason for you to start drinking beer with a group of guys," he chides.

I begin to protest, and James jumps in. "Hey, Chef," he reminds Ben, "she's part of the crew. Don't give her a hard time." Turning to me he says, "C'mon, you're a big girl."

I want to be here, having drinks with these four men: Ben, Phil, Corey, and James. James asks, "What can I get you?" as he steps up to the bar.

"Beer's fine. Please."

"My pleasure," he says, and his eyes laugh at me, at my manners. I am out of practice, I suppose, spending my days with a five-year-old and my nights working.

We sit in a large oak booth; beyond is the bar, also oak and rustic, glass and bottle laden. The lights are low, recessed in the walls around us, and the only attempt at decor; and if I squint my eyes to blur the light, I can make the beer in the glasses shine like amber, the rising bubbles reminding me of the dead insects and plants trapped in amber resin. By the time James is back from ordering the round, I feel adrenaline coursing through my body. All of us sit upright and alert, I notice, as Ben begins to talk about the night in the kitchen, deciding what went wrong, what could have been done differently.

"*Mise en place*," he states, using the kitchen term for preparedness. "The advance work wasn't there, no one was prepared, and we let everything get the better of us. It's been a long day," he sums up.

"I don't know," I reply, feeling the surge of energy within me. "Eventually it was kind of fun."

"Fun?" Ben asks, slaking his thirst with a long drink of beer.

"Yes, fun. And interesting. You have no time to think, you just react. Everyone was exuding energy; it was exciting."

"Look out, it's getting into your blood," he warns. "And it sounds like you've got it bad."

"She's right, though," adds James. "You get to a point where you're pushing yourself, going beyond what you thought you could do. Plus being creative, expressing yourself. Hoping someone likes what you put down in front of them." He stops a moment, resting into the bench back. "It has to get into your blood, you breathe food, eat and sleep it. It's addictive. Otherwise why stand on your feet twelve hours a day sweating like a pig?"

"But what part of it is addictive?" I ask. "That's what I haven't figured out."

"I think it's about taking risks," James answers. "Putting yourself out there, facing rejection, hoping instead the customer loves you, loves your food."

"Like telling someone you love them. Then hoping they won't laugh in your face," Ben adds.

"Maybe," I agree. "Do you ever feel silly, making food this important? Talking about it like this?"

Ben shakes his head, "No, because it *is* important, not the food on its own so much as the whole experience of eating, sharing. Hopefully the meal will satisfy something in someone."

"I only ask because I grew up in a home where we pretty much ate just to stay alive. But I remember food vividly, bad food for sure, but also good food. Like, I'd steal the neighbor's tomatoes. And I had another neighbor, a Jewish woman, who used to invite me in and let me taste all sorts of—what were to me—exotic foods. I remember thinking when I was young, How come this is so important to me? How come it isn't important to my parents? How come I'm so weird? I sure felt strange."

James asks, "You used to steal tomatoes?"

"Yup," I say. "And then hide in my yard and eat them like apples. There's nothing like it, one simple good-tasting food. Fresh New England corn, the sugar-and-butter kind, that's another good one."

"I like roasted red peppers," Ben says.

Corey jumps in, "Lemons, and the smell of lemon oil on your hands."

"Garlic," James adds simply.

Phil says, "There's nothing better for dinner than a roast chicken."

"Carnivore," I call him. "How about a really good pear?"

Ben agrees. "Or spring asparagus," he adds.

"Olives, either the briny Greek ones or the wrinkly black kind." Corey snaps his fingers for the name. "Gaeta," he announces. "Olives have to be about the best. They taste like sex."

"If this is about sex," James says, "how about any kind of cheese, runny, creamy, or tangy."

"Chocolate," says Phil. "It doesn't taste like sex, but my wife thinks it's the next best thing."

Ben tells me, "You've got to ignore these guys. They're trying to shock you with all this talk of sex."

"I don't shock easily," I reply. "Anyway, food *is* sexy. Maybe preparing food is sexy. Or sensual, if there's a difference. All these things we talked about—pears, olives, cheese—they're beautiful on their own. They taste wonderful, and you can just pick them up in your hands and eat them.

"Maybe that's it," I conclude. "Maybe they taste so good because you can eat them from your hands."

"You definitely aren't weird," James tells me.

"Finally, after all these years. Thank you," I say.

"Can I get you another?" Across the table James motions to my glass.

"God, no," I answer in surprise, looking down at my empty glass. "That would put me right to sleep. Is this some kind of test for the uninitiated?" I ask. "Let's get the new guy drunk?"

"Girl," he corrects me.

"Woman," I answer, and he raises his glass, tilts it at me, concedes the point.

Phil stands, excuses himself, says he has to get home. It is late, almost one, and we are all growing tired, contemplative. James slouches against the back of the oak booth, his legs stretch out, his feet touch mine tucked primly under my seat. Wondering if this is accidental, I look over at him, but he does not look at me. My thoughts feel thick with foamy beer, my movements slow, as if I am trying to walk under water, and I excuse myself for the rest room. When I return there are three at the table; we are dwindling in number, a reminder of the hour.

When I slide back into my seat next to Ben, he leans forward and taps my arm. "Do you want to go?" he asks.

"Not really," I declare, "maybe in a few minutes. It's been too long since I've done anything but go home to bed."

"I'm too lazy to leave right now," James explains. "Unless I'm in the way," he adds, looking across the table through narrowed eyes.

Ben and I look at each other and burst into laughter. Ben explains, "You are way off. Anna's like—"

"A sister," I finish for him, "or worse, a ward—a charity case."

"Sooner or later you'll stop feeling sorry for yourself," Ben tells me. "I'd like to get home, so if you want a ride—"

"I can take you," James tells me, "if you want to stay. They close about two. I'm gonna finish my beer, but then I can drive you home."

I look from Ben to James. I haven't been out in a few months, haven't been anywhere with grown-ups outside of work. And then there is the pressure of those feet; the feet intrigue me; right now James intrigues me.

"Okay," I say, and I slide out to let Ben leave. He kisses my cheek as he goes.

"You'll be all right," he says, more of a statement than a question. "Behave yourself, O'Brien," he calls over his shoulder.

"What does he mean?" I ask. " 'Behave yourself'? Should I worry, here alone with you?"

James sits up. "Must be that brother-sister thing you two were talking about. And to answer your question, I am perfectly harmless."

"Are you?" I ask, remembering his feet.

"I am now," he answers. "You see, I have sisters of my own.

Younger sisters. And I spent a lot of years looking out for them." He takes a long sip of beer. "I liked what you said earlier, about food, about one simple good-tasting thing. You'll work out okay."

"You haven't thought much of my work."

"You worked well today. Why don't you tell me what you were doing in . . . where?"

"Chicago."

"Chicago."

"Up to now, I've spent my time analyzing butter substitutes, figuring out what could be used in baking for people on low-cholesterol diets." I begin speaking of things I know well, filling the nervous air with words. "I used to do those protein exchanges and calorie counts you see at the end of recipes. Analysis. Stuff like that." I see James open and close his mouth, as if he had a question, then thought better of it. "What?" I ask.

"Which work do you like better?"

"Is one necessarily better than the other?" I ask.

"Not necessarily. But if you're making a meal, fatty acids and carbon chains don't matter a whole lot. You were a chemist, not a cook. Now you're a cook. Which do you like better?"

"They're both just jobs."

"Is it really just a job for you? Sometimes it looks like you're actually connecting with the work. Like tonight, in the kitchen, or here, talking about food. Other times I can't tell."

"You sound like such a snob when you say that," I say, shaking my head.

"What do you mean?"

I twist my empty glass on its coaster. "You make it seem like there's something wrong with me if I don't care about my job the same way you do."

James leans over the table; he speaks with open hands, palms up. "I've always loved to cook, I love combining great ingredients, feeding someone a meal, hoping they enjoy what I've made. I guess I expect everyone to feel the same way, but I don't think that's being a snob."

"But you don't even know what I feel. You're simply assuming my motives aren't as pure as yours. I have a daughter to support; maybe I just need the job."

"You're right," James agrees. "I don't know. I don't know anything about you. So why don't you enlighten me?"

"You're baiting me," I say, my mouth set grimly. "Are you trying to win an argument?"

"I'm not arguing. I'd like to know more about you; it was just a question."

"Nothing's 'just' anything."

"What the hell does that mean?"

"It means people never say what they mean. Why do you want to know more about me, so you can feel superior? 'She doesn't know what she's doing, she spent her days in a fucking lab, substituting fucking applesauce for butter.' What's so superior about what you do, anyway? Why is what you do any more important than my work for the magazine?"

"I never said that," James replies quietly. "Is that really what you think I'm doing? Picking on you?"

"Aren't you? You lied to me from the beginning. You made me think you were helping me, then you went to Ben behind my back and tried to get me fired. Why did you even bother working with me? I could have managed to look stupid enough on my own."

"Right after you started working, Ben asked me what I thought so, tonight, I told him. It's unfortunate that you were listening, but if you had asked me I probably would have told you the same thing. I don't know who you've been hanging out with, but I always try to say what I mean."

"Are you always this annoyingly calm?" I ask.

"Not always. Why? Am I annoying you?" I nod my head. "You're pretty annoying yourself, you know. You won't tell me a thing about yourself, and you jump down my throat when I ask."

"Haven't you figured it out?" I ask. "I don't have anything to say. At this particular point in my life I am deeply ashamed of myself. Why would I want to tell anybody anything?"

"I see what Ben meant."

"About what?"

"Someday you'll quit feeling sorry for yourself. Why don't you cut yourself some slack? There's no reason for you to think you can't make the same mistakes as the rest of us poor slobs," he tells me.

I look James straight in the eye. "Look," I begin, "I'm trying to believe you when you tell me you only say what you mean. But I don't understand that. I only know two things for certain: I have ten years' worth of a failed marriage under my belt and a five-year-old asleep back at my mingy little home. You'll have to forgive me if I'm not exactly dripping confidence." I hold his eyes frankly and humorlessly. "Maybe you don't really want to know who I am.

"Maybe," I continue, sliding out of the booth, "we should go." And before he moves, I stand and make for the door.

Waiting for James in the parking lot, I look around at the slush on the sides of the road, gray, heavy piles, probably gritty from the sand trucks. The worst part of winter, I think, is the end, as the snow gets dirtier and melts almost in resignation. There is no moon but it is a clear sky. I can see my breath and someone's cigarette smoke across the parking lot. I watch the last red embers as the cigarette drops to the blacktop.

James's truck is so much like most of his clothes, slightly dilapidated and worn. There is a dent in the passenger side, and the door creaks when it's opened. The ride is awkward at first until I break the silence.

"Look, forget it," I rush, catching my breath. "I'm sorry, I'm sorry. I shouldn't have let loose on you like that."

"Quit apologizing. You said what you felt, didn't you?" he asks with his eyes on the road as he makes the turn out of the parking lot. "I'm just glad you're talking to me about it now."

"Glad? You're glad? Why? No one's ever been happy to hear me pitch a fit. It's always, 'Be good and quiet, don't disturb things.' " I look down at my folded hands resting on my lap. "You were right; I *am* feeling sorry for myself. I'm sure you don't want to hear this."

"I'll hear whatever you want to tell me."

"Why don't you tell me something about yourself instead," I suggest.

"Okay, what about me then?" he says. "I'm from New Hampshire, mostly everyone here is a transplant or a tourist, but not me. I have eight brothers and sisters, a good Irish family. I think I like to cook as a sort of reaction to the assembly-line meals I ate growing up. Plus it was something to do, to get a job and get out of the house. Plus, I like it."

"Wow, nine kids," I say in amazement. "I'm an only child. Like Sara," I add.

"Yeah, you've got that only-child look about you," he says.

"What's that?" I ask.

"That nervous look you get when things get too noisy. I always felt bad for only children. No one to mix it up with."

"Is that so great?" I ask. "Mixing it up?"

"Well, it's nice to have my own place, but when my family gets together I realize I miss the noise, even the lack of privacy. Now, that wasn't so hard, was it?"

"What?"

"Telling me something about yourself, telling me that you're an only child."

I smile tentatively. "I think this is the first conversation we've had without one of us yelling or you pointing out something I've done wrong."

"C'mon, I don't yell. And it's my job to show you the right way to work. You have a ton of bad habits."

For a moment I turn from James to look out the window and point out my street. He pulls over and parks alongside the curb.

"All the time I've spent working alone," I agree. "I've never had to develop the right habits." I look at my watch. "I should go in, it's getting late." I look into his eyes for a signal, acknowledgment, and all I see are questions. "What is it?" I ask.

"I'm just trying to figure you out."

"Don't strain yourself," I tell him. "I'm not that difficult. Well, good night. Thanks . . . for the beer and the ride. I'll see you."

James lifts his hand in a wave as I close the truck door behind me. But I notice he doesn't drive off until I've unlocked my front door and then closed it firmly behind me.

I am awakened early by the telephone ringing.

"I'm not usually up this early, especially after a night like last night," proclaims a voice I recognize, a voice deep with sleep not yet shaken off. It is James. "But I can't sleep. Are you busy for breakfast?" he asks.

"Busy? I'm not even fully awake. Neither is Sara." I sit up in bed.

"Let me come over and make you breakfast," James suggests.

"Are you serious? I don't think I have much of anything to eat besides cereal, sliced bread, peanut butter . . . kid stuff," I reply.

"Let me look around my kitchen. I'll bring the food." Sensing my hesitation, James urges, "Anna, c'mon, I've got something I want to show you."

I don't know whether to roll my eyes or hang up. Instead I throw out, "The old 'I've got something to show you' line? Try again," and I don't budge.

"No, really," he insists, "I have got something I want you to try. I'll leave whenever you want me to. Promise." He waits through the dead air. "Well, what do you think?"

"All right." In spite of myself, I give in. "Give me half an hour?"

"I'll be there in about thirty minutes," James says before he hangs up.

I get out of bed to wash and dress, and by the time I have water on for coffee I hear a knock at the door. James hauls in two large bags of food. He works swiftly and wordlessly, unpacking, taking command of my utensils and dishes. I watch him put salmon he has cured himself, vivid orange, on a white dish. He piles a large plate with clusters of tiny champagne grapes, slices of mango, and cut black plums with gold-red flesh. He places a soft white cheese at one side of the plate; I notice the impressions of cheesecloth on its surface. James slices dark rye bread, and I smell the sour yeast across the table.

Sara wakes and pads into the kitchen, stopping in the doorway when she spots James. She scoots to the table and crawls onto my lap.

"Mommy, who is this?" Sara whispers.

"Sara, this is—" I switch in midsentence and address James. "Do you have a preference for what you're called? 'James'? 'Mr. O'Brien'?"

He rolls his eyes. "Mr. O'Brien is my dad. James is fine," he tells me. He bends at the knees next to Sara to be at her eye level. "Sara, you can call me James. I work with your mother. And I decided to bring you both breakfast this morning."

Sara looks shyly at James and then hides her face in my breast. I return the embrace, and she spends the next few minutes waking up while being nestled.

James gets up and puts a bunch of the tiny red grapes on another, smaller plate and sets it down in front of Sara. I shift Sara to her own seat, slide the plate over. Sara, fascinated with the doll-size fruit, begins to eat.

James places salmon, glistening in its cure, in the center of the table. The fruit is abundant, the cheese pristine. He finds a glass bowl and spoons blue-black jam into it. He hands me a plate and uses two forks to serve me salmon.

"Gravlax with dill, rye bread, homemade yoghurt cheese, fruit, blueberry jam I made myself last summer. Now eat," James commands.

"Made yourself?" I raise an eyebrow.

With his fingers he picks up a slice of soft, unctuous salmon for himself, and drops it into his mouth, bypassing plates and utensils. He grins at the tang of the brine, the heat of the vodka. James cuts into the soft cheese and spreads it on a slice of bread. He spoons jam on top and savors every bite.

My throat is momentarily too constricted to eat, and I fear I won't be able to taste any of this beautiful food. I watch Sara munching her grapes and bread spread thickly with jam. I watch James eating slowly and licking jam from his fingers.

Suddenly I am hungrier than I've been in a long time, and I try everything in front of me. James rests back in his chair, sated, and watches us. Sara, tired of breakfast and the grown-ups, slides off her seat. I kiss the top of her head as she passes by on her way to her room.

"So what are you doing here, James?" I set aside my knife and fork.

"Ever since I met you, I thought, There's someone who could use a good meal. What have you been living on?" he asks, shifting in his seat. His eyes travel along my body. I am self-conscious of my bones, certainly thin and fine. "Toast? Cereal? For someone who makes her living preparing food, that's kind of pathetic. I could snap you like a twig."

"Pathetic, huh?" I look down at my hands in my lap. The rings on my left hand are loose. "So you think all my problems will be solved if I just fatten up a bit?"

James shrugs, "Can't hurt. If there's one thing I can do, it's feed you up."

"Please don't feel sorry for me, it's too seductive. The last thing I need is someone who wants to take care of me."

"What if I want to? What if I think you want me to? What if I think you just need a good cooking lesson?" He isn't smiling but his eyes crackle and hold mine.

I ask, "Is this about last night? All to prove a point?"

James answers, "You don't give up, do you? It's not about arguing with you, Anna, it's about feeding you. It's about food. Look at everything. It's beautiful. There's more to eating than just staying alive."

"I know that," I tell him. "My mother was—is—a horrible cook, and my father was a terrible eater, very fussy. We ate the most god-awful food, mostly tasteless and overcooked, so I grew up thinking I could do better, that I *would* do better. It's always been important to me."

"There we go. You've finally told me something that matters to you."

"Keep feeding me like this, and I'll tell you anything," I say. "Anyway," I continue, looking down at the table, "I always tried to cook nice things for Michael. Toward the end, our dinners became quiet, if we even ate together. Before we separated we had friends over, and Michael fell asleep right at the table. That's when I finally got it. It was all for show, those meals, each one perfect, with the table looking like a painting. You know, a still life? You look and exclaim, 'The color! The abundance!' But then you realize that no matter how much the painters loved that food, you can't smell or taste a thing. And that's not what a meal is about.

"You know, there's nothing quite so nice as seeing people enjoy a meal you've made, simple or elaborate—it doesn't matter. But then there's an awful emptiness when it's rejected. It's personal."

"It *is* personal," he agrees. "That's why when a meal works, the payoff is so great. Everybody's happy, satisfied. But when it doesn't work, you just have to keep trying. Or maybe," he adds with a grin, "you just need a new set of friends."

I smile at him, at his simple solution. "You know, If I were a bad cook, like my mother, I probably wouldn't care. I can't imagine her thinking about anything except her duty to keep the three of us alive. I guess I just had too much of myself invested in every mouthful. I wish—" I begin.

"What?"

"That I hadn't used the food as, well, good-looking props. To make my life appear like it was okay. See, after enough of these meals, no one cared, and eventually I could hardly taste a thing. Eating became so far removed from a basic enjoyment. I . . . I haven't been able to eat. I've lost my appetite."

"You ate this morning."

"It was so good!" I exclaim. James finds my enthusiasm very funny and he roars.

"Why is everything I say to you so funny?" I ask him. "You always get such a bang out of what I tell you."

"You sounded so happy, and I'm happy that you liked your break-fast."

"I swing back and forth between self-pity and rage. I haven't been happy. This morning was a nice change." Looking around the kitchen, I take in all the dirtied dishes and the extra food to be put away. "I really hate the way I sound: bitter, unhappy, complaining, and I don't know why I'm telling you all this. I think I've probably said enough." I get up to stack dishes and carry them to the counter. James looks at me a moment longer, then rises and steps through the kitchen door to the back porch while I clear the kitchen.

I watch him through the window above the sink. In his easy way he leans his backside against the porch rail. Everything he wears has at least one hole in it. His heavy boots are scuffed, and I can see where one of them is separating from its sole. His navy blue crew neck sweater is oversize and misshapen, with a stretched neck that exposes his white T-shirt. The left sleeve has a moth hole at the elbow. I am touched by this; without knowing how, I long to darn it for him. Even in these worn-out clothes, James is attractive.

I spend a lot of time thinking of this as James lolls on my back porch, as I've watched his large hands placing beautiful food delicately on my plates. After our breakfast I begin to wish he would place those hands on me. What, I wonder, is this attraction to James all about, where has it come from? What is attraction, anyway? A chemical re-action, a series of hormones triggering nerve synapses, instigating a chain reaction with various other organs? Is the answer in anthropol-ogy? Some primal urge to continue the species? I am not even sure I like him; most of our conversations have been contentious and defi-nitely not relaxed. I do not trust attraction; it's gotten me into a lot of trouble already.

When he comes back in and sits down, I finish wiping off my counter and sit down with him.

"So what happened," he persists, "after all these pointless meals? Why are you here and your husband's back in Chicago?"

"I couldn't possibly . . ." I begin. "Why do you want to know?"

He ticks off his fingers. "I work with you. I'm here with you right now. I'd like to know you better. Three pretty good reasons."

"Have you ever been married?" I ask.

"Why do *you* want to know?" he replies.

"Very funny," I tell him.

"Well, you still haven't answered me."

"Answers," I say. "I don't have any."

"Try," he presses me. "Did you want to leave?"

"I knew better what I didn't want, what I really didn't want, was to make so many mistakes. But fixing, staying for so long, was humiliating. Leaving, I suppose, was the only thing to do. But then leaving meant admitting to years of mistakes and that's brought me just as low. I'm still humiliated. I've got a lot to figure out. I'm a mess," I conclude.

"And what have you figured out so far?" he asks, ignoring my last remark.

"After a month? You must be joking. Well, have you?" I ask again to change the subject. "Been married?"

"No. Not even close." He doesn't offer any more information, and I realize I am hungry to know more.

Then he asks something that really shakes me up. He leans forward, his arm on the table in front of him, and asks me, "Can we do this again?"

Not long after my breakfast with James, Ben calls me in to talk about sending me to a weekend-long food and wine conference in Boston, only weeks away in mid-April. My life begins to assume a shape into the future.

In Ben's office, as I half listen to him tell me about the conference, my eyes drift to a framed photo on Ben's desk. James, Ben, and I appear in the photo, taken at a wine tasting shortly after I began working at the restaurant. My cheeks are alcohol-flushed because I refused to spit the wine for fear of being photographed with my head in the spit bucket. In the picture I am trying to catch Ben's eye to avoid looking directly at the camera.

"Anna?"

Startled out of memory, I apologize. "I'm sorry, I wasn't listening. What did you say?"

Ben sees me looking at the picture. He picks up the frame, saying, "I said, I'd like to send you to the conference, you and James. There are some discussions I'd like you to sit in on." Ben hands me the photo. "I think he seriously likes you," he tells me as an afterthought as he points to James's image in the frame.

"Oh, please," I say, setting the picture down on Ben's desk.

"You mark my words, he does," warns Ben, like a prophetic old woman. "Only he doesn't know what to do about it."

"Seems to me he's done pretty well for the first month, criticizing my work. Or when he's not criticizing me, he's laughing at me."

"Exactly. The last woman I thought of hiring? James told me he'd work with her only if she wore a dress in the kitchen."

"That's a very highly evolved reaction," I quip. "Ben, actually I can't believe he'd say that. I complain about the criticism, but he's been . . . he's treated me very professionally."

"That's what I'm telling you. I see him trying to be different. For you. I have to assume he's doing it for you."

I consider this and say, "Maybe it's not a good idea to send us together."

"And why isn't this a good idea?" Ben moves out from behind his desk, and rests his backside against the front of it, his arms crossed over his chest.

"I don't know, exactly. You see," I begin, "he came over last Sunday, early, to make us breakfast." I pause, unable to articulate anything more for the moment.

"Breakfast?"

"He brought over all sorts of food; he took over my kitchen. Everything tasted wonderful. I don't know, I felt . . . I liked him, after he left I felt maybe I'd made a friend. But I'm already having a difficult enough time working out my problems without encouraging a new relationship. Maybe it's not such a good idea for me to go away with James. You could send someone else with him. You could go."

"James is going in my place. And you're the one who'll benefit,

Anna. It makes sense to me. It's three days, you'll be back on Sunday. Besides, going away with him doesn't mean you're signaling the start of some relationship you aren't ready for. Forget O'Brien for the moment. I want you to go to Boston if you're staying on with me. I'd like you to stay; you're good. You can be even better." He looks closely at me. "Unless you think you won't be here long term."

"I love working here, I see myself staying here. It's just that now you're adding more variables. James is a new variable. Every day all this stuff covers me like a blanket until I'm stifling."

Ben answers me calmly. "Anna, life's messy, and I know right now yours probably sucks. I understand why you feel overwhelmed, but you're gonna have to work it out. I'm asking you, do you want to stay?"

"Stay," I answer.

"Then go to Boston," he says slinging his arm around my shoulder, pulling me to him in a rough embrace before leaving his office for the kitchen.

I pick up the photo again and look at myself, glass in hand with Ben's arm around my shoulder, looking in his direction. I study Ben, short, sturdy, and completely carefree, smiling directly at the camera. James stands slightly to one side although clearly a part of the three-some. He reaches one hand for a bottle to pour, while the rest of him is turned to me and Ben. Three people enjoying the food, the wine, one another's company.

But what I remember now is this moment after the picture was taken: I move my head slightly after the camera's flash. I see James, whom I have seen every day, as if for the first time. His eyes—did they see food between my teeth, wine splashed on my work shirt?—penetrate me as certainly as his ever-present chef's knife slices flesh. I feel the scrutiny briefly, and almost as quickly someone comes up behind James and claps him on the back, the connection broken.

James strolls the food displays in the morning, he visits with food purveyors, tastes samples, takes business cards. I am cut loose, taking some remedial lessons in food and wine pairing and attending a demonstration of kitchen prep work. This is a much smaller, streamlined version of the expansive national shows I have attended in Chicago. Rather, this is assembled locally by a group of city chefs interested in getting together and sharing ideas.

James and I meet up once during the first day, sitting in on a discussion of current food trends led by a local newspaper's restaurant critic. He informs us that extra virgin olive oil is a hot item; almost worshipfully the writer tells how the trendiest restaurateurs place shallow white saucers on dining tables, with slices of rustic bread for dipping.

"What an ass," James mutters so that only I, seated next to him, can hear, and I stifle a giggle. He whispers in my ear, "I hate this, hate when one item is glorified in this way.

"Worshiping at the altar of the olive," he snorts. Raising his hand, he begins, "Excuse me but . . ." and he pauses, organizing his words. "I like olive oil; I think it is an essential part of some kinds of cooking. But don't you think when you place it on its own, give it so much importance, that you're encouraging a certain snobbism? And that snobbism takes good food and enjoyment one step farther away from the diners? We're telling them it is more important to have this one product—olive oil or whatever is the flavor of the day—than it is to enjoy the meal as a whole." He leans forward in his seat and looks prepared to debate. "Don't you think?" he finishes.

All around us voices erupt as opinions are expressed, both in support of and dissenting from James's statement. I lean back in my seat and close my eyes, hearing the energetic hum of passionate voices all around me. Right now this is the only place for me, and I am very, very happy to be here.

At the end of the first day there is a cocktail party, a mixer. I watch James from across the room, shaking hands and talking with acquaintances from culinary school and chefs he knows by reputation only. Salespeople talk to me briefly until they learn I have no authority at all; then they move on.

"We women are outnumbered here." I turn at the voice behind me.

"Hi," she says, introducing herself with an outstretched hand. "Patty. For some reason they never want to believe we might actually be the decision makers."

I take her hand. "Well, in my case they're absolutely justified. Anna. Rossi," I add, testing out my maiden name.

"In that case I better call security, get you thrown out. Shocking who they're letting in these days," she teases, making me at this instant heartbreakingly homesick for Colette. "Seriously, what do you do?" she asks.

I tell her where I work, why I'm here, and I'm a little surprised to learn she's heard of Ben's. "What about you?" I ask.

"I'm a pastry chef for one of the hotel dining rooms. I'll actually be giving a demo and talk—you know, a question-and-answer type of thing—tomorrow."

"I'm signed up for that session. I'm trying to get all kinds of information under my belt," I explain.

"Who needs it? You can learn a lot on the job if you really want to. Though sometimes the cooking-school types feel superior."

"I know what you mean. At first I felt like the kitchen mascot, or everyone's little sister. But I was the least experienced person joining an established kitchen; probably much of it was my own insecurity.

"But being here, this is like heaven to me. It helps me feel I belong," I say. "All these people in one place talking about food. How frivolous and self-indulgent, but how wonderful," and I smile at Patty.

"Tell me about your work," I prompt, and I listen with one ear, lulled by soothing words like "ganache," "marzipan," "genoise." "Tempering," "folding," "baking blind." With my other ear I pick up sounds from around the room: laughter, the rapid sales pitch, forced enthusiasm, low, serious tones. The sounds and sensations of the cocktail party are the same wherever you go, no matter what the mix of people. There is a whoop of laughter from the other side of the room. I strain for James's voice, by now so familiar, and I think I can find it beneath the other voices; like a bass line issuing from a stereo, it finds me, vibrates within my chest like a second heartbeat or a dangerous arrhythmia. Next to me Patty talks on about *pâte brisée* and American-style pies. With a huge, goofy smile plastered on my face, I breathe in deeply, then sip a delicious chenin blanc that tastes of melon, and relish its slightly sweet taste on my tongue.

James picks this moment to finish mingling, and he comes to collect me. I feel his hand on my back as he puts his lips close to my ear. "Ready for dinner? I am. I'm starving."

His words, teasing and tantalizing with a concrete promise of dinner, break into the pastry-speak and I am happy to say good-bye. Offering my hand to Patty I promise to attend her session tomorrow.

James and I walk out into the night.

We walk up the street and slip into a restaurant that is dimly lit, already late evening within its doors. Outside, sleet shoots down from a dark gray sky like icy needles: an unusually raw April day. Many people take refuge indoors, either in the few remaining open stores or in cafés drinking cups of coffee for the sake of warmth. A few, like James and me, head for the comfort of an evening drink and a warm meal. My temporary freedoms—from work, from motherhood (with Sara once again at my mother's)—are clear and sharp before me like the falling ice. Freedom propels me through the doors.

"I'd like a drink," I say across the table. "Something to warm me on the way down, like tequila. I'm freezing. But I'll settle for red wine."

As the overhead lights dim, waiters move around the dining room lighting candles. James calls our waiter over and orders wine and an appetizer.

"After a certain point I hate cocktail parties," James tells me. "It makes me itch to sit around someone's restaurant and talk to people about what they're cooking in their kitchens. Taste their food."

"I know what you mean, but I've been to worse. Where wives would congregate, talk about their cleaning ladies, or where to get the best bikini wax in Chicago."

"Bikini wax, huh? What is that exactly?"

"Not polite dinner conversation, trust me. Anyway, I enjoyed hearing about desserts. Oh, look, our food!" I exclaim, clasping my hands.

"Good thing, I'm hunnngrrry," James growls, and his feral animal drawl makes me smile.

The thin slices of raw beef on James's plate, the flesh bruise purple, glisten with olive oil. Shaved Parmesan lies scattered around the plate in large curls. The cheese, at room temperature, releases its oil; it, too, shines, and it crumbles when James picks up a piece. With his fingers he offers me a slice of beef, which I lean across the table to take from his hand. I watch as he piles carpaccio onto French bread and licks olive oil from his fingers.

"This is really good," he says, grinning, and I lift some cheese from his plate, nodding in agreement while I watch the muscles around his jaw contract and relax as he chews.

"I'd like to work in the city one day," he continues. "Maybe have my own place. But then I'd have to decide to leave the fresh air behind me. Which I don't know if I really want to do."

"Why the city?" I ask.

"There's always room for one more; everything's changing here."

"What kind of place would you have?" I ask, finally tasting my own first course of braised leeks, which feel like silk in my mouth.

"A small place, a little out of the way, maybe in a neighborhood. Where people could come for a good meal as well as the friendly atmosphere. A place where I could take some risks, push myself, come up with my own ideas." He stops to mop the plate with some bread and takes a drink. "There's a guy I know. I went to school with him in Rhode Island, and he now owns the kind of place I'm talking about. He's married, he and his wife met in school. She works front of the house while he manages the kitchen. They have a real partnership. It's beyond work, it's their life."

"And that's what you want?" I ask.

"I think so."

"Wouldn't you have to get married first?" I tease. "Or at least be serious about someone? When I asked you if you'd ever been married, you said, 'Not even close.'"

"Up to now with my job, I've worked crazy hours. Some girl will find this attractive and exciting for a couple of months, at which time she begins to calculate that that will leave about four hours a week for her, most of which is spent climbing in and out of bed. The excitement wears off quickly. So I made a habit of picking the ones who didn't really care that it was for the short term."

"Okay. Without talking numbers here, of all the women you've ever gone out with, there hasn't been one, no one you've been serious about?"

"That's about right. It's always been easier not to get too involved."

"So, you go for the easy relationships with lots of women."

"Jesus, Anna, I'm not, like, a monk. And I never said 'lots.'"

"I'm not judging you, really, I'm only trying to understand you better. Not too long ago," I tell him, "Ben told me something you said, about female staff members wearing dresses in the kitchen."

"Ben talks too much. And I didn't mean all women. What happened was, he thought of hiring this female, and I thought she didn't really want to get her hands dirty. So I told Ben if he hired her maybe she'd like to wear a dress to work. Now, he can hire whoever he wants, but I have to get the work out of them. I questioned her commitment; it was my way of pointing that out to Ben. I meant what I said, though. In that case." He pauses. "So you heard that from Ben, and what? Decided that I have an attitude problem, about women?"

"No, I don't think that. I do think you're tough to figure out. A tough boss, a thoughtful friend, a hard worker in the kitchen but maybe not in your personal life? A mass of contradictions. Add to the mix that you always say what you mean, and I'm at a total loss."

"What do you want me to say? I've made some poor choices. I'm convinced finding someone is all trial and error, and I'm just stumbling around like everyone else. But since my last relationship, I've decided to hang back a bit."

"Tell me about her," I urge.

"I went out with this girl at work, Christine, for about six months last year. She worked front of the house."

"Waitress," I say, and James shrugs his assent. I can picture her, long-legged in black pants and white blouse, taking orders, unruffled and competent. For some reason I see myself in contrast, in my back-of-the-house gear—baggy checks, filthy white shirt, clunky clogs—and I'm filled with inadequacy. The inadequacy greets me like an old friend; this territorial thing, however, is very new. I feel like circling James, marking him with my scent.

"But it was over a long time before. . . . Look," he tells me, "we fought all the time."

"We argue."

"Fought, not argued," he clarifies as I start to open my mouth again. "We didn't like each other, which is much different than disagreeing."

"So why did it last six months?"

"Because I found her attractive, and the mutual dislike was kind of exciting for a while," he tells me plainly.

"That is so shallow," I laugh. "I can't believe you told me that."

"I told you I'd tell you the truth, remember?" James asks. He continues talking to me, but I detect a change in his tone, an impatience that wasn't present in our earlier banter. I think of my own decisions and wish I could take back my words. "Have no illusions about me, Anna. I'm flesh and blood and full of flaws. Sure, I'd like to find what my friend has with his wife, but I haven't. That doesn't mean I prefer my life this way."

"What would you prefer?" I ask, and I reach across the table to touch his hand. His eyes meet mine.

"If two people in our business work together, they're spending time together. Plus they're doing the same work, so they feel more connected. It's still hard work, but with a common goal. That's what I'd like."

"Do you think it would be incredibly stressful, having your relationship so closely tied in with your livelihood?"

"There's risk and sacrifice in everything. Maybe you give up a little of your leisure time, or you have more joint worries about money, but it seems to me by working together, two people who really want to work together are gonna have the communication thing figured out. My friend? He and his wife have different responsibilities, but they operate as two halves of one terrific team. When it works, it's gotta be pretty amazing. And from where I stand it looks pretty good."

The waiter arrives at this moment with our dinner: a very simple piece of grilled salmon, a brace of tiny quail resting on a puddle of demiglace. I taste my food and, laying down my fork, look across the table at James. He breaks the leg off a tiny quail. I have felt these same hands, gentler, on me, guiding my own hands with a knife, showing me the way to work and what to do. I try to imagine the softness of his skin, perhaps the skin of his back, smooth and warm, right then as if my fingers actually lay on him.

Then I shake my hands out, shaking off the sensation.

After dinner James suggests a walk. The sleet stopped sometime during dinner and the clouds shifted, leaving a crisper, clearer night sky. Shoving my hands in my pockets, I leave my coat unbuttoned and flapping open to feel the cold air rushing through my clothes to find my skin. We cross the neatly plotted streets of the Back Bay, passing boutiques and brownstones, and stroll up the Commonwealth Avenue mall with traffic passing on either side of us. At the Ritz we jaywalk through the traffic and walk into the Public Gardens, where our pace slows. Despite the freak freeze, the grass is turning emerald green, though still thin, tenuous new growth. We stop at the bridge over the duck pond, some people pass us walking purposefully, with destinations in mind, to the subways, buses, taxis; others appear to be as aimlessly strolling as we are. The air smells of spring, of earthworms rising out of the ground with the rain.

Next to me James stands looking over the bridge into the murky water. His jaw is clenched. I can see prominent tendons in his neck and the muscles tightened around his cheekbones, as if he is turning over a decision in his mind. I lean my back on the railing, look away from his face, and breathe in the night air.

"It's turned into a beautiful evening," I say, considering my next words. "I'm sorry that I called you shallow earlier. I shouldn't talk; after all I'm coming to terms with marrying Michael because (a) I liked sex, and (b) because it was something to do to avoid being on my own." I give a short, wry laugh, but at my sides I make my hands into fists. "Aarggh! I hate having to admit that."

"Anna," James begins. When I face him he asks, "What would you say to bagging the rest of this workshop?"

"You mean going home?" He nods in reply. "Well, I kind of like the conversations, and I'm supposed to be here to learn a few things. Ben might object."

"Ben won't mind too much. I've found a couple of new suppliers for him, and as for learning, I believe I could teach you more. We could cook together after work. You'll get more out of that, and by working in the restaurant every day, than you will by sitting in on a few demos."

"So you want to, what? Give me lessons? Like private lessons?"

"Not lessons, exactly. You don't really need lessons, you know that. It would be adding to what you already know, building on your skill."

"As your protégée?"

"I was thinking we could try to work more like partners."

"Partners?"

"I like working with you," he says simply.

I rest my back on the railing again and look up into the black sky. A plane is flying above, descending into Logan, and I watch the flicker of its external lights. Wordlessly I tap James on the arm and point to the plane with my finger. As he, too, rests his back against the railing, his arm rubs my shoulder, and we stand side by side following the plane's descent with two pairs of eyes until it disappears behind buildings.

"The planes have to fly right over the harbor to reach the runway," I say to James. "Landing here has always made me nervous. For a few seconds it looks like the plane will land right in the water, and it's always a relief to me when the wheels slam into the runway."

"I know. I hate flying," he tells me. "I get sick."

"I've flown a lot, but I'm tired of traveling," I continue. "All I've been doing is looking around for something to give my life meaning. I'm the only one who can do that." As I speak a cloud of vapor forms around my mouth. "What you said at dinner? About your friend and his wife? From where I stand it looks pretty good to me, too. You really want to drive back tonight?" I ask.

Next to me I hear James's quiet "Mm-hmm."

"We have to stop for Sara on the way back." I remind him.

"Already thought of that," James answers.

"Which will probably freak my mother out. We aren't very good at short notice. Well, then," I say, pushing away from the railing, "let's go." I hold out my hand, which he takes in his own.

Taste this," James encourages me, "and tell me about it."

He has just finished chopping, mashing, squeezing, mixing. The skin on his fingers is green and slick from peeling avocados. He is in my home after work; he hasn't even changed from his work clothes. For the past twenty minutes I've watched him moving at the counter, his feet bare, his white work shirt unbuttoned at the neck. His shirt is tired, his baggy checked pants are stained, but his movements are vigorous and purposeful beneath the limp cloth.

Before he offers me a taste, he's dipped his finger in the bowl. He tastes and corrects the seasoning, more sea salt, more lime juice, a couple of shakes of Tabasco. Then he comes to me, seated at the table, quiet and watchful; he holds the bowl in one hand. His other hand is extended to me, two fingers topped with avocado. For a few moments I don't understand his offer, then he says, "Taste this. And tell me about it." He stands expectantly, innocently hopeful, like a child.

Closing my eyes, I take his hand, bring his fingers to my mouth. I smell citrus oil on his skin, smell without seeing, taste blind.

"Bland at first; oily, rich and creamy; the green onions taste like grass first, then onions; the lime explodes; Tabasco nips at the back of my throat; when I swallow there's heat. If I stretch, I can taste a little lingering sweetness of tomato. But I taste the flavors all at once, it all works together even though I recognize the individual parts." I open my eyes, look up at him.

"Very good," he tells me.

We've been eating this way for a few weeks now, since we returned from Boston. We eat late into the night, clean up, say good night only to see each other at work the next afternoon. If it seems strange that we cook all day and come back to my place only to cook some more, it never occurs to me. I can't tell if he's testing me or teaching me or simply sharing; I haven't asked, haven't decided, as I am learning to eat, if any one of these intents really bothers me. Tonight is the first time he's fed me from his fingers. I hesitate about letting my tongue stay to lick the salt and citrus from his skin, but it tastes so good. My response, James's offer, both change the direction of this particular meal. I don't want him to leave.

"Can I have another taste, please?"

"I could feed you the whole bowl this way if you want." His eyes are boring into me.

"I couldn't possibly eat the whole thing," I answer, because I am full, not because I am embarrassed by my request.

"Just one more?" he asks, handing me another taste.

He takes his finger from my mouth and traces my lips. He sets the bowl down, leans over, and gives me a kiss. His tongue passes into my mouth, and he is tasting me.

The thing about James is, he knows—always—what I want even before I've said, before I've even fully formed the words in my brain. Before it is even verbal, when it's only an urge, a desire. Like with the lime, way back when I first met him, didn't yet know him, and he offered to squeeze a lime in my soda water.

And just a few days ago, when he found me sitting alone in the empty restaurant dining room right before dinner, taking a break with a cup of tea, he came up to me, wordless, and placed in front of me the most beautiful assortment of cheese—Maytag Blue, Montrachet, Tillamook Cheddar—all in small wedges or disks on a dessert-size plate. There were a few grapes, a few slices of fresh pineapple, a sprinkling of raspberries, five dry round water crackers. It was a restrained plate, it looked designed to tempt a small child or a person heading back to food after a long illness. Still it was beautiful, the shades of white, chalk, and cream, the yolk yellow of the cheddar cheese, the lighter yellow pineapple. Each thing said, *Look at me.* I ate a grape, put a piece of blue cheese on some pineapple, and the blend of salt and sweet brought tears to my eyes.

I tell him it's a gift he has, his intuition. He tells me I don't know the half of it; then he laughs and draws me into his generous, engulfing arms. These things I don't know about him frighten me, but his arms are a safe place. I am also nervous about needing to feel safe.

For me, James is a dangerous street. By May we are eating together nearly every night. My mind is preoccupied, dangerously distant from the mundane, and I have to force myself to concentrate on everyday details. During my workday I find it hard to concentrate on my job. The sight of his hands working so near mine makes me long to sit next to him, holding those hands. I am quite often exhausted, too, for after work, late into the evening, James prepares strange meals out of foods he selects just for me. He feeds me small fruits, like clementines and fresh figs, pungent wedges of ripe cheese, and triangles of sand-wiches held together with salty olive spread. He lounges, watching me eat, often reaching over to share food from my plate. I learn to be protective of my meals, but with a look James can pluck one of the tastiest pieces for himself. James has a smile as powerful as a train wreck.

He is chaos, too; he causes me a great mind storm. I often think of him as an opium den, myself an addict. He is the place I return to, night after night, drawn to him like an intoxicating drug. When he leaves in the early hours of the morning, I think if I open all the windows, sleep off the remnant desire, I will awaken later in the day cured. But like a drug addict, I find that the next day only brings more craving.

In this way James becomes a part of me, like a limb or blood, James and his good food, and his kisses, which are like the taste of a simple, wheaty bread after a long hunger.

James and I kiss. He touches my body longingly; I could ask in a thick, strangled voice, "Please." And I do want him; I'd like nothing more than to lead him down the hallway to my bedroom, closing the door firmly behind us. I can imagine the snapping spring of the doorknob, a kind of starting gun. I want to see his body; I've touched it so much I imagine I know what it looks like, but I also know it will surprise me. But my ratty serviceable bedroom shames me as it reflects my emptiness. I can't lead him there. It is a depressing place to me, as empty as a novice's dormitory, left unfinished back when I moved in. I still haven't raised the mattress off the floor or added anything personal to the stark chair and dresser.

I have been separated for more than three months; I am trying to succeed at managing my new life; and I am working with someone whose proximity at this moment is nearly bringing me to my knees. So while I want him, I make myself not have him. All my instincts are questionable. Because he, my need for him, makes me angriest of all, angrier than any mistake I've made with Michael. Like a mirror, he shows me my weakness.

When summer swoops in, muggy and sultry, the kitchen becomes unbearably hot. But we cook on.

At work I am aware of curious stares. James and I, quite uncon-sciously, begin to touch each other, some spillover from our late-night dinners. I will reach out and rub his arm if he is next to me; I can feel his muscles relax if I touch him when he is tense. Sometimes when he stands behind me, with his arms around me to show me a chopping technique, I want to move back into him. I long to reach up and grab his neck, bring his mouth to my ear. I know if I back up, I will fit nicely into the V of his planted legs; I know I will feel his erection. But we never go this far; at work we haven't moved beyond the simple reassuring touches. It is new for me, moving slowly. For James, too. Still, as we begin to go places together, work together so closely, every-one assumes we are sleeping together. My denials, however, are re-ceived with amusement especially from Ben, who tells me, "You look good. Really well." And I do feel better. My clothes fit better.

Sara, too, seems swept along into this idyll, responding perhaps to my happiness and relaxation. I take it as a good sign that her night-mares have decreased and her brow more often looks smooth and un-lined. Although she isn't aware of the long, late hours I spend with James, she becomes accustomed to his presence during the daytime and on the weekends. As it warms up, the three of us spend more time together out of doors looking for shade on wooded trails. One Saturday in July we take a day off, and James drives me and Sara across the Maine border to a town with a flea market. When we stop to look around, Sara tugs me in the direction of ice cream. James just laughs his hearty laugh and says he'll walk around, meet us back here. Sara, with an unerring sense for sweets, plows through the crowds and leads us to a stand.

As we eat our ice cream cones, Sara so involved in catching all the drips in this heat, I wander the stalls, stopping at some green glass plates. They are smooth on the surface but embossed with a leaf pattern on the underside. The woman has eight for sale, along with some stubby, thick-stemmed goblets, which look something like a simple horn standing on its end. I can't decide if they are ugly or endearing, but I am enchanted by the color, the true green of an ivy leaf. I lick ice cream and ponder buying myself these as a present.

I smell James, the particular soap he washes with, before I feel his arm at my back, his hand on my rump. He looks pleased with himself.

"I found some basil over there, there's a farmer's market." From behind his back he pulls a bunch of basil leaves wrapped like a bouquet.

Sara tells him, "We found ice cream."

"I see you did. Can I have a taste?" Sara lifts her cone, and he takes a lick. "Delicious," he says. "Much better than these old leaves," he tells her, wrinkling his nose.

"What about you?" he asks, facing me. "Can I have a taste?"

I shake my head no. "I won't share," I tease, but then I laugh and hand him the entire cone.

"Thinking of buying?" James asks pointing to the glass with my ice cream.

"Thinking, but I haven't made up my mind."

"I don't know if it's occurred to you," he says, "but everything you own is white. The color makes kind of a nice change."

"What do you think red wine would look like through that glass?" I ask him.

"Probably mud."

"Exactly what I was thinking. I think I'll take all of it," I tell the woman. I add to James, "Just to see what that wine will look like." We wait while she wraps the plates and glasses in some old newspaper.

"Anything else you want to see?" I ask James. "Besides the basil?"

"Oh, I've done my shopping," he tells me rather cryptically. "There's a place I know, between here and home. I thought we could stop for lunch. Have our lunch on a rock next to a stream. How 'bout it, Sara? Want a picnic?"

The day suddenly feels long and lazy, as if there's nothing to do for almost forever, no work, no baby-sitters, just time. I look at my daughter, a grubby ring of chocolate ice cream around her mouth, sun shining off her dark hair, and I am gloriously happy.

On the way to James's truck, I stop short in front of some furniture. Resting against the canvas and metal framework of the stall I see a huge oak headboard—it is very plain, simple, except for carvings like

Celtic knots around its rectangular border. Lying behind is the bed's frame. And I must have it all.

"A bed?" James asks.

"I need it," and I turn from him to the salesman. He helps us carry it in pieces to the truck. James shifts something wrapped in brown paper from the truck's bed to the front seat.

"I saw a mirror and I wanted it, so I bought it," he explains.

"A mirror and a bed. And all this green glass. We're crazy."

"Maybe," he says, opening the cab door for Sara and me to slide in along with our packages.

Forty-five minutes later we are eating bread and fruit by a stream, as James promised. Sara asks where the stream comes from, and James holds out his hand, saying, "Here, I'll show you." He leads her off, and I quickly pick up peels and cores, leftover bread, and pack everything in the bag so I can follow. We walk along the stream to its source, a place in the earth where it bubbles up from the rocks. "It's a spring," James tells Sara. "Underground water. It finds a place to push out above ground and runs along that downhill path, making the stream." He points back to the path with his left hand.

"Can I drink the water?" Sara asks.

"Sure," James answers. "It's a kind of natural water fountain."

Sara gets down on her knees and takes a sip. "It's cold, Mommy. How can it be cold? I thought the inside of the earth is hot."

I do my best to explain, then I say, "Sara, I haven't had a taste yet. Tell me what it tastes like."

From behind me James wraps me in his arms, drawing me into him, kissing the side of my neck.

"It tastes like rocks. Like cold rocks," she pronounces.

"That's the granite, Sara," James explains. "It has to travel through granite. Very good."

"Rocks, hmmm?" I say. "Sounds good, sounds like I need to try some."

James releases me and bends at the knees. At this moment I love the look of his thighs, his knees pointing out over his toes as he squats with his hands cupped under the spring. He brings the water to my mouth as Sara drops to take another sip. His hands smell like basil and sunshine. The water is cool, and it does, indeed, taste like rocks, flinty cold and earthy.

We've been out all day and it is almost five o'clock when James stops outside my building. We all get out of the truck, I pick up my package of glass gingerly as I climb out. Sara follows and races me to the front door. I start after her, thinking James will follow too.

"Hey, Anna," he calls from the truck, motioning me back. "I'm gonna need a hand," he tells me. "With the bed. And the mirror. It's for you."

"For me?" I ask in disbelief. "You bought me a mirror?"

"Don't just stand there," he adds. "Can you give me a hand, maybe open the doors?"

I look into the pickup. Everything must weigh a ton. "Why did you buy me a mirror?"

"Because you don't have one, because you need one. You don't even own a freakin' mirror outside the bathroom. Your house looks like a sensory deprivation chamber, like you're punishing yourself. And sleeping on the floor," he scoffs. "Next thing you know you'll be wearing a hair shirt and beating yourself with willow branches."

"Don't think I haven't thought of it. Actually, I was trying to simplify."

"Well, there's simple, and then there's masochistic." He lifts this mirror out of its packaging and rests it against the passenger door. "Can't even see how good you look these days." James stands behind me, his hands on my shoulders push me forward so I can see my reflection. It's true: My clothes no longer hang or gap. I'm fuller somehow, all over, and I have a tan, and the word that comes to my mind is healthy.

"Look at you," he says. "You're beautiful," and he traces my cheek, my jaw, my neck. Finally I recognize the person I see: no more bones and hollows and angles. It's like I've been away and now I'm back.

I accept the gift and—emboldened, unafraid—ask him to put together my new bed. I bring James beer as he works on in the heat of the evening. The beer bottle is slippery with condensation, James's back with sweat. Sara takes a tepid bath, and while she swims in the tub I sip wine from one of my new glasses. We were wrong about the color. Through the glass the wine looks as glassy black as obsidian.

Once Sara is tucked in, I find James slouching against the door-frame of my bedroom, beer in hand. He asks if I can help with the mattress and box spring, which I do. Standing back, I'm surprised by the bed: This behemoth is lovelier than I gave it credit for when it was lying in pieces in the back of the truck. James has rubbed it with oil soap, buffed it with an old soft towel I use for dusting, and the oak is honey colored.

"You could strip this and put on a new finish, if you wanted," he suggests.

"I think I like it the way it is," I answer, knowing I won't do a thing to it.

We make up the bed silently by fixing the sheets that slipped when we shifted the mattress. He offers me a sip of beer, and I shake my head but move around to stand next to him. I move my fingers along his back, which is covered with his perspiration. His skin is cool.

He draws me to him, folds me snugly in his arms. "Hungry?" he whispers into my hair and, even though it is late and we are tired, we eat because it is what we want.

For a little while I watch James cook without his shirt on; I can see the interstitial muscles and tendons at work across and underneath his shoulder blades as he pulls his arms back, elbows bent. Looking away because my breathing becomes shallow, because I feel lightheaded with watching the harmony of his bone and muscle, I chop a few herbs, mix together a simple salad dressing, pour another glass of wine. There is a familiar quickening in my gut, and butterflies. Every motion, sound, smell, assaults me; I feel each as if it were a hand on me. Behind me

I hear the rapid springing of a whisk against a glass bowl. I will not look but allow myself to imagine the contours of a bicep as James purposefully beats air into eggs for an omelet. The sizzle of butter hitting the pan. The eggs firming instantly. James works quickly moving eggs around the pan. The grind of a pepper mill. I drink, feel the buzz of alcohol, but everything gets sharper, not dulled. Plates, silver. James tasting the vinaigrette, his finger dripping. He serves me supper. I try to take a deep breath, watch as food passes his lips. Our eyes lock.

"This is very, very good," I tell him, but my voice betrays me; I am not in the least hungry for dinner. It is James—watching, hearing, smelling, feeling him prepare anything—that has me hungry. Finally I want only to taste him. I touch his upper arm, feel where muscle joins the bone, notice that his right arm, his right hand are marginally larger, better developed than the left. He puts his elbows on the table, lets me draw a line along his arm. When I stop, he groans, but I am only taking his utensils away from him. We hold hands, walk down the hall to my new, absurd bed, the bed I don't know I want so badly until we fall into it.

Everything has come to this, every experience in my life has led my to being in this bed with James. It is as if we are swimming together, at first long, lazy, big strokes. An easy swim, no fatigue, we work together; we don't race. It's just slow and easy, swimming ahead like we're trying to reach something, then slowing up: stretching, reaching, then retracting. I forget that the water pouring from James's skin, from mine in this muggy July heat isn't the ocean, and so we move across a soft pool until we're both there, where we want to be, gasping and surprised; now we're clinging to each other, washed up, enfolded, entangled, entwined, kissing, and exactly where we want to be.

"I can't sleep," I tell James later that night after he's placed his hands, his mouth, all over my body until I am full with him, covered with him, hardly know where he ends and I begin.

James turns over and puts a hand on either side of me. Raising himself up on his hands, his elbows locked, he looks down on me. "You can't sleep?" he asks.

"I'm worried. About sleeping with you."

"It's a little late for that now," he says, and, kissing my cheek, he lies down next to me.

"I mean it. Both of us have so much . . . stuff . . . behind us. With other people. Mistakes, maybe. I don't want to make mistakes with you."

"It's okay to make mistakes. Besides, why are you even thinking of other people? It's like you're bringing them into bed with us."

"It feels that way to me, right now, as if they *are* all here."

"You know," James says, "at first I didn't want to get involved with you." He rolls onto his back and speaks up into the air, "I didn't know how . . . there'd never been anyone I . . . It was easier at first, at work, to believe you were screwing around, passing time while you sorted out your life.

"Then I saw you were good at it, I saw you were serious. The food we prepared, your company, our conversation—everything came together. And I thought, 'We can do this together.' I watched you watching me. I liked the way you looked at me."

"How did I look at you?"

"Like this," and he shows me with his own face now above me again, his eyes reading into me. "Like you meant it, like you really thought I was okay."

"You *are* okay," I tell him. "You are better than okay." And I kiss him hard, pressing into his teeth. I bite his bottom lip as if it were a piece of fruit.

"Don't hurt me," he teases, but then the smile fades, and I can see that he means it. "The past, Anna, it's all part of us. It makes us who we are together; we can't get away from that. But short of you developing amnesia, is there anything we can do to put all these people—and mistakes—away, at least for the night?"

"Well, maybe there is something you can do."

"Maybe?" he asks, an eyebrow raised. But before I answer, his mouth is back on me, his finger stirring me into a kind of boiling soup, and I've forgotten what it was I felt afraid of, anyway.

PART FOUR

The Lone Wolf

Dear Anna,

My state of mind is for shit, like a bomb has dropped in my head and left me with only shreds of facts and truths which taken together make no sense. Driving away from New Hampshire I had some direction and energy. I understood that in separating we made the right decision, the only decision.

But when I got home, after I played off the answering machine tape and heard your voice in the house one last time, it was so quiet here. I started wondering if maybe the perfunctory conversations we've had lately, maybe even hollering at each other, would be better than this ringing silence. This really sucks.

I've always been good at constructing a theory of the case, at stringing together various truths into a big picture so the jury has a story, a way of understanding what happened and why. Maybe there's no theory here for me to fall back on. Do you know what this feels like to me, creating a new life? Used to be I could come home, count on dinner and you and Sara. For even though we hadn't much to say to each other, it was something to build a life around; it was familiar and expected, comforting even in its unremarkable routineness. Someone, maybe it was Julie, told me my newfound singlehood should be liberating—all this time to do exactly what I want to do, when I want to do it: work, maybe a little golf on Sunday when the weather improves. But I hardly know anymore if that's exactly what I want to be doing with my life. Maybe what I want has something to do with you, me, and Sara, home-cooked meals, and someone to talk to after a long, hard day. But what a fantasy, huh? We didn't have that, either, and now it's just me and my tendency when alone to drink my meals because I'm too lazy or too scared to make the effort.

There's so much gray. I'd love to point to something and say, There, that's it: We screwed up at that exact moment, and now I can move on. Like Julie says, feel liberated. But my life passes by and I remain, day after day, behind my desk at work early in the morning and long after the support staff has gone, in a sticky molasses of feelings, unmovable, immobile, paralyzed.

Dear Sara,

As I sit to write to you, the house is very quiet. I will tell you about my days if you promise to write back and tell me what you are doing as winter ends in New Hampshire. As I said, the house is very quiet. Every once in awhile, I turn to tell you something, or I turn at what I think is the sound of your footsteps, but then I remember you are not here. That's when I pick up a pen and write my letters to you.

I am very busy at work, so busy that most days I eat all three meals at my desk. Sometimes I go to Uncle Barnaby's house for dinner. Aunt Maddie prepares very healthy meals because of the baby—lots of broccoli, which is rich in calcium, she tells me. But it's hard to fill up on broccoli, and I always leave their house a bit hungry. But it's nice to have the invitation.

Every day now I get my own coffee. While the water heats, I head out to the back porch to smoke. There's no one here, no one to object to my smoking indoors, but I can't get used to smoking in the house. Actually I'm trying to quit because it is a hard habit to keep, especially on the colder mornings, not to mention terrible for my lungs. But as I watch the smoke drift through the porch screen out over the backyard, at least my hands are busy.

The hum of the teakettle draws me back in the house, so I take the water off the boil and spoon coffee into the filter. My coffee is not as good as your mom's; I haven't gotten used to this contraption she was so attached to, and I never use enough coffee. No matter how much I put in, it's never enough. But my mind spreads out slowly like jam as I watch the coffee grounds wet and swell. I think of the day ahead at work, I think of you.

As I sip the weak coffee, enjoying at least the feel of the warm ceramic mug between my hands, I listen to the cars passing through the slush on the roads. I hear birds tricked out of their shelters by this teasing thaw. The only other unseasonable February I can recall is the one the winter after you were born. It was so mild that your mom turned to me and said, "We could paint the baby's room." She was right; it was warm enough, at nearly sixty or sixty-five degrees, to throw open the windows and let the paint dry, let the sweet smell of paint out of the house. We moved your crib in with us for the week, all three of us unused to each other as roommates, until your room was done and rid of any chemicals. Then the weather turned nasty, as it will in March. Still, maybe this year we will have an early spring in the city.

I miss you, Sara-girl, but I am happy when I think of you opening my letters. If I close my eyes I can see you reading them with your mom. If I leave my eyes closed a bit longer, on the back of my eyelids I can play out what I imagine you are doing: reading this letter, playing with your doll, snuggling into bed with a nighttime book, building snowmen. Do you have lots of snow? A good-size yard to play in? Has your mother taught you to make snow angels? When I played in the snow with my brother at your age we stayed out until our toes stung. After we came in the house, Grandma made us put our stockinged feet below the radiator in the kitchen, and as we sat we sipped hot chocolate she had warmed while we stripped out of our wet snow pants. I still remember that cocoa—warm, slightly bitter, with marshmallow fluff melting into a foamy layer on top—and my burned tongue from gulping that first mouthful in my eagerness to warm up.

What happens as we grow up and forget these early days of childhood? Why do we forget such simple pleasures, replace them with more complex ones? After all, what could be better than drinking hot chocolate and warming toes by a radiator through bulky dry socks? The hiss of the radiator as Mom turned it up or down to suit us meant, to me, she loved us. Our toes would tingle, then itch, then swell as they thawed. Grandma made us wear plastic bags between socks and boots, but that's as waterproof and protective as it got. No such thing as polar fleece back then, no knowledge of wicking fabrics or layers.

I'd like to stand at a window, as I know my mother did while we played, and watch you across the yard as you romp in the snow. I would like to be with you, whatever it is you are doing, and I am sorry we are so far apart right now.

Dear Sara,

Guess what? I had a weird dream last night, kind of scary, although I can't say why. [Actually, I wake every night, startled by my dreams until I have to sit upright and breathe deeply to quiet the pounding in my chest.] I was in a theater, like a movie theater with rows of seats and dim floor lights along the aisles, listening to a talk about architecture—the history of the buildings of Chicago. The lecturer was a big-shot Chicago architect with owly glasses, and we listened to him go on and on, and he got really boring after a while, until it seemed we would fall asleep in our seats. Then all of a sudden the group was outside. Do you know that dream thing, Sara, when without warning the scene shifts?

So now, part of the lecture becomes a walk through the city using the buddy system, walking two by two. I'm paired with a woman who looks familiar but I can't place her, can't put a name with her face. But it's no longer Chicago we're in, Sara, it's New York City [that old "dream thing" again] and I don't know why since I haven't been to New York in years. We keep walking, listening to the architect guy ramble on as we head for a gray stone building with lions on either side of the entryway. He tells us this is some fine example of public sculpture. I raise my hand to object, I'm thinking of all the finer pieces in Chicago, the Picasso, the Miro, the Calder, but my partner yanks me by the arm before I am able to speak.

She leads me from the group. She says, "Let's grab a bite to eat." And I go along, without a word, but I'm thinking, "Yeah, I could use a sandwich." I could eat, I realize, while walking on the sidewalk with crowds of office workers shuffling around me, just an anonymous member of the throng. It's only alone, in the quiet of home, that I can't figure out what I'd like to fill me up. As we move in closer to the building, looking for a fast-food place, we're approached by policemen who appear out of nowhere to tell us, "There's a quarantine here. This whole block is shut down because of an outbreak of scarlet fever." And this is the part that made me feel scared. I started thinking about you, Sara. Is she safe, I wondered?

Ask your mother, Sara, about the time you had scarlet fever. We took you to the children's hospital in the middle of the night with a huge fever that we couldn't bring down, but no one thought to give you a throat culture. When they looked in your ears and your throat everything was clear, not inflamed. The docs insisted you were fighting off a viral bug, and they got the fever down quick enough with ibuprofen and popsicles so we believed them. Then three days later your fever was back up, you were throwing up and nearly delirious. When we got you out of your pajamas the trunk of your body was covered in shocking red pin dots. Covered. Your mother knew what it was immediately. But I was speechless. And frightened. And feeling *so very guilty until your mother told me to quit beating myself up. "How could we have known," she insisted. But can you see why the dream would frighten me?*

Ask your mother, Sara, ask her this: How do we survive our kids? Ask her: How do they manage to survive us?

Chicago, 11 March
Dear Sara,

As I sit to write to you, the house is very quiet. I miss you, Sara-girl, but I am happy when I think of you opening my letters. If I close my eyes I can see you reading them with your mom. If I leave my eyes closed a bit longer, on the back of my eyelids I can play out what I imagine you are doing: reading this letter, playing with your doll, snuggling into bed with a nighttime book, building snowmen. Do you have lots of snow? A good-size yard to play in? Has your mother taught you to make snow angels? When I played in the snow with my brother at your age we stayed out until our toes stung. After we came in the house, Grandma made us put our stockinged feet below the radiator in the kitchen, and as we sat we sipped hot chocolate she had warmed while we stripped out of our wet snow pants. I still remember that cocoa—warm, slightly bitter, with marsh-mallow fluff melting into a foamy layer on top—and my burned tongue from gulping that first mouthful in my ea-gerness to warm up. Anyway, I will tell you about my days if you promise to write back and tell me what you are doing as winter ends in New Hampshire.

I am very busy at work, so busy that most days I eat all three meals at my desk. Sometimes I go to Uncle Barnaby's house for dinner. Aunt Maddie prepares very healthy meals because of the baby—lots of broccoli, which is rich in cal-cium, she tells me. But it's hard to fill up on broccoli, and

I always leave their house a bit hungry. But it's nice to have the invitation.

Your mom tells me you're having bad dreams. At first when I heard this, I thought I'd tell you some of my own (yes, grown-ups have them, too). My idea was if I told you mine, and you told me yours, we could take them away from each other. But when I looked at what I'd written down, it scared even me. I said to myself, "Sara doesn't need to hear my dreams." So I'll be the strong one, Sara, the someone to take your dreams away.

I remember you waking in your old bedroom here in Chicago with nightmares. Remember? I'd come into your room? Because I was always up late working, I'd hear you first. I'd come in and ask you to wrap up your dream, close it up, and give it to me. I must have taken quite a few packages of dreams over the last five years. And I'll still take your dreams from you, Sara; you can box them up and send them even though I'm not close by. Give them to your mom when you wake in the night, draw them in a picture or describe them for a letter, and Mommy will send them to me.

It's good to picture something really fine after a bad dream, when you're lying in your bed after you've given the dream away and your mom's next to you, maybe holding your hand or rubbing your back. You can imagine something truly beautiful, like the most perfect birthday cake. And when you think you have all the details just right, then add something more beautiful—another pink rose, another layer of cake, a bigger scoop of ice cream. Pretty soon you'll fall asleep with this beautiful cake filling your mind, something to stay with you long after Mom's gone back to her own bed.

And you can always fall asleep remembering how much I love you.

When I was a kid, maybe just a little older than you,

I had such a vivid dream about magic. A wizard talked to me in my dream, told me to reach under my pillow and I'd find his magic wand. And then, he said, all my dreams and wishes would come true. I remember feeling under my pillow in my sleep and waking up just as I was reaching further and further under for that wand. Have you ever dreamed of magic, Sara?

Daddy

Chicago, 7 April
Dear Sara,

Thank you for the beautiful drawings. I thought of hanging them in my office, but I put them in the kitchen at home instead. I'm wrapping up a big case, and I didn't want your work lost in the swamp of paper in my office, only to end up in a storage facility somewhere west of Itasca. You should see the office. Stacks of file folders, boxes of discovery documents: what a load of paper I generate! But it may be that the case will wrap up sooner than we all expected. The secret is, no one wants to go to court, and we wait to see who wants to go the least. Personally I am tired of this one, but I work on. Looks like I may be going to Seattle sometime soon to depose a few people—ask them questions for the record in advance of a trial, that is. I've never been to the West Coast, so maybe the trip will be interesting.

Your pictures of the mountains and the trees reminded me of when I spent vacations in New Hampshire with your mother long before you were born. We took lots of photographs. In this package you'll find some of them; tell your mom I dug them out of some photo albums while I was sitting around the house after work yesterday. You can see how young we looked! Look at me in shorts—did you ever see such knobby knees on any human being in your life? And such white skin! Your mom was the one who tanned. And just look at her on top of the mountain! Can you see the beautiful fall colors behind her in the valley? The trees begin to shut down, store up energy for the winter—and that simple thing makes such a colorful fall in the mountains. Think of all the people who drive through the valley and as far as Crawford Notch in October simply to watch the leaves change from green to yellow, orange, red, maroon, then brown.

Once I had finished with the travel photos, I took your baby albums out, too, and do you know what I noticed? I'm not in many of them. There was you on a changing table, standing in your crib, throwing laundry from a hamper, in Halloween costumes, blowing out candles. I'm in maybe a half dozen pictures. How did that happen? Then there are the photos of you in your mother's arms, and I know I must have taken those, but still I'm not in them. I'm glad, though, for the pictures of you; it's better than seeing my own face staring back at me. You were a very pretty baby, big slate gray eyes. We thought for sure they'd stay gray or turn blue. What a surprise when one day they appeared newly brown, like a deer's, like your mother's, soft and anxious and quick.

I've enclosed a few disposable cameras. I thought maybe you could take pictures around the house or on a day trip. Or ask your mom to take some pictures of you, maybe dressed for your first day of school, when that rolls around this fall. Then if you send the camera back I will have the film developed, see what a big girl you're getting to be since, without proof, I can hardly believe you will be six. Where have the years gone?

Uncle Jim has invited me up to their cabin in Door County, Wisconsin, for Memorial Day, and I am looking forward to the long weekend and forcing myself out of the office. You see, it's the start of cherry season: First small white flowers yield a hard green fruit, littering the ground below with white petals as the green gives way to ripe red cherries in the presence of sunshine. There was a cherry tree in my backyard growing up, so I know all about cherries, and I think you would like, as much as I did when I was young, pretending that the petals were spring snow.

Love from,
Daddy

Eagle Harbor, Wisconsin, 24 May
Dear Sara,

Uncle Jim's house was very cold and musty when we got up here, but we shouldn't've been surprised—it's been locked up all winter. He and Aunt Julie invited me along for Memorial Day weekend, for their first vacation of the season. The sun has been shining, although the early mornings are still so cold I can see my breath when I walk out the front door for firewood.

I helped to air the place out, cleaned up a bit, gathered and chopped some wood. Other than sweeping away cobwebs and lazy brown spiders, the biggest project has been clearing out the fireplace. I began pulling out leaves, twigs, twine, and decided something had built its nest in the chimney, probably last fall. We needed to light a fire, so I kept going, removing layer after layer of bird evidence and dreading finding the actual bird. But the former inhabitant had, as it turned out, scarpered long ago.

There are signs of mice present, however—droppings, paper and fabric shreds, tiny scritching noises of unknown origin. I haven't actually seen the animals but Aunt Julie has; she swears they come out just to taunt her. And while none of us has the heart for traps or poisons, Aunt Julie threatens them when she's held hostage on top of a chair or table. I believe we will eventually scare them out of sight, our big human noises so disruptive after many months of quiet. Right now, though, I get an odd enjoyment from us humans not being the only living things in the house.

I remember my childhood vacations on Cape Cod began much the same, in an emptied house. I'd spend the entire spring sitting in a classroom, antsy, daydreaming about the beach, warm water, swimming, fishing, and crabbing. When I got a little older it was girls I daydreamed of: girls vacationing for the summer just like me and my brother. I imagined John and I would impress them with our swims across the channel that fed into the bay. (And maybe we did manage to impress one or two.) Before Grandma and Grandpa moved there permanently, we'd rent a house, my dad would drop us and come up for weekends, until his two-week vacation started in August, after which we'd all drive back together, back to friends, back to school.

One summer day, I was about ten or eleven, I took the fishing pole and went out by myself. I had some grand idea of feeding the family with my catch, wanting the look of admiration on their faces when I came home with dinner. Have I ever told you this story?

That day, I caught nothing but two smallish eels from the mud at the bottom of the channel. Eels, Sara, are pretty disgusting creatures, hardly even fish, which can be so beautiful, but I took them from the hook myself, laid down my pole, and put them into a bucket. I decided to celebrate catching something, anything!, with a swim—I was hot and tired and lazy from standing quietly in the early morning sun. Even my feet were tired from gripping the shifting sands. So I walked out onto the boat dock and belly-flopped into the water to cool off. Immediately I felt the coolness of the water, and then a spreading fire radiating from my belly. I wasn't far from the shore so I swam straight in. My stomach was just a mess of red rash. Without looking first, I had jumped right in on top of a jellyfish.

I ran to the house so fast that my father had to go back for the eels and the fishing pole. But you know what? That night, he cooked those bad boys; he cleaned them outside under the cool, running water of the hose, cooked them on the grill, and ate them. No one else did, but my dad said he enjoyed every bite. For an eleven-year-old boy, that was pretty cool. Funny what I remember while I'm writing to you.

How are you, Sara? I think of you while I'm reading or working. Some nights I look for you to tell you something, I forget sometimes you're so far away even after so many months apart. For a moment I believe we are still all together in Chicago.

I couldn't sleep the other night, Sara, and you know what? I thought of what I tell you when you are restless, I thought of something beautiful. I cleared my mind and then thought of the beach. A beautiful, calm beach at low tide. There was beach glass everywhere, in colors I'd never seen before—red, amethyst, gold. There was enough to fill buckets. I began collecting the glass, looking at each piece very carefully. I felt the rhythm of the waves behind me, the rhythm of stooping and collecting. Can you imagine pieces of red glass, blue glass, even shards of pottery and terra-cotta tiles? It was a beautiful beach and I was able to get back to sleep. Thinking of you helps, too.

Remember I love you, sweetheart.
Daddy

Dear Anna,

Do you think if I wrote to you asking for recipes you'd write back? I went through your cookbooks and your extensive recipe files tonight, looking at all the things you loved to make. Recipes and menu ideas and notes handwritten in the margins of cookbooks and these dinner party notebooks you kept. Recipe cards written in felt-tip marker, which, when I mistakenly laid them down on a damp patch of counter, began to bleed, words running into words, lines dissolving, instructions gone.

You see, I'm hungry. I mean, I eat at work: breakfast coffee on the run, sandwiches around the conference table at no set time once or twice a day, just one of the many who sit working and eating. It's laughably like a restaurant, a neighborhood hangout some days, and just like I told you some time ago, this simplifies my life. I don't have to rush home and sacrifice the billable hours. Anyway there's no longer any need to rush home. But I am hungry for something real, and I thought maybe I could learn to make a meal for myself. But I don't know what, and to tell the truth I'm a bit intimidated and feel a bit foolish with making a well-rounded meal to enjoy in the company of myself. It's easier to be one of the crowd at work than to imagine one lamb chop, one chicken breast, one fish fillet, one potato, one serving of vegetables, one small salad. A clean plate, a cloth napkin, silver? Absurd.

I made an attempt, I went shopping and filled the refrigerator, but the food went untouched. When finally I remembered what I'd bought, a lot of the produce was spoiled: brown mush at the cores of my apples, fresh herbs edged in black slime, moldy tangerines, sprouting potatoes. I've seen it all.

Where do I start, Anna? Where did you start, when you were young? I remember you telling me about when you began to be interested in food and cooking, sneaking food at a neighbor's house. And when I wrote to Sara I told her about catching eels and watching my dad eat them. He enjoyed them. How do I get back to that place, that early place before I forgot how to enjoy myself in such a basic way?

Seattle, 17 June
Dear Sara,

Remember that case I've been telling you about? The one that was winding down? I think we've finally got it nailed, more or less forced a settlement after taking depositions that no one wanted to participate in. Remember I said no one wanted to go to court? Well, they really didn't want to go through days of being deposed, either. After the first day of calling witnesses in and questioning them for the record, the group we're disagreeing with has asked for a break. They're also asking to talk, to work out some kind of agreement, which feels pretty good after all the time we've spent trying to get to this point.

I flew out to Seattle two days ago and I'm still here, but mostly enjoying my free time as I wait around for our talks to begin. Coming from the East, even Chicago, which is not so much a Midwestern city as it is a world-class city, Seattle seems small and provincial. By provincial I mean not terribly sophisticated—which, don't get me wrong, is not a bad thing. The city definitely has its own flavor: youthful and laid-back, and all of this settled in between some beautiful scenery. In fact I can't think of a prettier backdrop: the Olympic mountain range to the west, the high peaks of the Cascades east and south into Oregon, the inlets and tree-covered tiny islands of Puget Sound. But the feeling I have when I walk the main streets or climb the hills up side streets or hop the buses for rides through the neighborhoods is: Am I missing something? That's it; I have this feeling that somewhere something interesting is going on but no one's telling me about it and it's too hard to find. Or maybe my feeling simply means, what you see is all there is.

I walked through Pike Place Market earlier today, the big tourist draw. Rows and rows of food stalls filled with every imaginable flower, herb, fruit and vegetable, every

jam, flavored honey, and baked good ever made. There is
even a fish stall where the salesmen toss whole fish around
to each other as they package them up for customers. It
bothered me, seeing the fish sailing through the air, it
struck me as kind of irreverent and disrespectful of the fish,
because it was so obviously an act for the gathering crowds.
I left in a hurry, and afterwards, I just walked and walked
some more, jostling with the crowds, knocking elbows and
shoulders and stalling behind large groups of tourists who,
like me, tried to take in the abundance of colors and aromas until our senses felt overloaded.

I left the market out one of the side doors at this end.
Behind the market there are several more small stores along
a walkway, more food, prepared foods to take away, strange
mottled and pockmarked Asian vegetables. There were
street musicians: a Peruvian group, a blues singer. I even saw
a juggler who reminded me with his bad joke (What's the
only thing you can't eat for lunch or dinner? Breakfast!) that
I hadn't eaten. It's quite a custom here to stop in for big
milky coffees, which seem to provide a meal's worth of cal-
ories in a cup, and I've had many. I'll never master the lingo
though, beyond asking for "skinny," which means skim milk.
The mochas are good; they kind of remind me of the chocolate cake your mother makes with the curls of chocolate on
top. Maybe she flavored it with espresso, I'm not sure.

I wandered a few streets over, looking for some bakery
or other where I could grab something, anything starchy, to
fill me up. Something to eat with the rest of the city bustling
about me. Bagels, croissants—so much to see, but you know
what? Nothing appealed, so I went back in the direction of
the hotel. By now my feet ached, and I thought of flopping
on my bed up in the hotel room, kicking my shoes off, and
resting. The hill between First Street and the hotel is a
killer; I am used to *flat*, but all around I saw people making it
up: standard shift cars stopping and starting at lights, bicy-

clists, other pedestrians. On every corner on the way up the hill there stood groups of men, and even this early in the day they were smoking and hungover, panhandling for change. Maybe they have no daughters, or sons, to write to or think of and instead they find other hardluck men to hang with. Life is truly difficult for some people, and just when you think you've got it bad, you find someone who's worse off. I remind myself of this anyway as I climb the last few steps into the Four Seasons luxury hotel where I have the luxury of putting my feet up to wait for our opponents' call as they prepare to talk large cash settlements; the hotel where, when I rest my head back, I am free to think of you, to think of what I will tell you about once I pick up my pen and writing pad. How lucky I am.

All my love,
Daddy

Dear Anna,

Earlier today, when I broke off from writing Sara's letter, I took a small nap only to be wakened by a business call. We're wrapping up our business tomorrow morning; I may even leave directly after so perhaps I'll be back in Chicago tomorrow evening, back in my own bed. After the phone call I heard my stomach growling, and I knew it was time to eat. I've been eating with the masses on planes, in hotel dining rooms. I've eaten at my desk with only paperwork for my companion. I've had many quick sandwiches with the associates or with the opposing side during fifteen-minute meal breaks. I remembered the market, looked around my spacious and comfortable room, and decided I'd go shopping on my last day here, shopping to bring back groceries to the room. I'd make myself a meal which I'd then eat by myself. Of course, I can't cook in the room, but I figured I could find good foods I could kind of slap together and which

*also would taste like a meal rather than filler: empty space filler,
time filler, conversation filler, stomach filler.*

*At the market, Anna, I bought a loaf of bread. I found some
honey and picked one from bees that had feasted on lavender pol-
len. I found boysenberry preserves, purple-black and syrupy. I
found some goat's cheese and a few nectarines. At a small grocery
store on the way back to the hotel I stopped and picked up a bottle
of Thomas Kemper raspberry wheat beer, chilled from the refrigerator case, and I had me a small feast back in my room. I don't
recall when anything tasted so good—bread and jam, bread and
honey, bread and cheese, all washed down with this good beer. I
don't recall when I've felt this good, either, just by myself. I ate
until I was full, after I'd tasted everything there was to taste. I
finished feeling I'd made some good choices—better, that I am
capable of finding good, simple things.*

*I find myself looking forward to tomorrow, to finishing up
the work here and going home.*

Chicago, 6 August
Dear Sara,

Boy, is it hot! Reminds me of your first summer and the
few days the mercury hit 100 degrees. The way a young
child's head gets sweaty in this heat, fine hair plastered to
a scalp. Aunt Maddie had her baby—three weeks early—
but she and the baby are fine. It's a little boy, he weighed
almost six pounds when he was born. They're calling him
William Michael (yes, after me), and I am also to be god-
father at the christening in a few months. So Uncle Barnaby will be the last consecutive Barnaby in the family.
Aunt Maddie put her foot down; I've never seen her so
adamant about any one thing before, but she says she can't
call an infant Barnaby. They'll call him Will, which really
sounds like a proper little boy's name.

Will was born last weekend on a hot day like today.

Uncle Barnaby and I were golfing by the lake trying to catch a breeze and hoping to cool off—which was sort of working—when he got beeped. We picked up Aunt Maddie and I drove them both to the hospital and stayed. The baby came quickly, and after, while Maddie fed the baby and slept, I took Barnaby to our house and cooked him some dinner. He had so much nervous energy left over that we sat at the table talking, laughing, remembering old times. Everything a meal with a friend is supposed to be.

Since returning from Seattle I've mastered a few simple things in the kitchen. I now make good poached eggs and very good potato pancakes with lots of scallions. Fortunately the potato pancakes taste good with the eggs, and that is what we ate. We sat around the table with this good food and talked about trips we'd taken in the past. We talked about you, your birth, which made me think of my own childhood. As we ate this simple supper in the kitchen I told Barnaby about dinners I enjoyed as a boy. If Grandma and Grandpa were going out, Grandma would feed John and me in the kitchen. Our favorite was pancakes, sometimes with blueberries dropped in and always drenched in syrup. But we also ate fried-egg sandwiches, something I haven't tasted in years. Grandma managed to cook the yolks through with out frying the life out of the egg. She called these basted eggs. We also had shepherd's pie, ground meat and mashed potato, which we loved. We could sit in the kitchen and push that soft food into mounds on our plates and then race to see who'd finish first. On these kinds of nights Grandma would never scold us for playing with our food. We were left alone, which was heaven; maybe better than the food itself was being outside the scope of manners and beyond scrutiny.

There are a few pictures of baby Will in the envelope. None of Maddie—she won't have her picture taken, she says, until she looks better-rested (something about circles under her eyes and a trip to the hairdresser), but I think they both look fine. Please share them with your mom, and tell her Aunt Maddie was asking after her, wondering how she is faring at work.

Love from,
Daddy

Eagle Harbor, Wisconsin, 5 September
Dear Sara,

I'm sitting on the porch of Uncle Jim's summer house, smoking. A cigar, actually. Someone at the local bar gave it to me last night after we shot a friendly game of pool. Jim and I go into town in the evenings, shoot some pool with the locals who aren't ready to concede the town to tourists yet. We play for small change, and they enjoy taking my money. Then we watch whatever sports happen to be on cable TV. Mostly I listen to so many predictions about the next season for the Cubs and the Brewers. Most of which, I think we can all safely say, won't come true. And forget it if they start in on the Bears vs. Green Bay! I brought my notebook and pen to the bar and pool hall last night, too. As I sat there writing, the regulars looked at me like I was crazy. They were itching to get back to the pool table and glasses of beer while I sat, largely ignoring my fish sandwich, and wrote letters to my daughter.

Tonight, I'm in charge of dinner and I have some time to write while our steak is grilling on the barbecue. Your mom will be amused I'm sure to hear that I've even attempted her potato salad tonight. Labor Day weekend is the last hurrah for the old cabin this year and besides cooking, I've been busy helping Jim buy materials for a mud room on the back of his house, which he intends to slap up in the spring. This is the kind of mud room the locals should call entryways, but don't. Jim and I have no idea what to call it either. It seems he's just as busy during the week as I am, and so appreciates the cheap, accessible labor.

Speaking of cooking and hard work, are you learning to cook too? Do you help your mom? She mentioned something about you accompanying her to work in the afternoon once school starts. What do you think of this? Will Ben let you help in some way? Will you eat dinner with the cooks before the restaurant opens? I can picture you seated on your mother's lap, picking things from her plate; I can see your mom with her arms around you before she has to get back to work. This must be quite a time for you, Sara, both of you. No, all three of us.

I took Jim's truck out yesterday. But, city dweller that I am, I wasn't used to driving a pickup. Of course, it's all Jim's fault for pressing the truck on me . . . but I drove it into a ditch. It had stalled on a hill, and I was restarting the engine. So, I guess you might say it rolled back into a ditch. The truck was lodged at a forty-five-degree angle to the road. I spun the rear wheels till they looked surprisingly snug and at home in their ruts. The truck pointed slightly upwind and was half in the road. (I guess this is dangerous.) Thinking I'd tip the truck over if I stayed in the driver's side, I got out.

Fortunately the hill was on the way to the house, so I decided to wait for Jim. I figured if I was gone long enough he'd take my car and come looking. But Jim didn't drive by, not while I stood beside the truck out in the rain, anyway. So I got back in the truck and played my final card: four-wheel drive. I felt it was the only way to pop that sucker out of the mud—figured the risk was worth it—and you know what? It worked!

Jim and Julie recently returned from a trip to Scandinavia, which began in Iceland, of all places. Sounds so remote, but they say it was beautiful. Treeless, windy, rocky like the moon, but also starkly beautiful. Part of their trip made me think of you. They flew to the Westmann Islands from Reykjavík, a chain of small volcanic islands off the southern coast. Puffins nest and lay eggs in the cliffs of the islands during the spring and summer, and on Heimaey in August the baby puffins (about one to two months old) learn to fly and swim by being shoved out of the nests by their parents. The infant birds are supposed to fly towards the sun over the ocean, but occasionally they get fooled by the lights of the town and fly in the wrong direction, where they would be easy food for the roaming cats and dogs. So the town's children get to stay up late during this part of August. They collect baby birds in boxes at night and take them to the beaches the next day, where they toss them into the air to release them. I had a picture of you, of standing with you on the beach like one of the Icelandic children. Maybe one day we could do this. Or any other thing together.

We will have lots to talk about when I see you, which will be soon, I promise, as the holidays approach. I do not like being so far away from you, I do not even like telling you this all the time. So quit talking about it and do it is what I must say to myself. Being alone at work, at home, makes me know what is important. Even being with friends can't hide the fact that my life is pretty meaningless if I am so far away from my daughter. I am beginning to think through plans for Thanksgiving and Christmas, and once back to work, once the case files from Seattle are packed for cold storage, I promise many thoughts on how we will arrange our time together.

All my love,
Daddy

Dear Anna,

I have just gotten in from a partners' dinner, something we are trying to do once a month to keep on top of cases, and I found I couldn't get home fast enough. We all take turns picking a restaurant or a private club; tonight's selection was a monument to excess. Course after course, wine after wine, and then no time [or energy or brain capacity] after all to have any meaningful or worthwhile discussion. I think this was supposed to replace or substitute some partners' desperately lonely home lives. I understood that if no one else did. I felt, about halfway through the evening, like a sick person or an invalid just wishing to be alone in bed. Or really, alone at a table with a plate of scrambled eggs, some fried potatoes with onion and garlic, a few shots of Tabasco over all— as a kind of bridge between flavors. Instead I had sautéed foïe gras [which only made me feel sorry for the geese when I recalled what you told me in Paris, about their feet being nailed to the ground as they are force-fed]. We had fish floating in infused broths, medallions of game meats strewn with unidentifiable red berries, plates designed with sauces so that they would look more at home hanging on the walls of a modern art museum instead of on a table in front of me. And I can guarantee you, it brought none of us closer; probably most of the partners were so overwhelmed that we were rendered senseless, sluggish, dulled. I'm just learning to be comfortable eating by myself, I shouldn't have to work so hard to be uncomfortable with others. Maybe when it's my turn I can invite them to dinner at home. Let's see . . . we could have grilled cheese sandwiches, cups of tomato soup, a green salad, and a few laughs.

Before you get upset with me for knocking all this fancy food, I must apologize if this is what you find yourself preparing these days. Somehow I can't imagine it, you cooking all these rich foods for the sake of the food rather than the experience. I think it must be something for you to put a meal on the table of strangers and make them happy. Make them feel part of *something larger—culture, civilization. Something for both the diner and the cook. I had to go way back to relearn in a sense what I liked, just to be here now, even considering that I could get a group together in the house for soup and sandwiches.*

Chicago, 29 October
Hey Barn,

Thanks for dinner over the weekend. I was beginning to feel like a loner, wolfing down solitary meals at my desk or worse, drinking them in front of the TV set at home. Wow! Real food and real human contact. Maddie looks well, really radiant, and the baby's beautiful. You guys are very lucky.

About what we discussed, it's now a reality: I humbled myself before Bill, asked for the transfer to Boston, so part of the time out there will be ironing out details with my new office and getting an apartment for me, and for Sara when she visits. Enclosed are a more formal letter, and power of attorney charging you with temporarily managing our personal accounts. For your file, I've photocopied all pertinent correspondence—utilities, credit cards, the bank, the post office, even Hank, the caretaker. What a lot of paper! But everything should be in order. I'm leaving in a few days for a respite at my folks' between the holidays.

'Cause, Barnaby, I am self-destructing, I really am. Picture this: I sit across a wide desk, I am hunched forward slightly, my clasped hands resting between open knees. My knees are shaking because I am bouncing my feet out of nerves, fear. I have no shred of composure left to allow me to sit up straight or relax in front of this man, Bill, who's been so fair to me, always. I come like a penitent, like a man humbly seeking parole, and I am afraid of what I am about to say.

I ask him for the transfer, I explain why, and I decide that I hate him, hate the stupid prick as he sits there, that stupid signet ring on the small finger of his stupid manicured hand. I am so crazy that I think I see him make a show of listening to me, a show of sympathy. What's he really thinking? You screwup, that's what. Or maybe that's what I am thinking about myself.

Or how about this one: Over Labor Day weekend, Julie and I were sitting on the porch of their cabin, drinking, smoking together, talking. It was like old times, sitting around student digs drinking cheap wine. Except no Anna, and Jim was out with the kids at a parade. Can you see where this is going? Before I really thought it through, we're in a liplock. Of course, this wasn't the brightest idea I'd had in a while—ranks right up there with taking the truck out with three or four beers under my belt, but that's another story—but it felt so good to actually feel something, however brief. And it was brief. First we're sitting on the porch, all this incredible energy in the air, and I lean in and kiss her, I smear her lip gloss, which she hates. I remember this from law school, I kissed her once, when I was still pretty newly married, and I remember how, even back then, she hated to have her lips messed up. And how Anna never wore any lipstick, her lips were always available to me. And I have to wonder, after agreeing with Anna that our marriage had run out of something essential, after months of practicing how to get by on my own, even learning how to eat alone, I have to wonder this, another how: How the hell did I get here, so screwed up and lonely that I'm kissing my friend's wife and actually considering the offer she just made?

She offered to sleep with me, and the thing is, she doesn't care, she really doesn't care about lack of commitment between us. A quick fuck: I could be a project for her. I think she believes my loneliness is weakness, as if with every thrust she would be allowing me to reach in and take some of her backbone. And another question: Why? Why would I consider, however briefly, her offer? Some would argue that the why is irrelevant. Anyway, I know. I've spent months running away, avoiding spending time alone with myself. She's just another way for me to avoid thinking about what went wrong. Good story, huh Barn? I've gone about as low as I can; I've allowed such mess in my life.

In my mind, in the darkest hours of the day with the quiet all around me, I see Sara's eyes on her anxious face watching me as I got in the car to drive to the airport, leaving her behind. I write to her; the pretty things I tell her, the ugly I struggle to leave out. Like, I'll tell her how funny it is to be the city slicker stuck in the mud with Jim's truck, but I'll edit out the beer that made me think I could take the truck out in the first place. Briefly I feel better, imagine myself a better person. But I know I failed, and the failure is alive, it's like a boa wrapping around my heart, spine, liver, and squeezing until I'm numb but leaking bile. The only person I can tell the failure to is Anna, maybe the only person who can understand; instead I write her letters I'll never send because somehow I know, truly, I can only help myself. I'm trying hard to get the control back, put the pieces of my life back together in a way they make sense. Eventually I suppose I'll revert to type easily enough; I'll put my head down and slog on like I've always done. But if I've learned anything over the past months it's what I believe in, and that's my family, or holding together what's left of it.

Now that the divorce is a reality, despite your best advice about custody, I've got to work something joint out with Anna. I miss my daughter. I've worked too long in this business, and I know once people go down the road of custody battles and recriminations, there's almost no turning back; and that route is not about Sara. At some point I've got to think and feel and express myself like a human being. Right now a stay at my parents' looks pretty good, a new job, too. It's unfamiliar territory and new routines. It's time, man, to start over.

Thanks, pal, for agreeing to write the checks after I'm gone. You're a brick.

Mike

Chicago, 29 October
Dear Anna,

Of course by now you know Maddie had the baby, a beautiful baby boy who looks like neither of them and both of them at the same time. When Barn told me they would call him William Michael I nearly wept. I haven't felt very worthy lately of any kind of human contact, let alone simple affection, and the gesture moved me. It's very nice to have a friend. And be one back.

I ended up being the chauffeur and hung around the hospital waiting room to make sure everyone was okay. They let me in briefly to see Maddie holding the baby just after he was born. A pretty teary experience; Barnaby was beside himself. I recognized Maddie's distance; it was as if she were in the room with only the baby. The rest of us might not have existed. She didn't even notice as she nursed the baby that I took Barnaby home with me to feed him. Her head didn't lift as we walked out the door. I thought of you and Sara, your bond, your exclusivity, your tiny circle of two. Then I thought of me and how badly I want to be let back in.

Anger, I have found, is sometimes an adequate substitute for energy; a good mimic, it helped guide me back home into some initial acceptance of your suggestion to separate. But right now I can't feel angry anymore, it is a poor imitation for action. At first it felt right to get away from you, then once I got here, home to this ringing silence—there was no noise in the house, can you understand that?—I missed you. And Sara. I can't begin to say what this emptiness feels like, especially missing Sara, but I'll try.

What did I miss (do I miss)? The people we were when we started out, back when the two of us sat on the beach and I asked you to marry me and you said yes. Back when you looked at me with eyes full of questions that for you had no answers. I was simple enough back then to think I could help you with the answers, help you feel something positive after the blankness of your father's death. I miss you looking to me for the answers, for even towards the end when your eyes were full of questions again—What's happening to us, Michael?—even then when I wished you would stop looking at me that way, I liked it that you looked. For whatever's happened, wherever we've diverged, we're still a family and I still believe in that as an eternity, a forever kind of thing. Forever, as in our child.

Now that Barnaby's selling the house, now that we know we will split everything down the middle and walk away from what we built up together, I'd like to talk to you—just you and me, no lawyers—about custody. Joint custody. I can move to Boston; it's in the works already, in fact, a transfer to the Boston office. Can we do this, talk and listen to each other without anger? Can we break our polite, written communications? I'm willing, Anna. Please tell your lawyer to go away, and you can talk to me. If you were here now I'd say, Look at me, Anna, I'm down on my knees. Can you believe as I do that we'll get through this if we keep a common goal in mind? Sara.

M.

Chicago, 10 November
Dear Mom and Dad,

It was great to hear your voices. I'm glad I decided to call,
if only to wangle an invitation for Thanksgiving dinner
from you! If you'll have me, I'd like to come east and stay
for a few weeks. My big news? I'm planning to transfer from
Chicago to Boston. I got the go-ahead from both offices
after Anna and I—Bigger News—decided to try and work
out a joint custody arrangement. To tell you the truth, I
am looking forward to a little bit of mothering (hate to
admit this at my age). The beach. The smells of the hon-
eysuckle and beach plum when summer rolls around, even
low tide. And Sara, the proximity to Sara is the best reason
of all. I think I'll hang for a while, wrap things up here,
help Barnaby get the papers in order to sell the house in
my absence, then I'll fly east mid-November, in plenty of
time for Thanksgiving.

I've been longing for a good, home-cooked meal. I even
salivate when I think of creamed onions, and I know I used
to scoff at those when I was young and obnoxious. I remember pushing them around my plate, all shiny white and slimy.
I was fascinated by the slide of each separate layer as I ap-
plied the pressure of my knife or fork. I swear, this year you
won't have to yell at me to not play with my food.

Up until recently, meals have been sketchy at best. The
more I stop in at cheap restaurants, the more convinced I am
we have four new basic food groups: grease, salt, sugar, and
air. On my best days I used to stop at a grocery store and
stock up on cheese, fruit, yoghurt, and bread to eat at my
desk, but even this gets old after a few days.

While at friends' homes, I've sometimes eaten pretty
well, I've even turned into a decent plain cook, mastering
steaks and fish on the grill. Most days, though, I've endured
strange things: Julie's vegan messes up at the cabin during her

"healthy food for Michael phase," like eggless soy milk quiche with strawberry tofu pie to round off the meal quite nicely. Anna would have freaked at the thought of serving two pies in one meal. But I'm not knocking a free meal in the company of good friends. Still, I need to learn to cook for myself, sit by myself in my own place, and feel comfortable.

Actually, I'll be standing in a diner or a fast-food joint, waiting for the next greasy burger or grilled cheese sandwich, and I'll think of Anna's roast chicken. Vegetables all caramelized from a long, slow roasting. Or a plate of spaghetti, a simple salad with homemade dressing, bread warm from the oven. These are things I dream of, long for, things I could learn to make for myself.

But, please Mom, for Thanksgiving creamed onions will be just fine by me. Turkey, stuffing, potatoes—the traditional things I can fill up on and satisfy my hunger with. Just a good meal to make up for months of unsavory, sometimes unspeakable, food.

Michael

Falmouth, Massachusetts, 26 November
Dear Sara,

Happy Thanksgiving! What will you and your mom do for the holiday? Are you having dinner at the restaurant, or is your mom cooking at home? Or will you go see your grandmother? You see, Sara, I have too many questions for you. What I really need is to have you close enough to hug, and I would like to come and see you before Christmas. I was feeling sad for a while, but I'm much, much better now as I realize how soon I will see you. And of course, writing to you helps lots.

Grandma Costello cooked a huge dinner, and I'm sitting in the den now, trying to digest after such a big meal. It's a great time to write to you—the house is quiet except for Grandpa's snores. No one even thought of turning on the TV. It's cold but I may go out for a walk on the beach later with Uncle John, Aunt Kate, and your cousins. Who are not nearly as cute as you, may I add, but don't tell anyone I said so.

I've been collecting some marine samples for you from all the beaches I've visited. Maybe we can put them into a shadow box and label them all someday. I've found crab shells picked over and then discarded by hungry gulls. I find the most interesting rock samples, rocks from the beach in all colors: mauve, dark gray, white, granite pebbles shining with quartz, feldspar, and mica. Someone, a fellow beach-comber, told me that olivine can be found quite readily, so I am on a new quest to add that to our rock collection. I found one rock, roughly the shape of a heart, pinkish brown with intersecting lines of white mineral running through it. It is a very unusual, beautiful stone and I'm saving it for you.

I can walk through marshland—wet, tall, scratchy brown grasses—and reach the small beach near Grandma's house. The days are very gray and cold now, not much sun. The waves have been rough, tossing small fishing boats around a bit. Every day the tide brings in shells of scallops, quahogs, hermit crabs, even horseshoe crabs.

When I first saw a horseshoe crab at age four or five, I thought I'd found a monster. Some older kid picked it up and chased me with it, telling me it would sting me with its long stick. Of course, it was dead, washed up on the shoreline and dried out—but I didn't know that, and it scared me. Such an ugly, ancient creature. Sweetheart, the natural world is a strange but beautiful place. I can't wait to share these treasures with you.

I'm enjoying my holiday so much that I'm thinking of taking a month or so (maybe six weeks?) off from work between Thanksgiving and New Year's. I have the time coming to me. And the best news is, I'll be in Massachusetts with Grandma and Grandpa, close enough to drive up and visit you. This winter there will be a comet passing through the western skies; scientists are already tracking it. I want, on a clear cold night, to be able to get you out of bed in your pj's, bundle you into boots and a jacket so we can watch the comet and its tail of galactic debris fly through space. There's so much I want us to do together.

Now, Sara, I know your mom has been talking to you about why we don't live together anymore. I've also been doing a lot of thinking about being away from you. Your mom and I know we need to work together to keep you as close to both of us as we can; the one thing in all of this upset that we still do well together is look out for you, Sara. Part of the reason for my long vacation is also to talk with my law firm's Boston office about a transfer, working in Boston from now on instead of Chicago. With my big case wrapping up, it's a good time to move. This means more big changes, selling our Chicago house and finding a new house for me in Boston. But we'll be closer, you can spend some time with me and some with Mom, which isn't the same as being all together but it's the best we can do. And we want to do the best.

I hope at Christmas you'll come with me to look for a house that has a bedroom in it just for you.

Hugs and kisses from,
Daddy

Anna,

Dad's still a champion snorer. Mom can't abide the noise, says he drives her out of the room. But I find the drone a comfort, almost lulling. It's great to be here, to see them together, the same old routines. Dad's got a bottle of Poire William [eau de vie? I figured you'd know] that they brought back from their trip to Europe earlier this year. Never been opened, and we're cracking into it now. It's supposed to help the digestion, I understand. You would like the slim-necked, clear bottle, the pale gold liquid, the spidery foreign printing on the label.

I've cut way down on drinking over the past couple of months, but I can't give this a miss. Not to worry, it's under control. I'm calmer, I feel better. At night, when I try to fall asleep without a drink, I see Sara. I know I need to be well enough to be a father to her, and I'm trying.

I wanted to tell you these things in person. I drove up; in fact, I filled the car with Sara's Christmas gifts not long after we spoke on the phone. Your voice. Something in your voice—contentment, kindness, generosity, I don't know how to describe the tone—made me brave, hopeful. And of course I was also ecstatic about our custody agreement and couldn't see Sara soon enough. I got what I wanted, I saw you, but you weren't alone, and finally I could do nothing but drive back home.

Today, thinking about you, I left my parents' house and walked through the marshes to the cove that is their beach. It is a quiet, empty, gray place now, beach grass brown and trampled in the sand dunes. I reached the beach, and the waves were rocking into the shore, hard and gray and resolute. Anna, it was cold, about forty degrees, but no real wind and none of the snow that's falling everywhere else. I stood there, looking, just looking as I've been doing so well over the past year. I took off all my clothes, down to my boxers, and stepped in. I thought of those old guys in South Boston who walk into the water every winter. I thought briefly that the shock of the cold water might bring on a heart attack. But maybe feeling something—even pain—is better than feeling nothing.

I waded in up to my waist. My shorts clung to my legs, flapping against me like tangled, wet seaweed. I looked out over the ocean and, holding my breath, dunked in up to my neck. I could imagine hermit crabs underfoot, schools of minnows like I used to see as a kid, darting silver and quick around my legs, and real seaweed touching my ankles like limp hands. My large human body was so invasive in their world. The water was damn cold, but the air as I stood felt colder. Of course, when I got back to the house, clothes wet through, my mother was certain I'd finally cracked. She brought me some dry clothes and some tea and made me get under a wool blanket.

And maybe I have cracked. All because of what I saw when I saw you across a dark parking lot. Or maybe I've found my way through the murky water. Maybe hope is next, hope that we can make this new life work.

PART FIVE

Mise en Place

Since April I have meandered with change, I've rolled with it and let it roll over me. Now, nearing the holidays, I am forced to count and measure the changes in our lives.

Perhaps the biggest change of all as I approach my one-year anniversary in New Hampshire is the divorce. Every day now is like a step closer to the final paperwork, and as we get so near to the end the steps are small and precise, deliberate and full of direction. No more aimless rambles, we are on course.

Marrying a lawyer and socializing with many others has not prepared me for being a plaintiff, for being the client. Having a person feel outrage on my behalf is both attractive and frightening. My lawyer believes I am entitled to compensation for the years of law school when I worked so Michael could study. It takes all my effort in the face of this well-financed indignation to keep Sara in mind as we go down this road of heated disagreements over the pecuniary.

I realize how little I need or want beyond what I have or what I can make with my own two hands.

But finally agreements are reached and terms drawn up: I tell the lawyer to ask Michael to sell my vast collection of things, which has spent months in storage, for I don't want any of it; Michael agrees to sell the house, too, and all proceeds will be divided. The last step of the process is arranging for custody of Sara, which, of course, is much tougher than selling a few pots and pans.

Michael writes to her all these months, letters full of love and plans for the future. In October, he breaks down and writes to me with words that approximate falling prostrate at my feet. Over Barnaby's protests, he informs me. He begs me to consider joint custody. He has a plan, a solution, can we talk, without lawyers, without any baggage, just talk and listen? Can we do this? Can we break our restrained, polite, brokered conversations? And with Michael's written questions I begin to acknowledge change.

I pick up the phone and dial a series of numbers as familiar to me as my own name. It is a brief call, this one, placed to Michael at the house we no longer own together. Miraculously, he is home and he answers.

"It's Anna," I say.

"Oh. Good. Hey, hold on," he says, and I hear the rustle of his hand covering the mouthpiece, I hear him clear his throat before he gets back on the line.

"Did I wake you?" I ask. "You sound sleepy."

"Reading. I dozed off," he explains. "But I'm awake now. Is Sara okay?"

"Fine. She's fine. But she's feeling the . . . breakup more than she lets on. Michael, she misses you. I called because, well, what we—you—talked about? In your letter? Moving, custody? Well, I wanted to say, you do it, Michael, you look for a place, and we'll work it out. The details of sharing Sara, I mean. I'm not doing this very well."

"You're doing fine," he assures me. "I should have called you sooner."

"No, I should have called you. Will the move be okay for you? It's a big change, Chicago to Boston."

"I can work anywhere," he replies. "Actually I'll be happier in Boston. I've had a lot of time to just think. Alone. And it'll be nice to be closer to . . . family. But you know what? We can talk more in December. Christmas vacation is cool with you? If I pick her up and bring her to the Cape?"

"Mm-hmm," I assent. For a minute I do not trust my voice to form words that may choke like a bone in my throat. I recover, though, enough to add, "We'll be at Mother's on Christmas Eve. Why don't you drive up on the twenty-fifth? I'll have Sara ready."

"It'll be like this, summers and school vacations," he reminds me.

"I know."

"And then for me, during the rest of the year."

"I know. Hey, I've got to work in the morning, so I should—"

"Yeah, hang up," Michael finishes.

"I'll call you from my mother's," I say. And very softly before laying the phone down I also say, "Good night."

I stand in Sara's doorway watching her sleep before I head off to bed myself. In the dark of my room, under the down covers I find James, sleeping and warm, and I press myself into his body until I, too, am anesthetized, asleep.

"I hate you!"

At this moment, my daughter's small face and body amaze me; twisted and contorted with rage, she fills the room with an over-powering energy. Rage spills from her in waves, it radiates, it strikes me. Like a flat, rushing palm, it has the power to pin me against the wall. I am weakened before her. Before I am able to utter a syllable—in soothing, in protest—Sara flees the room, slamming her bedroom door behind her.

James sits in the corner of the room quietly regarding his nails, waiting perhaps for me to speak.

We finished our dinner and I had just gathered Sara up with me on the couch to read Michael's most recent letter to her. He is at his mother's as I knew he would be, one state away, a three- or four-hour drive. Together on the couch we read of his progress from Illinois to Massachusetts, this relocation in order to share custody as the finalization of our divorce grows imminent. Her reaction to the news, therefore, surprises and stuns me: I expected a simple joy at his nearness; I am unprepared after our idyllic summer for the force of her disapproval.

I stop to pick up the leaves of Michael's letter from the floor where Sara flung them. Taking a seat next to James I finish reading, going over and over the words to find clues to her reaction. I fold the letter neatly and slide it into its envelope, this lovely letter, full of expressions of love and also promises for Christmas. I rest my head on the back of the couch.

"What was that about?" I wonder aloud.

"I could ask you the same thing," James responds. He sits forward with his elbows on his knees and his eyes probe me. "I'd try and offer an answer, Anna, but this is all news to me, too. Maybe if you had thought of sharing your plans with me I could have helped with Sara."

"Is everyone angry with me now?"

"Baffled. What? Did you talk to your ex-husband? When did all this happen?" he asks.

"He wrote with the suggestion and I called him. He thought—I agreed—getting along and working together would be best. For Sara. Michael wanted to be the one to tell her once he was settled."

"Seems that idea worked really well, doesn't it?"

"I could do without the sarcasm," I snap back. "Custody was my decision to make, and I made it."

"Fine," he replies, holding up his hands, "I'm a wiseass and I apologize. You're right, it is your decision to make. I guess all I'm saying is I'd like to be involved. It would have been nice to know."

"I didn't tell you because it didn't cross my mind. She's my daughter, mine and Michael's, and in this instance I didn't think. . . ." James shakes his head, only slightly, but enough for me to register his frustration with me. "I feel like a blind person, James, stumbling through an unfamiliar room. But I'm doing the best I can." I rise from the couch. "I've got to talk to Sara; right now she's the one who needs the explanations."

Carrying a glass of water, I knock on Sara's door. I hear neither greeting nor refusal so, encouraged, heartened, I enter her room.

"I used to slam my door, too, even when I was much older than you, I'm ashamed to say. I thought it would get my mother's attention. You already have mine."

"No, I don't. You talked to Daddy, and you didn't tell me," she accuses.

We think we have done so well, Michael and I, we are so civilized in our breakup, we are humane. Except that Sara has become a pas-

senger on our bus, or worse, we pick her up and carry her along carefully like a piece of valued luggage. We forget how we tower over her,
that our conversations out of her earshot or carried on above her head
keep her removed. I should have remembered a child's confusion.

"You're right, I didn't tell you. And maybe I should have. Daddy
and I thought he would surprise you. I'm sorry if it was the wrong kind
of surprise." I ask her, "The letter made you miss your daddy, didn't
it?"

She rolls her eyes at my dense question. "I always miss Daddy.
Every day. Don't you, Mommy?"

"When I think of him," I hedge, "I wonder how he is."

"When will I see him? When can I see him?" she needles.

"He wants you to come to Grandma's for Christmas. And after,
for your school vacation. I'm sorry we didn't tell you right along what
we've been thinking. We've been talking it over, we are trying to work
it out that you live with him part of the year."

"Don't you want to see him, too?"

I repeat the words which are supposed to comfort, explain. "Daddy
and I decided not to see each other for a while, but I'll see him when
he picks you up for Christmas."

"But then you won't be with us."

"No, Sara, I won't. It'll be you and Daddy. And Grandma and
Grandpa, too."

"But not our family." Sara slides down under her covers. "I do hate
you," she repeats.

"Sara—" I begin.

"You can go now." She turns her face to the wall and closes her
eyes. I have been dismissed.

When Sara started first grade in September, I exchanged my late shifts
for a stint in pastry. Our schedules now dovetail: We leave together
for school and work in the morning; Sara's school bus drops her near
the restaurant, where she spends until four in the afternoon with me
as I finish up for the day. In the only kitchen job that begins and ends

in the early hours of the day, I find an enjoyable solitude. My work—with bread dough, cakes, sauces, many varieties of fruit and chocolate—is essentially autonomous and undisturbed. Best of all, I am able to be home with Sara at the end of a school day and then most evenings during the week.

Today after school I meet the bus and hug my stiff and distant child as she climbs off. She has barely spoken to me since yesterday's tantrum, holding Michael's letter and our custodial decisions against me. Ben notices, too, as soon as we walk in the door without our usual laughter or chatter about the day. I meet his raised eyebrow with a shrug as Sara throws her backpack and coat to the floor and walks from me to sit on a stool at a corner of a stainless counter.

"It's polite to hang your things up on the coatrack rather than leaving them lying on the floor," I admonish. "Come on back and take care of them."

"You do it. You're closer," she answers back.

"Now, Sara," I say firmly. But she is just as firm in her refusal.

"Why should I do anything for you when you won't do anything for me?" she demands.

Ben picks up the coat and pack and walks with them over to Sara's spot at the counter. "Everyone who works here," he tells her, "is responsible for their belongings. We all hang our things up, you know that; so you take care of it and we'll see what we can find for you to do this afternoon."

Her argument is not with Ben, and she considers him only a moment as he places the coat and bag at her side before taking her things without further fuss.

"I felt my blood pressure rising," I say to Ben as Sara leaves the room. "You know, all the parenting books tell you not to argue with a child, and I see why. I felt as young as she is. And sillier."

"What's wrong?"

"She's angry at me. She had a fit last night over a letter Michael wrote and the custody decisions we're making, keeping her in the dark. I can't say I blame her for feeling angry, but she won't hear my apologies."

"And 'Apology accepted' would make you feel better, wouldn't it? You aren't supposed to feel better. You're the mother."

"How'd you get so smart? You don't even have kids."

"That makes me smartest of all," he grins.

"I think I'm beginning to hate you."

"All this anger! How about an outing instead?"

"An outing? Where?"

"If you've finished most of your work, I'm going over to check out a fish farm, a new guy. He's closer than my current supplier, and he wants to do more business in the area. The two of you wanna come?"

"Yes, I'll go, I love fish. But why don't you ask Sara." I motion with my head as she returns from her task.

"Hey, Sara," Ben asks, "wanna go see a man about some fish?"

We watch as gallons of water pour through wide pipes, spewing along with it thousands of tiny fish into rectangular holding tanks. Breeding has taken place in a tank farther back; they're here now to grow. As the fish flap, squirm, pile, splash, and land every which way with their tails bent, heads down, bodies instantly submerged, Sara looks on, fascinated. "Why do they farm fish?" she asks.

Ben explains, "Because sometimes there aren't enough fish in the sea or lakes or rivers. Or people don't want to overfish. Look." He points. "These are trout, and over there," he points again, "are the salmon. That's where we want to be. With the grown-up fish. I see my guy now."

I take Sara's hand, and we walk with Ben to another set of tanks where the fish farmer waits. Over at one corner they begin to talk business with a shake of hands. Sara and I lean over a rail and look in at the larger fish. The water is clean but dark and dense with fish and the depth of metal tanks. We see fish by their movements only, dark shadows in the viscous water. They swim close together, passing, dodging, darting away.

"I love fish," I tell her. "I would love to swim like a fish. Watch them push off with a flap of their tails." And with my arm, I whoosh a serpentine figure through the air, my pointing fingers leading the way as surely as a fish's own head. Sara copies me, faster, slower, up, down, and straight ahead. For the first time in nearly a day she giggles, and I laugh along with her. My arm fish lunges for her belly and gives her a tickle until she grabs me around the waist in a hug. We hold on to each other until Ben calls, "Sara, come here. You want to hold one?"

We walk toward the men. Ben holds by the belly a trout with a few spots, random like freckles. Extending his arms, he beckons to Sara. First she pats it along its spine. "It's wet. And smooth," she tells me.

The fish is so beautiful, and without hesitation she slides her hands under, clutches its silver-white camouflage belly alongside Ben's larger hands. As if it were in my hands I feel the course of its blood through its blood-rich gills, the flick of the membrane of its eye, the synapses of its brain as the sensation of being held passes along its lateral line. I touch the skin and brush my hand the length of the fish with the nap of the scales. It is smooth, cool, and as slippery as a bathed infant.

Ben's struck a deal to take a few fish back to prepare tonight; if he's satisfied he'll continue to use this new supplier. Maybe later I'll find myself flaying any one of these creatures, or more likely James will. He'll remove the flesh from the bone, or perhaps hold a cleaver over the large body of the salmon, cutting it into three segments to roast it on the bone. Its fat will keep it from drying out; cooking on the bone will impart such flavor.

Before I can ask Sara to replace the fish, it plops from her hands to the cooler at Ben's feet, with a snap first left, then right. She looks from her empty hands to me; surprised by the sudden strength with which it escaped her, her eyes open wide with wonder. She looks up at me and smiles, and I smile back.

As we drive to the restaurant, Sara sits with the cooler next to her on Ben's backseat; her right arm rests on its lid as she keeps it from sliding. I break from making small talk only once to turn around and watch Sara holding the cooler of fish protectively. "Hi, Mommy," she says.

I look at Ben. "Thanks for letting us tag along. It was just what we needed."

Ben looks ahead as he drives. His eyes squint as he looks well off into the distance, up into the mountains. "Looks like snow," he says.

The snow begins in early November, and, fall by fall, all New England is soon buried under inches of it, heavy and compacted. Here, up north, the ski resort owners are ecstatic. Every night as the weatherman predicts more powder, cheers go up in the bars and pubs and restaurants. Shop owners, innkeepers like Nora and Hugh, restaurateurs like Ben, all speak in excited, giddy tones as we gear up to handle the influx of tourists so early in the season. Everyone agrees this promises to be a busy and profitable winter once the snow stops and the sun shines.

Except that the sunshine is rare. The sky is heavy with snow for days at a stretch. Darkness settles in earlier and earlier, and the atmosphere is oppressive. The feeling of being trapped under these weighty nimbus clouds combines poorly with the pent-up frenzy of anticipation, as if we live as floating particles in some kind of unstable emulsion. Suspended, waiting.

And along with the colder weather and hovering over us like the snow is reality. The cold touches me and chills me awake after a warm, comfortable dream.

 As Christmas approaches, Sara lets go of her resentment and begins, instead, to look forward to visiting her father. I am buoyed by her eager anticipation. As it snows steadily, a few new inches every other day, I hear from the cooks and the waitstaff about the crazed evenings, of party after party of large groups, five, six, even eight, all skiers who are perhaps a shade too jolly and loud from a few beers in taverns as they wait for the skies to clear and the ski runs to open. Most of the evening is spent turning tables over in record time, and pushing them around the floor in various configurations to accommodate the

larger parties, a waiter complains. He adds that these impatient customers complain of slow service and vent their anger at the kitchen tableside. There are scarcely any deuces, he moans—the quiet romantic couples who drink wine in quiet toasts and tip well.

From James I hear about the lot of the cooks, who have to hustle to get up to eight meals to the table at the same time. The waitstaff is the chef's enemy, bringing in order after order and therefore subjecting themselves to poisonous glares from the hot and sweaty line cooks. According to James, the kitchen staff believes the waiters themselves are standing on the street corners like barkers beckoning to new customers. While my workday stays constant and I am insulated from the mayhem, James's day increases until he is working twelve or more hours daily, and on the evenings he makes it to my house, I cook for him. We no longer have the relaxed tastings of the summer, and the meals I make keep body and soul together. I look at him across my table, I watch him eat, he talks to me between mouthfuls, his elbows set on the table in front of him, his hands held up and clasped together after he lays down his fork. He talks to me and I listen. Seated at his side I reach out as I listen and stroke his arm. I feel his muscles relax under my fingers.

We know we will not have Christmas together. Sara and I will spend Christmas Eve at my mother's, since we are her only family, and I will cook a lavish, indulgent meal: small amounts of several tempting side dishes and a pork loin rolled and stuffed with dried apricots and prunes. It's all planned. With my mind on the menu, it's easy to ignore that Sara and I will be apart on Christmas Day for the first time in her six years, or that Michael will pick her up on the twenty-fifth and take her for the whole of her school vacation as he camps with his parents and searches for a place to live.

James offers me his truck for the drive to Boston if, first, I drop him off in southern New Hampshire, where he will spend Christmas with his large family. I like to imagine that his house will be a messy, noisy one over the holiday. When I speak this thought aloud, he insists that Sara and I stop in to meet his family, to see for myself just how noisy a big family can be.

After a late meal as we talk this over in bed, the plan begins to terrify me, and I tell him so. "Your mother will hate me," I argue.

"Your lack of self-confidence is such a turn on," he teases. "Come here and whisper more of those snappy put-downs in my ear."

"Okay, she'll love me, but she'll hate that I'm getting a divorce. I know mothers. Okay, okay, it's me," I relent when he glares crossly. "I'm nervous."

"How 'bout if I change the subject. Remember my friend," he asks, "the one I told you about who owns the restaurant with his wife?"

"Uh-huh."

"Want to see the place?"

"When?"

"Monday, when we're closed."

"This Monday? Because next Monday is our staff party, remember?"

"This Monday. He wants me to drive down. About once a year he asks me to change jobs. This is it."

"Are you thinking of leaving?" I sit up in bed.

"No, I never do. When I leave my job, it'll be for my own place; he knows that. But it's this thing we do, anyway."

"We'd just drive down for the day?"

"Just for a few hours. Hit him up for lunch, then drive back."

"Maybe it'll be less snowy south of here. I'll call Trish tomorrow, see if she can sit."

"Sara can come, if you'd rather. They have kids, they wouldn't mind."

"No, I think I'd like to spend the day alone with you."

"Now *there's* an offer," James says as he pulls me on top of him.

The door to Billy and Monique's brownstone is impressive: broad, tall oak that dwarfs anyone, like me, who dares approach it. Even before it is swung open in welcome, I know it will be inches thick, a fortress door, a door designed to keep the home's inhabitants safe. James has dropped me off in front to save me the walk from the back alleyway, where he parks to be off the street. I wait for him on the sidewalk, too shy suddenly to knock on the door without him.

It is snowy here in the city, too, steadily snowing and persistently gathering. Our feet, as James meets up with me and takes my hand, make the first disturbance in the clean white blanket on the walkway. On the landing before this massive door my footprints, slender and small, look insubstantial next to James's lug-soled ones. He wears new boots, Thinsulate-lined and made for this weather. However, snow slides easily over the tops of my flats, then slides inside and dampens my socks. I have worn the wrong shoes and I can't keep from looking at my chilly feet, comparing them to James's warm and dry ones.

"Look at your feet," James says, ringing the doorbell. All this time he has been looking down with me.

"I know. How stupid of me," I admit.

He smiles as we hear footsteps, skipping, hurrying down an interior flight of stairs. Returning his smile, I feel his hand at my back and watch—uncomprehending—as he squats to sweep me from behind my knees until I am suspended above the snowy landing, safe in his arms. He bounces me once to firm up his grip, and I feel I am falling, like a roller-coaster drop with my stomach struggling to catch up.

Panic invades my giggle, my involuntary initial response. "Please," I beg, "put me down. Please? I don't want—"

But my plea is interrupted by the opening door and Monique's concerned entreaties. "Come in. Come in, quick," she insists. "Take those wet things off."

—*Your friends to meet me like this, feet first*, is exactly what I had wanted to say. I had imagined we'd meet as equals, all food lovers, all brought together by our common fondness for James. Instead, self-consciously, I am the center of attention, of too much care. I'd like to leave and come back, start over, maybe wearing a more sensible pair of boots and not requiring this fuss. Monique removes the shoes for me, and James places me down in the entry. Behind us, she sets my shoes in the corner to dry and closes the door; it closes quietly for one so heavy, with an air-lock seal like a vault.

"Billy?" Monique calls. "James is here, James and Anna." She turns to me. "He's in the kitchen with the children, they're getting lunch on the table. Dinner, really," she explains, "like in Paris, on a Sunday afternoon."

James laughs at her quick, breathless speech. "Okay," she says, blushing as she nudges him with her elbow. "I realize I'm rambling; I do it all the time. So let's start over. How are you, James?" she asks. "You look terrific, all happy." She pauses to kiss him before taking me by the arm and leading us all to the kitchen. "And Anna? It's wonderful to meet you. Ever since James told us about you, we've been looking forward to this afternoon together.

"Billy, our guests," Monique announces as we enter their large kitchen. At a work island in the center of the room stands a husky, dark-haired man. Seated around him, giggling but focused on washing and tearing lettuce leaves for a salad, are three round-cheeked, round-eyed, curly-haired children. Cherubs.

Billy wipes his hands on a kitchen towel. In three great strides, he crosses the kitchen to exchange a quick embrace with James. "Man, it's good to see you. It's always too long. And Anna," he says, gathering me up in his arms, "we're especially glad you're here." He is so large I feel swallowed whole.

Monique herds the children over and introduces them to me, one by one. They, too, are infected with their parents' good natures; they smile warmly at me and extend their arms up to James for lifts and hugs. Once the greetings are finished, Monique sends the children back to their work and stands at her husband's side. Billy takes his wife by the waist and pulls her close. "Billy." She frowns up at him, "We should have shoveled. Why didn't we think of it? Anna's feet got all wet."

"No, please," I say. "It's me, my fault. I was hoping there'd be less snow down here, and I didn't dress properly."

"Still," Monique insists.

"You might as well let her fuss over you," Billy tells me, grinning. "It's what she does. You should see her with the customers. It's what makes them want to come back!" He bends down to kiss his wife. She closes her eyes and meets his mouth with hers. She makes the kiss last, letting her lower lip linger and hold his. I remember longing for a home like this once, trying to create this perfection once, with Michael. And as I watch, it is also as if I am looking into the future—my own future—with a husband who will give me three perfect, happy children; one who will care about shoveling the walk for my friends. A husband who will carry me through the snow, and who loves me because I fuss. And I watch them kiss until, finally, I have to look away, reminded only of failure.

We dine on slices of very rare breast of duck with turned new potatoes in a delicate but flavorful demiglace, and crème brûlée for dessert. James's friends are charming, the town house they've converted is idyllic, the French-influenced food is flavorful yet restrained. Their angelic children, also charming, babble excitedly about Christmas and beg to show me their favorite possessions. I yearn to let go, to enjoy this meal in the company of such a warm and welcoming family. James's friends. But it's too soon for this meal. Suddenly eating with strangers—even strangers so willing to become my friends—seems more intimate than sex. The wonderful food brings us so close so fast that I feel naked in front of these people; I am sure that they can see all my flaws. Together in this haven of a kitchen sealed off from the rest of the imperfect world by the protective front door, I am not prepared enough in my stockinged feet. I couldn't even wear the right shoes, I chastise myself. At the table I listen to the conversation and smile at the right moments, but I contribute little.

When the grown-ups' table talk turns coercive, with James as the object of pressure, I pass on coffee and leave with the children, who take me to see their rooms upstairs. I've been ignoring James. I know, he knows, and he raises an eyebrow as I leave, but I let myself be flanked and swept along without a word.

The stairway smells like demiglace, the childrens' bedrooms like burnt sugar crusts. When I sit on a twin bed surrounded by stuffed animals I speak of Sara, my sometimes moody, sullen Sara. They ask if she has brothers or sisters, and when I shake my head no, they stare collectively, as if they cannot believe me. For a moment I feel I would not be surprised if they all opened their mouths to speak and French spilled out. *Mais, Madame, çe n'est pas vrai*, they would say. *Pas des soeurs? Pas des frères?* Truly, I would answer. I mean, *Vraiment*. I feel I am in a foreign land. Or another planet. None of this seems familiar—this cozy home, the elegant food, these charming children.

I know James has again, good-naturedly, refused a job, a lateral move to sous-chef in his friend's restaurant. I hear him say so upon my return to the kitchen. "I couldn't save any money down here, and you know when I move," he says, "it'll be for my own place. Anna and I . . ." and his voice disappears suggestively so that when I reenter, they greet me in a new light, with a different scrutiny and an even warmer embrace. *Welcome to the club, to the inner circle, to the idyll.* Or maybe I hear this, too, in French. Or Old Norse. As we leave, his friends stop at the door and kiss me on both cheeks as the French do; they pump James's arm in friendly goodwill. I step quickly into my waiting shoes and through the door onto the walk. But when I move, keeping warm as I wait for James, I notice that the indentations left by my shoes fill quickly. The snow leaves no trace.

On the trip back, alone again with James, I am quiet. He looks at me, every once in a while taking his eyes from the road. "Talk to me," he urges. "What is it, Anna? What's wrong?"

"I can't say, exactly."

"Try," he insists.

"I felt . . . that this entire afternoon was like being in the middle of a propaganda film," I say, breaking my silence.

"I don't know what you mean."

"That you three were presenting a united front."

"And that would be for whose benefit?" he asks.

"Mine, I guess. Perfect couple, perfect home, perfect meal, perfect children. Like you needed to show me, 'All this can be yours.' "

"What's this really about, Anna?"

"I told you, perfection. I'm not perfect."

"That's a relief."

"You asked, now don't joke. I feel . . . you're pushing me too hard."

"Pushing?"

"Moving too fast."

We drive on without speaking for a few more minutes. The muscle along James's jaw is taut and pronounced. "I only wanted you to meet my friends," he tells me.

"Maybe it was all too—" I begin.

"Perfect?" he asks sarcastically.

"Stop it."

"Look, I'm sorry I said that, but what have the past eight months been about, if not moving forward? A relationship—business, personal—it doesn't move backward. There's only forward or over. And now you want to slow down; is *that* what you're saying?" James brings his hand down hard on the rim of the steering wheel.

"You're angry."

"Of course I'm angry. I'd be an idiot if I didn't feel angry. When did this happen, this indecision? Why haven't you said anything?"

"I'm trying, right now, to tell you. But I don't even know if I have the words." I pause and take a deep breath. "It's hard to live up to, that's all I'm saying."

"Live up to what? There's no formula here, it's all new. I wish I could understand what you mean. I wish you'd tell me."

"I wish I knew," I say to the side window as I hide my face from James.

James and I speak at work when our workdays overlap in the mid-afternoon, before I leave and right before he starts. But all contact outside of the restaurant has been suspended. I would like to believe, it would be easy for me to believe, that he is making a point by withholding his affection. But I know well the difference between the silent treatment and utter bewilderment. We are both baffled. How can he know what to say to me when I don't even understand what I was saying?

Ben asks me to stay late on the Sunday before Monday's staff holiday party. The restaurant is hopping with large groups and he's extremely shorthanded. So I work on after asking Trish to stay a little later with Sara. There is no rhythm in the kitchen, or I have trouble finding it after being away from evening work since September, and by nine o'clock we are feeding off each other's nerves. Ben barks orders, his temper remains high. Everyone is making stupid mistakes: Food is not getting out on time, the cooks could definitely be better organized. With Ben on the line James oversees all of the kitchen staff, making some repeat tasks. He takes Phil's knife from him at one point to show him what he's doing wrong. With the knife poised above the cutting surface, he lifts his eyes and sees the prep cook taking slices from a larger piece of meat. James isn't happy with the way it is being cut up, and he hollers, "Put the knife down and don't move until I get there." Muttering under his breath, "fucking idiot," he wipes his hands and demonstrates the right way to take slices.

Because he doesn't often lose his patience at work, I look up at him, I watch him as he returns to the chopping. His eyes move from his task for a moment, and as they meet mine, his concentration goes out the window. Somehow on the downstroke, the knife goes the wrong way and clips him between thumb and forefinger on his left hand. It is such a sharp blade that there's no blood visible for a few seconds. "Shit," he says, as he starts to bleed; it's a long one, stretching from the lowest knuckle of his forefinger through the fleshy part around his thumb's joint.

Next to James, Phil is staring, incredulous, at the amount of blood when it eventually does flow. I haven't moved, I can't get near him through all the movement, the flying arms and legs and hands. Ben has to yell at him to shut down his station because it's bloody; he yells for a towel. His voice stirs me, and I quickly step to James's side with a stool and force him to sit. I take his arm and hold it out to Ben, while Ben begins to bandage James as well as he can. James insists he will be able to make the rounds, give instructions, but then it is obvious to everyone that the bleeding won't stop on its own. Ben looks around, quickly decides who's least busy, and instructs him to drive James to the emergency room for stitches. "We can't spare you for long, so get back here after you've dropped him," Ben calls as they leave the building. The rest of us, horrified, keep going.

The accident subdues us, the frenzy finally comes under control, and we finish the evening quietly cleaning up.

At the hospital James has six stitches placed in his hand, has it more professionally bandaged, and gets sent home with Tylenol with codeine, antibiotic cream, and spare dressings. I hear about this when, after work, I drive his standard-shift truck very poorly to collect him at the emergency room. Under the harsh fluorescent lights he waits slumped in a chair, looking very tired and gray. And very sheepish when he sees me; he gives me an embarrassed half smile.

"I can't drive," he says, holding up his bandaged left hand.

"Good thing," I reply. "You don't look in any condition to get behind the wheel."

"And I didn't know if anyone would remember that I was here."

"Poor you," I tease. "I remembered. How do you feel?" I ask, taking the seat next to him, holding up my own left hand in sympathy.

"I'm all doped up, and I feel like an idiot," he says. "I haven't done anything like that in a long time."

"There was some bad energy in that restaurant this evening. Everyone was all spun up." I smooth down his hair and take the paper bag of supplies from him.

"My hand aches," he tells me. "But I didn't hit any tendons. Good thing." His eyes fill up with tears. "Anna, it's killing me. Can we get out of here?"

My bad driving, sloppy clutch work, the stall-outs, James notices none of it during the short ride to my house after the effects of the painkillers. By the time we pull alongside the curb, he's exhausted and snoring a drug-induced snore. I wake him and walk him right past a surprised Trish to put him to bed, but before he drops off to sleep he notices I still have on my work clothes. They are spattered with drops of his blood, now dried maroon, which dripped on me as I held his arm while Ben wound on the towel. He touches the spots with the fingers of his unbandaged hand, says, "Sorry," and leans back in my bed to fall asleep.

By three on Monday, Ben and I have prepared the restaurant for about thirty people. As he said weeks ago when the snow started and he began planning, "There is no good time for a party this season, so we might as well stick it right in the middle of the madness."

With Sara playing beside me I've uncorked and recorked many bottles of wine, iced cases of beer in large metal tubs and in the kitchen sinks, and laid out fresh bread, cheese, and hors d'oeuvres. Ben does not speak to me beyond simple directions and questions as he strings Christmas lights in the windows and over a tree by the bar. Before I go home to change and meet Trish, who will mind Sara, I pick up the end of one strand of electric lights and plug it in, and the tree glows. Sara, deprived of a tree until we get to my mother's on Christmas Eve, stands mesmerized. She squints her eyes at the lights.

Beside me Ben asks, "So how's the hand this morning?"

I turn to him. "Painful. He's in a lot of pain. Look, I'm so sorry," I say, "about last night."

"Accepted. Hey, it would have been just as crazy without you."

"Yeah? Me being there didn't help. All because we had this . . . this fight last weekend." I rest against the bar. "And over what? A beautiful dinner and lovely people who only wanted to make me welcome in their home. What was that all about?"

Ben laughs. "Are you asking me? Or yourself?"

"Sometimes I look at James, who always says what's on his mind, and I think: I'm almost there. I say to myself, I've always wanted that, to be open like he is. And sometimes it seems I am *that close*." For Ben I pinch my fingers so close together that only a speck could pass through. "But then I meet his gregarious friends, or I piss off my kid by acting like my own parents—something I swore I'd never do—and I realize, Who am I kidding? I'll never learn, I'll never catch up. Let's face it: I lived most of my life with two people who never actually spoke to each other. What do I know?"

"And I thought you'd retired the self-pitying act. You trying to scare everyone away?"

"I am pretty frightening at times, Ben."

"So you're purposely trying to make it tough for anyone to care about you?" He walks over and stands next to me. "You and James? You remind me so much of each other it isn't funny. I've known him for a few years, I've seen him do a few crash-and-burns of his own. And now you. It's like you're driving fast down a highway, driving as fast and hard as you can to get something behind you and to hell with the consequences. My point is, James isn't so different, or wasn't. Until he met you and started looking a little harder at his life. And I think he helps you relax, focus. You're good for each other."

"I didn't want to fight with him. Maybe it's the damn snow," I joke. "All this snow."

"That would be easy, blame this depressing weather and the crazy fool it brings out in all of us. Anna, you've got a nice life for yourself here, your work, your kid in school, your friends. That's a nice foundation. And I'm happy for you, both of you. When I look at the two of you," he continues, "I can see you leaving in a year or so, opening your own place. I'd be first in line, your first customer. Maybe that's why I'm worried, because I can see you seating me, making me a fine meal. You owe me." Even though there is a gleam in his eye as he says this, I hear a serious concern beneath the teasing.

I take Sara's hand, help her on with her jacket and hat. "Oh, Ben," I sigh as I stand up, ready to head out the door.

"Anna," he answers, "Get out of here. Go home and clean up; then let's have a party."

Tables and chairs have been pushed around the perimeter of the room; the restaurant is transformed by a crowd of our coworkers, their families and friends, all concentrating on cutting loose after weeks of hard work. The lights are low, people gather and talk and laugh around the bar, through the kitchen, and in clusters at the back of the room. Ben greets us at the door, and he whispers in my ear, "Remember to help me kick everyone out by ten. I need a decent night's sleep." I squeeze his hand in a pact.

James is grouchy; his hand still throbs, he tells me. He's not taken any codeine so he can stay awake and drink beer. He points to an empty corner, away from anyone else. I am wearing a simple black sleeveless dress, a bright green scarf around my neck, hanging long, and he winds the scarf over his bandaged hand. We stay attached to each other like this for awhile, wordless, face-to-face, his hand winding and unwinding, and we touch for the first time in a week. The Christmas lights stretching around the windows twinkle, and their flickering reflection in the glass flashes over our clothing, our arms, James's hair. I offer to get him a drink because he looks pained, but he says, "Stay, just another minute," so I do. Around us people are laughing, drinking, talking, as the evening swells and expands. We catch a draft from the front door as another large, noisy group wanders in. Someone turns the sound system on, and we have music, Billie Holiday's beautiful sad voice surrounds us until I hear Ben's voice insisting on cheerful Christmas music and the CD is stopped midtrack. James rests back against a table, scissoring me in his legs, and I am very comfortable.

"I've missed you," James tells me.

"Come here," I say, and he stands to move in close to me. "James," I begin, putting my finger on his lips, "I need to say something."

He holds on tighter, and my hands snake up under his arms and grip his shoulder blades. I cannot see his face, but I feel the expression of his warm breath behind my ear as he leans close to me. "Everything's converging. Divorce. Sara. Michael. The future."

"I know."

"I'm not handling any of it well, and I don't know why. Something about meeting your friends and feeling so inadequate next to that perfection set me off, made me want to scream."

"They're not perfect. They've worked hard."

"But I only saw those wonderful kids. And the smells. Their home smelled like a fairy tale. Yes, this is incredibly irrational, and I hate it. And I hate myself for feeling this way."

James lets me go when I finish speaking; he holds me at arm's length.

"Anna, sweetheart," he says, "I could really use that beer."

After returning from the bar where I've pried off the beer bottle's cap, I sit sipping wine while James slugs beer, sullenly, thirstily. We sit now in quiet, quietly drinking.

"I don't feel so well," James says, breaking our silence. "My hand is fucking killing me." He drains the bottle. "And I wish you'd brought back two," he says, holding up the empty. "I'm in a lousy mood; I shouldn't have even come here tonight."

"If I were an insecure person, I'd say it was me."

James bursts out laughing, and it is so infectious I laugh along with him. "Thanks for that," he says, "for making me laugh."

"That's refreshing. You haven't laughed at me in quite a few days. You know," I tell him, "I definitely didn't want to fight with you last weekend; it was as if I couldn't help myself.

"We've been in our own little world, James. You, me, Sara, home, work: a small circle. Last week I felt as if I was on display, exposed, and that I couldn't possibly measure up. It wasn't your friends; I *wanted* to meet your friends. I got scared. Of us." I put my face in my hands. "I don't know what to think anymore, except that I think too much," I say through my fingers. "And it's all so painful."

"It can be, but the flip side of painful is happy. You like me? You like your job? You're happy? Just be happy."

"I'd like that, and I am happy, but lately I find myself falling into old habits, the silent fuming, the inability to express myself. I don't particularly like the person I became with Michael, and I don't want you to see that part of me. More than that, though, I don't want to be that way with you. But here's the thing: What if I'm incapable of being anything different?"

"Is that what this is all about?" I nod. "Come here," he says, "I'm tired of you standing so far away." He takes me on his lap and places his unbandaged hand at the small of my back.

With his hand holding steady and firm and hot, imprinting the skin beneath my dress with its heat, I explain, "Sometimes the life I

want seems ... unattainable because so much crap is so deeply in-
grained in me. What if I am only able to screw things up for myself?
That's ... perverse."

"So you're perverse. I can live with that."

"It's not funny."

"I'm not laughing, we all screw up. God knows I'm not perfect."

"But you are so open, everything around you—you hold everything open to me. Like a gift, every day. I wonder what I give you,
and it's daunting."

"So what? So I can tell you what I think. You wanna know something about me? Every time I've gone out with someone I've been able
to tell them exactly what I think. Like, 'This isn't serious' or 'I can
guarantee you this won't last.' Now that's communication. You're im-
pressed that I can say what I think? I say, Big fucking deal. For a long
time what I was thinking wasn't worth anything. It's hard for you?
Well, it's hard for me, too."

Surprised by the fire in his voice, I can only manage a limp "Oh."

"Maybe you stayed for the wrong reasons, but don't walk away for
the wrong ones, either. You wonder what you give me? Just think about
it. See," he continues, "I've been trying to tell you, I've always walked,
always found women I could walk away from. But this is about trying
to do a little better, you make me want to be a better person ... I want
to try, anyway. With you," he says as we sit there wrapped together.
His hand, still hot against my skin even through a layer of clothing,
reminds me of the heat of sex. With each second we hold on, our
embrace shifts subtly from comforting to sexual. James feels it too; I
hear him acknowledge the change in the husky, thickening voice with
which he suggests, "Could we maybe get out of here?" before shifting
me to my feet.

As we leave I apologize to Ben for skipping out before ten, but he
simply waves me on. As I reach for James's hand at the front door,
Ben calls, and I turn to see him surrounded by friends with a wide
smile, a child's Christmas smile, on his face. He says, "And Anna?
Merry Christmas."

"Merry Christmas, Ben," I reply as my fingers light on James's, as they crook together, as we walk with fingers linked together through the door.

Outside in the parking lot I hear the soft pop of a car door opening, then closing again. Across the black expanse I see clouds of hot breath in the cold air as around us people come and go. We walk, arm in arm, slowly through the icy lot, me careful in my heels. James's arm is up under my coat, gripping my waist, reminding me there is warmth even in the wintry night. We stop at his truck, and he tosses me his keys after I rest my back against the driver's door. Before I can open the door to drive, he leans into me with the weight of his body. His right hand holds my shoulder while he props his left against the truck above my head. My knee moves up the inside of his thigh.

For the first time I tell him, "I love you."

James's hand heals quickly in the week before Christmas, and he makes me a special meal that we eat late at night on the floor of my bedroom. Propped up against my bed we eat hungrily and laugh together over the haphazardness of this spread of pots, pans, the jumble of plates and utensils, and the open bottle on the floor. Before our drive south I give him a present, a blue cashmere scarf to wear against the cold. I wrap it around his neck; it is the blue of lapis, like the dark ring around his paler blue iris.

I wrap new bandages on his hand, too; I've changed the dressing for him every day, watching as the skin around the sutures went from pink and swollen to dry and yellowing and puckered. Eventually the stitches dissolved, but each day as I put on new gauze and tape, I looked carefully for the bright red striations of infection; I brought the skin to my lips to feel for an uncommon heat in his flesh. But he heals well. By Christmas, when we separate for our family gatherings, his skin is grown together nicely, a thin raised line of shiny new skin the only mar remaining on his lovely hand.

We pull off the highway outside of Manchester. James's muscles ache from this long drive, and when we finally stop, he jumps from the truck to shake out his arms and legs. Stopped in the family's driveway, Sara is asleep next to me, and there is a ball of fire at the base of my spine, too, with the tension of being thrust into the middle of James's large family. I haven't been introduced to parents in years, and I am scared, worried I will not pass.

He is wearing his new scarf and his big navy blue sweater and a huge grin as he walks toward me in the truck. His hands are behind his back and I can tell he's up to something. That grin. From behind his back he holds up an enormous snowball. He looks about twelve, and I am intensely in love with him at this moment. His arm rears back, he makes as if to throw the snow. I stick my tongue out at him and lock the doors, at once safe behind the windscreen, windows up. So he drops the snow, holds his arms up in surrender. He walks to the driver's side window.

"Let me in," he speaks through the glass. I shake my head no. "It's cold. I want to warm my hands," he says. Laughing, I unlock the door, slide over closer to Sara, who is buckled in and still sleeping. James climbs in next to me. "Hi," he says. He puts his hands on either side of my face and they are cold, so I take them in my gloved hands, blow on them, hold them tight.

Leaning over, he kisses me, and his lips are warm. Beside me Sara stirs and rubs her eyes. "Hey, Sara," James says. For a minute she is disoriented, so I take her hand, too. We three sit quietly, joined in the middle by me, until Sara wakes a little more. "C'mon in," James urges. "It's cold out here. Come meet my family."

"Oh, God," is all I can say.

Alone at the kitchen table with Mrs. O'Brien, we sit and drink tea, good and hot with lots of milk. James has enticed Sara outside with the promise of a snow fort, and from the backyard I can hear her chatter and lots of laughter. When we hear James's deep voice giving instructions, Mrs. O'Brien and I smile at each other.

"My middle child," she says, smiling and nodding her head to the window overlooking the backyard. "Always up to something. More tea?" she asks.

"Yes, please," I answer, sliding my cup across the table.

"This is nice, being able to sit," she tells me. "The holidays are crazy, grown children, grandchildren, even with everyone helping out it's exhausting. But we all love it. We're used to each other, the noise. Don't tell anyone, though, but I do enjoy a quiet moment and, now and then, the chance to sit down."

I lift my cup, sip the strong tea. "There will only be three of us at my mother's tonight. Tomorrow, only two. Growing up for me it was always three, too. Funny—I can't even imagine what a large family is like."

"Mostly exasperating." She laughs. "But I can't imagine anything different either."

From outside we hear, "Get him, get him! Now duck, Sara, get down!"

"He's probably got her throwing snowballs at anyone unfortunate enough to walk by," Mrs. O'Brien observes. "Only two for Christmas dinner?" she asks.

"My mother. Me. Sara's going with her dad for Christmas and the next two weeks." Resting the cup in its saucer, I say, "You know I'm separated. Divorcing," I clarify, as if it makes any difference.

"James did say," she answers.

"When he asked me to meet you, my first thought was you'd be

horrified by the divorced girlfriend. Maybe barring the door, not wanting me to blacken your house."

Mrs. O'Brien laughs at me.

"Your son finds me very funny, too," I tell her. "But what was I
supposed to think? Nine kids, an Irish family. Even my own mother is
in denial. I've been dreading this visit. I certainly didn't think we'd be
sitting together so comfortably."

"Do you know, Anna, how many of his girlfriends he's brought
home to meet his family?" Before I have a chance to speculate, she
answers her own question. "Aside from one date in high school, and
that was about fourteen, fifteen years ago, none. You're the first. All
my other children, they'd bring girlfriends, boyfriends by. I watched
them all struggle along, some getting engaged, then married.

"But James has always gone his own way. I knew he had a social
life, he was never at home, so I asked him once why we never met
any of his girlfriends. He just laughed at me, told me there wasn't
anyone he'd want me to meet, although I had my suspicions he simply
wasn't interested in the hard work. I suppose I don't have to tell you
marriage is hard work. Anyway, occasionally I would despair that he
had no one special enough to bring home. And now, after all these
years, here you are."

"He's kind of taken me by surprise. I mean, I was only trying to
work, get our lives settled. I wasn't looking for anyone to . . . well, take
care of me. I mean, he made me talk to him. He's very persistent." I
shake my head. "I don't know why I'm telling you all this, you barely
know me."

"I know all about his persistence. And I think you're trying to
reassure me: 'Mrs. O'Brien, I'm not taking advantage of your son.' No
one wants to see their children make mistakes or get hurt, but like I
said, I trust he's able to make up his own mind.

"When you have nine kids," she continues, "you just work hard
day in and day out feeding them, keeping them in clean clothes, getting them through school. You have very little time with them as
individuals, so you kind of cross your fingers and hope everything
you've done has helped make them capable of taking care of them-

227

selves, capable of making good decisions. And he's done all right for himself so far."

There is no irony or malice or resignation in her tone and she looks upon me with kind blue eyes, James's eyes with the darker edge. As we sit together, I can see where he's come from: her eyes, her laughter. She pours herself more tea and takes a sip, pursing her lips with the astringent tannin from the tea's long steep in the pot. I find myself wondering as I watch her flinch at the unexpected bitter taste what it was like for James to have a parent like this, one who would let her nine children explore the world on their own terms. She interrupts my thoughts, adding, "I think your Sara is lovely."

"She is," I agree. "She's kept me going on days I didn't want to get out of bed."

"Children will do that, keep you busy with their needs. There's no time for anything else."

At once there is a flurry of war whoops from the yard. We rise from our seats, Mrs. O'Brien and I, and stand together at the window. She points, saying, "Look." And I look out to see two of James's brothers lurking at the corner of the house, engaged in fierce snowball combat with James and Sara. James steps back, locates me in the window, and calls to me, "Get out here, you coward, and help us against these two idiots." A white snowball flies in a perfect arc and strikes his shoulder.

"Go on out," Mrs. O'Brien urges.

"Let me help you clean up," I offer.

"Anna, the dishes will be here when you get back, if not these ones, then others. Go out and have fun."

I enter the white, the back of my black coat soon covered with powdered snow as I run for shelter. Behind the wall of white snow blocks sit James and Sara, a huddle of color: navy blue under a rare water blue sky, the snow clouds vanished; red and orange fleece, blue-black hair, the yellow glare reflecting off the snow; gray-white steam rising from two, now three, mouths close together. I am accepted in, enveloped, and we join strengths against the onslaught. The four legs of his two brothers come crashing into our wall, toppling mounds of snow over onto us. Sara breaks free and, laughing, runs into the house. James wraps me in his arms and we tumble away over and over in the snow. I am laughing and shrieking with cold and snow down my neck and the kisses he's planting all over my face until he stops us, digging his elbows into the snow, and I am under him strangely blinded by the sun but looking up into his eyes, which might as well be the sky because I can see a long, long way.

In front of me is a plate with Stilton cheese and toasted walnuts. The cheese has been sitting out for about forty-five minutes; it is both creamy and sharp. The walnuts have mellowed from toasting, the oil is leaching a bit, and they, too, are creamy. I am picking up a bit of cheese with my fingers, piling it onto a walnut half and popping it into my mouth. I need to lick my fingers after each taste. My mother suggests getting me a knife but I tell her no, and continue to eat, offering her some. But she declines. Even Sara will eat this cheese, although it is strong stuff. Sometimes that's what children go for, like sour dill pickles, the peppery bite of radishes, salty brined olives. She's even finished a plate of caponata, full of capers and eggplant. I am lucky, having a child who eats without fuss.

Meanwhile my mother is still pushing bits of meat around her plate. I've poured wine, but she drinks water.

"Anna," my mother says as she lays down her silver, "I'm thinking of having a memorial service for your father this year."

I look up from the plate of cheese, waiting for more information. My mother looks older since my last visit only a few months ago. Her skin is pale, papery around the eyes. I notice a slight tremor in her hands, which she stops with the effort of clasping them before her plate, her wrists daintily touching the edge of the table.

I swallow, take a sip of wine. "Why this year?" I ask. Father has been dead eleven years this January.

"I should have arranged it last year, on the tenth anniversary," she begins. "But I didn't, and this year you and Sara are here. So I thought, why not?"

"I'll be in New Hampshire, and Sara will be on the Cape, remember?" I remind her.

"I know, but if I can plan the service for the the last weekend of her vacation, you can come down, and Michael can drive up. Anyway, I meet with Father Dolan next week." She looks over at Sara, who is draining her glass of milk, and touches her dark, glossy hair. "This is something I want to do, Anna."

My mother is sixty-seven; eleven years ago she was a fairly young widow. In that time, she's never remarried or dated, preferring to live her solitary life with memories and specters and volunteer work at the local hospital. Even the house remains stuck in the past: There is a broken barometer on the wall, kept for looks rather than utility, a built-in corner hutch holding curios, china, salt and pepper shakers I have never liked, blue glass under a filigree of silver. The room is so remarkably unchanged that for a moment I expect my father may slide the dining room's wooden door into its slot in the wall and step through to join us.

"Okay, fine. Of course, do what you want to do," I answer.

Mother picks up her knife and fork, cuts her meat into even smaller morsels, and contemplates putting something into her mouth, the utensils frozen over her plate.

"Is there something wrong with your dinner?" I ask.

"No, no, it's fine. It's just a little . . . different, that's all. But very good. It's all very good. You're a lovely cook," she tells me. "I never was, I never had much imagination when it came to food, but he didn't mind that. Your father wasn't much of an eater." She sets down her silver once again. "He used to think pork would give him tapeworm," she shrugs.

"That's a very primitive, very old-fashioned notion." I laugh.

"You never knew your grandmother," my mother continues, "your father's mother, but I ate there once or twice. Your father wasn't exaggerating when he said the woman couldn't cook," she continues. "Once I went over and saw our dinner meat thawing on the counter. I touched the package; it was no longer cold. Lord knows how long it had been sitting out. It must have been terrible growing up like that. It's a wonder they all lived.

"Later we could laugh about it. He never laughed about his childhood until he met me," she says. "Your father wanted to do things differently in his house, so I made a point of learning what he liked, cooking the way he liked."

"You did," I agree, both surprised and pleased with her sudden openness. Her attraction to my father, their marriage, had always been a mystery to me. I would like her to keep talking, and I choose my next words carefully. "He would have hated the idea of me cooking for a living."

" 'Hate' is the wrong word. I think he just wouldn't understand it. We used to wonder where you came from, talking about food the way you did. Besides, cooking seemed so menial, like the cooking and cleaning our grandparents did when they arrived in the States. He just wanted better. He wanted the best for you, Anna."

Sara, with impeccable timing, begins to ask about dessert, so I excuse myself to clear the table. My mother follows me to the kitchen; while she runs water to rinse the plates, the telephone rings.

"Maybe it's Daddy," Sara hollers excitedly from the dining room.

But it is James, and I wave my arms to get my mother to turn off the faucet. "Tell me about your day," I say. Mother remains in the kitchen next to the sink, waiting to complete her task. Through the telephone wires I hear about his meal, punctuated by stories of his brothers and sisters, and their juvenile squabbles make me laugh. He describes to me everything he is making, everything going on in his mother's kitchen. I find his voice soothing, so I lean back against the counter and listen.

"I miss you," he says when he finishes.

"I miss you, too."

"I don't like the idea of sleeping alone."

"No," I agree.

You won't forget to pick me up tomorrow? To avoid the crowd here?" he jokes.

"I won't forget you. But I've got to go now. Sara's practically banging the table for her dessert," I exaggerate.

After I hang up my mother begins rinsing plates again, she scrapes food from her plate into the sink until all the lovely but untouched leavings mingle in a pile in front of the disposal. Without lifting her eyes from her task she says, "That wasn't Michael, I think."

"No, it wasn't. It was someone I work with, the man whose truck I drove. James. Well, you know, you met him briefly in April, on our way back from the conference in Boston. I'm picking him up on the way back," I explain. "He's become very—" I begin but my mother cuts off my words with a shake of her head.

"I don't want to know," she tells me.

I take ice cream from the freezer, let it soften a bit as I slice a pie. "How about this," I propose, changing the subject. "I can collect Sara here after her stay with Michael, like you suggested. Then we'll stay on for the weekend, for the memorial service." My mother turns to me, pleased, but I cannot look at her face for long. She looks tired, the skin of her cheeks slightly mashed as if she has slept funny. The pie, the plating of dessert, provides an easier place to focus my eyes, and I continue, "I shouldn't have too much trouble from Ben over the extra day or two. He'll just have to work me like a dog when I return," I try to joke lightheartedly, passing my mother to reach for silver in the drawer. But her hand stops me; she holds my wrist lightly.

"You're staying in New Hampshire, then, indefinitely?" she asks, the first time today either of us has referred to the future.

I nod my head. "You know I've decided. Ben asked me to stay on months ago. He likes my work and I like it, too."

"I see," she says. "What will you do? About your husband?"

"The divorce will be final soon, as soon as he moves, as soon as we work out the custody. We're being very civilized. Amicable," I add defensively, as if I expect her reproach, shock, or resistance. But surprisingly, uncharacteristically, my mother offers none.

"You know," she says, "he's always been good to me."

"I know, Mother. Michael is a fine person. But I don't think we're fine together."

"Until then you're still married, in some eyes you'll always be married," she reminds me with a more familiar warning. "I can only hope you're not rushing into anything."

James, I think, wishing I had him back on the line, Why can I talk to you? Why could I never speak here? I'd rather be home with you, foraging for one of our meals, touching you, or even working together. I want to tell her about you, that we sleep together and I've never been so happy. I'd like to tell her how you touch me. I could tell her, just open my mouth and blurt out the words. Instead, I let her drive me crazy. Instead, I quiver inside because my mother ignores me, reduces my life to a young girl's decisions.

Finally I look at her face, the sorrowful eyes, her slackened skin, the hang of her head. Walking closer, I take her awkwardly into my arms, kiss her cheek, which I am surprised to find is wet. Slowly I wrap my arms around her, grasp her in a way I haven't since I was a child. Her spine is unyielding under my fingers, vertebrae hard and knobby beneath my hands. She is no longer soft and young, and I realize it's been too long since we've embraced; we've forgotten how.

I wait for something whispered softly in my ear.

I wait.

Nothing can prepare me for seeing Michael after nearly a year, nothing. Not his voice over the phone during the past few weeks to outline the details of shunting Sara, nor the pep talks I've given myself since yesterday realizing he'd be here soon to take her away (It's a day like any other, Anna; it will only be two weeks, Anna; everything will be okay). He's made himself as unrecognizable as possible with a new dark beard. His presence is a shock, although he looks entirely natural sitting here, and I float a moment, suspended between the reality and the unreality, as I adjust. My husband, yet not quite. My ex-husband, nearly. No longer a lover, not even a friend, but also never a stranger. It confuses me; I don't know what to do or to say to this man who sits leafing through one of my mother's magazines, a cup of coffee steaming at his side, recently poured, so Mother must have clucked over him, fussed, and settled him in the comfortable chair and then fled. Perhaps she was hopeful as she did so, hoping that the normalcy of it all would prompt us out of our fancy or, in her eyes, the nightmare. He stands as I walk into the hallway from playing outside with Sara. Her bags, packed and ready, are beside my feet.

"Hi," I say softly, as I hang up my coat. "New beard?"

Michael shrugs, "Not really." His eyes look around the room and beyond me, anywhere but directly at me.

"If you're looking for Sara, she's still outside. She'll be right in. We didn't know when exactly to expect you, so we took a walk after opening presents. She's been up for hours." I smile hesitantly. "Why don't you sit?" I prompt. "Can I get you more coffee? I'll have some with you, something to warm me up." Like my mother, I look to routines and rituals, to fussing over this man for comfort. Or perhaps I simply need something to do with my hands.

"No, no more, thanks. God, this is awkward!" he exclaims.

"Yes," I agree in relief. "Why don't I just sit, too?" And I take a seat in the corner of the sofa.

"Daddy?" We turn our heads at the sound of Sara's voice coming from the front hallway.

"Hey, big girl," says Michael. "Look at you."

Sara walks to me and stops at my side, resting her hip against the arm of the sofa.

"I don't like your beard," she tells him.

"Well, then, I'll just have to shave it off." He asks, "Can I have a hug?"

"Don't scratch," Sara warns, wagging her finger at him as she steps tentatively into his arms.

Which is, after all, what this is all about. Not me, not Michael, or our sudden shyness, but Sara. She walks him by the hand to show him her Christmas presents, the new school clothes, and the doll she will hold on her lap during the car ride to the Cape.

After, he finds me in the kitchen, hunched over the steam in a cup of coffee.

"I'm—we're—ready to go," he says. "Sara and I."

"She's all packed," I tell him as I stand. "Let me—"

"Your mother's reading her a book. Giving us some time, I think."

"Time?"

"To talk. She's pretty transparent, your mother. About what she wants."

"I know what she wants," I tell him. "She disapproves. But we'll all have to adjust to change."

He nods. "Speaking of which, I start the new job right after school vacation. I'll be renting an apartment in the city, temporarily, which will give me time to look for something to buy. A place Sara will feel comfortable in." Michael looks closely at me. "You look really well, Anna, you've put on some weight. It suits you."

"Thanks," I answer. "I guess I'm eating well. Cooking and eating well. Oh," I blurt, "this small talk is hard for me. Sara's leaving is—"

"You haven't been apart, ever," Michael interjects.

"No."

"This first time, watching her drive away, will be tough. But we'll get used to it."

"Yes. It'll be okay, Michael. I know we're doing the right thing. I'll be back at work tomorrow, and the time will fly."

"We'll adjust," he emphasizes. "So what's the plan? For the return trip?" he asks.

"I thought . . . well, Sara needs to be back to school on the fifth, and Mother wants to do some memorial service that same weekend. She suggested that we meet here, that way Sara and I could go to church with her before going back to New Hampshire."

"A memorial service?"

"For my father. Ten years, one year late," I joke.

"I can stay. For the service," Michael offers.

"You don't have to. After you bring Sara back, you can be on your way. There's no need."

"But I want to. Why wouldn't I? I was there with you eleven years ago. You can't just erase me from that experience, too."

"I'm not erasing you from anything. I didn't think you'd want to be there, that's all. I don't even want to be there."

"But why? He was your father."

"Exactly. I lived through it, isn't that enough? I mean, he's dead, and I don't see the point in bringing him back every ten years or so. It's macabre. And pointless."

"Pointless," Michael repeats.

"Yes, pointless. He's gone. We've all had to move on. We do this, this memorial service, and it's like we're stuck. I hate it."

"You told your mother you'd go, didn't you? You didn't tell her what you told me?"

"Of course I agreed to go, without a fuss. But that doesn't mean I have to like it."

Michael reaches across the table for my hand. "I'm sure it brings up lousy memories for you—you watched him die and you couldn't help him—but maybe it's a way to put it in perspective. A way to put it all to rest."

"Lousy memories?" I ask, pulling my hand back. "Memories. Memories of *what*? Watching him *die*? Is that what you think? Michael, when we were on that beach after the funeral, what did you think I was telling you? That I looked on helplessly? That I felt *helpless*?"

"Didn't you?" he asks.

Our voices have risen, escalated along with the conversation, the sound waves reverberate with the force of our words. We sit and look at each other, and our last words seem to hang in the air as an echo. I realize I am breathing hard and scowling. I put my head in my hands for a moment and squeeze my eyes shut. I breathe more slowly. In and out. Then I raise my head.

When I open my eyes, behind Michael and framed by the doorway is my mother. She holds Sara by the hand, she has my girl dressed and ready to travel in her fleece-lined jacket and hat. Sara clutches her doll in a football hold under her other arm. She looks from me to my mother, who is frozen in the doorway with her eyes wide and yet bizarrely unfocused. How long has she been here, and what has she heard, what can she possibly think?

I rise from my seat and Michael turns his head with my movement; he looks with me over his shoulder. Just in time to see my mother crumple to the floor, her hand dropping from Sara's on the way down.

The eyes are closed, the mouth, slightly open to expose teeth, looks ready to emit a snore. The man lies on his back, a perfect rest: undisturbed, peaceful, undisturbable. The sheet is white and pulled up to the chin. Look closely and you won't even see the rise and fall of his chest. Take note of your surroundings, and you'll realize this room has none of the personal touches of a bedroom. You have been left alone, you'd like to wake him because it's too eerily quiet in here. Until, that is, your mother enters.

She can cry, touch him, kiss him, but you dread skin that feels as cool and waxy, as unnatural as a waxed and polished apple skin holding brown rot at its core. "Don't touch the sheet," you warn, your voice sharp and insistent for you know what lies under there. Perhaps the chest was cut open, the ribs yanked back until they cracked, no better than Styrofoam, certainly not what we think of as strong bone, under purposeful and well-trained hands. They've made everything nice for you, Mother, you long to say, they've covered up their messes and their intrusions, but the truth is it was a battle to find that heart and attempt to start it pumping again. So for God's sake, don't touch the damn sheet.

The problem with this memory is it always comes back in the second person, as if I claim no responsibility, no links to the man lying under the coarse hospital-grade sheet on this bed with its stainless-steel sides. But I always felt, even then, that it was someone else there, not me.

Did I say earlier I couldn't reach him? What did I say, that I was stuck outside the bathroom because his body wedged the door? That I hoped he wasn't sad or lonely as he lay on the cold tile floor, ceramic tiles impressing themselves, checkering the skin of his back even as blood pooled under that skin, forming huge bruise like stains as it gathered? That I listened to the life leave his body, that I knew he was dying at home, dead before reaching the hospital, knew it by the even, regular clicks at the back of the throat regularly counting off last vital seconds.

Because, if I did, then all of this is true.

But it is also not true.

From the warmth of my bed I hear voices in the hallway. As always now, my childhood bed feels strange after months of my dormitory mattress. Also I am not used to sleeping alone. This January is cold, but I have a window open above the radiator for circulation. If I wrap the blankets about my neck, my head, my ears, I can muffle the nervous rustling, the pacing back and forth between my parents' bedroom and the bathroom. I can barely hear the beeping of the home blood pressure monitor or my father's liquid coughs. In and out I fade, waking, sleeping, burrowing, listening. I am both comfortable and unsettled.

I hear loud thuds as if someone has dropped something heavy, ungainly, and it hits the floor beginning, middle, end. I am scared but frozen. Because I am sure it is my father who has fallen. Because I can hear my mother calling his name, softly but firmly; she wants a response. I think, Maybe he is dead. It is dangerous, this mixture of fear and apathy that I hold inside like an extra-hard-edged organ; it is both paralyzing and decisive. I decide to pretend I haven't heard until the knocks come at my door and I can no longer ignore what is happening.

"No, I didn't hear a thing," I lie.

"I can't get in there," my mother says, so I crack the door. There is a heavy, labored but regular intake of breath; that's good, I think, he's breathing.

"What happened?" I ask.

"I think it's his heart," she says. We waste precious seconds as she reconstructs events for me.

"Look, sit, and I'll call for an ambulance," I command. It is easy to take charge, to give the appearance of being helpful. I am scared at how naturally it comes to me, this dissembling, because I know just how culpable I am. I know just how much earlier I could have gotten here.

After I leave the phone, my mother is back by the bathroom door. I do not want her to hear death, so I tell her to go away, go sit. I open the door again. Yes, he is lying with his head against the door, I see this much reflected in the bathroom mirror: his body splayed out the length of the bathroom floor all the way to the tub. Yes, I hit his head each time I crack the door, slide his head into an uncomfortable angle. Maybe it hurts him. Still, I could open the door enough to squeeze through, maybe climb onto the sink's counter, then drop to the floor. I could hold his hand. Maybe he would know someone was there, maybe he wouldn't. But I'd know.

And yet I don't move.

When the paramedics arrive and have to take the door off its hinges to reach him, I feel relieved of my guilt. But inside I know I am lower than a coward; I am not merely scared, I am passive. But passive is the only response I know to impassive, untouchable, unknowable, and ultimately unreachable, especially in death.

I chose instead to stay outside the door, to keep my mother away, to listen to the heavy intakes of breath turn to gurgles, then to rattles, then to a click at the back of the throat. To talk through the door, reassuringly but pointlessly, "Someone's coming, keep breathing. I'm here, Daddy. Daddy, I'm here. Daddy?"

Michael sits with Sara in the waiting room, and after I have answered insurance questions and provided billing data, I am allowed in to see my mother. At first I see her through a flood of doctors, nurses, information; I cannot get any closer. I hear about treatments, progress, prognosis.

Talking with the doctors at the hospital, I hear their fervent assurances. "It is wonderful," they say, "that she can speak. Other than an ever-so-slight muscle loss from minor nerve damage, your mother," they repeat, "should make wonderful progress. Blood thinners," they tell me. "Have you heard of Coumadin? It will help the flow of blood to the brain." I know just enough anatomy to know about her carotid artery and blockages, to know the mechanics of the stroke. But I listen, try to, patiently. They speak so fast, these doctors, or is it my mind, slow to comprehend? I am taken by surprise; it seems I am playing catch-up—absorbing what's happened, not yet ready to discuss treatment.

My mother lies in the hospital bed. She is sleeping now. Earlier she kept trying to apologize to me, as if she could have controlled the seizure. She asked about Sara.

"Hush," I told her, "please don't worry about Sara. She's fine, she's with Michael."

"I'm so sorry," she said, "for scaring Sara."

It seems to be good that she has spoken, that she has asked for me and Sara before drifting in and out of sleep. They tell me if I wait outside someone will get me when she wakes, so I agree to leave.

As I walk to join Michael and Sara, I look at my watch, trying to calculate how long we've been here, waiting. I feel ill.

Michael offers to take Sara for something to eat. He asks if I want coffee. "Anything?" he presses.

"No," I tell him, "but what would I do without you?" And I mean it. I have no idea.

My elbows are on my knees, my forehead on my fists, I am hunched over in a waiting-room chair. How long have I been sitting like this, I wonder, sitting, waiting, thinking, trying not to think? Sara. What will I do about Sara if I am at the hospital every day? Then I recall she was almost out the door with Michael. Will he whisk her away to the Cape as planned? If so, I imagine it will be quiet there in my mother's house, I imagine moments of pure peace after days of frantic care taking, traveling back and forth from the hospital. Perhaps I will sit every night alone with a cup of Earl Grey tea; is it supposed to be calming, this tea infused with bergamot, I wonder?

I will live in Mother's house after Sara is off with Michael and his parents; there will be no little-girl sounds, no humming from distant rooms, no more incessant questions as I go about my chores. My own mother will lie tucked into bed, sleeping off the effects of her trauma, maybe in sleep escaping for a time from the new course of her life. As she mumbled to me out of one side of her mouth when I found her at the hospital: "My new life sentence, Anna."

And I will have elected to be there, in my childhood home, becoming the keeper of the parent, fixing meals, coaxing a sluggish appetite, learning how to mete out blood thinners, stealing a quiet cup of tea. And very much alone.

I can't bear the thought of Sara leaving.

Then I think of James an hour or so away at his parents' house, waiting for me, expecting me to drive up in his truck all smiles at the sight of him. After I find a pay phone, I dial. On the fourth ring, the O'Briens' phone is picked up.

"Is James there?" I ask, moving past niceties. "Anna," I answer, adding, "Please just get him on the line."

"You're chickening out, aren't you," he jokes, no greeting, just his rumbling voice booming over the wires.

"James," I rush, "my mother's had a stroke. I'm at the hospital, and I can't come to get you. I know I promised but I-just-can't-get-there." Although he can't see me, I use my hand to punctuate the words in my crisp, firm, staccato delivery, which helps me hold myself together.

For a few moments there are no sounds, not a breath or the clicking of a tongue in disapproval, only the blankness of someone mulling over a question. I wonder if he has set down the receiver gently, perhaps walked away from the phone. But then there is the rustle of a hand muffling the mouthpiece, and I hear James holler, "Will you keep it down? Can you shut up? Anna, are you still there?" he asks when he gets back on the line.

"I'm here. There's nowhere to go."

"Can you tell me what happened? What happened? When?"

"Please, I can't talk now. I wanted you to know why I'm not there, and I'll . . . I'll call you back later. From the house."

"Anna, don't hang up," he insists. "I can get a ride. There's bound to be someone here who'll give me a ride. It's an hour. Anna?" he asks when he hears nothing in reply.

I want to be able to handle this, to know that I can take care of my mother and my daughter without falling apart. And it's Christmas, his family deserves better than this—my mess intruding on their holiday.

"Please don't come," I urge.

"I want to come. I'm coming. I'm there. What about Sara?"

"Michael's here, with Sara. He was taking her when . . . ," but I cannot finish the sentence; I can only rest my head back against the wall behind the pay phone, the metal cord pulled tight around my chin.

"Are you able to give me directions?" he asks, and before hanging up I do my best to tell him where to find me. Standing in front of the inert phone, lifeless plastic and metal, I put my face in my hands, give a grunt of frustration, then settle myself to wait some more.

I hear footsteps approaching, I feel a hand on my back.

"Have you seen her again?" Michael asks, walking out from behind me.

I shake my head. "Where's Sara?"

"Over there," he points, and I see her sitting quietly watching the television on the other side of the waiting room. "I figured a little television right now wouldn't be the worst thing. Is everything okay?" Michael asks me.

"No, everything is not okay. I hate hospitals, they remind me of my father. And I've been obsessing all day, wondering what might have happened if this had occurred while Sara was home alone with my mother. Did I ever teach her to dial 911? I can't remember. Plus, my mother's recovering from a stroke." Michael doesn't miss the sarcasm in my rising voice, and he puts his hand on my back; he rubs it gently to calm me.

"That came out wrong; I'm sorry. But you said 'recovering'—does that mean the doctor feels positive?"

I nod. "She spoke, slightly slurring her words, but they think that may be temporary muscle loss, which may improve. Her speech center probably isn't affected. Or maybe it is, I don't know. I guess I didn't take everything in when they told me. Could you sit down?" I ask him. "I don't like looking up at you."

As he sits next to me I reach my hand out to his face, touch the scrub of his beard, feeling the coarse hair nip my fingers. His chin tips down reflexively to protect his neck.

"It really looks fine," I tell him. "Sara will get used to it." My hand drops to my lap, clasps the other as I begin to cry with fatigue, all the uncertainty catching up with me. "I don't know how long this will be, Michael. I have no idea what's in store."

"It's all right," he croons, and he takes my hands. From eleven years ago, my father's funeral, I remember this gesture, how good he is at being strong.

"All I can think is how quiet the house will be, how empty when I go home at night. I don't want Sara to leave; am I being incredibly selfish?"

"Not incredibly. But Anna, she's frightened. She was badly fright-ened by your mother's collapse. Maybe if I take her to the Cape, she'll be able to calm down." He pauses, thinking, "Or maybe she'll just fret more if she's away from you, I don't know. Maybe . . . ," he begins and then hesitates.

"What?"

"Maybe we could stay up here with you, in your mother's house. I'd be able to see Sara, Sara would still have you, you wouldn't be alone."

"Maybe. I don't know, either," I answer. But I do know, I know him, I know this support. "Okay, yes, for a few days anyway. We'll see how it goes."

"Mommy?"

I look over at Sara. Near her, standing in the corner out of my way is James; he leans against the wall, biting his thumbnail, waiting.

"Michael," I add, standing, "thank you."

"Anna, Anna," James calls, trying to break through to me, but I am in a single-minded daze striding through a maze of hallways to find either a doctor or my mother's room to help me decide, stay or leave. Which?

"Let me help," he says. "Slow down, and let me help."

Earlier, the neurologist approached us in the lounge. He suggested to Michael that we leave; he hoped my mother would rest through the night, uninterrupted, and he urged us to do the same.

"I'd say she'll most likely be fine for the night," he hedged while attempting to reassure.

Michael immediately took Sara back to the house, although I stayed, unable to leave my mother. Before he came to the hospital, James found himself a hotel room. He asks me now to come back with him and rest.

"No. It's okay. I can do it; I should stay." It is like I don't know him. I don't want it to be like this. "People die from strokes, right?" I ask James.

"I guess they can. But you won't know what's going on until you hear from the doctors. Tomorrow. Tonight, you should rest."

"I would like to see either her or the doctor again before I leave, just to be sure."

"Sure of what? The doctor already told you to go home." I feel his hand on my elbow, turning me. "Anna," James says calmly. "Don't you think it's kind of weird that you agreed to let your husband stay here with you and Sara?"

"Weird? The entire day has been weird. Horrific. Besides, Michael was already here, he was taking her anyway. He offered."

"I could have stayed."

"Work," I conclude. "You should get back."

"You don't need to decide for me when I need to get back to work. I want to help you."

"I know. I know you want to help. But it's what we thought of, it was arranged. I just needed to have something arranged. I had to do it. And then I didn't want her to go; I didn't want to be alone."

"You wouldn't have been alone."

"But I wouldn't have had Sara."

"Okay," he relents, holding up his hands. "But come with me tonight and I'll take you to the hospital tomorrow. I'll stay until I know you're settled. You've got to let me help you."

He takes me in his arms, and I'd like nothing better than to feel his warmth, the pressure of his muscle and bone on mine, but I seem to have grown a shell, a rigid exoskeleton that protects against any sensation.

"There's nowhere to eat on Christmas, nothing's open. I have nothing to give you," James apologizes as we enter his hotel room.

"I'm not hungry," I answer as I walk through the small room, drawing the drapes shut. I turn out the light and return to James in the dark. I unbutton his shirt. I am practiced; I do it well.

Without Sara in the next room we should feel uninhibited, but we are quiet as we begin to make love to each other. I feel extraordinarily absent tonight, physically performing, mentally detached. James is patient, though, moving slowly with me, looking, touching, stroking, trying to relax me with his words. Even his manner is different: hesitant, shy, deferential. How I hate myself, my body and my mind, for failing me at this moment, even my voice for neglecting to say, "Please stop. This isn't what I want. Tonight."

When I close my eyes my imagination runs. As we kiss each other, remove clothes, caress each other's skins, even though he's right next to me, I see James in my mind with another woman. It is not me, I cannot see myself in this picture. Instead, this woman looks like Christine, his former girlfriend: long, blond hair hanging straight from a side part, hair that was probably worn up in a sleek French twist when she worked, as she moved with ease from table to table. And I wonder if someday I will face this—that he will move to Boston to work, that a pretty girl will walk into his own restaurant looking for a job.

I try to focus on sensation, make the right sounds at the right times, move in the right ways, but now I see him with a young, pretty wife, who also looks like the Christine of my mind. I see a couple of blond children who are his own, with his own brilliant blue eyes. Not someone else's wife and child. Maybe I can see nine kids, like his own family, and it is noisy and James is laughing at the noise, at his happiness in the company of his family. This is how it will be in the end, I am certain as I lie here, and if I look hard enough I see him in his kitchen cooking for his family. It is not me he cooks for.

I know if I ask he will stop. I know, too, that if I had said no to begin with, he would have lain with me, held me; he would have fallen asleep holding me. Instead I lie back, I part my legs, which in the end is easier than trying to understand what it is I really want.

I am wretched as I make love, full of doubt, unworthy. This imaginary girl will have no history of poor decisions, of a bad marriage, to erase. He will look in her direction and hire her because I am not there. Her past will combine easily with his, and they will walk out into the evening as one whole being. Maybe this girl will not need to be taken care of; they will divide the tasks and take care of each other.

These thoughts, rampant now like wild animals, pull my heart into little pieces. This, tonight, is all I feel.

PART SIX

Hunger

I am five, and my father picks me up from my morning kindergarten.

"We are going to see your mother," he tells me. "She is in the hospital."

I have not seen my mother in a week, and I miss her. It takes a long time to reach the hospital, it seems to me, because we've been stuck behind a bus making frequent stops. But finally we pull into a parking space near the building, which is shaped like a capital Y lying on its side. Standing outside one of the wings Father looks at his watch.

"We're a little early," he says.

As I look around the snow on this gray day, I feel Father tap my shoulder. "It's time," he says, bending at the knees; I follow his raised arm, follow his pointing finger up to the "one-two-three-four-fourth floor," he counts to me. "There she is, Anna, in the window. There's your mother. Wave now, so she can see you."

She wears a light-colored gown, one arm waves, the other is bent at the elbow and cradles her waist. I blow kisses, and Mother pretends to catch them. Once more she waves, and then she is gone.

"I'm sorry you can't go in," Father says. " 'No children,' it's the rule."

"When will she be home?" I whine.

"In a couple of days."

"Father, why is Mother in the hospital?" I ask him. No one has said.

"She needs to rest, she'll be home soon," he repeats, taking my hand.

"Why can't she sleep at home?" I wonder in the car. Father looks only at the road, stretched out before him as we drive away, leaving Mother behind us somewhere but no longer in the window.

Mother's crying. She won't come out of her room today. She came home from the hospital three days ago, and today Father has to go back to work. He tells her she'll be fine, and he leaves after drinking some orange juice. After the door closes behind him, I hear my mother call to him, "I will *not* be fine." But only after he is gone.

No school for me today. I finish the cereal Father poured before he left, then I play in my room. I take out all my dolls and animals and line them alongside my bed. I speak to them. Their grunts and growls and baby lisps fill my room as they talk back to me and keep me company. I do not want it to be quiet so I keep them talking.

I tell them all, "I do not like my mother. She is being naughty. I will not talk to her today." But I cannot keep my promise. I climb the stairs and stand by her bedroom door.

"Mommy," I call, my lips pressed up to the keyhole.

"What is it, Anna? Can't you go play?"

"I'm lonely." No answer. "I'm hungry," I try. But again I do not get a response.

"Please go play, Anna. I am not well. Be a good girl and go away."

I am a good girl.

I go away.

 I have showered and dressed and now I kneel on the floor whispering to James, who is sleeping curled on the hotel's firm mattress. "I can't stay . . . ," I breathe into his ear.

He looks at me through sleepy eyes, startled by my voice and temporarily disoriented. Like an apparition, I have spoken, waking him from a deep sleep. "Give me a minute," he says, struggling to wake up from his fugue.

"It's okay. Go back to sleep. I'll get a cab, but I've got to go." As I began dropping off to sleep, I fell into memories of hospitals and Mother, and right now I need to get out of here and find Sara. Right now I can't believe I have left her behind. If I am this frightened by old memories, she must be terrified by the realities of the day. I rub my temples as if I can erase the picture of a six-year-old's shocked face looking over her fallen grandmother. And as I kneel here, I remind myself, I have no idea whether my mother is dead or alive.

"You don't need a cab. There's the truck. Let me get dressed and I'll drive you," he says as I move to wait by the door. I watch one leg and the next as James steps into his jeans, I watch in agony the slow deliberateness with which he laces his boots. When he pats his pockets futilely for the car keys I bang my fist on the door in frustration. James looks up at me before pulling on his sweater.

"I have no idea who you are," he says. Spotting the keys on the dresser, he slides them into his fist and passes me at the door. "Let's go."

He hasn't seen what I've seen, he doesn't know what I've heard or felt, the hospital window high above my head, the arm crossed protectively over a waist, closed doors, disembodied tears, a wrenched wail, a hand on my shoulder. And I do not tell him, for tonight I've put my fear, as solid as an object, in the way, stopping all forward motion.

"It's my new life sentence, Anna," my mother slowly speaks to me after I've pulled up a chair to her bedside. I don't say, "You told me that yesterday. Tell me instead what you mean." Rather than question, I take her limp left hand in mine. Before leaving us alone, the nurse hovers in the doorway to tell me that Mother slept well over night.

"Used to think life was penance. But now I think . . . more like prison." It takes her a long time to get these words out; she forms each one slowly and carefully as if I am a lip-reader and she must enunciate. Or like the slow-motion speech of a nightmare.

"Mother, please don't talk," I say, holding her hand.

"Must talk," she insists. "Must get well."

"Look, I'll be with you for a while; I'll be here every day. So why don't you talk a little at a time, but only after you've rested. All I've got is time for you, Mother."

"Anna," she speaks, and I watch a single tear travel down her cheek, a small drop contained only by surface tension.

"You haven't touched me today," I observe. "I miss you."

"After last night I wasn't sure you wanted me to," James answers truthfully. "You look alike, you and your husband. All that black hair."

James arrived minutes ago as Michael gave me a brief supportive hug before taking Sara to the cafeteria for some juice. Perhaps our hair mingled as we held each other and James looked on.

"His isn't really black," I correct, "just dark brown."

"Are you glad to see him?"

"It's nothing, James."

"It may be a few things, but nothing isn't one of them. And you haven't answered my question."

"Michael? I'm glad he's here with Sara through this madness."

"That's not what I asked."

"But that's exactly why I'm glad to see him. And I did want you to," I add. "Touch me, I mean. Of course I do. Why would you think I didn't?"

"Because," he answers, "I can feel you pulling away from me."

"Wait a minute—" I begin to protest the raising of our voices in the busy hospital waiting room with a television blaring and people milling about, arguing as if it is only the two of us, alone.

But he holds up his hand. "No, you wait a minute. I've tried to be cool about all this contact with him lately, and maybe the tension is just catching up with me. Maybe I'm out of line, I don't know. But you were a million miles away in bed last night. You ran away, and you keep pushing past me when I try to help. I meant what I said: I don't recognize you. We talk, Anna, we work together, we share everything, but lately you are a stranger. What's going on?"

"Nothing. Nothing's going on. My mother's ill, and I feel like I should handle this myself, that's all. I can't keep relying on men like you and Michael to make things nice for me."

"Is that what you think I'm doing? Trying to make things nice for you?" James frowns.

"Don't look at me like that," I tell him. "Explain to me when I've ever taken care of myself."

"I'm sorry that you think all I've been doing is taking care of you. Look," he says, forcing me to meet his eyes, "I'm not Michael, Anna."

"No, you're not Michael. And this isn't about him. Or you, even. It's about my mother, taking care of my mother."

"Then why is he here, this man you've been divorcing for nearly a year, if you're so determined to do this on your own? Why is he here, and why are you all of a sudden . . . playing house with him?"

"That is not fair. I told you why he's here. Besides, I want to do this. I can take care of my mother. I can handle this."

"I've watched you do it for nearly a year; I know you can. You don't have to prove to me that you don't need anyone."

"Please." I step forward, grasp his upper arms. "Understand me."

"God, Anna, I understand you. I can practically smell what's happening. I can smell your fear. Don't do this because you're scared."

"Scared?"

"Of not being a good girl. Christ, you aren't six anymore! You don't have to do what everyone expects of you."

"And *you* have no expectations? Come off it. You're standing right in front of me, telling me what you expect me to do."

"That isn't the same thing, and you know it. Of course I have expectations, but I only expect you to be yourself, Anna. I love you. Did you hear me?" he asks when I make no response. "I said I love you. Don't ignore that."

"I heard you. I have to know you heard me, too."

"All right, fine," he gives in. I watch his shoulders drop; as the anger leaves his body, he only looks fatigued, resigned. "I'll go back to New Hampshire today; since you don't need me here, I'll get back to work. What d'you think, Anna? What should I tell Ben?" he asks as he takes his jacket from the back of a chair and slips into it.

"Tell him I'll call him as soon as I can. As soon as I know how my mother is and what I have to do for her."

"I'd like you to come back, I think you know that."

I nod my head. "I know."

"I can recognize scared, 'cause maybe I'm scared, too. You and he have a lot of years behind you. You have a kid. Maybe I can even recognize the road you're heading down, and it scares me," he says, and he stops at the door just as Michael and Sara are returning. "Just call me if there's anything—anything—you need. I can be here within a few hours, you know that." As I nod my head once again, I imagine him walking back then touching his lips to mine gingerly, as if I am the patient. However tender, brief, fleeting the brush of our lips, this kiss would speak to me of longing and would leave me breathless. But he is too far away and instead I watch him leave, stopping only to give Sara a hug. Part of me goes with him.

The doctor tells me, "Mrs. Rossi is really making remarkable progress. She's lucky of course that it was only a mild stroke. Her speech center is unaffected, it's the nerve damage that bothers her speech, her mouth. With physical and occupational therapies it may be she won't have any lingering effects. I can't say for certain now, but judging by past patients with similar episodes, I'd say it's likely. Just keep her talking." He grins at me like a cocky young boy.

"We talk whenever she wants."

"Good. You can help her with the light exercise the physical therapist has suggested. And when you take her home, keep her eating. She's a little on the thin side, and we don't want any broken bones."

"She says she's not hungry, but I'll try," I tell him.

"It may be she's self-conscious about eating in front of you. Chewing, you know, like speech, is difficult. But see if you can't get her over that. Other than what we've discussed, soon she can start being up and around more, getting ready to leave the hospital for a rehab center, trying to get back to full mobility."

"Doctor," I begin carefully, for there is one thing I want to ask without sounding uncaring, "I'd like to know what I can expect. I mean, as far as my mother being able to take care of herself. You see, right now I live in New Hampshire. I can't stay away from work or caring for my daughter indefinitely, yet I need to know if she needs someone long term."

"The future," he muses, sitting back in his chair.

"Yes."

"One possibility is that she makes a good recovery, takes her medication, and sees me regularly for monitoring. She may be able to live on her own quite successfully.

"But there's always the possibility of more episodes, maybe not so small next time." He leans forward, "Is it just the two of you? She has no other family?" I shake my head. "She could try assisted-care living," he suggests. "A kind of apartment complex with some home help and medical facilities nearby. She'd still feel independent, but secure."

"She could live with me, too," I think aloud, "or at least closer. I could even stay."

"Of course," he agrees.

Mother rests on in the hospital, nearing one week, and I occupy her house. Me, Michael, Sara. Michael suspends his own house search and watches over our daughter full-time. During the day after he drops me at the hospital, he takes Sara to the aquarium or to the Children's Museum, to the library or on shopping trips. I give them lists of things I think of, things I believe I need, like ingredients for soup. I prepare and freeze lots of soup to feed my mother, thinking, perhaps, that good soup will course through her body, fatten her up, nourish her, make her better.

Over the past few days I have collected many kinds of bones: ham hocks, beef shanks, a chicken carcass left over from dinner. I even send Michael out to hunt down veal bones, which were hard to find and required a trip to an out-of-town butcher. In our evenings together, Michael and Sara watch as I break the poultry bones in half exposing the marrow, then cover them with water and let it all simmer. The beef, the ham, the veal, all yield up a gelatinous soup when simmered. But then I wonder if perhaps the cholesterol in marrow is counterproductive to the Coumadin or harmful to a stroke patient, so I end up freezing my beautiful stocks.

Sara loves the excursions, to her they are like treasure hunts, and she is so proud to return to me after successfully finding what I need. Michael and I listen; he sits at the table while I stand over a stockpot, stirring and smiling at her as she babbles on about standing in line at the butcher shop, the look on the butcher's face as a small girl demands in an imperious tone, "Best veal bones, please," when Michael lets her place the order.

I feel more at ease with Michael; after tucking Sara in, we sit awhile longer and he speaks to me with an animation I haven't heard in his voice for a long time. He tells me more details of their days, we laugh together over the many things Sara has told him, her funny observations. We sit at the large dining table; he pours me wine, brews tea for himself, and we talk with a bowl of polished fruits between us. At the end of the day it is easy, as I sip my wine and talk with Michael, to ignore that I have a mother in a hospital up the road, that soon there will be decisions to be made.

Cooped up at the hospital all day and then again at home in the evenings, a nostalgia sometimes overwhelms me, a longing for Chicago in winter. Maybe Michael's presence reminds me of the city, how at this time of the year I could be walking along busy sidewalks, pushing through excited crowds at after-Christmas sales, taking in the last few nights of twinkle lights on the branchy bare trees on Michigan Avenue. Since our house sold quickly, I have no more connection, no place to live there. No more job, which I don't miss. I tell myself it is my friends and images like a night full of glittering artificial lights in place of stars that I truly miss. In the quiet of my mother's house, I call Colette. I miss her now as I haven't in months, not since I first moved to New Hampshire and had to work at settling in.

She is full of news. They have replaced me at the magazine, she tells me, with someone she can't stand. "Do you mind?" she asks.

"That they've replaced me or that you can't stand her?" I tease.

"No, no, of course not. I wouldn't go back to work there, anyway." And I tell her about the stroke, my mother's prognosis, that I live day to day until I know what arrangements to make for her.

"Did you have to quit your job?" she asks.

"No. Not yet. Maybe I won't have to, but when I think of the future I can't see what else I can do but be closer to my mother."

"Surely you're not considering staying on with her?"

"It's one thing I have to consider, if she's impaired."

"I thought your mother made you nuts."

"She does, she did. She can't talk well enough now to drive me crazy. Anyway, my mental health seems secondary right now," I conclude. "Enough about me. I called to forget about myself. Tell me everything," I urge. For the moment, I escape.

Colette tells me Tom has moved in, that he speaks of marriage. She tells me in a voice of barely contained enthusiasm, "I never thought, after my ugly divorce, that I'd want to remarry, you know?"

She says there was an ice storm not long ago that blew in freezing rain that covered trees and power lines in a hoary, slow-melting frost. "Tom and I were trapped in my place, no phone, no electricity, for three days. When I looked out the windows the trees reminded me of Merlin, with these long white frosty beards and white robes hanging down from scrawny limbs. It was beautiful, magical, like a fantasy forest, and imagine! In the city! We even cooked over the fire in the fireplace!" she exclaims. "Canned soup in a pot, like camping." She giggles, and I laugh with her.

"I should have FedExed you the tons of soup I have in my mother's freezer. Homemade. Forget it," I laugh when she asks why I have a ton of homemade soup in the freezer. "You know me: When in doubt, cook. So all is well between you?" I ask, changing the subject.

"Let me put it this way, when everything thawed out, he didn't leave. And I wanted him to stay. It's nice, Anna. We still sneak off at work, we'll hear our names being called while we're in a corner necking, but we ignore everything. It's just the two of us. And then he comes home with me. I tell you, it's very nice."

"I know, I can imagine it's very nice," I agree, but in my heart I feel unsure. Hearing the joy in her voice, I want only to be happy along with her, my friend. Instead, I find myself wondering if she knows true happiness hiding out from the world while trapped alone with Tom. Or is it an illusion, this otherwordly haven they have made? Part of me feels compelled to send a warning: The world will intrude, will come crashing in in the form of an illness or an ex-husband, an earthquake or some other natural disaster. Something. While talking to her I realize that my own impossible situation, my confusion, impairs me as a friend, as a human. And I know I must get off the line. "I'm so happy for you, really. Will you give Tom my love?"

"Sure I will. But what about you, dearest? You haven't said a word."

"It's so crazy here, Colette, and I thought of you, how good it is to talk to you. I wanted a friendly voice."

"What about your chef's friendly voice?"

"James? He's back in New Hampshire, back at work."

"And you're all alone? In between that house and the hospital? Where's Sara?"

For a moment I consider telling her about my strange arrangement with Michael and Sara, playing house, as James put it, but I cannot face the surprise or disapproval—though it's not Colette's inevitable and biting judgment I fear. It's my own I dread, once the reality is put into words. After all, I tell myself, it is nothing, this arrangement, nothing but convenience, and no explanation could ever adequately capture the subtleties of our pact, not for my ears anyway.

But without waiting for answers, Colette asks, "Will you be okay?"

"I'll be okay. Talking to you has helped, as always."

As I wrap up this call, I take the phone to the couch, and I lie down, close my eyes and think of all the people I've left behind, like Colette now taking a big risk and sounding so happy for it, while all of my life has been a forward motion or one extended departure. "I need to be up early tomorrow. I need to hang up." Under my eyelids I feel the needling tears welling.

"I'll let you go," Colette says. "Good night, Anna."

"Please don't forget to hug Tom for me. And Colette? I miss you."

Food does not tempt my mother, but I am not surprised; it never has. It is still difficult for her to eat, her facial muscles are uncooperative. There are some beautiful soft foods, though, and when I lie in bed at night waiting for morning and another day at the hospital I list many of them in my mind. Blancmange, pale and wiggly, a sick person's pudding, like in *Little Women*. There is its eggy cousin, the floating island, poached egg-white meringues floating in a pool of pale yellow custard. Or just baked custard, a little nutmeg sprinkled on top. Maybe mashed potatoes alone, like I ate while I was pregnant, or even a shepherd's pie, the ground meat piped with mashed potato. I could send Michael out to find good meat—lean young lamb—I could grind it at home, which no one ever does anymore. I could take out the old aluminum meat grinder, heavy and dense, clamp it to the counter, and grind away. Each night I list these and more as I drift off to sleep. And of course there's soup.

I stand at the kitchen counter, chopping a cheap but flavorful cut of beef into tiny cubes, preparing to let it stew slowly in its own juices, rendering a kind of beef broth that, later in the day, I hope to serve to my mother in a mug through a straw. Old cookbooks call this beef tea. The color of a wine called Sangre de Toro and not unlike bull's blood, it will build her strength; it is healthy food, sustaining. The beef is lean and I am only rendering up its juice.

When I bring the beef tea in to my mother at the hospital, she is sitting up in bed.

"You look well today," I tell her.

"I feel better," she replies.

"You know the physical therapist will be here later?"

She nods yes, motioning with her head to a chair at the side of the bed for me to sit. So I do.

"And Sara would like to visit," I say.

My mother asks, "Do you think Sara will be f-f-f . . . ," she struggles to form a word.

"Frightened?" I finish for her.

She nods. "Of me?" she asks.

"No, not now, I don't think. She was frightened at first. She'd had a bad shock. But she's not scared of you. It's the suddenness, I think, that scares young children.

"Mother," I continue, "something's been on my mind since you came to the hospital. I remembered being here, visiting you, when I was young. Father picking me up at kindergarten. Were you in the hospital then? Can you remember?"

I notice her eyes leave me, move to settle on the wall or closet beyond my shoulder.

"Don't you want to talk now?" I ask.

"I can't talk fast." She shows me a twisted mouth, the left corner droopy, as proof.

"Take your time. I can wait. Here's what I remember. It was a gray day, like this," I point to her window and the pewter sky beyond, dull with low clouds. "I stood outside, looked up when Father pointed, and there you were, waving."

"I wasn't always a good mother," she says, not answering my question. "I tried."

"Were you sick? I was so young, that's a long time ago now, and I didn't understand. Father didn't explain."

"Your father."

"He went to work after you came home from the hospital. You stayed in your room, I remember that. Were you still not well?"

"Why do you . . . want to know?"

"The memory still bothers me. Because I was alone, I remember being left alone. And that I didn't like it."

"He left me alone. He died."

"I know; I know you must miss him," I tell her. "But I'm here."

"I'm tired now," she says, ignoring my attempt to comfort her.

"Are you hungry? I brought some broth." I hold out the thermal mug and urge the soup on her, holding the straw up to her lips in my hands. I help her with the straw and wipe her chin when soup dribbles from her clumsy lips. When she's had enough she turns her head. I raise the napkin to clean her mouth, but she snaps, "I can do it." I have overstepped trying to help, so I back off, realizing how little I understand.

After a late dinner Michael and I drink coffee. Sara is in bed, exhausted after an afternoon of learning to ice-skate. She and Michael discovered an old pair of my double runners in the basement. The skates fit well enough, and he took her to a flooded and frozen-over field. While they described the afternoon to me over dinner I perceived Michael as a kind of tour guide or events planner, amusing Sara, keeping her every second busy and focused, which made me cross. I am in a black mood after this afternoon's circular and unsatisfying conversation with my mother, and only one step away from becoming cutting and sarcastic. After packing Sara off to bed with uncharacteristic swiftness, I reclaim my seat at the dining table, and Michael observes me over his coffee cup.

"What about you?" he asks after I drain my coffee.

"What about me?" I snap back.

"How was your day?"

The way he asks this question reminds me of too many dinners we've shared in the past; in confusion I don't know whether to take comfort or weep.

"Awful," I answer. "And I'm in a pissy mood."

"It's got to be frustrating for you. Waiting for your mother to improve. It's catching up with you," he pronounces.

"She's improving; it's not that."

"What is it, then?"

"You'll think I'm silly, but when she was first admitted to the hospital, I remembered something. I visited my mother here years ago. We had to stand below her window and wave. But I don't remember why she was in the hospital. Why would she have been there?" I ask him.

"I don't know."

"Why won't she answer my question? How awful can it be? I mean, it's not like it would surprise me that she, say, had a nervous breakdown. Or even that she was admitted to a psych ward!" I blurt.

"I think that's the most ungenerous thing I've ever heard you say," Michael admonishes. "And why does it even matter? It's your mother's business, not yours, and if she doesn't want to talk, you should let it go."

"Let it go?"

"Get over it. Say you get her to talk," he leans in over the table. "Then what? Where does talking get you? You'll never be satisfied, and you'll have stirred up things your mother never wanted to mention in the first place."

"A person should be able to talk to her mother," I insist.

"A person, maybe, but maybe not you. Face it: You've got the relationship you've got. What's the sense of pushing for change? It'll make you crazy that you can't change her."

"How come I feel it will make me crazy if I don't at least try?"

We face off across the table, staring over coffee cups, napkins, and red apples striated with the palest of green. I give in first and look away to the one patch of wallpaper that had been hung upside down years ago and never corrected. The repeating stripes nearly hid the mistake unless you looked and looked, as I had with so many years of practice looking at this same wall during conversations with my father. Something about the direction of the climbing vine in the center of the stripes nagged at the eye.

"You know I'm right," Michael concludes, staring at me. But my eyes are elsewhere.

We shuffle sleeping quarters a few days before Mother comes home, just to be prepared. Michael takes the couch, gladly giving up the guest bed; I move to the guest room in anticipation of her return. She's been in the hospital ten days, and during the last few visits I heed Michael's advice. I remain quiet, unquestioning, I try to appear nonchalant, no longer interested in asking any more questions, no longer even acknowledging there are questions to be asked. Time no longer has any meaning; the rise and set of the sun are only different casts of shadow. Michael and I have not discussed the nearing end to school vacation. Soon Sara's teacher will expect Sara back at her desk, Michael will need to begin his new job, yet incomprehensibly we have made no plans. Ben does not phone, nor does James. We three in our borrowed home might be castaways or survivalists: insular and self-sufficient. I wonder if they think we prefer it this way. I wonder if we do.

Today, as Mother sits up in bed with a pair of fat knitting needles moving slowly up and down in her hands, I sit with her, marking her progress. Knitting is one of the recommended therapies, something to do on her own between the physical therapist's visits. Mother throws herself into her rehabilitation with single-minded purpose. She makes a poor patient, she wants little assistance. Submitting to help with dressing and bathing has been humiliating for one so modest, and I believe she works in a fury mostly to regain mastery of these two chores.

She does not move swiftly in her task, and the needles click like a clock not quite keeping time. I look up from my book, look up at my mother's face now less ravaged than after her collapse. She can wrinkle her forehead over the chore of knitting. She's chosen a scarf for Sara, a simple straight stitch, knit two, purl two, which will be quite a length if she keeps at the work. Pink, a baby pink I never would have chosen even in Sara's infancy. The pink that announces "baby girl," a pink that will clash with her orange fleece jacket and her olive complexion.

I look up from my book and continue looking up from my book, for the words on the page will no longer string together in a meaningful way for me. I have been exemplary, I have listened to Michael and probed no further because, as he asserts, I am certain to be frustrated. And I continue to acquiesce until I hear these ticking needles, like the hands of a stopwatch counting time just for me.

"Mother," I say.

She looks up from the fluffy cloud of pink in her hands, and she stops knitting but the wrinkle remains.

"I need to know why you were in the hospital."

It seems an eternity before her brow smooths and before she acknowledges my question. Then with her sigh of impatience, the younger mother I remember is back, the one who sighed with every one of my questions.

"I lost a baby," she tells me. Her speech is much better now, still slow, but clearer as the nerves and muscles start to cooperate. "It wasn't the first time. So I had surgery."

"Surgery?" I ask.

"No more babies," she states. She looks at her hands and the knitting in her hands. Her eyes, cast down, search for dropped stitches.

"I am so sorry," I whisper.

"No," my mother says forcefully. She looks at me, her daughter. "I was . . . glad."

At home that evening I take a bottle of wine and a glass to the dining room. I lay some food out for myself in case I feel hungry; I even begin to slice some bread and watch as the crisp crust shatters. But I sit for a long time without eating, without turning on lights, until it gets so dark I cannot see anything in front of me. Only the street out the window illuminated by street lamps. And sleet falling around the large lightbulb, more snow.

Pouring one glass and then a second, I move to the living room. I do not know where Michael and Sara are as it begins to get so dark and snowy outside. During the second glass of wine I decide it must be my last. My eyes feel heavy, tired, but instead of clouding over or closing in sleep they see, over and over again, my mother, me, the private hospital room. Sara. I see Sara as if for the first time, as if I am looking at her for the first time in my own hospital room.

When I went to the toilet for the first few weeks of my pregnancy, I expected, and often hoped, to see blood. It is a mistake, I remember telling myself, this pregnancy, perhaps a false, hysterical one. Maybe my body is reacting to the base fear that oozes from my pores just thinking about being pregnant, stopping itself up in reaction, forbidding flows. Surely if there is a baby inside it swims with damaged neurons, perhaps an imperfect heart or something that will turn into a cleft palate. Over and over I told myself these things until I expected my body would reject this growth, this nonviable embryonic human. I expected to sit and expel my own waste only to find blood and tissue in the bowl with urine, a quick flush swirling it all to the sewers. I thought of aborting, quickly, before Michael knew or suspected, having everything vacuumed out. And then, cleaned up, I could come home. Start over. Childless.

I didn't think I wanted a child. I did not know if I wanted a child I anticipated would be hurt by all the alcohol I had recently consumed. I even wondered whether I could care for a child—if I could love, hug, protect, reassure, build confidence. If, even, I would be able to remember it. My worst fear, the one I dreamt about during those first few weeks, was that I would leave the baby behind somewhere, forgetting him until I got home. Or maybe I would get up, go to work, and leave the baby behind in his crib, to wet and soil himself, to cry until he turned an angry boiled purple. People had done it, abandoned their young. Would I?

Michael would look at me accusingly, his eyes would shame me.

Or he'd look at me with disinterest when I told him, and that would be worst of all, his back as he left for work expressing his demeanor: cool, detached. I never wanted a child anyway, his back would say.

So that when I looked at her for the first time and she was perfect, when she presented herself, plump and rosy, I was amazed. Amazed and grateful.

Tonight, though, I mostly see my mother and my own self. Our faces are a little fuzzy, even mixed up—hers on my body, mine on hers. Maybe it's the wine. Or maybe we've changed places, my mother and I, with no discernible difference.

"Glad?" I asked earlier, needing her to repeat herself, not quite comprehending her response.

She spoke to me clearly as she sat there, she answered me succinctly in short sentences. "There were two, before you. Then one after. I thought I would . . . lose you too. I lived with that. It was awful, to fail. So no more. And I was glad."

"Three miscarriages?" As my words tumbled out I heard the shock in my voice, harsh and almost accusatory. But of whom, or why, I hardly knew.

"The doctor said to stop. Trying. I agreed," she continued. " 'Take it out,' I told him the last time."

"Take it out? Your uterus?"

"Your father wanted children. Lots. We were always . . . trying." As she spoke I remembered a child's nightmare and after, in a search for comfort, the looks on my parents' faces as I walked into their bedroom. The look of sex, the need for privacy.

"So you had a hysterectomy? In this hospital? That's what you wouldn't tell me?"

"No point. I put it behind. Your father, though. He was . . . ," she paused to search for a word.

"Sad? Disappointed?" I asked, helping her.

"Angry, I think. At me. My choice. No more chances." Here the dispassionate report yielded to the first spark of anger and frustration. Her hand gripped the knitting until the knuckles turned white. "After you I asked him, 'Aren't you glad about Anna?' But he had to try. Make me try."

"You cried. He left for work and you cried."

"He made me take care of you. I couldn't. You reminded me—"

"I reminded you. I reminded you of *what?*" Again my voice rose, demanding; I sounded shrill, the words ringing in my own ears. I was shocked at how much had gone unsaid in our lives. I softened my tone. "Of what?" I asked again.

"Of blood. All the bleeding, each time. I never really wanted children, after."

"But then you had me."

"With you I was always scared. Even after you came. Didn't really know what to do with you." Then my mother shook her head, her mouth pursed as if with the taste of bitter foods. She put her hand over her mouth so I wouldn't see. Or maybe only to tell me that she was finished.

I sit now, alone in the dark, with my fantasy that my mother's illness would somehow be a bridge between us.

I could have told her then about Sara's first picture, how my eyes dropped to the black-and-white image of the sonogram to see a grainy but unmistakably human form. Michael was there with me, I remember the squeeze I gave his hand, which nearly crushed the metacarpals and turned my knuckles white. He must have known that squeeze wasn't from my discomfort, lying there as I was with a bursting bladder and cold under the tech's gel; it was from pure terror. Of what we'd see as the image appeared on the screen. Did we imagine two heads? Or none at all? Perhaps no brain, a deformed spinal column, stumps for arms and legs? Who knew she'd be perfect?

I could have told her this was on my mind every day and night for my entire pregnancy. How she was conceived, a fact of my life, an eternal shame: that she should come to us through some drunken fumblings, a stuporous lack of will, a totally loveless, numbed, drunken fuck.

For the first time I could have shared how, when I met Michael, I was hungry, ravenous even, for the closeness of our bodies. How he'd never met anyone like me, he said; he said that the way I would take off all my clothes and appear so comfortable showing myself to him was a revelation.

I could have told her that I was surprised Sara didn't grow out of that heat, that nothing did, although those were times that seemed so fertile. That in one sterile night, in carelessness, she should be conceived. That she was a constant reminder of the mistake. That Michael chose to stay away from home, to stay away from Sara. And me.

That we really never recovered from Sara, did we?

Because every time he held me, I knew what he saw and felt; he knew why those spaces between my ribs were there, the hollows where my femur joined my pelvis, the right angles that masqueraded as my elbows. At those moments there was always so much to say, always the instant, the empty air in which to talk, and yet it was so hard for us to get the words out. It was as if everything that went unsaid between us ate me from the inside. And Michael? The unspoken words stayed with him like an undigested meal, until he had no room left for anything else.

But I didn't say any of this.

Instead I sit now, alone in the dark, until Michael walks in with Sara hanging limply in his arms. With the harsh light of the hallway on her face, her hands, she looks dead. From my distance I cannot see the rise and fall of her chest. For an instant I am sure she is dead, that he is carrying her to me dead, like an offering to lay at my feet. Until Michael stamps the snow off his feet and Sara makes a small whimper and shifts a bit in his arms.

"Movies," he says. "I took her to McDonald's and a movie. She fell asleep in the car," he explains.

"Tuck her in," I tell him. "I'm going to bed."

That night I have a dream about my father. In my dream he tells me, "Your mother never wanted you, but I did." We are fishing; he stands next to me at the river's edge catching fish he will never eat. "You heard her," he says, " 'You forced me,' she said. What kind of mother feels forced, Anna? But that's all right because I love you."

In my dream I am a child having a bad dream, and no one answers me when I call in my repetitious drone, "Mom, Mommy, Mother." So I slip out of bed to my parents' room. Their door is closed securely, and I have to turn the knob with two hands to open the door into darkness. As I scan for my mother's bed, I am blind. "Mother," I whisper. "Mother, I'm having a bad dream." I kneel beside her bed, feel for her shoulder to wake her because she does not answer. But her bed is empty, and the room holds the unnatural, uneasy stillness that follows in the wake of halted motion and muffled whispers.

"Anna, over here." My father breaks the silence with his hissing, throaty whisper, and I follow his voice. At his bed I stop. I can see, like a cat now, the outline of my mother lying with her back to my father's chest in the twin bed.

"Did you have a bad dream, too?" I ask her because she is being held the way I would like to be held.

Father shifts under the covers, he pulls Mother in closer. "What is it?" he asks. His face is ashy, and his voice comes out in shallow bursts of breath.

"My dream," I whine.

"Go back to bed," says my mother almost lovingly. Her eyes tell me a secret. The secret is no one can come lie with me now. Father shifts again, and Mother's gentle lips iron out, a longer thinner line of lips stretched over teeth, like tried patience, like pain.

"Get to bed," she tells me, more firmly this time. "You'll be fine."

"And close the door," my father adds.

Then my father is in the sickbed, not my mother, and he cannot speak as I stand over him, yelling. Instead he cowers.

"How do you love me?" I demand of him. "All I can remember is your hand on my shoulder, keeping me on my knees. What bad thing could I have done at six or seven. Or at sixteen and seventeen? My body? Boys? I was just a kid. Was everything I felt or did wrong?" With a face full of fear, he presses a buzzer at his bedside, and my mother appears to get into bed with him.

"Leave your father alone. He is a good man," she tells me, looking at me with a victorious look in her eyes. "Go away," she says as he takes her from behind. "Leave us alone," she speaks through teeth clenched in pain.

Next I follow my father through city streets. He has Sara by the hand, and they stop to wait for a bus. I can't get to the bus stop fast enough, and their bus pulls up to the curb while I struggle on down the street. When I look up I see their faces in the wide back window. With her eyes Sara follows my father's outstretched arm, his pointing finger. The bus pulls out into traffic beyond my reach. I call out, "No!"

I touch my cheek, thinking I am awake because there are real tears on my face, wetting my pillow.

Am I awake? There is movement in my room, I hear a rustle. Lying on my back I prove to myself I am in fact asleep; I can feel my eyelids clamped shut. But I can also reason with myself, I can converse with myself in my head. So could it still be a dream, or am I awake?

The movement creates a draft, a breeze of air wafting above my bed. I am only dreaming the noise and breeze, it must be. But I hear a voice I have not heard in years. "Anna," he speaks, firm, clipped, spoken low. My eyes are closed, I am sure of it, but I see nonetheless a man, a form in underclothes going from closet to dresser, putting away clothes, preparing for bed. He speaks to me in my dead father's voice, I hear him as if he were in the room. Which of course he is not, because I am asleep.

Am I?

I hear the voice prattling on, but I cannot make out the words no matter how hard I strain to hear. He walks to my bed, still talking. I listen closely; maybe there is wisdom in the words, the key, the answers, but I do not understand. Please speak up, I think, until I remember I am asleep.

He lifts a corner of the covers. "You are not real," I say. He gets into bed. Remember this is a dream. When I feel the pressure of a sinking mattress, I make sure I keep my eyes shut and will the dream away.

In the morning I move slowly from heavy sleep to wakefulness. As I turn to face the window where the sun beats in as it reflects off the snow, I brush with my shoulder a warm body next to mine. James, I think, and a smile of satisfaction creeps over my lips. He whispers, "You had a nightmare."

"Mm-hmm," I agree, my eyes closed as I prolong the last moments of sleep. "I did. It was awful." The sun through the shades is orange. I think as I wake of blinding snow, needing sunglasses, a clear blue sky after the weighty skies of snow. It must be cold outside, it always is when the sun comes up immediately after a snow, but it is warm in here. Fingers graze my side, tentative touches flutter on my skin, hesitantly. Usually James grabs my hip, pulls me to him; we laugh when he grabs; his hand is so firm and assured of me, my response. He knows I will burrow into him, press my back and bottom into his flat, warm belly. These fingers question, "Is this all right? And this? And what about this?" They lightly touch the small of my back, my waist, the curve of my buttocks. I wait for the firm hold, sliding me in closer, accepting me. I wait to recognize his warm smells: the soap, the sleep, the garlic that never seems to wash away. I like nothing better than opening my eyes surrounded by muscle molded to mine and comforting smells. But I recognize none.

"Are you okay this morning?" he asks.

I open my eyes and look over at Michael.

"You had a nightmare. At first I thought it was Sara when I heard the cries. I couldn't wake you when I got in, so I stayed. I slept. You were sleeping. We were just sleeping."

"Michael . . ."

"What is it? I told you nothing happened."

"I was scared. I had a terrible dream, and then there you were. You weren't supposed to be there. At the very least it was disorienting."

"Is this about your boyfriend?" He spits the word at me, making it sound absurd, even obscene, for someone my age.

We sit at the dining room table with breakfast coffee and the remnants of my last night's solitary attempt at a meal littering the table: a cut loaf of bread, shards of crust crumbs, a piece of cheese with dried, waxy edges. My wine glass, stained grape at the bottom of the bowl. The bottle I set aside, left uncorked. Neither of us is hungry this morning. The fruit in the bowl looks tired. Put out to encourage snacking, it has, instead, gone untouched. The nut bowl with its nutcracker has been here since Christmas Eve. The bowl of lemons I put out for a shock of color holds a few rinds brushed on their undersides with the gray-white bloom of mold. I'll need to throw everything away.

"James has nothing to do with this. This is you and me, Michael," I say, looking over the mess on the table.

"James. And you're right; he left anyway. I'm here and he left. That should tell you something."

"I asked him to leave."

"And I wanted to stay."

"I know we've been getting along, sometimes even feeling comfortable, but for you to come in my room last night . . . We are no longer married, not in any real sense, Michael, and I don't know what you were thinking." I try to rein in my temper. "This is bound to be awkward, seeing each other for the first time in almost a year, but—"

"That's not quite accurate," he cuts in.

"What isn't?"

"It's not the first time in a long time. I saw you," he says, "only a couple of weeks ago. I drove up here to bring Sara her Christmas presents. On a whim."

"But we'd decided—"

"I know what we decided, but you and I had been talking, and I thought of the idea. Spur-of-the-moment. Once I'd talked to you after Thanksgiving, once we made the arrangements, I found I didn't want to wait." Michael brushes some crumbs into a pile and sweeps them into his cupped hand.

"But you never came."

"But I did," he says, walking through to the kitchen where he tosses the crumbs into the sink. He stays in the doorway. "On a Monday. I drove by your apartment building, but it was kind of late. I thought, 'Tomorrow's a school day,' and I guess I lost my nerve. I went to Ben's, drove to the restaurant, and parked. I don't know what possessed me, I didn't even know if you'd be there."

"We're closed on Mondays."

"Not this Monday. There were plenty of people, people coming and going, but I waited in the car because all of a sudden I didn't know what I'd say to you if I went inside."

"Our holiday party, it must have been that Monday." I attempt a sip of coffee, for something to do as I wait, recognizing Michael's habit of building a story and the way he picks just the right facts to make his case. The coffee is warm, no longer hot, and easy to swallow. "You were just going to show up?" I ask after setting the cup down. It squeals into its groove in the saucer, making me grimace.

"Just show up. I was . . . encouraged by our phone call. It was so surprisingly civil. I liked the sound of your voice. I missed Sara. So I made the drive." Pulling out his chair, Michael sits again. He leans forward over the table and the seat groans with the shift of his weight. He asks me, "Ever had an image trapped in your mind, Anna, so deep that you can't shake it, can't will it away? Maybe you do, from last night, like after a bad dream when you can't fall asleep without getting right back into the scary part?"

I nod my head.

"Good, then you'll know what I mean. Anyway, here's what I see," he continues. His eyes crackle with the promise of a gripping narrative, and I cannot look away. "I see a woman stepping out into a restaurant parking lot. And there's a guy with her, draped on her like a piece of clothing. They are so close, walking together, that not even a breeze could pass between them."

I sit up straighter, caught up in the beginning of his story, seeing two people as he sets the scene with his rapid words. "James," I say aloud.

"Like him, right." Although his eyes are piercing, Michael's voice is low, modulated, not threatening, although by now I know what is coming. My brain pulls up a memory of sound, of a car door opening across a black parking lot, its dull vacuum pop as it closed again. That night, leaving the restaurant, I was not dressed in my work clothes. I had on my black coat, the one from the vintage clothing store, the one with the black plastic beveled buttons, the one I wear with different scarves, the one with the amber brooch on its lapel. The brooch Michael gave me on one of our anniversaries. I recall my coat, unbuttoned, and how the wind reached under to my skin, under the dark, fitted dress with its scooped neck. I remember how well the dress fit me, and the green scarf I wore with it, and how, earlier, James's bandaged hand wound in and out of that scarf. Because, of course, I wasn't alone.

"Anyway," Michael continues, interrupting my memories, "they reach a beat-up old truck, and they separate only briefly. Only until the guy pins one of her shoulders to the window. He stands in front of her, his legs slightly apart. I wait for her to kick him in the nuts, or scream, and then I see it: Her knee moves up between his legs. I think, Okay, now you've done it, you asshole. She's gonna get you right in the balls. And man, if I didn't think he deserved it. I started to put my hand on the door handle, like this," and he squeezes his hand tight to show me. "I was ready to spring on him from across the parking lot."

The curl of his hand makes me ask, "Should we wait to talk about this? Save it?"

"Save it? I thought you wanted us to talk, that's what you wanted months ago. No, I've kept it in for a couple of weeks." He relaxes his fingers and reaches across the table to brush the hair from my brow bone. "I'm not angry now; you can tell I'm not angry, can't you, Anna? I've told you so much in letters; I've written you all sorts of letters I haven't been able to send. Let me try now. I just need to tell you what

I saw, what I knew," he pleads. He's right, I see no anger, only passion, his passion in this attempt to make a connection, to tell me something. Important. To him.

"I know what you saw," I answer.

"Please."

"All right, Michael, you tell me."

"It was you. I saw you, you were stroking the inside of his thigh with your bent knee, and it hit me: This is my wife, my wife is fucking this guy."

Thinking of our child upstairs, I flinch at his words. "Michael, Sara could . . . at any moment—"

"You know, for a minute," he ignores me, "as my hand squeezed the door handle, I thought about jumping out of the car and pounding the guy, but the weight of it all pinned me to my seat. I pulled the door closed; my hand dropped from the door handle. I couldn't move. I simply sat for a while after you drove away, maybe five minutes, just breathing."

"Why are you telling me this?" I ask.

He looks away from me to his hands now resting, palms down, on the table. When he looks up his eyes are wet with tears. "Because," he says, taking a deep breath, "because I knew when I saw you that you were sleeping with him. I mean, I slept with you for—how many years?—anyway, it hasn't been so long since I slept with you myself that I couldn't recognize that look you get. So I thought, 'She's fucking someone. And that someone sees my daughter every day, while I don't. Can't. How do I feel about that?' What do I let myself feel, Anna—Anger? Betrayal? Jealousy? Should I feel those things? Because, after all, it's over, right?"

That was the night I first told James I loved him. We hadn't been together in a week, and at the truck, his hands held me gently, not against my will. I wanted it. My leg wasn't moving with enough speed or force to clip him good and hard. In fact, I needed to touch him that tenderly, needed to feel the heat of his thigh through his clothes, and later, at my home, the heat of his skin directly on mine.

"Yeah, it's over," Michael concludes, answering his own question.

His face is contorted with stifled tears. "Except now it's like a movie in my head."

Yes, Michael, I should tell him, I see it, too: me, James, our walk, my stockinged leg running up his thigh, his eyes when we broke apart, my mouth still slightly open with the kiss.

"See?" he asks, and he wipes the falling tears from his face with the back of his hand. "That's what it all comes down to. I thought you were right about us. Until I saw you. And I wanted it all back."

I take his wet hand between my two, which are still warm from holding my coffee cup, and I knead my knuckles into his palm. I bend his fingers over my hand. Michael brings his face up close to mine until our foreheads touch; he says, "Anna.

"I want . . . I've been so lonely, day after day, eating alone, putting one foot in front of the other to get out the door. I suggested sharing Sara, I figured that would help structure my days and nights, that moving closer would help me feel part of a family again. But now? Being here? Taking care of things for you? It's more than just keeping my days occupied, it's what I know how to do. I've missed it."

I am overwhelmed by his emotion, as raw and available as the first time we kissed, then fell into bed. As if he holds it out to me, something to show me, in the palm of his hand. Closing my eyes, I brush his forehead with my lips, I linger there a moment as Michael takes a few breaths. He continues, "When we were splitting up last winter, I told you I really needed the stability, the familiarity of a family. Someone to come home to, to grow old with. All this with someone I know. I know you. I know this life. I don't want to start over."

"What exactly are you saying, Michael?"

"I'm saying I felt sorry for myself for days after seeing you in that parking lot. Seeing you kiss him. I drove home in a state, and the next day I went to the beach and walked out into the water before going back in to my mother. She said, 'What do you expect?' So I asked myself, What did I expect? I guess after being alone, coming home to an empty house, I imagined you were alone also, raising Sara, working. Maybe, too, I expected through Sara we'd get back together."

"For Sara?"

"Sara, the future, all of it. Even now, we could settle here, near our families, make a clean start. I'm telling you, I saw you and I don't care. We can put it all behind us."

A fresh start after wasting the past ten years recreating my parents' marriage, substituting my own misunderstandings, miscommunication, and bitterness. My mother lies recuperating in a hospital bed and she will need my attention. What care can I give her if I am self-involved, absorbed in a new life? My future with my mother, getting to know each other, deserves time. My time and attention. I think of James, who has not called me; I contemplate all my recent fears of maybe making a new set of mistakes with him: wasting another block of years, his time and mine. And Michael? I know what he means; I, too, know this life, the ease of navigating life with Michael.

"I'm so tired, Michael, tired of not knowing what to do, and I'm tired of people telling me what to do. I'm worn out with the possibility of more bad choices. I woke up exhausted after last night's sleep. Maybe I can't do this alone." I let go of his hand and fold my hands together on my lap. "Maybe it's a start. Making peace," I tell him.

"It does seem a pretty good place to start."

I walk with Mother to the dayroom. Her doctor cornered me on my arrival at the hospital. "It's time to prepare for her release," he informed me. "She's well enough to leave, make a few trips a week for rehab and physical therapy. Talk to her about it. Put some plans in place," he calls over his shoulder as he walks briskly away from me down the corridor, already mentally with his next patient.

Though I sit only two feet from her on a sofa in the sunny dayroom on her floor, she is behind a locked door and I cannot reach her. I can see a three-quarter view of her face as she turns. And even though I am close enough to reach out my hand to hold hers if I merely exercise my muscles—flex and extend—it is as if she has closed an actual door effectively and irrevocably to keep me standing on the other side, waiting.

She doesn't want me.

Minutes ago I began discussing her future, our future, as Sara played in a corner of the room. Sara is with me today, we are within reach of each other.

"Mother," I say, "I have given this some thought. I'd like you closer by, in case you need help. I could stay on with you. Anything you want."

"My home," she states.

"Do you want us to move in with you? Sara and I will do that, if that's what you want."

"You need to get back to work."

"Eventually. Maybe." I pause. "Michael is lonely, Mother, and he wants us to get back together, he says. He thinks that we can compromise and build a future together. He thinks this makes more sense than starting over with somebody new."

Mother nods, her head still partially turned from me. "That's the choice I made," she tells me, and I recall the times I heard her crying behind the bedroom door. I think of myself as a child, bewildered and alone, but it is Sara's face I see.

"What if that happened, and we moved? You could come with us. You could sell the house. Or you could keep it; it's paid for. Maybe you could go back once you're better. But for now—"

"Anna," she interrupts, "you try too hard." She looks away, over to Sara jabbering away to her doll, knees bent under her as she plays in the sunny corner. "I'd like a nurse," she continues. "A visiting nurse. I'd like my own home."

"Oh. But I thought . . . after yesterday, our talk."

"You thought what? That I'd keep talking? I have no more to say."

"But I do, there's much more I want to say to you. So much that I want to know." Mother shakes her head, but I press on, "When I was pregnant with Sara, Mother, at first I wished she would disappear. I know how you must have felt because I felt it too," I whisper so Sara in the corner will not hear. Mother shakes her head again, slowly, deliberately. Her mouth is in a sympathetic, lopsided smile, pitying. I feel like a fool, unable to comprehend what she means. "But look at her." I point, my voice barely above a murmur. "Look. Imagine that corner empty, I can't. I can't."

"Then you can't understand me. Not really." She still cannot bring herself to look me straight in the eye.

"Your life sentence? Me?" I ask, stroking her rigid hand on her lap. "Your prison? Is that what you meant?"

"Just alone," she answers. "With everything."

"But you don't have to be alone."

"It's my choice," my mother says. She is not crying now like she did years ago when I played with my dolls, but she is just as far away.

"We could all live together, you, me, Michael, Sara. I could cook nice meals for us. We could be happy."

Finally Mother looks my way. "Too, too hard." She smiles. "Go home now. Plan a nice lunch. Talk to Michael, over a good meal. Do what you like to do." She puts her hand to my face, passes it a bit clumsily over the wrinkles above my questioning eyes. "Never knew where you came from, Anna. You loved food and people in ways we . . . your father and I . . . didn't understand. You can't live in my life. You can't live my life. And you should go. Before you can't leave."

We all give the gifts we can.

I analyze everything. I've said this before in the context of my former work as a food scientist. But I suppose there is no small measure of truth in this: that the scrutiny extends to my life and other's lives and the universe of life around me. In many ways, although I have veered from the path I set out on years ago, I am still the scientist, a curious observer, an inveterate hypothesizer. I need to know. I can't help myself.

Except there is one part of my life that, by willful and blind avoidance, goes largely unexamined. I've thought for so long that—no, it would be more accurate for me to say I've blamed this for so long on the adults around me. This, the unexamined part, being of course my complicated relationship with my father. Even now I plan to set aside the tough questions for the moment in the hope that reaching a different kind of understanding will bring me a bit of peace with him— eleven years dead and yet more alive than ever.

Imagine: A child tears out of a mother's body, both part of that comfortable home and yet separate, individual. From the first days, of conception, of birth, this relationship is in a very real sense parasitic: Blood from one passes to the other, cords connect; nutrients break down in one set of organs and are stolen, absorbed by another, smaller, needier set; milk flows with little preparation between one flesh and separate, eager, sucking gums. They steal the best of us, children do, the grown-up body's humors, its elasticity, its immune system, even sometimes its strength and health. The way I and my unborn siblings sapped my mother, the grown-up forever after exists both at the will of another and at the mercy of an imperfect, aging body. And then there's another wrinkle in this bizarre contract between parent and child, that sooner or later the parent is going to have to let the child go, and the child is going to want to leave the parent in the dust. It's our nature, this recipe for growing up.

But what if, also in our nature, is reluctance—reluctance to be a parent, reluctance to show emotion? And what if that reluctance shames us until we temper it with control, so that control masquerades as caring?

I suppose when I learned about Sara taking up residence in my body I was reluctant to have her because of what I learned in childhood: Listen, Quiet, Follow, Don't ask. Until something inside me, maybe Sara herself, understood and then transmitted to me that I was not my own parents, that I could do things differently with her, that I could make her a part of my life by listening but also make her strong enough to live separate from me. After that, it was easy; I have followed my instincts with Sara, and maybe generation by generation that's what we do as parents: as much as we can for ourselves and more for our children, so that someday they will do even better for theirs.

In some sense when Michael tells me I must get over my past troubled relationship, he's right. When he says I have the relationship I have with my mother and can't expect to alter it, he's also right.

And I have, in this one area, believed I could simply forget. How many times have I said, *Father is dead and no amount of thought will bring him back?* And I had Michael, after all, for ten years to help me keep the questions at bay; with his unwavering belief in strength and forbearance, he did all the right things for me, made it so I could go on forgetting, by diagnosing and then proposing a course of treatment. "You're in a state of shock, so let's get married, and I will keep you busy, keep you from thinking."

Only thinking is what I need to do: It's who I am.

My parents, if they couldn't quite get me to stop thinking, did manage to keep me from asking. They kept me in line; I let Michael step in and do the same with me. It's what I knew, it's what I trusted, the control. What I perceived about myself—my sexuality, my love of good food as some kind of basic, glorious human need for communion with others, even my need to take care of another person—these I recognized but never trusted. I could see these qualities as you see features in a mirror, or the outlines of a flat human form in a photo, bearing resemblance to me but separate, trapped elsewhere.

Why, then, why if I can see the efficacy of Michael's solution to put my father behind me, why now does my father keep returning? He is hidden in every memory I have dredged up, lurking, waiting, until it is not so easy to put his ever-present shade away in a nice, neat, labeled box. Because I feel it was him with me in my mother's guest room, although reason tells me I mixed up a horrible half-sleep dream with Michael's presence on the night of my nightmare. But sometimes, even for a scientist, reason can't explain everything. And I felt him, I heard him, I knew I was awake even though I knew I had to be sleeping. He was there and he was trying to tell me something. And since I'll never really know, I'll have to guess. Hypothesize.

How I'd like to leave this unexamined, to say they fucked me up, my parents did, that they are somehow responsible for my passive role in every aspect of my life, from my father's death to the lack of success in my marriage. But the truth is, I function; even as handicapped as they were, they raised a daughter who can earn her living and raise her own daughter. Who can feel love for many people, maintain friendships, and even, on occasion, balance her checkbook. They even taught me something about need; even as they discouraged need and emotional mess they showed me how much I need despite their austere lessons.

And I do need.

I've heard it said—think I read it written or expounded by some marriage counselor somewhere—that if people put half as much effort into saving their first marriage as they do into a new relationship, then the marriage would never have broken up in the first place. The theory goes, or I understood it to mean, that people will make compromises and adjustments in a second relationship that could just as easily have been made in the first. This is so much common sense. No one is perfect, and a relationship is always work, there is always conflict to resolve, there is an ebb and flow, acknowledged good patches and bad ones. So why start over?

There are plenty of arguments to support this, too. People argue for the children, for the future, for companionship. Maybe this is what my mother told me in answer to my unasked question, the question she knew I longed to ask but never would. "Why, Mother, why when you had all those troubled pregnancies and Father wanted you to keep trying; why, after you locked yourself in your room and cried and then got over it to subject yourself to his pressure and anger again: Why did you stay?" "That was my choice," she told me, giving me the answer to my unspoken question. Meaning, perhaps, *There was you, Anna, and the prospect of life alone, and it was a life I knew and felt comfortable with. And perhaps because I loved your father despite his limitations, loved that he wanted to keep on trying with me, that he wanted me; and he loved me because I could and would cook exactly the way he liked and therefore brought to his life a simple act of comfort and caring.*

That's as close as I'll ever get to an explanation of their lives: "That was my choice, Anna." I can only now deal with mine.

Someday Sara will wonder, no matter how open Michael and I are with her, what happened between her parents during the year that their marriage took a bad turn and they lifted her out of a secure life, separated her from her father, and caused her to have nightmares and temper tantrums. Maybe she, too, will blame and blame and blame, and obsess until she comes out at the other side of that very dark tunnel of examination into the light, to reach her own understanding and a livable comfort. For even if, as Michael suggests, we reconcile, she'll carry the burden of our passive mistakes as I expect I'll carry the guilt of my father's death as my burden. These facts will be our touchstones. Forever. I know she will wonder, I know she will carry anger; she will see us as we are, imperfect. But the big difference will be, I expect and I do truly believe, that her questions will not knock around her head and her sore heart unasked. Maybe she will have pain, but also she will have a voice; she will be able to ask and I will answer: *There is pain in life, painful decisions, painful mistakes, but if you feel pain you are very close to feeling great joy.*

She will learn something from me about need, the need to speak and ask, and the need for connection with another human because his presence completes you rather than creates you, and I will have taught her by my example.

 I wait until Michael and Sara go to bed, and then I call James because he does not call me. I call him because I need him, I need him as I need food or air or blood or Sara. Not as my strength but as my human, vulnerable weakness. I already know he needs me; everything he's done—and said—has told me so.

Mother suggested a meal, and I turn to James for help. It is late, and I catch him at home after work, a time, I can't help thinking, we would be together eating and talking about work.

"Help me," I say, "I want to make a fish soup. Like a bouillabaisse, I guess, but with local fish."

Jane Ward

"Hello, I miss you, too. Me? I'm fine, a bit cold tonight but otherwise fine."

"I know, it's late, and I'm manic. But I really want to make this."

"Tonight?"

"No, but maybe tomorrow. For our lunch."

" 'Our' lunch?"

"For Michael and me. We need to talk. I'm comfortable over a meal."

"You want my help making lunch for your husband?" I have to hold the phone far from my ear, James is laughing so hard.

"Is that an angry laugh?"

"It's a laugh laugh. I can live with you making him lunch. I was angry when I left. I was, in fact, an idiot, but I'm not so angry anymore. When I calmed down I understood what you were asking me. 'Understand me' you said, and I do. Now I'm just lonely. Feeling unbelievably sorry for myself. And hungry. I'm hungry all the time."

"So you'll help me?" I demand.

James yawns, calm, relaxed, still sleepy, and very much at home talking with me about good food. "Okay. Basically, you're making a fish fumet with aromatics like fennel, add some herbs, then whatever fish and shellfish you want. Mussels are good, a good firm white fish or maybe bluefish. Squid. Do you like squid? Even Atlantic salmon would hold up. You need fish that will hold up because you have to bring your broth up to boil, throw the fish in, cover the pot, and take it off the heat. It should sit for about five minutes, covered. The last thing you want to do is boil the life out of your fish."

"Myotomes," I say, referring to the chevron-shaped flakes of fish muscle, the building blocks of a fish's flesh, which become prominent once it has been cooked. The word pops into my head after so long; it's been a long time since I thought of words like "myotomes," relying as I have on my eye and a quick finger poke for doneness. "Fish muscles," I explain to James.

"Whatever. Maybe a thread or two of saffron. Just play with it."

"Of course," I agree. Trust myself, I think. "Yes. Thanks. I can do it."

284

"What is it, why are you up so late worrying about fish soup?"

"Because I'm crazy," I tell him. "You know what? Fish stock is the only stock I haven't made since I've been here. I didn't even think of fish bones. I've bought chicken, veal, beef, even ham. Lamb soup sounded disgusting. I guess there's Irish stew and Scotch broth, but the idea of boiling a big, gamy lamb leg . . . ugggh. Anyway," I continue, "maybe I am soup obsessed, making something to feed my mother. All I think of is soup."

"Soup?" he asks me.

"But she's not hungry. Besides, I don't think she likes me to see her eat. She dribbles," I explain. "Not that I care. But she does. Even though I just want to help her, I have to respect what she wants. And she doesn't want me, or my help. James? It's physically painful for me to be held back like this, wanting to help, not being allowed. So instead I make soup. And manic phone calls. Late into the night."

"Painful, huh? Yeah, now I remember you. You're that woman I used to cook with."

"And I think I remember you, too, Chef. You're that guy who only wanted to help me. Was it this painful for you?"

"It's killing me, Anna. But I never thought of making soup." He is quiet for a moment, then asks, "So, what are you going to do with all this bouillabaisse?"

"Serve it for lunch."

"All this for what? To prove a point?"

"I think we've had this conversation before. No, not to prove a point. It's just soup."

"I seem to remember someone saying nothing's 'just' anything. You know, Anna," he hesitates, "you could always come back here and cook for me."

"I could, couldn't I?"

"And I could cook for you."

"Yes, you could," I agree. "I'd need a ride."

"You would, wouldn't you?"

I lift the lid of the stew pot and crumble two threads of saffron into the tomato-rich broth. I stir the bouillabaisse, quickly add the fish and shellfish, replace the pot lid and remove the pot from the heat. I set the timer for five minutes and pour myself a glass of wine. As I stand at the sink looking out over my mother's frosty backyard I see a pair of cardinals, resident birds, the brilliant male, his gray-pink, less showy mate. The sky is a promising blue, and the sun's reflection turns the snow-laden branches and ground to glass. From this angle it nearly blinds me.

"Standing there, you look impenetrable." Michael's voice startles me, giving lie to his words.

"Hardly," I laugh. "Your voice made me jump."

"We keep on surprising each other," Michael replies. At this truth I smile, gentle and kind, and the curve of my lips puts Michael at ease. He relaxes visibly and takes a seat at the kitchen table. "Sara got tired of me, I think. She's up in her room with her dolls."

"For now, anyway. We'll be eating in about five minutes." I look down into my glass of wine and ask as an afterthought, "Would you like some?"

"No thanks. I'm really trying to cut down. Have you noticed I've quit smoking, too? And I definitely don't drink in the middle of the day anymore." He stops when he sees me contemplating my own glass. "Not that I think you're wrong," he adds.

I wave off his apology. "You do what makes you feel better," I answer, and Michael nods. I set my glass down on the counter and ask, "What did you mean by 'impenetrable'?"

"You looked like I couldn't know you, or what you were thinking."

"Ah, that's the secret. I wasn't thinking about anything. Just enjoying the frost outside, the sunshine. My glass of wine." I smile at Michael. He looks up, he holds my gaze steadily over his clasped hands, his strong hands made even stronger with the fingers woven together. Strange, what I remember most: Michael contemplating something, a problem, interlacing his fingers, sliding back in a chair, quietly thinking and forming a solution, rubbing his eyes and brows with his thumb and forefinger, running a hand through his hair. These gestures are

Hunger

strongly imprinted on me; there are things I will never forget.

"This is nice," he says, "you, me, Sara playing in her room. She's happy."

"I think she'll be okay," I agree.

"We could have another, you know," Michael suggests. His voice takes on an oily, seductive tone as if he is offering a treat: a rich ice cream, creamy chocolate, another child. "If you come back."

For the moment I ignore his offer, and with a quick look I check the time left on the kitchen timer. Four minutes. I am tempted to lift the lid and smell the broth, but remembering James's instructions, I turn instead to Michael. "Can I tell you something, Michael?" He inclines his head to me, telling me to go ahead. "Remember when you told me that if I asked my mother for answers I'd never be satisfied? You were right. I asked, I pushed, and she finally answered me. And all I learned is that someone else's marriage is essentially unknowable, a complete mystery."

"I thought you asked her about being in the hospital years ago, not her marriage?"

"Turns out it's the same thing. The big secret was, my father wanted lots of children but Mother had trouble carrying them. She said he was angry when she had to have a hysterectomy."

Michael shakes his head. "This is what you were aching to hear? That your mother had a hysterectomy? Anna, I told you it would be personal, that you—"

"I remember what you told me, but you know what else?" I continue after cutting short his admonition. "Despite all the conflict, she still misses him, every day. And what do I make of this? That my father was a domineering jerk? That my mother was crazy for staying with him? I don't know. Somehow I don't think it's as simple as that, as black and white, good and bad. But I'll never know, really, what kept them together, will I? I'll never have the answers."

"Why do you have to make anything of it? This was years ago, and you know you've got to move on. You said so yourself, remember? Your father's memorial service, your memories? 'Pointless,' I think, is what you said."

287

"Not so pointless after all." I sip some wine and twirl the liquid in the glass before setting it down on the counter behind me. "You are so adept at summing everything up," I say. "Like when my father died and I told you I felt nothing. You told me it was shock, you gave it a name. It can't just be nothing for you, you have to label everything: This situation, that feeling, you process it and package everything up nice and neat, then you put it away and move on. Well, I've tried, but I can't do that, not with all this information, it keeps coming back to me anyway. And you can't do it for me, no matter how hard you try."

Michael stares on, he leans back in his chair with his legs stretched out before him, and he takes in everything I have to say. "They are my parents, Michael, they made me, and I have a lot of feelings that aren't that easy for me to comprehend. It isn't easy for me to say that maybe I loved him because he was my father but I was so absolutely paralyzed by him that I couldn't get out of bed to help when he was dying. And it isn't easy to need my mother to love me because I'm her daughter, and know she never will because I remind her how she let my father down."

Michael pulls his legs in and sits upright. "What do you mean, 'know she never will'?" he asks me. "Of course your mother loves you—she's your mother."

I give a short, wry laugh. "Somehow I don't think that's a guarantee of anything, but maybe I'm wrong. I do know, though, that she doesn't want my help. She wants to do this on her own with a visiting nurse, and I also know I have to listen to what she wants. She wants me to go home."

"Home?" For an instant he looks hopeful.

"New Hampshire."

"Anna—" he begins, but the stove's timer buzzes and interrupts his protest. I switch off the insistent, annoying hum and ignore lunch for the present.

"I don't think it makes sense to talk like this," he tells me.

"I know it doesn't make sense to you, but it makes perfect sense to me. I think if you are serious about starting over, we might as well start by being able to speak to each other," I counter in a lowered voice, listening as I do for a sound, a hint, that Sara may have ventured down the stairs. "You're talking about loneliness and second chances and second children, and we haven't even talked about what this means for us. Or Sara."

"She is the reason to keep trying."

"She could be," I agree. "Why didn't we have a second child, Michael? Did you ever wonder? What another child would have meant?"

I step across the kitchen and slide the door into its place in the wall, sealing off our room from the dining room and the rest of the house. Sara will not hear what I did as a child; I will not even raise my voice. "Remember her sonogram?" I ask. "I kept that picture, I kept looking at it for days just to reassure myself that she was normal. All because we'd been drinking and careless and kept on drinking, because who would have guessed I was pregnant?" Michael stays mute, he offers no response to my barrage of words. "How do I get through to you?" I wonder aloud.

"Did you think I'd forgotten? Besides," he counters, "it all turned out fine. She was fine. And you love Sara, you loved her from the start."

"Yes, I love her. And when I knew she was healthy, I just held on and kept on holding. She was my chance, does that make sense? We both love her, no question. She is the best of us."

"Some people don't even have that," Michael contends.

"I know."

"We knew we wanted kids," he reminds me.

"I know, but we never spoke of when. A second child, a planned child? Might have meant, I suppose, that we loved each other enough."

Michael looks away, he spreads his legs and again leans back into the chair. Remembering our lunch, I step over to the stove and lift the pot's lid. A garlicky steam assails my nose; breathing deeply, I feel lightheaded with the mingled scents: briny fish, garlic, onion, tomato, aromatic fennel. I gather together the salt and pepper and correct the seasoning, but as I start to taste I halt the spoon before it reaches my lips. In the pot, mussels lie, shells open, and their tiny coral bodies remind me of a child's plump earlobe. I reach one out with the spoon; its bottom shell sits in rich broth scattered with flecks of finely minced onion. I turn and hold the spoon out to Michael.

"Here, these are beautiful. Taste. Tell me if I need to add anything."

He looks at the proffered spoon. His fingers still clasped, he makes no move. He looks puzzled, unsure of what to do, so again I urge the spoon on him. He shifts around in his seat and looks behind him at the table, which isn't yet set.

"Pass me a plate or something? Can I have a plate?" In a panic, he tries to take the spoon by its handle, but my grip remains firm.

"Just use your fingers. Go ahead, let me feed you," I urge.

"Are you kidding? It'll drip all over. Let me take the spoon." His hand covers mine and this time I release my hold.

Now that my hands are free, I bring a bowl and a small fork to the table. Then I tear off the end of a loaf of bread and hand this to him, too. Michael drops the mussel into the bowl and sets the bread next to the lone creature. To me, it looks forlorn sitting in its small puddle. Michael carefully removes it from the shell and swallows the tiny thing quickly.

"I don't know. Tastes okay," he answers as he chews. "Needs a little salt, maybe."

"What does it taste like, Michael?"

"It's good. Tastes fine. There's something funny, though."

"Funny?"

"Different, I mean. Like licorice."

"That's the fennel," I retort, whisking the bowl away from him. I pick up the piece of bread and mop the broth from the bowl, biting in, chewing slowly, savoring. I taste everything in the small mouthful of broth-soaked bread, everything that has gone into the soup. It needs nothing, even from this small taste I know it is perfect. As I eat, Michael watches. Although fleeting, I identify a flicker of confusion, disbelief, maybe even disgust at my hungry tasting. At this moment

I'd like him to know hunger is different from greed, but I know no other way of telling him, no other way to help him understand.

As I finish my taste, Michael leaves the table. He slides back the door and stands in the doorway, letting air into the steamy, perfumed kitchen. After ladling soup into three bowls, I slice the rest of the bread neatly, on an angle, remembering how it felt under my hands last night, marveling at the chemistry of baking. Although I feel bread dough every day, that something could go from feeling like pliable flesh to rough wood still amazes me.

Michael faces the dining room, I face the stove; we stand with our backs to each other. He says, "She is something, Sara is, something for us to build on. If we're patient, if we give each other time, I know we can get to a better place."

"I'm sure we could," I agree. "People do it every day. My own parents did. Like my mother told me yesterday, 'That was my choice.' "

"Then you know I'm right."

"You are so sure." I smile at his words.

I set aside a large bit at the end of the loaf and put it at my place, where soon I will tear it into ragged chunks. It reminds me of the rough meals with James, the often unmatched plates, the hastily gathered pots, bowls, bread boards, silver, wooden spoons—everything piled on the table, sometimes on the floor or the bed. He never wanted anything fussy, only beautiful; he was in too much of a hurry to eat and share to bother with napkins that matched placemats that matched tablecloths. Bringing the bowls to the table, I lay them down and move to stand next to Michael in the doorway.

"You know," I tell him, "I heard words like 'patience'—'be patient,' 'calm down,' 'be good and quiet'—all my life, and I followed those instructions. So well, in fact, that I was able to sit passively by while my father died. Now when I hear words like 'patience,' they're like words delivered at my eulogy, because I might as well be dead."

At my side Michael says, "I don't understand you."

"I can't go on feeling . . . nothing, simply because feeling nothing is easier than feeling pain. It's like the difference between eating to stay alive and eating to take part in something bigger than you are." I continue because Michael looks puzzled, "Basically it's the difference between fear and joy."

"That's a big difference."

"Exactly."

I turn to look at the table behind me set for lunch. It looks so different from all those table settings in Chicago. I recall all my prized possessions from the coach-house kitchen, now all locked up behind a metal door awaiting sale, within a chain-link confine no doubt, with a key pad at the gate and a security guard on duty. I know just the kind of place, although I've never been to this particular storage facility—and probably never will—on the outskirts of the city. Above our heads, interrupting our thoughts, we hear a dull thud, a toy being thrown or dropped, and the padding of small, quick feet. Michael and I smile and shake our heads at our daughter thundering across the house.

"You were right about Sara. She is something for us to build on. She's pretty great."

Michael places his left arm over my shoulder and draws me close like an old friend. "Oh, God, Anna, our marriage. We hadn't been good together for a long time, had we?" he asks.

I put my arm around the small of his back and hold his waist. "No, Michael, not for a long time," I agree, "and, no, we can't go back."

We stand with our arms around each other for a few more seconds, not quite ready to let go.

I hear Sara's feet pelt down the stairs and cross the living room heavily, as only a barefoot and hungry child can tread through a home. She races to the kitchen doorway and comes to a sharp stop right before Michael, holding out her arms to be lifted.

"What's for lunch, Mommy? I'm hunnnngry!" she drawls as Michael hoists her up. In Sara's words I recognize James's baritone call and the way he always comes in on a Sunday morning saying, "Where's breakfast? I'm hunnnngry," drawing out the word until it sounds like an animal's growl, an instinctive groan for food.

I smile. "Me, too, Sara. I'm hungry, too."

PART SEVEN

Gifts of Food

A father comes to his daughter's bedroom door one summer afternoon. He arrives home early from work, and he stops to ask her if she would like to go fishing with him the next morning, a Saturday. He has very recently taken up fishing, but only clients have ever been asked along. Eagerly she nods her head yes.

"We must leave at four, and you must be very quiet out on the river. Can you do that?" he asks her. Again she nods.

Her mother sets about laying out clothes, rubber boots, even a sweater, because sometimes a summer morning is heavy and damp with vapor, especially at this woodsy part of the stream. Her father packs rods, hooks, extra line, salmon eggs and corn for bait; he asks his daughter to dig for nightcrawlers, which she does eagerly, not long after the sun sets, with a flashlight. It is late when she gets to bed, but she's filled a coffee can with worms.

In the morning her father shows her how to bait the hook, how to cast the line, how to stand perfectly still, how to wait patiently. When she catches a fish the father puts his hand on her shoulder; he pats it, wordless, because they must remain very quiet. She can take the fish off the hook; she is not squeamish. She places it in his basket, wicker, vinyl lined, with a leather closure, and breathes in the smell trapped inside: the fresh fish smell of stream, flesh, and metallic blood. She does not get bored, although they stand there, staking their part of the stream, for hours.

When they arrive home with nine fish, she pulls up a stool and stays with her father as he eviscerates them under a flow of cold tap water all at arm's length, his elbows locked, his head turned slightly, and his nose wrinkled against the smell. The trout, gutted and clean, lie in a haphazard pile on a wooden board, their eyes fixed and glassy, shining and bright. As the girl looks closely she sees the lie of the scales and on some a rainbow sheen; she sees each fiber of the tails and fins like flattened paintbrushes; she sees connecting membranes. They are beautiful, these fish: sacrificed to be ultimately enjoyed. Her father scales them, then removes their heads. The smell permeates the kitchen.

"Are we going to eat them?" she wonders.

"No, I'll give them away to a couple of clients," he answers.

"They smell good."

Behind them the mother snorts. "All that blood," she says, nodding at the stringy entrails flushing down the sink.

Something about the girl's face must have made her father think, for he breaks from his work to look at her a moment or two.

"Well, I could split them four and four," he considers, his arms back in the sink, his face again turned from her to his task. "That would leave one—it would have to be the smallest one, though."

She realizes what he means, that she may have a fish. She picks the small one, the runt; it is speckled and brown and beautiful to the girl, with its silvery sheen and pink flesh. He washes his hands well after cleaning and packing his fish for the freezer. Dropping a knob of butter in a frying pan, he sets the fish in, cooks it until the skin crisps, browns, and the feathery tail curls. His daughter has never before seen him cook. He helps her peel back the skin to expose the cooked flesh, once like the insides of seashells, now creamy colored and dotted with bits of browned butter and done all the way through. For her lunch after their morning together she eats the fish from the bone, until all that is left is skin and skeleton. She tastes the stream, the trees, the sunshine breaking through them, all in the body of this fish. All the father does is watch, his brows knit in a puzzled way: uncomprehending but indulgent, maybe even loving.

Full from her lunch, the girl skips out to play. She sees her dying neighbor, Mrs. Klein, sitting on her porch and she waves.

Mrs. Klein calls to the young girl through the screen. "Good morning," she calls in delight.

"Hello, Mrs. Klein," the girl answers.

"And how are you on this beautiful morning?"

"I've been fishing already. With my father." She adds, "We've been up since four."

"Fishing? Up so early and not yet tired?" Mrs. Klein wonders. When the girl shakes her head no, Mrs. Klein chides herself, "My dear, it is too lovely a day for me to be so gloomy. Won't you come in and visit?"

The girl hesitates; she can see as Mrs. Klein's head rests on the chair back that her friend is tired.

"Come in, come in," she urges, lifting her head as if reading the girl's thoughts. "I mean it. You do me a world of good." Mrs. Klein has not yet dressed; she is still in her nightgown, which the girl sees hanging below the hem of her bathrobe. No wig this morning, her head is wrapped in a beautiful scarf of red and gold, although the scarf's vivid color highlights her thin, white skin. She smiles at the girl's arrival, and her face sings with joy. "Although I have nothing very tasty to offer you today. There are, however, some candies," she gestures to a ruby red cut glass dish as the girl walks in through the porch door. The dish is filled with jellies: spearmint leaves and orange slices. "But nothing for lunch."

"I've eaten. I had a fish," the girl answers. "I'm full."

"A fish? A whole fish yourself?" Mrs. Klein shakes her head. "What it is to have an appetite. It is a wonderful gift, an appetite. If I were hungry . . . ," she begins, and her eyes go far away, as if she is seeing a table spread with treats. The girl sees memory cross the woman's face and longs to cook for her, wishes she could cook something her friend could eat and keep down, maybe the very thing that would make her well again, make her live a good long time.

"What are you thinking of, Mrs. Klein?"

"That if I could eat one thing, it would be blintzes. My aunt's blintzes, like when I was a girl," she replies.

"What are blintzes?" the girl asks.

"Ah, let me tell you a story," Mrs. Klein begins.

"When I was a little older than you are now, my aunt began teaching me to cook. She was famous for so many things, but my favorites

were her cheese blintzes. The cheese was sweet and tangy. I could sit
and eat one after the other, sometimes with sour cream, sometimes
with cinnamon sugar on top. Not what you'd call health food these
days. But it felt healthy, being fed with love.

"She loved to cook, she loved to feed us. She wanted me to know
this, too, to know how to cook. And I wanted to learn. So I stood
very close to her and watched. She wore a housecoat, I remember, and
she . . . perspired. But I didn't mind. It was hot, tedious work, you see,
and she was always at that stove." Mrs. Klein stares off into space, back
into her memories, and smiles. The girl tries her best to wait for more,
but she is impatient for the story to continue.

"Mrs. Klein?" she reminds her friend. "The blintzes?"

"Yes, I remember, the blintzes." She touches the girl's hair, fixes
her with an indulgent smile. "It is a thin pancake, and you must make
one at a time in a frying pan. My aunt had a special pan for her
blintzes, a small, flat frying pan. Before we began, she heated it well.
She said to me, 'It needs to be good and hot. I test it with a drop of
water.' And she showed me how to sprinkle the drop of water. 'The
water should say *Psssst!*' she told me. 'It should dance. Like this.'
And—*pssst!*—just like she said—that drop of water sizzled, that's how
we knew the pan was just right.

"The batter, it is a runny mixture, yellow from many eggs. My
aunt explained, 'We must work quickly,' then she poured in a small
amount of batter, and lifted and tilted the pan. She turned her wrist
this way and that, showing me how to quickly coat the pan." And
with her own fineboned wrist, decorated with pronounced blue veins,
Mrs. Klein shows the girl what she means.

"When one side had cooked," she continues, "my aunt flipped the
circle to cook the other side, then she lifted it hot from the pan to
show me. The first one was golden, speckled with brown. 'Too much
brown,' my aunt told me. 'But go ahead, you hold it. The first always
has too much butter from the pan, so we don't eat it. But you must
know how that looks, too.'

"My aunt worked on while I watched, making one at a time, working through the bowl of batter until she had a plate stacked high with

pancakes. Then it was my turn. I poured in batter and swirled it, like I saw my aunt do, and yes, my wrist moved easily like hers. This time my aunt stood beside me and watched. When I was done she said, 'Yes, Sari, my girl, just like that.' And she let me eat the very one I had made, filled with sweet cheese." Mrs. Klein's voice trails off, tired from her story. She rests her head and her eyes a moment. With her head back and her eyes closed she speaks, "It is that I remember, that first taste. My cooking—it is what I hope my family remembers. About me. I think food makes good memories." Below the scarf's edge, through the pale skin, the girl sees blue veins beating at the woman's temples. Even with her fatigue, Mrs. Klein manages a smile. "I still have the pan, my aunt's flat frying pan, you know."

"Mrs. Klein," the girl asks, "why are you so happy?"

"Because, little one, my daughter and son will be home from camp tomorrow, because you are here visiting me, because I can still recall the sweet creaminess of cheese blintzes. And because I am still alive." She laughs, and the sound reaches across the room to touch the young girl like light fingers. "It's a good thing to be alive," she says.

It is a good thing, the girl thinks, to be here with Mrs. Klein, and in that instant she understands that soon her refuge, these visits to Mrs. Klein on both good days and bad, will be closed to her. She defines death as an empty porch, the end of this good conversation about food.

The girl says simply, "I wish you were my mother," and this time Mrs. Klein does not laugh. The woman touches the girl's hand; she cannot grip with any strength but her eyes press into the girl with great vigor.

"You are a good, dear child," she says, sitting back now in her lounging chair, spent from her last movement. "And please, call me Sara. Friends should always use each other's names, I think. And I am also very happy to have my friends." Before she asks the girl to leave she whispers, "You be happy, Anna. Be happy, too."

They stand together on the granite rocks that look over the ocean near the abandoned quarry. A mother and a father, side by side in a slight September wind which catches spray from the waves, return to the ocean as a reassurance that summer is indeed over. The remains of lunch are spread out behind them, papers and cloths and food containers anchored with large smooth beach stones: the chicken salad, golden with curry; leftover brown rice, nutty and toothsome, hastily tossed at the last minute with a few roasted vegetables, cold lentils, and a tart vinaigrette made with lemon juice; the chewy roll, which should have teased out Sara's tooth; and the homemade bread and butter pickles which eventually did. She bit down on a crisp pickle and found her tooth lying on her tongue. Like so many children, she simultaneously laughed and cried with the surprise, until both her parents hugged her. Now, her surprise completely forgotten, she tries to whistle through the gap, she calls up to the birds with the shrill hiss of wind passing through the wide opening. She is happy she's lost a tooth, not the first, but gloriously, proudly this time, top row, front and center.

The tooth rests now in her father's pocket, not the one with the loose change and car keys where it might get banged around, but the one with the handkerchief. He wrapped it for her, and she must remind him to hand it over when he drops her at home later. As he keeps the tooth safe, he pats it from time to time, this transient piece of his daughter—her bone—now safe just beneath his own bone, the bone of his hip.

Anna would like to hold the tooth, she thinks of arguing with Michael, territorial, proprietary, but then thinks better of it. There have been other teeth, ones he hasn't held, and there will be many more.

Michael suggests they begin packing up. The gulls are emboldened, brazen, circling, swooping lower and lower; the sun, too, is lowering in the sky; the tide is venturing in. The remains of lunch should be packed into the basket and then piled into his car. When Sara hears this plan she begins to look intently at the tidal pools, moving farther and farther from her parents, hoping to prolong this day of picnicking.

She fools no one, but no one can be angry with her, either. They let her be, to explore, to find tiny fish trapped between granite slabs, seaweed anchored to the sides of rocks, patches of white foam bubbles that may be the waste breathing of all the life under the water but remind Sara of the toothpaste foam she spits into the sink. For a good long time, observation—just looking—occupies every fiber of her: from her squatting, springy knees to her rolled shoulders; from her acute eyes to her quick, connecting, linking, hypothesizing mind.

Before leaving, before calling Sara back, Michael and Anna stand silently, thinking of lunch, the mist, each other, the ocean, their daughter before them clambering over the rocks. They turn to face each other and smile, still shy but not so much today. The wind today blows steadily across them and brings with it autumn air. Anna slips her arms into the sleeves of a sweater which has been draped over her shoulders.

"Just a few more minutes," she pleads. "It's so beautiful here. I know I should feel cold, and I do, but I don't really mind it. I'm happy standing here even with the wind."

"Maybe we both are," Michael thinks. "Happy." He speaks this last word aloud.

She mistakes his last word for a question, and nods her head in reply. She squeezes his arm as she looks at his profile, his face meeting the ocean breeze head on.

Behind them, their daughter slips on a rock and scrapes her knee. She howls, piercing the ocean air with life. They go to her.

After closing, the chef sits at a dining table, writing menu and preparation notes in fierce, silent concentration. Finding him alone, his wife comes up behind him and lays her hand on his shoulder. She has finished tabulating the receipts for the night, she has checked on the kitchen staff's progress with cleanup. She has even prepared for her husband a plate of sandwiches from the night's leftovers; now she wants him to put away his work, too, and eat something. He looks up at her and smiles; he covers her hand with his.

"I'm almost done. Sit with me, see what you think," he says, sliding the papers scribbled with tomorrow's menu ideas across the table to her. Their fingertips touch as one gives, the other receives. There is a current still between them, even after a number of years of this hard work and a few professional disagreements; and this jolt, this desire transmitted through fingertips despite the late hour, is a renewal.

She slips on reading glasses, which are new, and makes to brush hair off her forehead. But there is a haircut, also new, although the sensation of hair still exists, and she smiles to herself at her mistake. He likes her private smile, he relaxes back into his seat. His back is tired and his feet sore, so perhaps it is time to hire someone to take over the bulk of the physical work, he thinks. Concentrate on the creative side and the staffing. When he looks up he sees her pointing to a line in his notes and shaking her head.

"Maybe not this," she says. "We tried something similar and it didn't sell, remember?"

He nods. She doesn't cook much for the restaurant anymore, unless they are understaffed or in a bind, and he knows if he insists it will go on the menu, this preparation similar to one they tried before but couldn't sell. He looks over at his wife a moment, deciding. She slides the plate of sandwiches over to him.

"Grrrr," he utters from somewhere deep in his throat. Warm grilled eggplant and cheese; flaked poached salmon bound with a little mayonnaise, some capers, and scallions; a bit of mushroom ragout on toasted bread: He tries them all. "These are delicious," he tells her, talking with his mouth full. "You are so great."

"I know."

"Thank you," he says, "for thinking of me. I was starving. It's exactly what I wanted." He smiles his disarming, slaying grin to which she is still susceptible.

"I know," she says.

Taking the paper back he makes a pencil line through the questionable idea; he squeezes his eyes closed to picture the fish and the produce being delivered in the morning. Furiously he scrawls down what he sees in his mind's eye, passes the paper back, and this time she nods.

"Perfect," she tells him. "Now come."

They clear the plate but leave the notes behind on the table for the morning, and they walk with arms around each other's backs to switch off the lights. They say their good nights in the kitchen, reminding the sous-chef to lock the back door after everyone has gone, and walk up the kitchen stairwell to their home above the restaurant. Inside it smells of garlic and spice, roasting meat and baking bread. They wash quickly then remove their clothes, stained and sweat soaked and clinging after a night of cooking, standing over a hot line, walking, running, even yelling. She loves the smell of her husband before he showers and has on occasion asked him to come to bed without soaping up, without rinsing the scent of hard work down the drain.

Tonight she smells his hands, the open palms pressed to her face, and takes in the garlic he has tried to wash away with soap and then mask with lemon oil. It is no longer sharp or pungent, but the trace scent brings tears to her eyes as she recalls the first smell of his skin in her nostrils. A few years ago now. She would like to take a picture of him, she thinks, or pictures, of his hands feeling the heft of food, washing, peeling, chopping, seasoning, grilling dangerously close to flames, placing food on plates, many pictures in sequence from start to finish, but then the pictures would never capture this smell. And she breathes again deeply.

The chef, noticing the tears in her eyes, holds her face in his capable hands, he kisses her wet eyelids and a tear drops from her eye, falls on an old scar on his hand, runs along its fissure. Whispering *hush* in her ear, he begins to make love to her. With him she becomes all states of matter: solid, then liquid, then vapor. Of course she knows in the light of day that this is not strictly, not scientifically true, and a picture would prove, would document this: his hands on her skin, solid; her skin and his touching, solid; their bodies entwined, ever solid. But in the dark she knows as they touch each other, as they move together, that their molecules are moving faster, shaking, keening, until they separate, drift, melt, then faster still take bits of their corporeal selves up into the surrounding air.

Acknowledgments

Stephen Elmont gave me my first break into the world of catering and taught me a thing or two about the importance of feeding people well; Christian DeVos took a chance on a young woman who hadn't the first clue about the catering market in Chicago; The 95th Restaurant's talented chefs tolerated my endless questions—even during the busiest meal times—and never shooed me away; Mark and Claire Rabin convinced me to bake at Quebrada Bakery, a truly happy place to work; members of the now-disbanded Keflavik Writers' Circle read and commented on so many drafts of this novel; Professor Pamela Bromberg graciously allowed me to do my first public reading at Simmons College; Dr. Elizabeth Landis, pediatrician nonpareil, took time out of her busy day to answer my last-minute medical questions; my editor at Forge, Stephanie Lane, guided me with her strong and excellent suggestions throughout the revision process; my agent, Carolyn Jenks (all the flowers in the world can't convey my gratitude, Carolyn), believed wholeheartedly in me and my manuscript; Patricia Crawford, Patricia Easterly, and Robin Kielty hold joint title for the best friends anyone could ever hope for. My thanks to you all.

And finally, special words to John, Emma, and Bennett: I love you.